NTC

Vocabulary Builders

Annotated Teacher's Edition

Lime Book

National Textbook Company
a division of NTC/Contemporary Publishing Group
Lincolnwood, Illinois USA

NTC Vocabulary Builders

Building Vocabulary the Natural Way

- New words are embedded in strong, carefully crafted contexts that allow students to unlock the meanings independently.
- Consistent emphasis is given to roots and word parts and their application to English words.
- Reading selections in the humanities, social studies, and sciences parallel the pattern of readings employed in SAT tests while reinforcing cross-curricular learning.
- Focused theme lessons examine words related to a particular area of experience or content, thereby allowing students to differentiate subtle shades of meaning.
- After unlocking the meaning of new words, students immediately apply their knowledge in reading and writing exercises.
- Special features heighten student interest in words while providing valuable practice in language and dictionary skills.
- Frequent "Mastering Meaning" features offer a variety of opportunities for using the vocabulary words in realistic writing situations.
- Practical test-taking strategies and practice test questions help students perform well on standardized tests.
- Regular Assessment pages provide tools for ongoing assessment; four more broadly-based tests are included in this Annotated Teacher's Edition.
- A dictionary of all the words studied in this text gives students a convenient means of confirming their hypotheses about the meanings of words, while offering a handy aid for independent review.

Overview of the Program

NTC Vocabulary Builders is a comprehensive vocabulary enrichment series for middle and secondary schools. Its consumable format and instructional strategies are designed to offer you the most effective, yet flexible, program available today. The seven books that comprise the series are recommended for the grades indicated below. However, individual classrooms vary greatly, and the highly readable nature of these texts makes them adaptable to other grade levels.

- Orange Book .... Grade 6
- Purple Book .... Grade 7
- Lime Book .... Grade 8
- Red Book .... Grade 9
- Blue Book .... Grade 10
- Green Book .... Grade 11
- Yellow Book .... Grade 12

The Lessons

Each text offers 36 instructional lessons covering a total of 360 words. These words are based on careful examination of adolescent and adult reading material and recent standardized tests. There are three types of lessons:

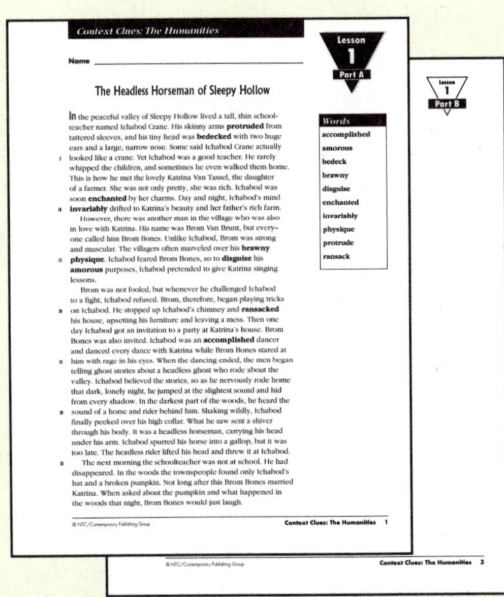

Context Clues: The Humanities

Lesson 1 Part A

Name ______________________

The Headless Horseman of Sleepy Hollow

In the peaceful valley of Sleepy Hollow lived a tall, thin schoolteacher named Ichabod Crane. His skinny arms **protruded** from tattered sleeves, and his tiny head was **bedecked** with two huge ears and a large, narrow nose. Some said Ichabod Crane actually looked like a crane. Yet Ichabod was a good teacher. He rarely whipped the children, and sometimes he even walked them home. This is how he met the lovely Katrina Van Tassel, the daughter of a farmer. She was not only pretty, she was rich. Ichabod was soon **enchanted** by her charms. Day and night, Ichabod's mind **invariably** drifted to Katrina's beauty and her father's rich farm.

However, there was another man in the village who was also in love with Katrina. His name was Brom Van Brunt, but every-one called him Brom Bones. Unlike Ichabod, Brom was strong and muscular. The villagers often marveled over his **brawny physique**. Ichabod feared Brom Bones, so to **disguise** his **amorous** purposes, Ichabod pretended to give Katrina singing lessons.

Brom was not fooled, but whenever he challenged Ichabod to a fight, Ichabod refused. Brom, therefore, began playing tricks on Ichabod. He stopped up Ichabod's chimney and **ransacked** his house, upsetting his furniture and leaving a mess. Then one day Ichabod got an invitation to a party at Katrina's house. Brom Bones was also invited. Ichabod was an **accomplished** dancer and danced every dance with Katrina while Brom Bones stared at him with rage in his eyes. When the dancing ended, the men began telling ghost stories about a headless ghost who rode about the valley. Ichabod believed the stories, so as he nervously rode home that dark, lonely night, he jumped at the slightest sound and hid from every shadow. In the darkest part of the woods, he heard the sound of a horse and rider behind him. Shaking wildly, Ichabod finally peeked over his high collar. What he saw sent a shiver through his body. It was a headless horseman, carrying his head under his arm. Ichabod spurred his horse into a gallop, but it was too late. The headless rider lifted his head and threw it at Ichabod.

The next morning the schoolteacher was not at school. He had disappeared. In the woods the townspeople found only Ichabod's hat and a broken pumpkin. Not long after this Brom Bones married Katrina. When asked about the pumpkin and what happened in the woods that night, Brom Bones would just laugh.

Words
accomplished
amorous
bedeck
brawny
disguise
enchanted
invariably
physique
protrude
ransack

© NTC/Contemporary Publishing Group — Context Clues: The Humanities 1

Lesson 1 Part B

© NTC/Contemporary Publishing Group — Context Clues: The Humanities 3

Context Clues Lessons embed ten words in an interesting and timely essay or familiar story in one of three curricular areas— the humanities, social studies, and science. Occurring in a regular cycle, these essays provide strong contexts that allow students to unlock the meaning of the words being studied.

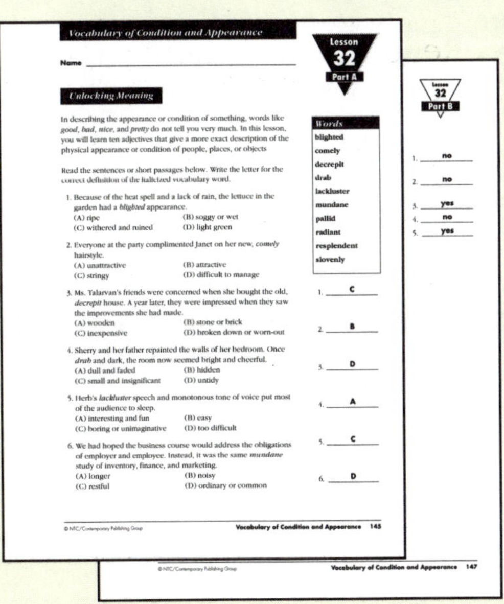

Vocabulary of Condition and Appearance

Lesson 32 Part A

Name ______________________

Unlocking Meaning

In describing the appearance or condition of something, words like *good*, *bad*, *nice*, and *pretty* do not tell you very much. In this lesson, you will learn ten adjectives that give a more exact description of the physical appearance or condition of people, places, or objects

Read the sentences or short passages below. Write the letter for the correct definition of the italicized vocabulary word.

1. Because of the heat spell and a lack of rain, the lettuce in the garden had a *blighted* appearance.
   (A) ripe (B) soggy or wet
   (C) withered and ruined (D) light green
2. Everyone at the party complimented Janet on her new, *comely* hairstyle.
   (A) unattractive (B) attractive
   (C) stringy (D) difficult to manage
3. Ms. Talarvan's friends were concerned when she bought the old, *decrepit* house. A year later, they were impressed when they saw the improvements she had made.
   (A) wooden (B) stone or brick
   (C) inexpensive (D) broken down or worn-out
4. Sherry and her father repainted the walls of her bedroom. Once *drab* and dark, the room now seemed bright and cheerful.
   (A) dull and faded (B) hidden
   (C) small and insignificant (D) untidy
5. Herb's *lackluster* speech and monotonous tone of voice put most of the audience to sleep.
   (A) interesting and fun (B) easy
   (C) boring or unimaginative (D) too difficult
6. We had hoped the business course would address the obligations of employer and employee. Instead, it was the same *mundane* study of inventory, finance, and marketing.
   (A) longer (B) noisy
   (C) restful (D) ordinary or common

Words
blighted
comely
decrepit
drab
lackluster
mundane
pallid
radiant
resplendent
slovenly

1. C
2. B
3. D
4. A
5. C
6. D

© NTC/Contemporary Publishing Group — Vocabulary of Condition and Appearance 145

Lesson 32 Part B

1. no
2. no
3. yes
4. no
5. yes

© NTC/Contemporary Publishing Group — Vocabulary of Condition and Appearance 147

Theme Lessons focus on the vocabulary of specific areas of content or meaning. For example, in the Lime Book students examine the vocabulary of mood and behavior, work and workers, and anatomy.

Root Lessons approach words through prefixes, suffixes, and one or more Latin or Greek roots or word parts. These roots and word parts are the key to understanding not only the words in the lesson, but hundreds of additional English words.

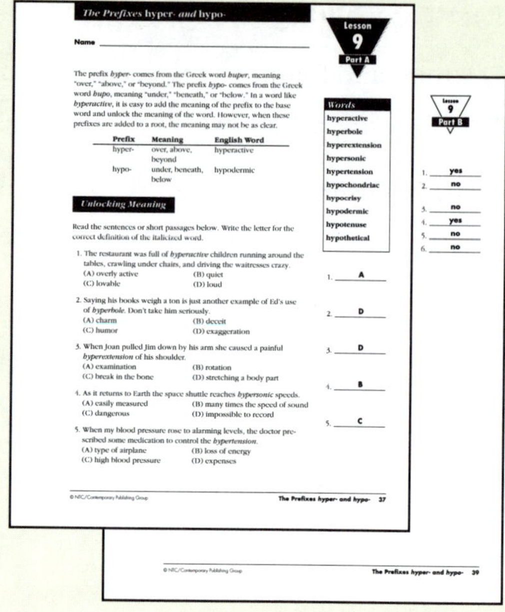

The Prefixes hyper- *and* hypo-

Lesson 9 Part A

Name

The prefix *hyper-* comes from the Greek word *huper*, meaning "over," "above," or "beyond." The prefix *hypo-* comes from the Greek word *hupo*, meaning "under," "beneath," or "below." In a word like *hyperactive*, it is easy to add the meaning of the prefix to the base word and unlock the meaning of the word. However, when these prefixes are added to a root, the meaning may not be as clear.

Prefix	Meaning	English Word
hyper-	over, above, beyond	hyperactive
hypo-	under, beneath, below	hypodermic

Words: hyperactive, hyperbole, hyperextension, hypersonic, hypertension, hypochondriac, hypocrisy, hypodermic, hypotenuse, hypothetical

Unlocking Meaning

Read the sentences or short passages below. Write the letter for the correct definition of the italicized word.

1. The restaurant was full of *hyperactive* children running around the tables, crawling under chairs, and driving the waitresses crazy.
   (A) overly active (B) quiet
   (C) lovable (D) loud
2. Saying his books weigh a ton is just another example of Ed's use of *hyperbole*. Don't take him seriously.
   (A) charm (B) deceit
   (C) humor (D) exaggeration
3. When Joan pulled Jim down by his arm she caused a painful *hyperextension* of his shoulder.
   (A) examination (B) rotation
   (C) break in the bone (D) stretching a body part
4. As it returns to Earth the space shuttle reaches *hypersonic* speeds.
   (A) easily measured (B) many times the speed of sound
   (C) dangerous (D) impossible to record
5. When my blood pressure rose to alarming levels, the doctor prescribed some medication to control the *hypertension*.
   (A) type of airplane (B) loss of energy
   (C) high blood pressure (D) expenses

1. A
2. D
3. D
4. B
5. C

© NTC/Contemporary Publishing Group — The Prefixes *hyper-* and *hypo-* 37

Lesson 9 Part B

1. yes
2. no
3. no
4. yes
5. no
6. no

© NTC/Contemporary Publishing Group — The Prefixes *hyper-* and *hypo-* 39

The Strategy

Each lesson consists of two parts, **Part A, Unlocking Meaning**, and **Part B, Applying Meaning**. Each part is printed on a single perforated page to allow easy removal and filing. In addition, individual lessons can be tailored to the unique needs and pace of your class.

Part A Unlocking Meaning

The first two pages of each lesson are devoted to helping students learn the meaning of each word on their own. Using context and/or information about roots and word parts, students choose from several proposed definitions, hypothesize about meanings, and use the dictionary at the back of the book to confirm their understanding.

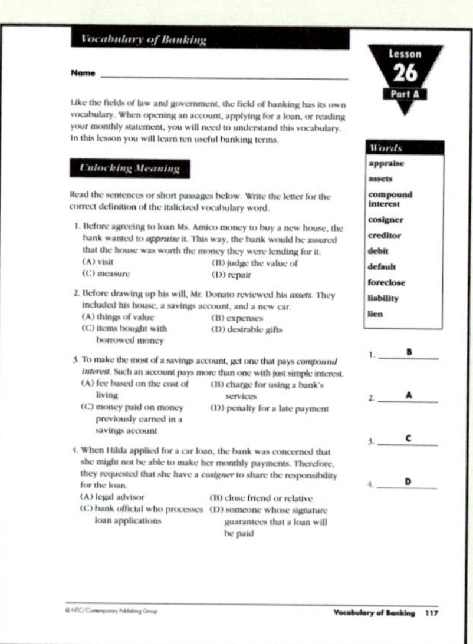

Vocabulary of Banking

Lesson 26 Part A

Name

Like the fields of law and government, the field of banking has its own vocabulary. When opening an account, applying for a loan, or reading your monthly statement, you will need to understand this vocabulary. In this lesson you will learn ten useful banking terms.

Words: appraise, assets, compound interest, cosigner, creditor, debit, default, foreclose, liability, lien

Unlocking Meaning

Read the sentences or short passages below. Write the letter for the correct definition of the italicized vocabulary word.

1. Before agreeing to loan Ms. Amico money to buy a new house, the bank wanted to *appraise* it. This way, the bank would be assured that the house was worth the money they were lending for it.
   (A) visit (B) judge the value of
   (C) measure (D) repair
2. Before drawing up his will, Mr. Donato reviewed his *assets*. They included his house, a savings account, and a new car.
   (A) things of value (B) expenses
   (C) items bought with borrowed money (D) desirable gifts
3. To make the most of a savings account, get one that pays *compound interest*. Such an account pays more than one with just simple interest.
   (A) fee based on the cost of living (B) charge for using a bank's services
   (C) money paid on money previously earned in a savings account (D) penalty for a late payment
4. When Hilda applied for a car loan, the bank was concerned that she might not be able to make her monthly payments. Therefore, they requested that she have a *cosigner* to share the responsibility for the loan.
   (A) legal advisor (B) close friend or relative
   (C) bank official who processes loan applications (D) someone whose signature guarantees that a loan will be paid

1. B
2. A
3. C
4. D

© NTC/Contemporary Publishing Group — Vocabulary of Banking 117

Part B Applying Meaning

The third and fourth pages in each lesson provide opportunities for students to apply their understanding of the words in a reading or writing situation. Each lesson allows students to read and write the words in an original sentence. In this part of the lesson, students are also introduced to appropriate variant forms of the words. For example, students may study the word *indifference* in Part A and be asked to decide whether *indifferent* is used correctly in a sentence in Part B.

Name ______________________

Lesson 15 Part B

Applying Meaning

Decide which word in parentheses best completes the sentence. Then write the sentence, adding the missing word.

1. Potato crop failures in the 1840s were the _____ of Irish immigration to America in the 1850s. (antecedent; antidote)
   antecedent
2. Gwen had a strong _____ to air travel. (anticlimax; antipathy)
   antipathy
3. Jorge is not _____, but he had to work and couldn't spend the evening with his friends. (antiseptic; antisocial)
   antisocial
4. The antique dealer tried to _____ the historic document to make the buyer think it was much older. (antedate; antebellum)
   antedate
5. A weekend alone in the woods was the perfect _____ for the hectic week Julio spent in the office. (anticlimax; antidote)
   antidote
6. Because the risk of infection is so high, hospital rooms must always be kept in an _____ condition. (antecedent; antiseptic)
   antiseptic

© NTC/Contemporary Publishing Group **The Prefixes *ante-* and *anti-*** 67

Our Living Language

The prefix ***anti-*** is one of the most flexible prefixes in the English language. It is easily added to existing words to form new words that most people will understand immediately. During the 1960s the words ***antiwar*** and ***antiestablishment*** emerged. More recently, ***antiabortion*** and ***antidumping*** have become common.

Cooperative Learning: Work with a partner to write a dictionary definition and sample sentence for each of the following words: antibusiness, antibusing, antifeminist, antigun, antinuclear, antipollution, antismog, antitank

68 **The Prefixes *ante-* and *anti-*** © NTC/Contemporary Publishing Group

Special Features

Most lessons conclude with one of the following special features designed to heighten interest in words while adding power to the vocabulary.

- **Mastering Meaning** provides opportunities to use the vocabulary words in an original writing assignment. Each Context Clues lesson concludes with this feature.
- **Bonus Words** give interesting and unusual backgrounds for one or more additional words. These memorable word histories offer easy and practical ways to build vocabulary.
- **Our Living Language** highlights the dynamic nature of our language by focusing on words that have recently entered the language or whose meaning has changed over the years.
- **Cultural Literacy Note** explains terms frequently alluded to in writing that have taken on special meaning.
- **Spelling and Meaning** explains how the spelling and meaning of words change with the addition of various endings.
- **Using the Dictionary** provides practical instruction and practice in accessing the information available in a dictionary.

Teaching and Learning Aids

Test-Taking Strategies

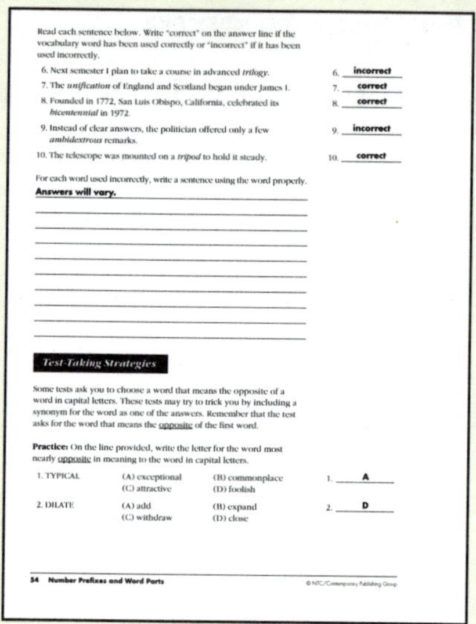

Read each sentence below. Write "correct" on the answer line if the vocabulary word has been used correctly or "incorrect" if it has been used incorrectly.

6. Next semester I plan to take a course in advanced *trilogy*. — 6. **incorrect**
7. The *unification* of England and Scotland began under James I. — 7. **correct**
8. Founded in 1772, San Luis Obispo, California, celebrated its *bicentennial* in 1972. — 8. **correct**
9. Instead of clear answers, the politician offered only a few *ambidextrous* remarks. — 9. **incorrect**
10. The telescope was mounted on a *tripod* to hold it steady. — 10. **correct**

For each word used incorrectly, write a sentence using the word properly.

Answers will vary.

Test-Taking Strategies

Some tests ask you to choose a word that means the opposite of a word in capital letters. These tests may try to trick you by including a synonym for the word as one of the answers. Remember that the test asks for the word that means the opposite of the first word.

Practice: On the line provided, write the letter for the word most nearly opposite in meaning to the word in capital letters.

1. TYPICAL	(A) exceptional (C) attractive	(B) commonplace (D) foolish	1. **A**
2. DILATE	(A) add (C) withdraw	(B) expand (D) close	2. **D**

54 **Number Prefixes and Word Parts** © NTC/Contemporary Publishing Group

Each text includes four special features designed to help students take standardized tests. Covering a wide variety of formats such as antonyms, reading comprehension, analogies, and standard English usage, these lessons familiarize students with test configurations and offer valuable suggestions for approaching each test and avoiding common pitfalls.

Assessment

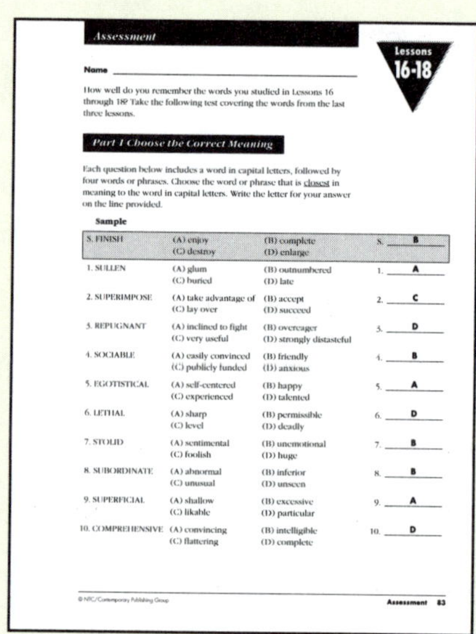

Assessment — Lessons 16-18

Name ____________

How well do you remember the words you studied in Lessons 16 through 18? Take the following test covering the words from the last three lessons.

Part 1 Choose the Correct Meaning

Each question below includes a word in capital letters, followed by four words or phrases. Choose the word or phrase that is closest in meaning to the word in capital letters. Write the letter for your answer on the line provided.

Sample

S. FINISH	(A) enjoy (C) destroy	(B) complete (D) enlarge	S. **B**
1. SULLEN	(A) glum (C) buried	(B) outnumbered (D) late	1. **A**
2. SUPERIMPOSE	(A) take advantage of (C) lay over	(B) accept (D) succeed	2. **C**
3. REPUGNANT	(A) inclined to fight (C) very useful	(B) overeager (D) strongly distasteful	3. **D**
4. SOCIABLE	(A) easily convinced (C) publicly funded	(B) friendly (D) anxious	4. **B**
5. EGOTISTICAL	(A) self-centered (C) experienced	(B) happy (D) talented	5. **A**
6. LETHAL	(A) sharp (C) level	(B) permissible (D) deadly	6. **D**
7. STOLID	(A) sentimental (C) foolish	(B) unemotional (D) huge	7. **B**
8. SUBORDINATE	(A) abnormal (C) unusual	(B) inferior (D) unseen	8. **B**
9. SUPERFICIAL	(A) shallow (C) likable	(B) excessive (D) particular	9. **A**
10. COMPREHENSIVE	(A) convincing (C) flattering	(B) intelligible (D) complete	10. **D**

© NTC/Contemporary Publishing Group **Assessment** 83

Following every third lesson is a two-page test covering the words in the three previous lessons. Employing standardized testing formats, these tests can be used as self-correcting reviews or as an evaluation tool. In addition, this Annotated Teacher's

edition includes four more tests, each covering nine lessons, or one quarter of the book. Because these tests appear only in the annotated teacher's edition, you can choose when to distribute them.

Dictionary

ex·pan·sion (ĭk **spăn′**shən) *n.* The act of growing in size, number, volume, or scope: *The expansion of the use of computers will continue into the next century.*

ex·pa·tri·ate (ĕk **spā′**trē āt′) *v.* **ex·pa·tri·at·ed, ex·pa·tri·at·ing, ex·pa·tri·ates. 1.** To remove someone from his or her native country. **2.** To voluntarily remove oneself from living in in one's native country. —*n.* (ek **spa′**tre it) A person who voluntarily lives in a foreign country: *During the French Revolution many French noblemen became expatriates in other European countries.* —

The dictionary in the back of each text includes every vocabulary word studied in the text. Each entry includes the pronunciation, definition, and any derived forms studied in the lesson. Students may refer to this dictionary when reviewing their work or to check their understanding.

Assessment Record

Name ______________________________ Class ______________

Periodic Tests

Page

Answer Key

Test A:	Test B:	Test C:	Test D:
1. B	1. B	1. A	1. E
2. C	2. D	2. D	2. B
3. A	3. A	3. E	3. A
4. E	4. E	4. A	4. C
5. B	5. A	5. E	5. B
6. D	6. C	6. B	6. D
7. E	7. D	7. A	7. A
8. A	8. B	8. D	8. B
9. C	9. E	9. B	9. C
10. D	10. C	10. E	10. E
11. B	11. A	11. B	11. D
12. D	12. D	12. D	12. B
13. E	13. B	13. C	13. A
14. C	14. E	14. A	14. E
15. A	15. B	15. A	15. D
16. E	16. c	16. e	16. f
17. D	17. g	17. b	17. b
18. D	18. a	18. d	18. d
19. A	19. e	19. j	19. e
20. C	20. b	20. f	20. j
21. D	21. j	21. i	21. i
22. B	22. h	22. h	22. g
23. E	23. f	23. a	23. a
24. A	24. d	24. c	24. h
25. C	25. i	25. g	25. c

Test A

Lessons 1–9

Name ______________________________

Part 1 Choose the Correct Meaning

Decide which definition best fits the italicized word in the sentence. Write the letter for your choice on the answer line.

1. After the accident, the managers began looking for a convenient *scapegoat*. 1. ________
   (A) the person who plans an an activity (B) someone who is blamed for the faults of others
   (C) source of information (D) type of report given after an accident
   (E) an illiterate person

2. The guide advised us that the trip could become *perilous* at times. 2. ________
   (A) exciting (B) expensive (C) dangerous
   (D) boring (E) overwhelming

3. The candidate hoped to *garner* a few extra votes before the election. 3. ________
   (A) earn (B) explain (C) deliver (D) steal (E) eliminate

4. For years Sheila held *menial* jobs in the hospitality field. 4. ________
   (A) meaningful (B) highly paid (C) related to computers
   (D) desirable (E) humble

5. The politician was *lionized* by the press for his position on the bill. 5. ________
   (A) ignored (B) praised (C) destroyed (D) explained (E) pleased

6. The main character declared his *amorous* intentions in the first act. 6. ________
   (A) evil (B) silly (C) hidden (D) romantic (E) noisy

7. The employer announced that he would not *tolerate* certain types of behavior on the job. 7. ________
   (A) encourage (B) insist upon (C) describe (D) reward (E) allow

8. The *preponderance* of evidence pointed to the defendant's guilt. 8. ________
   (A) majority (B) lack (C) cleverness (D) simplicity (E) necessity

9. Since his childhood, Edward has been something of a *hypochondriac*. 9. ________
   (A) one who commits crimes (B) liar (C) one who constantly feels he or she is ill
   (D) one who travels frequently (E) skillful swimmer

10. Her performance was interrupted several times by the *accolades* of the audience. 10. ________
    (A) rudeness (B) requests (C) demands (D) tributes (E) explanations

Part 2 Choose the Correct Meaning

Each question below includes a word in capital letters, followed by five words or phrases. Choose the word or phrase that is closest in meaning to the word in capital letters. Write the letter for your answer on the line provided.

11. MEDDLESOME (A) musical (B) interfering (C) interested (D) commonplace (E) expensive 11. ____________

12. APTITUDE (A) outlook (B) height (C) desire for food (D) talent (E) similarity 12. ____________

13. LABORIOUS (A) superior (B) organized (C) enslaved (D) proud (E) exhausting 13. ____________

14. LAGGARD (A) expressionless (B) sloping (C) loafer (D) carpentry tool (E) expert 14. ____________

15. HYPOTHETICAL (A) assumed (B) triangular (C) slow moving (D) sharp (E) easily recognized 15. ____________

16. BEDECK (A) place on a platform (B) flatten (C) expand (D) honor (E) decorate 16. ____________

17. PEAL (A) strip (B) attract (C) bring together (D) ring (E) guard against 17. ____________

18. REGENERATE (A) wicked (B) royalty (C) preserved (D) recreate (E) show openly 18. ____________

19. TRANSITORY (A) brief (B) small (C) related to trains (D) between nations (E) trapped 19. ____________

20. HYPOCRISY (A) religious belief (B) heavy weight (C) dishonesty (D) reputation (E) width 20. ____________

21. DESPONDENT (A) harsh ruler (B) letter writer (C) excited (D) gloomy (E) nervous 21. ____________

22. GERMINATE (A) wipe out (B) take root (C) protect (D) deliver (E) poison 22. ____________

23. GENTRY (A) bend at the knee (B) scholar (C) servant (D) distant relative (E) highborn 23. ____________

24. DISGRUNTLED (A) displeased (B) taken apart (C) supportive (D) crude (E) grooved 24. ____________

25. BOVINE (A) beloved (B) twisted (C) lacking in movement (D) juicy (E) dizzy 25. ____________

Test B

Lessons 10–18

Name ______________________

Part 1 Choose the Correct Meaning

Each question below includes a word in capital letters, followed by five words or phrases. Choose the word or phrase that is closest in meaning to the word in capital letters. Write the letter for your answer on the line provided.

1. AMBIVALENT (A) ambitious (B) undecided (C) talented (D) firm (E) able to use both hands 1. ________
2. SUPERFICIAL (A) sensible (B) thorough (C) spiritual (D) shallow (E) high official 2. ________
3. ALIENATE (A) set against (B) send abroad (C) embrace (D) express (E) provide comfort 3. ________
4. INDIGNANT (A) point out (B) secured tightly (C) amused (D) embarrassed (E) offended 4. ________
5. ABHORRENT (A) hated (B) excused (C) stopped suddenly (D) related to trees (E) vulgar 5. ________
6. FICKLE (A) easily broken (B) colorful (C) changeable (D) cheap (E) foreign 6. ________
7. ANTAGONIZE (A) cover with a protective shield (B) torture (C) express emotionally (D) provoke (E) pretend 7. ________
8. BIENNIAL (A) yearly (B) every two years (C) type of flower (D) twice a year (E) type of celebration 8. ________
9. STOLID (A) stolen (B) solid (C) quiet (D) rotting (E) emotionless 9. ________
10. REPUGNANT (A) easily angered (B) muscular (C) disgusting (D) favorably viewed (E) frightening 10. ________
11. ANTIPATHY (A) dislike (B) opposed to government (C) disappointment (D) purity (E) undesirable 11. ________
12. MUTATION (A) thick cover (B) pattern (C) loneliness (D) change (E) dark colors 12. ________
13. COHESIVE (A) living side by side (B) holding together (C) difficult to understand (D) loud (E) having a hard surface 13. ________

14. UNIQUE (A) imaginary (B) extreme (C) historic (D) easily bent (E) one of a kind 14. ____________

15. INCARCERATION (A) handicap (B) imprisonment (C) forward movement (D) business arrangement (E) printed material 15. ____________

Part 2 Matching Words and Meanings

Match the definition in Column B with the word in Column A. Write the letter for your choice on the answer line.

Column A	**Column B**	
16. mullah	a. split	16. ____________
17. antedate	b. break	17. ____________
18. cleave	c. spiritual leader	18. ____________
19. martial	d. superior to all others	19. ____________
20. breach	e. military	20. ____________
21. desecration	f. strength of character	21. ____________
22. subservient	g. date earlier	22. ____________
23. mettle	h. lower in rank	23. ____________
24. superlative	i. tell apart	24. ____________
25. differentiate	j. irreverent action	25. ____________

Test C

Lessons 19–27

Name ______________________________

Part 1 Choose the Correct Meaning

Each question below includes a word in capital letters, followed by five words or phrases. Choose the word or phrase that is closest in meaning to the word in capital letters. Write the letter for your answer on the line provided.

1. ADDENDUM (A) addition (B) musical instrument (C) number in math problem (D) leg muscle (E) letter 1. ________

2. UTOPIAN (A) foreign (B) make believe (C) historic (D) perfect (E) medical 2. ________

3. IRREFUTABLE (A) contradictory (B) unreasonable (C) cannot be bent (D) unusable (E) undeniable 3. ________

4. APPRAISE (A) place a value on (B) approve (C) explain (D) excuse (E) deny 4. ________

5. LUXURIANT (A) expensive (B) trimmed with gold (C) yellow (D) strange (E) abundant 5. ________

6. ASUNDER (A) beneath (B) apart (C) applaud (D) sunny (E) reasonable 6. ________

7. BULBOUS (A) bulb shaped (B) reddish (C) stretched (D) false (E) from the devil 7. ________

8. ESTRANGE (A) unusual (B) enslave (C) arrange in a line (D) separate (E) react suddenly 8. ________

9. ABRASIVE (A) well placed (B) rough (C) often criticized (D) cleaned (E) ruined beyond repair 9. ________

10. UNTENABLE (A) desirable (B) impossible to explain (C) dangerous to occupy (D) disorganized (E) indefensible 10. ________

11. BASTION (A) rod or stick (B) fortification (C) weapon (D) falsehood (E) level field 11. ________

12. DEFAULT (A) loss of moral values (B) break into large pieces (C) decline politely (D) failure to pay (E) celebrate a victory 12. ________

13. INDISCREET (A) powerful (B) industrious (C) thoughtless (D) amazing (E) sinful 13. ________

14. DISPARITY (A) difference (B) hopelessness (C) fairness (D) excuse (E) demand 14. ____________

15. ABDICATE (A) quit (B) criticize (C) forgive (D) remove (E) announce 15. ____________

Part 2 Matching Words and Meanings

Match the definition in Column B with the word in Column A. Write the letter for your choice on the answer line.

Column A	Column B	
16. abhor	a. harsh	16. ____________
17. narcissism	b. self admiration	17. ____________
18. irrelevant	c. cleverly planned	18. ____________
19. encumbrance	d. not applicable	19. ____________
20. serpentine	e. hate	20. ____________
21. exacerbate	f. winding	21. ____________
22. abstain	g. eliminate	22. ____________
23. inclement	h. do without	23. ____________
24. contrived	i. worsen	24. ____________
25. eradicate	j. barrier	25. ____________

Test D

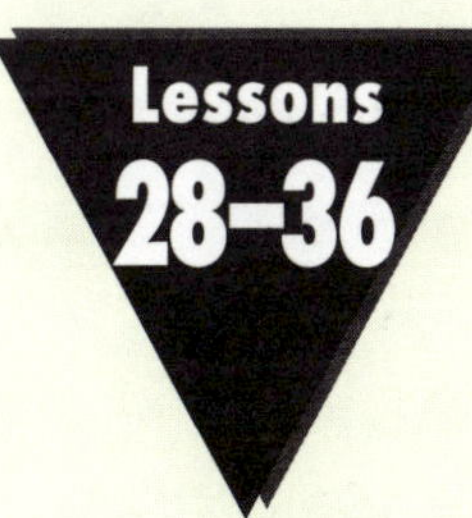

Name ______________________________

Part 1 Choose the Correct Meaning

Each question below includes a word in capital letters, followed by five words or phrases. Choose the word or phrase that is closest in meaning to the word in capital letters. Write the letter for your answer on the line provided.

1. IMPROMPTU (A) unlikely (B) simple (C) unattached (D) impossible (E) unprepared 1. ________

2. AFFLICTION (A) special interest (B) hardship (C) love (D) sharp noise (E) type of story 2. ________

3. LESION (A) wound (B) military group (C) foreign representative (D) unpaid debt (E) type of clothing 3. ________

4. LIBERATION (A) beverage (B) system for arranging books (C) release (D) productive soil (E) muscle tissue 4. ________

5. FERVID (A) solemn (B) eager (C) evil (D) costly (E) foul smelling 5. ________

6. COMELY (A) not trustworthy (B) well groomed (C) easily tricked (D) pleasing (E) defenseless 6. ________

7. ADVENT (A) beginning (B) invent (C) place a value on (D) conclusion (E) strong dislike 7. ________

8. ANECDOTE (A) type of medicine (B) story (C) perfect model (D) inexpensive gift (E) banking term 8. ________

9. SHREWD (A) troublesome nag (B) slice into small pieces (C) wise (D) uneven (E) colorful 9. ________

10. PULMONARY (A) related to the heart (B) highly polished (C) preventable (D) expanded (E) related to the lungs 10. ________

11. CONFUTE (A) confuse (B) refuse angrily (C) send away (D) disprove (E) take by force 11. ________

12. CONGEAL (A) show openly (B) harden (C) deliver (D) hid (E) give permission 12. ________

13. SCOFF (A) sneer (B) tear (C) explain (D) blame (E) send away 13. ____________

14. CAJOLE (A) celebrate (B) deny (C) replace (D) take in (E) coax 14. ____________

15. ADMONISH (A) pretend (B) admire (C) pierce (D) advise (E) disappear 15. ____________

Part 2 Matching Words and Meanings

Match the definition in Column B with the word in Column A. Write the letter for your choice on the answer line.

Column A	Column B	
16. scorn	a. seep through; penetrate	16. ____________
17. mundane	b. commonplace	17. ____________
18. capillary	c. agreement	18. ____________
19. demise	d. blood vessel	19. ____________
20. accentuate	e. death	20. ____________
21. resplendent	f. sneer	21. ____________
22. pallid	g. colorless	22. ____________
23. pervade	h. associate	23. ____________
24. affiliate	i. dazzling	24. ____________
25. acquiescence	j. emphasize	25. ____________

NTC

Vocabulary Builders

Lime Book

National Textbook Company
a division of NTC/Contemporary Publishing Group
Lincolnwood, Illinois USA

Project Development: Cottage Communications
Cover Design: Ophelia M. Chambliss
Cover Illustration: Sandra Burton

Acknowledgments

The pronunciation key used in the dictionary has been reprinted by permission from *The American Heritage* Dictionary of the English Language, Third Edition, © 1992 by Houghton Mifflin Company.

ISBN: 0-8442-0394-7 (Pupil's Edition)
ISBN: 0-8442-0395-5 (Annotated Teacher's Edition)

Published by National Textbook Company,
a division of NTC/Contemporary Publishing Group, Inc.
4255 West Touhy Avenue,
Lincolnwood (Chicago), Illinois, 60646-1975, U.S.A.

890 VL 987654321

Contents

Name ______________________________

Lesson 1
Part A

The Headless Horseman of Sleepy Hollow

In the peaceful valley of Sleepy Hollow lived a tall, thin schoolteacher named Ichabod Crane. His skinny arms **protruded** from tattered sleeves, and his tiny head was **bedecked** with two huge ears and a large, narrow nose. Some said Ichabod Crane actually looked like a crane. Yet Ichabod was a good teacher. He rarely whipped the children, and sometimes he even walked them home. This is how he met the lovely Katrina Van Tassel, the daughter of a farmer. She was not only pretty, she was rich. Ichabod was soon **enchanted** by her charms. Day and night, Ichabod's mind **invariably** drifted to Katrina's beauty and her father's rich farm.

However, there was another man in the village who was also in love with Katrina. His name was Brom Van Brunt, but every–one called him Brom Bones. Unlike Ichabod, Brom was strong and muscular. The villagers often marveled over his **brawny physique**. Ichabod feared Brom Bones, so to **disguise** his **amorous** purposes, Ichabod pretended to give Katrina singing lessons.

Brom was not fooled, but whenever he challenged Ichabod to a fight, Ichabod refused. Brom, therefore, began playing tricks on Ichabod. He stopped up Ichabod's chimney and **ransacked** his house, upsetting his furniture and leaving a mess. Then one day Ichabod got an invitation to a party at Katrina's house. Brom Bones was also invited. Ichabod was an **accomplished** dancer and danced every dance with Katrina while Brom Bones stared at him with rage in his eyes. When the dancing ended, the men began telling ghost stories about a headless ghost who rode about the valley. Ichabod believed the stories, so as he nervously rode home that dark, lonely night, he jumped at the slightest sound and hid from every shadow. In the darkest part of the woods, he heard the sound of a horse and rider behind him. Shaking wildly, Ichabod finally peeked over his high collar. What he saw sent a shiver through his body. It was a headless horseman, carrying his head under his arm. Ichabod spurred his horse into a gallop, but it was too late. The headless rider lifted his head and threw it at Ichabod.

The next morning the schoolteacher was not at school. He had disappeared. In the woods the townspeople found only Ichabod's hat and a broken pumpkin. Not long after this Brom Bones married Katrina. When asked about the pumpkin and what happened in the woods that night, Brom Bones would just laugh.

Words

- **accomplished**
- **amorous**
- **bedeck**
- **brawny**
- **disguise**
- **enchanted**
- **invariably**
- **physique**
- **protrude**
- **ransack**

Unlocking Meaning

Each word in this lesson's word list appears in dark type in the selection you just read. Think about how the vocabulary word is used in the selection, then write the letter for the best answer to each question.

1. If something *protrudes* (line 2), it _______. — 1. B
   (A) injures slightly (B) sticks out
   (C) causes laughter (D) is the source of admiration

2. Which word could best replace *bedecked* in line 3? — 2. D
   (A) dampened (B) alarmed
   (C) replaced (D) decorated

3. If someone is *enchanted* (line 9), he or she is _____. — 3. A
   (A) under a spell (B) singing a song
   (C) sleeping soundly (D) suffering from a disease

4. If something *invariably* (line 10) happens, it ______. — 4. B
   (A) rarely occurs (B) goes on constantly without change
   (C) cannot be counted on (D) cannot be seen

5. A *brawny* (line 14) person is ______. — 5. C
   (A) quiet (B) musically talented
   (C) strong and muscular (D) intelligent

6. Which words best define the word *physique* (line 15)? — 6. B
   (A) mental ability (B) the appearance of the body
   (C) medical history (D) religious beliefs

7. If you *disguise* (line 15) something, you _____. — 7. D
   (A) put it in plain view (B) destroy it
   (C) strongly dislike it (D) hide its appearance

8. An *amorous* (line 16) purpose is one that involves ______. — 8. A
   (A) love (B) money
   (C) danger (D) music

9. If you *ransack* (line 20) something, you _____. — 9. C
   (A) surround it (B) rebuild it
   (C) damage or destroy it (D) move it from place to place

10. An *accomplished* (line 23) dancer is ______. — 10. C
    (A) clumsy (B) unable to get a partner
    (C) skillful (D) poorly dressed

Name ______________________________

Applying Meaning

Decide which word in parentheses best completes the sentence. Then write the sentence, adding the missing word.

1. José finally overcame his shyness and wrote a(n) ________ poem to Maria. (amorous; brawny)

   amorous

2. Willard was such an ________ chess player, he could play and win ten matches at the same time. (accomplished; enchanted)

   accomplished

3. Returning from a long trip, we found someone had ______ our apartment and broken my favorite lamp. (disguised; ransacked)

   ransacked

4. Every year at Christmas, our village is ________ with colorful lights and banners. (bedecked; ransacked)

   bedecked

5. The football player's _______ body could not be hidden under his size XXXL uniform. (brawny; enchanted)

   brawny

Read each sentence or short passage below. Write "correct" on the answer line if the vocabulary word has been used correctly or "incorrect" if it has been used incorrectly.

6. Because of the expected cold weather, orange growers took several steps to *protrude* their crop. 6. **incorrect**

7. Whenever there was work to be done around the house, Josh *invariably* remembered some homework he had to do. 7. **correct**

8. In Mr. Hanson's class we studied gravity and other laws of *physiques*. 8. **incorrect**

9. The fairy tale took place in an *enchanted* forest full of elves and wizards. 9. **correct**

10. Many of Shakespeare's plays include comic scenes in which a character *disguises* his appearance to spy on someone. 10. **correct**

For each word used incorrectly, write a sentence using the word properly.

Answers will vary.

Mastering Meaning

Imagine that you are a reporter for the *Sleepy Hollow Gazette*. Write a newspaper account of the mysterious disappearance of Ichabod Crane. Include quotes from Katrina and Brom Van Brunt. Mention the rumors that both Mr. Crane and Mr. Van Brunt were in love with Katrina and the events at the party the night before Ichabod's disappearance. Keep your report factual and objective. Be sure to include the *who*, *what*, *where*, *when*, and possible *why* of Mr. Crane's disappearance. Use some of the words you studied in this lesson.

Lesson 2
Part A

Name ____________________

Our moods affect the way we act. It is not difficult to tell if someone is unhappy over criticism or upset with a grade on a paper. It shows in the individual's face, in movements, and in actions. While each of us is unique, moods and behaviors generally fall into clear categories. The words in this lesson describe certain moods and behaviors you will probably recognize in yourself and in others.

Words

amicable
berserk
defiant
despondent
disgruntled
exuberant
lascivious
loathsome
meddlesome
melancholy

Unlocking Meaning

Read the sentences or short passages below. Write the letter for the correct definition of the italicized vocabulary word.

1. Sandy cannot stand her cousin Jasper. Whenever Jasper visits, he always gets to watch the TV shows he likes and to sit in her favorite chair. Nevertheless, Sandy's mother makes her behave in an *amicable* manner because Jasper is, after all, a relative.
   (A) rude (B) loud
   (C) friendly (D) sneaky

   1. C

2. Coach Santos is usually quite calm and relaxed, but when the umpire threw his star player out of the game, he went *berserk*. Coach threw his hat on the field, kicked dirt into the air, and refused to leave the playing field.
   (A) into a wild rage (B) quiet
   (C) relaxed and comfortable (D) happy

   2. A

3. The more the police demanded the criminal's surrender, the more *defiant* he became. At one point he shook his fist at the officers and dared them to come and get him.
   (A) generous (B) resistant and unyielding
   (C) sneaky (D) foolish

   3. B

4. After his ideas were turned down by the group, Mike became *despondent*. He said little and left the meeting early.
   (A) excited (B) angry
   (C) encouraged (D) discouraged

   4. D

5. Four *disgruntled* workers walked off the job when the layoffs were announced. For weeks they had been unhappy, but when their friends and coworkers lost their jobs, they took action.
   (A) tired (B) simple
   (C) very displeased (D) amazed

   5. C

6. On the last day of the school year, a crowd of *exuberant* students gathered at the door waiting for the final bell to ring. When the bell finally rang, their cheers could be heard blocks away. 6. A

(A) wildly joyful (B) slow moving
(C) intelligent (D) confident

7. The city council passed a law to prevent stores from displaying *lascivious* books and magazines where young children might see them. Such material was felt to be improper for them. 7. B

(A) tattered and torn (B) containing sexual material
(C) educationally sound (D) costly

8. We were stunned when the bully took the child's bike and lunch box. We hardly knew what to do since we had never seen such *loathsome* behavior before. 8. C

(A) humorous (B) surprising
(C) extremely hateful (D) lazy

9. Hal had grown weary of Kim's *meddlesome* behavior. Her constant questions about his personal life were getting quite annoying. 9. D

(A) charming (B) athletic
(C) simple (D) interfering

10. Tears appeared in the eyes of several graduates when the *melancholy* notes of the school song were played. They knew they were saying good-bye to their carefree school days. 10. A

(A) sad (B) religious
(C) happy (D) piercing

Name ________________________________

Applying Meaning

Decide which word in parentheses best completes the sentence. Then write the sentence, adding the missing word.

1. In many cities it is illegal to display _____ magazines or other vulgar material where children might see them. (amicable; lascivious)

   lascivious

2. Kwan had been _____ for days because he was sure he had failed the test. (despondent; exuberant)

   despondent

3. However, when saw he had earned an A, Kwan became _____ and danced down the hall. (despondent; exuberant)

   exuberant

4. Refusing the blindfold, the condemned traitor faced the firing squad with a _____ stare. (defiant; meddlesome)

   defiant

5. Recalling his happy childhood, the elderly man began to feel a little _____ . (disgruntled; melancholy)

   melancholy

6. The heat and humidity caused the dog to go _____ : it ran in circles and growled at everyone. (amicable; berserk)

   berserk

7. Destroying the computers and painting racial slurs on the walls was a ______ act of vandalism. (loathsome; meddlesome)

loathsome

8. Even after days of talks, the strikers failed to reach an ______ agreement with management. (amicable; exuberant)

amicable

9. In this book a ______ woman constantly tries to make romantic matches among her friends. (despondent; meddlesome)

meddlesome

10. The plant had to close because a few ______ workers locked themselves to the main gate. (disgruntled; melancholy)

disgruntled

Cultural Literacy Note

The Humours

An old theory held that the human body was made up of four liquids, or humours: blood, phlegm, yellow bile, and black bile. One's personality was thought to be the result of these liquids. Someone who seemed sentimental and thoughtful was thought to have too much black bile. People of this type were called *melancholy*, a word formed from the Greek word *melas*, meaning "black," and *khole*, meaning "bile."

Do Some Research: Look up the meaning and history of these words: *sanguine*, *choleric*, and *phlegmatic*.

The Root -pel-

Name ______________________________

The Latin word *pellere* means "to drive" or "to push." It appears in several forms in English words, yet each form still keeps some hint of its original Latin meaning. It most often occurs as *-pel-*, as in the word *compel*. However, it sometimes becomes *-peal-* as in *appeal*, or *-pul-* as in *pulse*. Being able to recognize this root will help you unlock the meaning of a number of unfamiliar words. Each vocabulary word in this lesson has some form of the Latin word *pellere*.

Root	Meaning	English Word
-pel-	to drive, to push	compel
-peal-		appeal
-pul-		pulse

Words

appeal
compel
expel
impulse
peal
propel
propulsion
pulse
repeal
repulse

Unlocking Meaning

A vocabulary word appears in italics in each sentence or short passage below. Find the root in the vocabulary word and think about how the word is used in the passage. Then write a definition for the vocabulary word. Compare your definition with the definition in the dictionary in the back of the book.

1. To make it easier to reach those injured by the tornado, the mayor made an *appeal* for others to stay out of the area.

   Definitions will vary.

2. The new state regulation will *compel* all twelfth-grade students to pass tests in reading and math in order to graduate.

   Definitions will vary.

3. The lifeguard was able to *expel* the water from the victim's lungs. After that, her breathing became easier.

   Definitions will vary.

4. Seeing the beautiful ocean waves pounding on the shore, I gave in to a sudden *impulse* and dashed fully clothed into the surf.
Definitions will vary.

5. As the monument to the dead firefighters was unveiled, the *peal* of a single church bell broke the solemn quiet.
Definitions will vary.

6. A powerful engine *propels* a jet ski by taking in water at the front of the craft and rapidly forcing it out behind.
Definitions will vary.

7. Before the steam engine, horses were the most important means of *propulsion*. They pulled everything from trolleys to plows.
Definitions will vary.

8. By pressing an artery in my neck, the doctor could feel my *pulse*.
Definitions will vary.

9. Angry voters organized a drive to *repeal* the tax increase. If put to a vote, the increase would surely go down to defeat.
Definitions will vary.

10. For days, the defenders of the Alamo were able to *repulse* every attack. On March 6, 1836, however, the mission was overrun.
Definitions will vary.

Name ______________________________

Lesson 3 Part B

Applying Meaning

Read each sentence or short passage below. Write "correct" on the answer line if the vocabulary word has been used correctly or "incorrect" if it has been used incorrectly.

1. His work on the project earned him a *propulsion* to foreman. — 1. incorrect
2. The judge could not *compel* the witness to testify against himself. — 2. correct
3. The bells rang every evening at six o'clock. They would *repeal* two hours later at eight o'clock. — 3. incorrect
4. The losing candidate remained quite bitter. He always *repulsed* his old opponent's friendly approaches. — 4. correct
5. *Peals* of laughter filled the theater during the comedian's act. — 5. correct
6. It took every ounce of my strength to overcome the *pulse* to tell him what I thought of his rude behavior. — 6. incorrect

For each word used incorrectly, write a sentence using the word properly.

Answers will vary.

Follow the directions below to write a sentence using a vocabulary word.

7. Describe something you did. Use any form of the word *impulse*.

Sample Answer: When I found the wallet, my first impulse was to take the money and buy the CD I wanted. In the end, however, I returned the wallet to the owner.

8. Write a slogan for a worthy cause. Use any form of the word *appeal.*

Sample Answer: The flood victims need your help! Please answer our appeal for clothes and food.

9. Describe how a bicycle works. Use any form of the word *propel.*

Sample Answer: A bicycle uses the strength and power of legs and a simple pulley to propel it. It allows people to move more quickly than they could ever run.

10. Use any form of the word *expel* to describe something that happened at school.

Sample Answer: The principal had to expel several students after they set off a false fire alarm.

Spelling and Language

Adding -ed and -ing

When a one-syllable word ends with one vowel and one consonant, the final consonant is doubled before adding -ed or -ing. When a word of two or more syllables ends with one vowel and one consonant, the final consonant is doubled only if the final syllable is stressed.

skip	skipped	skipping
com**pel**	compelled	compelling
limit	limited	limiting

Add the Endings: Add *-ed* and *-ing* to these words: prefer, equal, shovel, bother, wonder, permit.

preferred, preferring; equaled, equaling; shoveled, shoveling; bothered, bothering; wondered, wondering; permitted, permitting

Name ______________________________

How well do you remember the words you studied in Lessons 1 through 3? Take the following test covering the words from the last three lessons.

Part 1 Choose the Correct Meaning

Each question below includes a word in capital letters, followed by four words or phrases. Choose the word or phrase that is closest in meaning to the word in capital letters. Write the letter for your answer on the line provided.

Sample

Word			Answer
S. FINISH	(A) enjoy (C) destroy	(B) complete (D) enlarge	S. B
1. AMICABLE	(A) talented (C) unusual	(B) kindly (D) late	1. B
2. RANSACK	(A) damage (C) forget	(B) put together (D) believe	2. A
3. DESPONDENT	(A) without hope (C) careful	(B) deep (D) energetic	3. A
4. DISGRUNTLED	(A) noisy (C) talkative	(B) ugly (D) unhappy	4. D
5. INVARIABLY	(A) different (C) skilled	(B) thoughtfully (D) without change	5. D
6. EXUBERANT	(A) spirited (C) uncovered	(B) cowardly (D) forgetful	6. A
7. BRAWNY	(A) blonde (C) brave	(B) muscular (D) tan	7. B
8. LOATHSOME	(A) lazy (C) hateful	(B) wealthy (D) old	8. C
9. BEDECK	(A) extend (C) beat	(B) overcome (D) adorn	9. D
10. MEDDLESOME	(A) playful (C) hardworking	(B) loud (D) prying	10. D

11. IMPULSE	(A) urge (C) memory	(B) smell (D) order	11. A
12. ENCHANTED	(A) long (C) spellbound	(B) rhymed (D) religious	12. C
13. REPEAL	(A) harvest (C) prepare	(B) cancel (D) save	13. B
14. COMPEL	(A) send (C) advise	(B) encourage (D) force	14. D
15. PULSE	(A) excuse (C) sound	(B) beat (D) smoothness	15. B

Part 2 Matching Words and Meanings

Match the definition in Column B with the word in Column A. Write the letter of the correct definition on the line provided.

Column A	Column B	
16. expel	a. to cause to move forward	16. j
17. defiant	b. in a rage	17. f
18. accomplished	c. the appearance of the body	18. g
19. propel	d. very sad	19. a
20. berserk	e. to hide	20. b
21. appeal	f. unwilling to yield to authority	21. i
22. disguise	g. skilled	22. e
23. physique	h. hateful	23. c
24. loathsome	i. request	24. h
25. melancholy	j. to push out	25. d

Name ______________________________

Current Trends

Too often, young people prepare themselves for jobs that are rapidly disappearing. This **tendency** is not hard to understand. When people think about good jobs, they think about ones they have heard or read about. They may even have had some experience with them. In other words they think about jobs that already exist.

However, the workplace keeps changing because the world keeps changing. Jobs in some fields are increasing, while those in other fields are disappearing. In the early part of this century, manufacturing jobs **dominated** the Help Wanted ads in newspapers. Factories hired huge numbers of people and paid them good money to build everything from automobiles to paper clips. However, by the 1960s machines were doing the work men and women used to do. **Automation** greatly reduced the number of manufacturing jobs. Moreover, businesses with factories requiring a large labor pool have moved to countries where labor is cheap. The number of manufacturing jobs available today is **insignificant** compared to those in other fields.

According to government figures, the **preponderance** of jobs in the next century will be in service-related fields, such as health and business. Jobs will also be plentiful in the technical fields and in **retail** establishments, such as stores and restaurants. The **expansion** in these fields is due to several factors: an aging population, numerous technical breakthroughs, and our changing lifestyles. The highest-paying jobs will go to people with degrees in science, computers, engineering, and health care.

What will employers of the future look for? Employers will want workers who are **flexible** and therefore able to change as business changes. The workers of the future will need to **tolerate** these changes. Many people will be expected to perform **temporary** jobs, then move on to new and different tasks. Each new task may involve new skills and understandings. The only thing that will remain the same is change.

Words

automation
dominate
expansion
flexible
insignificant
preponderance
retail
temporary
tendency
tolerate

Unlocking Meaning

Each word in this lesson's word list appears in dark type in the selection you just read. Think about how the vocabulary word is used in the selection. Then write the letter for the best answer to each question.

1. A *tendency* (line 2) is a(n) — 1. B
   (A) occupation (B) trend or direction
   (C) agreement (D) time of year

2. Which word could best replace *dominated* in line 10? — 2. C
   (A) misplaced (B) wrote
   (C) controlled (D) hired

3. *Automation* (line 14) means the use of — 3. A
   (A) machines to do work (B) wheels to move equipment
   (C) factories instead of small shops (D) education

4. Which word could best replace *insignificant* in line 17? — 4. C
   (A) magnificent (B) valuable
   (C) unimportant (D) beautiful

5. Which word or words could best replace *preponderance* in line 19? — 5. D
   (A) loss (B) description
   (C) smallest number (D) largest number

6. A *retail* (line 22) business is one that — 6. C
   (A) buys land for development (B) hires doctors
   (C) sells things in small, individual amounts (D) loans money to people

7. *Expansion* (line 23) means — 7. A
   (A) growth (B) value
   (C) sale (D) difficulty

8. If you are *flexible* (line 28), you can — 8. D
   (A) be on time (B) speak another language
   (C) work hard (D) change to meet new conditions

9. In line 29, the word *tolerate* means — 9. A
   (A) accept (B) dislike
   (C) avoid (D) talk about

10. A *temporary* (line 30) job is one that — 10. C
    (A) requires skills (B) lasts forever
    (C) is short-lived (D) stops slowly

Name ___________________________________

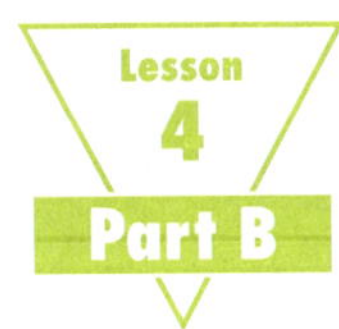

Applying Meaning

Write the vocabulary word or a form of the word that fits each clue below. Then use the word in a sentence.

1. An example would be a machine that fills bottles.
   automation Sentences will vary.

2. The leader of the wolf pack will do this to the other members of the pack.
   dominate Sentences will vary.

3. Someone who can change plans at the last minute might be described with this word.
   flexible Sentences will vary.

4. Things fitting this description will not last forever.
   temporary Sentences will vary.

5. It has a prefix that means "not" and comes from the word "signify."
   insignificant Sentences will vary.

6. You see these kinds of stores in malls and shopping centers.
   retail Sentences will vary.

7. The greatest in number, weight, or importance.
preponderance Sentences will vary.

Decide which form of the word in parentheses best completes each sentence. Then write the sentence, adding the missing word

8. A good education can _____ your chances of finding work. (expansion)
expand

9. I am very _____ of mistakes but not of lies. (tolerate)
tolerant

10. People in this neighborhood _____ to get along very well. (tendency)
tend

Mastering Meaning

One of your relatives owns a record store and hires students during the summer. You would like to be one of those hired next summer. Write your relative a friendly letter, explaining why you would be perfect for the job. Use some of the words you studied in this lesson.

Name ______________________

Work is an important part of everyone's life. It is not surprising, therefore, that many of our words deal with work and workers. Supervisors need words to describe the levels of skills of the workers. Workers need words to define the work they do and how well they and others do it. In this lesson you will learn ten words that describe work and workers.

Words

apprentice
aptitude
drudgery
journeyman
laborious
lackey
laggard
menial
nepotism
seniority

Unlocking Meaning

Read the sentences or short passages below. Write the letter for the correct definition of the italicized vocabulary word.

1. After graduating from a technical high school, John was eager to pursue a career as a plumber. To learn the trade, he became an *apprentice* so that he could learn from an experienced plumber.
(A) partner in a business (B) experienced supervisor
(C) paid advisor (D) someone learning a trade

1. D

2. Because of her natural *aptitude* for painting and drawing, Yolanda looked forward to a career as a commercial artist.
(A) lack of interest (B) curiosity
(C) ability or talent (D) fame

2. C

3. Carmen thought the job would give her the chance to use her creative talents. However, she soon learned that her job was *drudgery*, ordering supplies and answering the telephone.
(A) unpleasant, dull work (B) easy and fun
(C) full of opportunities (D) work requiring great personal skills

3. A

4. Building the cabinets required a knowledge of wood and exact measurements. Only a *journeyman* carpenter could be trusted with the job.
(A) uneducated (B) lazy
(C) skillful and experienced (D) unknown

4. C

5. Delivering groceries proved to be quite *laborious*. Kim found himself carrying heavy bags up several flights of steps in four-story apartment buildings.
(A) exciting (B) difficult and demanding
(C) relaxing and refreshing (D) interesting and informative

5. B

6. Ms. Santos did not want some *lackey* for her assistant. She preferred an independent thinker, not someone who always agreed with her. 6. A

(A) humble servant (B) troublemaker
(C) lazy or untrustworthy worker (D) lawbreaker

7. If the production line is to work properly, everyone must do his or her job promptly. One *laggard* will reduce output considerably. 7. B

(A) dishonest worker (B) slow worker
(C) careless worker (D) beginner or novice

8. Without a high school diploma, Freida was able to get only *menial* jobs running errands and mowing lawns. 8. C

(A) satisfying (B) difficult to learn
(C) simple and low-paying (D) highly desirable

9. After the new manager hired his wife for a high-paying job and promoted his nephew over more deserving workers, the union complained. Such *nepotism* had no place in the modern office. 9. D

(A) ability to think quickly (B) willingness to compromise
(C) ability to make smart business decisions (D) favoritism toward relatives

10. When layoffs began, those with the shortest amount of time on the job were let go first. Those with more *seniority* had more job security. 10. A

(A) length of service in a job (B) age
(C) sales and marketing ability (D) outdated skills

Name ______________________________

Lesson 5 Part B

Applying Meaning

Follow the directions below to write a sentence using a vocabulary word.

1. Write a sentence about a job you dislike. Use the word *menial* in your sentence.

   Sample Answer: Clearing tables and washing dishes is considered menial, but you can earn good tips.

2. Use the word *aptitude* in a sentence about a special skill you have.

   Sample Answer: My aptitude for numbers makes me want to study accounting and economics.

3. Use *journeyman* in a sentence about a worker at a construction site.

   Sample Answer: The work rules require that a journeyman plumber connect all pipes in the new building.

4. Write a sentence about a job someone had to perform. Use the word *laborious* in your sentence.

   Sample Answer: Digging ditches for underground cables during the hot summer was a laborious task.

5. Use the word *apprentice* in a sentence about a company that builds new homes.

   Sample Answer: As an apprentice carpenter with the construction company, Gabe learned many skills.

6. Use the word *drudgery* in a sentence about a boring job.

   Sample Answer: The drudgery of ironing shirts in the steamy laundry made Gloria decide to go back to school.

Decide which word in parentheses best completes the sentence. Then write the sentence, adding the missing word.

7. Our company treats workers fairly. All raises and promotions will be based on merit and _____ . (nepotism; seniority)

   seniority

8. Because she was so eager to please her boss, June became a hopeless _____ . (laggard; lackey)

   lackey

9. The sportswriter was a _____ whose copy was always late. (journeyman; laggard)

   laggard

10. Although her nephew was clearly the most qualified worker, Ms. Cortez was accused of _____ when she promoted him. (nepotism; seniority)

    nepotism

Our Living Language

The names for parts of the human body are often used in a figurative way to describe things around us. We refer to the *shoulder* of the road and the *eye* of a storm.

Make a List: Use each of the following names for parts of the body in a phrase describing something else.

finger	arm	nose
elbow	neck	lip

The Roots -gen- *and* -mort-

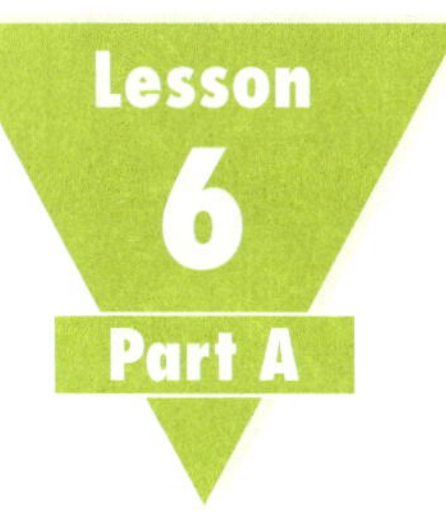

Name ____

The root *-gen-* found in a number of English words comes from two closely related Latin words. One is the Latin verb *gignere* meaning "to produce." The other is the word *genus*, meaning "kind" or "type" as in "I like that kind of pizza." This Latin word probably had its origins in the Greek word *genos*, meaning "race" or "kind." The Latin word for "death" is *mort*. English words with this root nearly always have something to do with death.

Root	Meaning	English Word
-gen-	to produce	regenerate
-gen-	kind, type, race	genetic
-mort-	death	mortality

Words

generation
genetic
genial
gentry
germinate
immortal
mortality
mortician
postmortem
regenerate

A vocabulary word appears in italics in each sentence or short passage below. Find the root in each vocabulary word and choose the letter for the correct definition. Write the letter of your choice on the answer line.

1. My *generation* takes space travel and computers for granted. My grandparents, however, are amazed by such things.
   (A) group of children (B) people born about the same time
   (C) foreign invaders (D) group of scientists

   1. B

2. It is easy to pick out members of my family. Our red hair, green eyes, and other *genetic* features make us stand out in almost any crowd.
   (A) beautiful (B) remarkable
   (C) foolish (D) inherited

   2. D

3. You could not ask for a more *genial* hostess than Fran. Her sincere smile and concern for her guests makes everyone feel comfortable.
   (A) intelligent (B) cheerful and friendly
   (C) exhausted (D) quiet

   3. B

4. Unlike Lincoln, Washington and Jefferson were members of the *gentry*. They came from educated families and owned large areas of land.
   (A) people of high standing (B) religious fanatics
   (C) royalty (D) leaders of a political party

   4. A

5. The rich earth and gentle rain caused the tulips to *germinate* early this year. We noticed their green stems poking up through the ground by the end of March.
   (A) die (B) become infected
   (C) begin to grow (D) take on bright colors

   5. C

6. Few who hear them will ever forget Martin Luther King's *immortal* words, "I have a dream." Even after this generation is gone, King's words will be quoted again and again. 6. **C**
   (A) illegal (B) confusing
   (C) living on forever (D) forgotten

7. Young people often feel they will live forever, so the death of someone close to them is a shock. It reminds them of their own *mortality*. 7. **A**
   (A) certainty of death (B) code of behavior
   (C) foolishness (D) memory

8. Jan's family owns and operates a very successful funeral service. Her parents want her to become a *mortician* and take over the business. 8. **D**
   (A) type of wall covering (B) someone with limited abilities
   (C) type of doctor (D) a funeral director or undertaker

9. A lengthy *postmortem* indicated that the puzzling deaths of two patients were both the results of heart attacks. 9. **B**
   (A) someone in charge of preparing reports (B) examination of a body to decide the cause of death
   (C) former member of a royal family (D) part of a hospital where dying patients are kept

10. Although his team was far behind, the coach hoped his half-time speech would *regenerate* the players' enthusiasm. 10. **A**
   (A) give new life to (B) put an end to
   (C) reduce or remove (D) explain

Name ____________________

Lesson 6 Part B

Applying Meaning

Read each sentence below. Write "correct" on the answer line if the vocabulary word has been used correctly or "incorrect" if it has been used incorrectly.

1. In some cultures it is not considered proper for women to appear in public alone. Such behavior is considered *immortal*. 1. **incorrect**
2. Good food, fair prices, and a *genial* wait staff are all necessary to make a restaurant successful. 2. **correct**
3. After the flood, the authorities asked all residents to *germinate* their water before drinking it. 3. **incorrect**
4. The speaker asked all of us to think of how pollution affects the world we leave for the next *generation*. 4. **correct**
5. Jeff's grandfather, a famous *mortician*, gave a great performance. 5. **incorrect**
6. Before the death could be ruled a murder, the police and the prosecutor needed the results of the *postmortem*. 6. **correct**

For each word used incorrectly, write a sentence using the word properly.

Answers will vary.

Follow the directions below to write a sentence using a vocabulary word.

7. Use any form of the word *generate* to describe a change you or someone else decides to make in his or her life.

   Sample Answer: Emily hoped some quiet time on the beach would regenerate her desire to finish her work at the shelter.

8. Use the word *genetic* in a sentence about something affecting a family.
Sample Answer: The researcher suspected there was a genetic link to Sean's disease since both his father and his grandfather had the same problem.

9. Write something a religious leader might tell his followers. Use the word *mortality*.
Sample Answer: Each of us needs to be reminded of his or her mortality and to prepare for what may come after death.

10. Use the word *gentry* to describe a group of people in history or in your community.
Sample Answer: In many societies, the gentry live very well, but the common people must struggle to make ends meet.

Test-Taking Strategies

Some standardized tests ask you to choose the best word or words to complete a sentence. Sometimes two or more words will fit the sentence. In these cases it is important to choose the best answer. This is usually the answer that is more exact.

Practice: Choose the word or set of words that, when used in the sentence, best fits the meaning of the sentence as a whole.

1. Faced with certain execution, Prince John decided to **C** his claim to the throne.
(A) prove (B) deny
(C) relinquish (D) renew

2. The high waves made me feel somewhat **A** about climbing into the boat and rowing across the lake.
(A) hesitant (B) puzzled
(C) shy (D) firm

Assessment

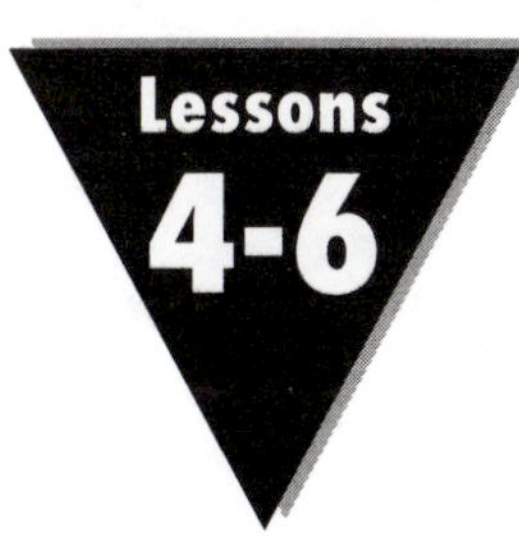

Name ______________________________

How well do you remember the words you studied in Lessons 4 through 6? Take the following test covering the words from the last three lessons.

Part 1 Antonyms

Each question below includes a word in capital letters, followed by four words or phrases. Choose the word or phrase that is most nearly opposite in meaning to the word in capital letters. Consider all choices before deciding on your answer. Write the letter for your answer on the line provided.

Sample

S. SLOW	(A) lazy (C) fast	(B) simple (D) common	S. C
1. TEMPORARY	(A) logical (C) everlasting	(B) punctual (D) cold	1. C
2. DRUDGERY	(A) easy and fun (C) useless	(B) without pay (D) boredom	2. A
3. INSIGNIFICANT	(A) written down (C) characteristic	(B) ancient (D) meaningful	3. D
4. TOLERATE	(A) oppose (C) line up	(B) consider (D) grow	4. A
5. MORTALITY	(A) house payment (C) eternal life	(B) coverage (D) signal	5. C
6. APPRENTICE	(A) teacher (C) woodworker	(B) cook (D) student	6. A
7. IMMORTAL	(A) short-lived (C) long	(B) powerful (D) religious	7. A
8. FLEXIBLE	(A) strong (C) useful	(B) rigid (D) tired	8. B
9. GENIAL	(A) magical (C) charming	(B) dignified (D) unfriendly	9. D
10. REGENERATE	(A) refuse (C) cool	(B) create (D) destroy	10. D

11. LABORIOUS	(A) supportive (C) silly	(B) easy (D) wild	11. B
12. EXPANSION	(A) without cause (C) shrinkage	(B) forever (D) lost	12. C
13. LAGGARD	(A) boaster (C) modesty	(B) hard worker (D) enemy	13. B
14. MENIAL	(A) kind (C) dry	(B) elevated (D) helpful	14. B
15. PREPONDERANCE	(A) lesser part (C) afterthought	(B) costly goods (D) invisible part	15. A

Part 2 Matching Words and Meaning

Match the definition in Column B with the word in Column A. Write the letter of the correct definition on the line provided.

Column A	Column B	
16. nepotism	a. funeral director	16. e
17. germinate	b. natural ability	17. h
18. dominate	c. control	18. c
19. automation	d. examination after death	19. i
20. aptitude	e. favor shown to relatives	20. b
21. generation	f. experienced worker	21. g
22. postmortem	g. people born about the same time	22. d
23. journeyman	h. to begin to grow	23. f
24. mortician	i. use of machines	24. a
25. seniority	j. being older or having more time on a job	25. j

Lesson 7 Part A

Name ______________________________

Tornadoes

Words

- **accolade**
- **colleague**
- **devastate**
- **extensive**
- **fury**
- **garner**
- **perilous**
- **primarily**
- **rashly**
- **transitory**

Filled with exciting special effects, the 1996 movie *Twister* attempted to show the awesome force of tornadoes. It also pretended to show how weather researchers study tornadoes. In the movie, fictional meteorologists actually "chased" tornadoes. Movie fans all over the world responded to the film with enthusiastic **accolades**. However, the film also **garnered** severe criticism from educators and meteorologists. Its fictional scientists did not act wisely or even realistically. In fact, they **rashly** put themselves in the paths of raging tornadoes over and over again.

Whirling with tremendous **fury**, at speeds of up to 500 miles per hour, tornadoes are nature's most **perilous** storms. In minutes, a tornado can **devastate** everything in its path. When a tornado touched down in Jarrell, Texas, in 1997, the destruction was **extensive.** A housing development was destroyed, twenty-nine people were killed, and hundreds were left homeless.

Shaped like a tall, thin funnel, a tornado's path is quite narrow and unpredictable. If a tornado strikes a neighborhood, for example, it might destroy houses on one side of the street and leave those on the other side of the street untouched. Although terribly destructive, tornadoes are quite **transitory**; most last only a few minutes.

Tornadoes can occur at any time of year and have been spotted in all regions of the United States. However, the most severe tornadoes occur **primarily** in the spring in the Midwest and Texas. Masses of hot, dry air exist in the atmosphere above the southwestern plateau of New Mexico. When these winds move eastward, they meet the humid, moist air of the Mississippi Valley and the Gulf of Mexico. The mixture of these air masses often leads to a violent thunderstorm, which can develop into a tornado.

Tornadoes form so rapidly that there is little warning. However, Dr. Joshua Wurman and his **colleagues** at the University of Oklahoma and the National Severe Storms Laboratory recently made a breakthrough in tornado research. They have developed a truck-mounted radar device that measures the wind speeds and the upward and downward drafts within a tornado's funnel. "With greater knowledge, we may one day be able to lengthen warning times from, say, five minutes to fifteen minutes," Dr. Wurman stated. "That margin could save lives by giving people a little more time to run to storm cellars."

Each word in this lesson's word list appears in dark type in the selection you just read. Think about how the vocabulary word is used in the selection. Then write the letter for the best answer to each question.

1. Which word or words could best replace *accolades* in line 5? 1. B
   (A) words of criticism (B) words of praise
   (C) questions (D) requests

2. Which word or words could best replace *garnered* in line 6? 2. B
   (A) gave (B) received or earned
   (C) was grateful for (D) looked forward to

3. Someone who acts *rashly* (line 8) is _____. 3. D
   (A) cautious and brave (B) scientific and professional
   (C) wise (D) reckless

4. Which word or words could best replace *fury* in line 10? 4. C
   (A) chill factors (B) duration
   (C) violent force (D) moisture

5. Another word for *perilous* (line 11) is _____. 5. A
   (A) dangerous (B) curious
   (C) gentle (D) rare

6. Which word could best replace *devastate* in line 12? 6. D
   (A) control (B) rearrange
   (C) affect (D) destroy

7. Which word or words could best replace *extensive* in line 14? 7. B
   (A) small (B) large and widespread
   (C) moderate (D) interesting

8. A *transitory* (line 20) tornado is _____. 8. C
   (A) violent (B) swirling
   (C) brief (D) colorful

9. The word *primarily* in line 23 means _____. 9. B
   (A) rarely (B) most often
   (C) sometimes (D) never

10. Which word or words could best replace *colleagues* in line 30? 10. C
    (A) ancestors (B) family members
    (C) partners (D) secretaries

Name ______________________________

Lesson 7 Part B

Applying Meaning

Follow the directions below to write a sentence using a vocabulary word.

1. Describe the foods you eat for breakfast. Use the word *primarily*.
   Sample answer: For breakfast I eat primarily cereal, fruit, and milk.

2. Write a sentence about two people. Use the word *colleagues*.
   Sample answer: Dr. Ramirez and Dr. Jones are colleagues at the medical clinic.

3. Describe an audience's response to a performance by a singer. Use the word *accolades*.
   Sample answer: At the end of Pete's song, the audience leaped to their feet, clapping and shouting accolades.

4. Give a reason for not doing something. Use the word *perilous*.
   Sample answer: Children should never play with matches because they can be quite perilous.

5. Use any form of the word *devastate* in a sentence about something that was reported in the news.
   Sample answer: Floods devastated all towns within 500 yards of the river's bank.

Read each sentence below. Write "correct" on the answer line if the vocabulary word has been used correctly or "incorrect" if it has been used incorrectly.

6. Holding her baby gently, Mrs. Peters sang a lullaby with *fury*. 6. **incorrect**

7. Perhaps spring flowers are appreciated more because they are so *transitory*. 7. **correct**

8. Helen wanted to save her money, so she spent it very *rashly*. 8. **incorrect**

9. Before buying the house, Jorge did *extensive* research on the area, its schools, and its taxes. 9. **correct**

10. Her excellent performance *garnered* hearty applause from the audience. 10. **correct**

For each word used incorrectly, write a sentence using the word properly.

Answers will vary.

Mastering Meaning

Do you think it is proper for moviemakers to change certain facts to make a more exciting movie? In the movie *Twister* the heroes studied tornadoes by chasing them. Scientists do not study tornadoes this way. This is not only inaccurate, it is dangerous. Write an essay stating your opinion of this practice. Use some of the words you studied in this lesson.

Vocabulary from Animals

Lesson 8 Part A

Name ______________________

Animals have always been important to humans as food, as helpers, and as symbols. For instance, snails are associated with slowness and foxes with intelligence. In this lesson, you will learn ten animal words that are used to describe people. The qualities these animals have—or are thought to have—are often associated with people.

Words

badger
beastly
bovine
dogged
lame duck
lionize
mammoth
scapegoat
sheepish
sluggish

Unlocking Meaning

Read the sentences or short passages below. Write the letter for the correct definition of the italicized vocabulary word.

1. The witness has answered that question three times. If you continue to *badger* her into changing her answer, the jury may begin to feel sorry for her.
   (A) flatter (B) bully
   (C) joke with (D) ignore

   1. B

2. Because of the *beastly* weather, we did not expect a large crowd at the parade. We were surprised that so many people showed up.
   (A) pleasant (B) dark
   (C) dry (D) disagreeable

   2. D

3. He spent the summer watching television, eating snacks, and sleeping. Thanks to this *bovine* behavior, he gained twenty pounds.
   (A) dull or slow (B) active
   (C) peaceful (D) exciting

   3. A

4. My cousin is not someone who gives up easily. Sometimes I find his *dogged* determination annoying, but he always finishes everything he starts.
   (A) friendly (B) silly
   (C) stubborn (D) angry

   4. C

5. Although she was defeated in the last election, Senator Walker still must complete her term. However, like most *lame duck* senators, she has lost much of her power.
   (A) good swimmers (B) defeated or helpless
   (C) speechless (D) effective

   5. B

6. Many people *lionize* athletes and actors while ignoring scientists and teachers. Yet scientists and teachers have a more lasting impact on our lives. 6. D

(A) rule over (B) make fun of
(C) do not notice (D) treat as important

7. I had no room for dessert after finishing such a *mammoth* sandwich. 7. A

(A) huge (B) dark
(C) vegetarian (D) old-fashioned

8. Although several people actually committed the crime, one person was made the *scapegoat*. He was sent to jail while the others were freed. 8. B

(A) lucky person (B) one blamed for the mistakes of others
(C) winner of an award (D) defender of animals

9. Elena asked everyone to help her find her glasses. She felt quite *sheepish* when someone pointed out that they were on top of her head. 9. B

(A) slow (B) embarrassed
(C) joyful (D) loud

10. Yesterday I swept and vacuumed the house, but today's heat makes me too *sluggish* to do anything active. 10. D

(A) clean and clear (B) sly
(C) slightly damp (D) drained of energy

Name ______________________________

Lesson 8 Part B

Applying Meaning

Each question below contains at least one vocabulary word from this lesson. Answer each question "yes" or "no" in the space provided.

1. If you needed to be rescued from a narrow cliff, would you want your rescuers to make *dogged* efforts to reach you? — 1. yes
2. When giving a speech, would you enjoy being *badgered* with interruptions? — 2. no
3. Would you enjoy being made the *scapegoat* for a class prank? — 3. no
4. Do newspapers frequently *lionize* successful local athletes? — 4. yes
5. If you had a *beastly* vacation at a theme park, would you want to visit it again next year? — 5. no

For each question you answered "no," write a sentence explaining your reason.

Answers will vary.

____

Read each sentence or short passage below. Write "correct" on the answer line if the vocabulary word has been used correctly or "incorrect" if it has been used incorrectly.

6. I awoke filled with confidence. I felt so *sluggish* that I was sure I would win the race. — 6. incorrect
7. Only one person can fit inside this *mammoth* tent. — 7. incorrect
8. Marge plays tennis and baseball every chance she gets, but her brother just watches her with a *bovine* stare on his face. — 8. correct
9. After announcing his plan to quit his job, Sam was treated like a *lame duck*. He was given no important assignments, and few people spoke to him. — 9. correct

10. No one had accused her of eating the leftover pizza, but her *sheepish* grin suggested she was guilty. 10. correct

For each word used incorrectly, write a sentence using the word properly.

Answers will vary.

Cultural Literacy Note

Dog in the Manger

One of Aesop's fables tells the story of a farmer who owned an ox and a dog. The dog liked to sleep in the manger, a box that held the ox's hay. One day the tired and hungry ox returned from a day of hard work and wanted nothing more than a few mouthfuls of sweet hay. The dog was not happy to be disturbed. When the ox stuck its head into the manger, the dog barked and snapped furiously.

The tired ox complained to its master. "The dog is truly impossible! It cannot eat the hay, but it keeps me from eating any!" Because of this popular story, "a dog in the manger" has referred to someone who spoils things for others, even though the spoiler can receive no benefit from it.

Write a Paragraph: Describe a situation in which someone acts like a dog in the manger. It might be a situation at school or at home. It might involve a real or imaginary person.

The Prefixes hyper- *and* hypo-

Name ______________________________

The prefix *hyper-* comes from the Greek word *huper*, meaning "over," "above," or "beyond." The prefix *hypo-* comes from the Greek word *hupo*, meaning "under," "beneath," or "below." In a word like *hyperactive*, it is easy to add the meaning of the prefix to the base word and unlock the meaning of the word. However, when these prefixes are added to a root, the meaning may not be as clear.

Prefix	Meaning	English Word
hyper-	over, above, beyond	hyperactive
hypo-	under, beneath, below	hypodermic

Words

hyperactive
hyperbole
hyperextension
hypersonic
hypertension
hypochondriac
hypocrisy
hypodermic
hypotenuse
hypothetical

Unlocking Meaning

Read the sentences or short passages below. Write the letter for the correct definition of the italicized word.

1. The restaurant was full of *hyperactive* children running around the tables, crawling under chairs, and driving the waitresses crazy.
   (A) overly active (B) quiet
   (C) lovable (D) loud

   1. ___A___

2. Saying his books weigh a ton is just another example of Ed's use of *hyperbole*. Don't take him seriously.
   (A) charm (B) deceit
   (C) humor (D) exaggeration

   2. ___D___

3. When Joan pulled Jim down by his arm she caused a painful *hyperextension* of his shoulder.
   (A) examination (B) rotation
   (C) break in the bone (D) stretching a body part

   3. ___D___

4. As it returns to Earth the space shuttle reaches *hypersonic* speeds.
   (A) easily measured (B) many times the speed of sound
   (C) dangerous (D) impossible to record

   4. ___B___

5. When my blood pressure rose to alarming levels, the doctor prescribed some medication to control the *hypertension*.
   (A) type of airplane (B) loss of energy
   (C) high blood pressure (D) expenses

   5. ___C___

6. A lifetime *hypochondriac*, my aunt Nell sees her doctor at least twice a week and always complains about her imaginary aches and pains. 6. C

(A) a person concerned about his or her health
(B) a person studying to be a doctor
(C) someone often convinced he or she is ill
(D) a close relative

7. Campaigning for animal rights while eating a hamburger seems to me the height of *hypocrisy*. 7. B

(A) compassion
(B) expressing beliefs one does not hold
(C) free speech
(D) honor and bravery

8. The immunization program required children to get a *hypodermic* injection. 8. A

(A) beneath the skin
(B) painful
(C) useless
(D) expensive

9. Today we learned the formula for calculating the length of the *hypotenuse* when the length of the other two sides is known. 9. C

(A) African water animal
(B) unproved theory
(C) longest side of a right triangle
(D) source of water

10. June used the *hypothetical* case of a person yelling "Fire!" in a crowded theater to prove that free speech is not always protected. 10. A

(A) an example used for the sake of argument
(B) far-fetched
(C) confusing
(D) too simple to be usable

Name ______________________________

Applying Meaning

Each question below contains at least one vocabulary word from this lesson. Answer each question "yes" or "no" in the space provided.

1. Does a measles shot require a *hypodermic* injection? 1. yes
2. Would it be wise to take several *hyperactive* children into a glass and china store? 2. no
3. Is a *hypotenuse* a large African water animal? 3. no
4. Might a healthy *hypochondriac* insist he or she has *hypertension*? 4. yes
5. Is the longest side of a triangle called the *hyperbole*? 5. no
6. Would you vote for a candidate with a history of *hypocrisy*? 6. no

For each question you answered "no," write a sentence explaining your reason.

Answers will vary.

Decide which word in parentheses best completes the sentence. Then write the sentence, adding the missing word.

7. The teacher tried to explain how a bill becomes a law with a _____ example. (hypersonic; hypothetical)

hypothetical

8. Her claim of being the fastest runner in the state was dismissed as _____ by most of her competitors. (hyperbole; hyperextension)

hyperbole

9. The equipment available in the laboratory was unable to measure such _____ speeds. (hyperactive; hypersonic)

hypersonic

10. The team trainer said the _____ the quarterback suffered would keep him on the bench for three weeks. (hyperextension; hyperbole)

hyperextension

Bonus Word

hype

One word that seems to be working its way into the English language is *hype*. It no doubt also comes from the Greek word *huper* and the English prefix *hyper-*. Although most dictionaries still classify the word *hype* as slang, it may eventually become accepted as standard English, especially if it fulfills a need to identify a certain element of modern living.

Write a Definition: Review the meaning of the Greek word *huper* and the English prefix *hyper-*. Then study how the word *hype* is used in the sentences below. Write a dictionary definition for this recently coined word.

There was a great deal of hype surrounding this year's Super Bowl.

All the magazine stories and television interviews are just so much hype for the new movie.

Lessons 7-9

Name ______________________

How well do you remember the words you studied in Lessons 7 through 9? Take the following test covering the words from the last three lessons.

Part 1 Choose the Correct Meaning

Each question below includes a word in capital letters, followed by four words or phrases. Choose the word or phrase that is closest in meaning to the word in capital letters. Write the letter for your answer on the line provided.

Sample

Word	Choices		Answer
S. FINISH	(A) enjoy (C) destroy	(B) complete (D) enlarge	S. B
1. PRIMARILY	(A) seasonally (C) mostly	(B) rarely (D) singularly	1. C
2. BADGER	(A) annoy (C) describe	(B) question (D) praise	2. A
3. PERILOUS	(A) dangerous (C) small	(B) valuable (D) safe	3. A
4. HYPERBOLE	(A) type of triangle (C) flattery	(B) sickness (D) exaggeration	4. D
5. COLLEAGUE	(A) school (C) doctor	(B) coworker (D) gardener	5. B
6. BEASTLY	(A) terrible (C) strange	(B) beautiful (D) musical	6. A
7. EXTENSIVE	(A) colorful (C) forgotten	(B) permanent (D) widespread	7. D
8. SHEEPISH	(A) embarrassed (C) loyal	(B) soft (D) adorable	8. A
9. FURY	(A) happiness (C) anger	(B) windiness (D) uncertainty	9. C
10. HYPOCRISY	(A) success (C) cruelty	(B) dishonesty (D) trickery	10. B

11. TRANSITORY	(A) changeable (C) short-lived	(B) simple (D) miniature	11. C
12. DEVASTATE	(A) enlarge (C) grow	(B) rebuild (D) destroy	12. D
13. MAMMOTH	(A) large (C) poisonous	(B) monthly (D) motherly	13. A
14. GARNER	(A) decorate (C) earn	(B) condemn (D) release	14. C
15. LAME DUCK	(A) fast (C) effortless	(B) powerless (D) small	15. B

Part 2 Matching Words and Meanings

Match the definition in Column B with the word in Column A. Write the letter of the correct definition on the line provided.

Column A	**Column B**	
16. hypothetical	a. to treat as important	16. g
17. hypertension	b. tired	17. j
18. lionize	c. someone who often seems to be ill	18. a
19. sluggish	d. stubborn	19. b
20. dogged	e. one who is blamed for the crimes of others	20. d
21. hypotenuse	f. overly energetic	21. h
22. scapegoat	g. based on a theory	22. e
23. hypodermic	h. the longest side of a right triangle	23. i
24. hypochondriac	i. under the skin	24. c
25. hyperactive	j. high blood pressure	25. f

Lesson 10 Part A

Name ______________________________

The Story of Icarus and Daedalus

King Minos was the son of Zeus, the most important of the Greek gods. Minos, who ruled the island of Crete, was a **fickle** ruler. He might love his subjects one day and **despise** them the next. Daedalus and his son Icarus were the victims of the king's changeable moods. Even though Daedalus had built the famous Labyrinth for King Minos, the king had Daedalus and his son imprisoned on an island. There Daedalus and Icarus spent their days watching seagulls float freely through the air. These birds gave Daedalus an idea for escaping his unjust **incarceration**.

Daedalus began to collect feathers and to form them into huge wings. Then he tied the feathers together with string and poured melted wax over them. As the wax cooled and hardened, it formed a **cohesive** glue. Next Daedalus fastened the wings to his shoulders and began to **cleave** the air by flapping his new wings back and forth. Slowly he began to rise from the ground and glide over his island prison.

When he floated back to earth, Daedalus immediately began to **mold** a set of wings for his son. Soon father and son were prepared to make their escape, but before taking to the air, Daedalus gave Icarus some final advice. "Remember, do not soar too high. The heat of the sun will melt the wax, and your wings will fall apart." Icarus was young, however, and he **disdained** all advice from his elders. Once he was in the air, the joy he felt over his escape and the power of his youth **prompted** him to sail higher and higher into the air. Nothing could **quench** his desire to reach the heavens.

The higher he flew, the warmer the air became. Gradually the wings grew limp, and then they began to **disintegrate**. Feathers fluttered to the ground. Icarus tried flapping his wings harder and harder, but it was of no use. He fell headlong into the sea. Hearing his son's cries, Daedalus began searching for him, but all he found were hundreds of feathers floating on the sea. He knew Icarus had drowned. So is it ever with youth who try to soar too high and too fast on fragile wings.

Words

cleave
cohesive
despise
disdain
disintegrate
fickle
incarceration
mold
prompt
quench

Unlocking Meaning

Each word in this lesson's word list appears in dark type in the selection you just read. Think about how the vocabulary word is used in the selection, then write the letter for the best answer to each question.

1. A *fickle* (line 2) ruler _____.
   (A) is the son of a powerful god
   (B) is just and fair
   (C) exists only in the imagination
   (D) frequently changes his or her mind.

   1. D

2. If you *despise* (line 3) someone, you _____.
   (A) have a strong dislike for that person
   (B) watch the person secretly
   (C) admire the person
   (D) have power over that person

   2. A

3. Another word for *incarceration* (line 9) is _____.
   (A) admiration
   (B) imprisonment
   (C) confusion
   (D) kingdom

   3. B

4. If something is *cohesive*, (line 13) it _____.
   (A) is difficult to understand
   (B) sticks together
   (C) cannot be found
   (D) falls apart easily

   4. B

5. If you *cleave* (line 14) the air, you _____.
   (A) cause it to become dirty
   (B) examine it closely
   (C) divide or split it
   (D) meet it face to face

   5. C

6. To *mold* (line 18) is to _____.
   (A) give shape to
   (B) force
   (C) forecast
   (D) destroy

   6. A

7. If you *disdain* (line 22) someone's advice, you _____.
   (A) follow it
   (B) listen to it carefully
   (C) reject it rudely
   (D) share it with others

   7. C

8. In line 24, *prompted* means _____.
   (A) frightened
   (B) tricked
   (C) warned
   (D) encouraged

   8. D

9. Another word for *quench* (line 25) is _____.
   (A) heighten
   (B) expand
   (C) deliver
   (D) satisfy

   9. D

10. If something *disintegrates*, (line 27) it _____.
    (A) comes together
    (B) falls apart
    (C) rises into the air
    (D) turns over

    10. B

Name ______________________________

Applying Meaning

Decide which word in parentheses best completes the sentence. Then write the sentence, adding the missing word.

1. A good leader cannot afford to be _____ in a time of crisis. (cohesive; fickle)

   fickle ______________________________

2. The mayor had come to _____ the newspaper's constant criticism of his actions. (disdain; disintegrate)

   disdain ______________________________

3. The Civil War threatened to _____ the Union into separate nations. (cleave; mold)

   cleave ______________________________

4. The coach had many talented players, but it would take weeks to teach them to play as a _____ team. (cohesive; fickle)

   cohesive ______________________________

5. Her father's sudden illness _____ Juanita to leave her job and rush to his bedside. (prompted; quenched)

   prompted ______________________________

Read each sentence below. Write "correct" on the answer line if the vocabulary word has been used correctly or "incorrect" if it has been used incorrectly.

6. After ten years of *incarceration*, the prisoner's conviction was reversed and he was set free. — 6. correct

7. The city notified the abandoned building's owner that she would have to *mold* it. 7. incorrect

8. No matter how much we dislike the umpire's calls, our coach will not allow us to *disintegrate* those decisions. 8. incorrect

9. American patriots had admired the skill and bravery of Benedict Arnold, but after Arnold betrayed his country, they came to *despise* the man. 9. correct

10. The Mars space probe is an outstanding example of science's ongoing *quench* for knowledge. 10. incorrect

For each word used incorrectly, write a sentence using the word properly.

Answers will vary.

Mastering Meaning

Think about the last sentence in the story of Icarus and Daedalus: "So is it ever with youth who try to soar too high and too fast on fragile wings." Does this statement apply to young people today? What does it mean to soar too high and too fast? What are the fragile wings? Write a short essay agreeing or disagreeing with the statement. Use examples from your own experience to support your position. In your essay, use some of the words you studied in this lesson.

Vocabulary of Faith and Religion

Lesson 11 Part A

Name ______________________________

Religion plays an important part in many people's lives. Whether or not you practice a particular religion, you will still read and hear many words that are related to faith and religion. Some of these words have more than one meaning. One definition may relate to something specific in the religion itself. The other meaning might be a more general term that is used in ordinary speech and writing.

Words

basilica
clergy
Koran
kosher
laity
mecca
menorah
mosque
mullah
sanctuary

Unlocking Meaning

Read the sentences or short passages below. Write the letter for the correct definition of the italicized vocabulary word.

1. The priest asked visitors to the *basilica* to dress in a way that showed respect for the members' religious beliefs.
   (A) form of transportation (B) type of church building
   (C) article of clothing (D) religious activity

2. Many members of the *clergy* wear special clothing when performing religious ceremonies.
   (A) people who build windows (B) people who sell things in stores
   (C) people accompanied by children (D) people authorized to conduct religious services

3. In this section of the library you will find the *Koran*, the Bible, and other religious books.
   (A) sacred writings of Islam (B) schedules for the week
   (C) window that opens with a crank (D) person who keeps records

4. Most stores and restaurants in Jewish neighborhoods offer a large assortment of *kosher* foods.
   (A) spoiled (B) exposed to strong light
   (C) meeting standards of Jewish dietary laws (D) necessary for good dental health

5. Front-row seats are reserved for religious officials. The rest are for the *laity*.
   (A) family from a foreign country (B) people who accept no religion
   (C) women in government (D) members of a religious group who are not officials of the group

1. B
2. D
3. A
4. C
5. D

6. Florida has become a *mecca* for students on spring break. The crowds of sun worshipers grow every year. 6. B

(A) source of difficulty
(B) center of important activity or interest
(C) classroom
(D) prison

7. When the last candle in our *menorah* was lit, we all agreed that it was a beautiful and inspiring sight. 7. C

(A) decorated eating tools
(B) furniture covering made of fine cloth
(C) candleholder used in Jewish worship
(D) string of beads used by several religions

8. This time of year has many holidays. It seems as if every church, *mosque*, and synagogue is filled. 8. A

(A) Muslim house of worship
(B) religious song
(C) container for jewelry
(D) place where clothing is hung

9. In certain Middle Eastern countries, few question the word of a *mullah*. His wisdom is considered supreme. 9. C

(A) place where people gather
(B) special holidays
(C) a religious teacher
(D) people who raise money

10. Some of the most important events in my life took place inside this church's *sanctuary*. 10. B

(A) collection of books
(B) sacred chamber or room; safe place
(C) storage area
(D) statue of an important person

Name ____

Applying Meaning

Decide which word in parentheses best completes the sentence. Then write the sentence, adding the missing word.

1. In many churches, the _____ receive not only a salary, but also a home and a car for their service to the people. (clergy; laity)

   clergy

2. Inside the _____ was a small courtyard. In the center of this stood a lovely fountain. (mullah; mosque)

   mosque

3. In many homes, it is the mother who lights the candles in the _____. (menorah; mecca)

   menorah

4. Prior to her wedding, Maria had been in the _____ only one other time, at her baptism. (sanctuary; Koran)

   sanctuary

5. The _____ had been built by local workers using stones from a nearby quarry. (basilica; menorah)

   basilica

Each question below contains at least one vocabulary word from this lesson. Answer each question "yes" or "no" in the space provided.

6. Would you expect to find writing in the *Koran*? — 6. yes

7. Would you expect to find many *kosher* restaurants in Japan? — 7. no

8. Is a holy city a *mecca* for devout members of a religion? 8. yes

9. Would a tired traveler try to get some rest and relaxation at a *laity*? 9. no

10. Would a *mullah* spend a great deal of time studying sacred writings? 10. yes

For each question you answered "no," write a sentence explaining your reason.

Answers will vary.

Our Living Language

inferno

The word *inferno*, meaning "a hell-like place of great suffering," is actually the Italian word for *hell*. It comes from the Latin *infernus*, which means "underground or lower place." The Italian poet Dante Alighieri used the word to describe his vision of hell in his epic poem, *The Divine Comedy*. The adjective *infernal*, meaning "awful" comes from this word.

Cooperative Learning: Obtain an illustrated copy of Dante's *The Divine Comedy*. How does the illustration of hell compare to the one you imagined?

Number Prefixes and Word Parts

Name ______________________________

When the meaning of a word has something to do with a number, it frequently includes a prefix from Latin or Greek. The Latin word for one is *unus*. The prefix *uni-*, meaning "one," can be seen in words such as *unicycle*, which means "a one-wheeled vehicle." Similarly, *bi-* carries the meaning "two," and *tri-* has the meaning "three."

Prefix or Word Part	Meaning	English Word
uni-	one	unilateral
bi-	two; twice	bicentennial
tri-	three	tripod

Words

ambidextrous
ambivalent
bicentennial
bilingual
trilogy
tripod
triumvirate
unification
unilateral
unique

Unlocking Meaning

Write the vocabulary word that fits each clue below. Then say the word and write a short definition. Compare your definition with the one given in the dictionary at the back of the book.

1. Many classical Greek dramas consisted of three plays performed in sequence. The Greek word for this performance was *trilogia*.

   trilogy Definitions will vary.

2. On July 4, 1776, the United States adopted the Declaration of Independence. This anniversary was celebrated on July 4, 1976.

   bicentennial Definitions will vary.

3. This word can be used to describe every word and every snowflake.

   unique Definitions will vary.

4. This word, which has something to do with government, contains a form of *vir*, the Latin word for "man."

   triumvirate Definitions will vary.

5. This word adds a number prefix to the Latin word *latus*, meaning "side."

   unilateral Definitions will vary.

6. I cannot make up my mind between two feelings. I don't know whether I am happy or sad to be moving.

   ambivalent Definitions will vary.

7. This word describes someone who does things equally well with the left or right hand. It includes the Latin *dexter*, meaning "skillful."

   ambidextrous Definitions will vary.

8. This noun is formed from the verb *unify*.

   unification Definitions will vary.

9. This word combines the prefix meaning "two" with a form of the Latin word *lingua* meaning "language."

   bilingual Definitions will vary.

10. The Greek word for "foot" is *pous*. You might use one of these to hold a camera steady when taking a picture.

    tripod Definitions will vary.

Name ______________________________

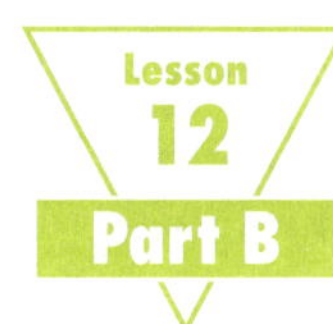

Applying Meaning

Decide which word in parentheses best completes the sentence. Then write the sentence, adding the missing word.

1. Although he is just a child, I feel quite _____ about forgiving Sam for losing my money. (ambivalent; unilateral)

   ambivalent

2. His disregard for the rules of punctuation and capitalization make e. e. cummings _____ among poets. (ambidextrous; unique)

   unique

3. The general warned the country not to _____ destroy its weapons. This would leave us helpless if attacked. (ambivalently; unilaterally)

   unilaterally

4. Power to govern the city was shared by a _____. (trilogy; triumvirate)

   triumvirate

5. Most international flights have _____ pilots and flight attendants. (ambidextrous; bilingual)

   bilingual

Read each sentence below. Write "correct" on the answer line if the vocabulary word has been used correctly or "incorrect" if it has been used incorrectly.

6. Next semester I plan to take a course in advanced *trilogy*. 6. incorrect

7. The *unification* of England and Scotland began under James I. 7. correct

8. Founded in 1772, San Luis Obispo, California, celebrated its *bicentennial* in 1972. 8. correct

9. Instead of clear answers, the politician offered only a few *ambidextrous* remarks. 9. incorrect

10. The telescope was mounted on a *tripod* to hold it steady. 10. correct

For each word used incorrectly, write a sentence using the word properly.

Answers will vary.

Test-Taking Strategies

Some tests ask you to choose a word that means the opposite of a word in capital letters. These tests may try to trick you by including a synonym for the word as one of the answers. Remember that the test asks for the word that means the opposite of the first word.

Practice: On the line provided, write the letter for the word most nearly opposite in meaning to the word in capital letters.

1. TYPICAL (A) exceptional (B) commonplace (C) attractive (D) foolish 1. A

2. DILATE (A) add (B) expand (C) withdraw (D) close 2. D

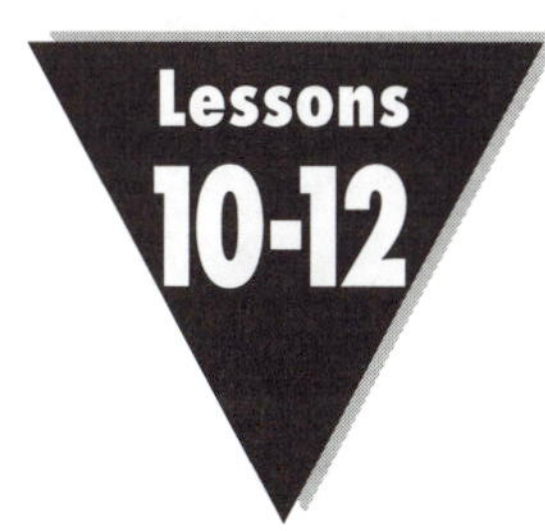

Name ________________________________

How well do you remember the words you studied in Lessons 10 through 12? Take the following test covering the words from the last three lessons.

Part 1 Choose the Correct Meaning

Each question below includes a word in capital letters, followed by four words or phrases. Choose the word or phrase that is closest in meaning to the word in capital letters. Write the letter for your answer on the line provided.

Sample

S. FINISH	(A) enjoy (C) destroy	(B) complete (D) enlarge	S. ___B___
1. BASILICA	(A) baseball diamond (C) priest's home	(B) baptismal font (D) place of worship	1. ___D___
2. UNIFICATION	(A) doing something alone (C) making a decision	(B) joining together (D) telling a tale	2. ___B___
3. MENORAH	(A) candleholder (C) noble act	(B) memory (D) stage light	3. ___A___
4. QUENCH	(A) extend (C) justify	(B) satisfy (D) relive	4. ___B___
5. INCARCERATION	(A) imprisonment (C) repayment	(B) rebirth (D) forgiven	5. ___A___
6. AMBIDEXTROUS	(A) skillful (C) skilled with either hand	(B) unclear (D) having high hopes	6. ___C___
7. BICENTENNIAL	(A) 200th year (C) antique	(B) celebration (D) patriotic	7. ___A___
8. DESPISE	(A) ignore (C) enjoy	(B) respect (D) hate	8. ___D___
9. UNIQUE	(A) matchless (C) simple	(B) common (D) interesting	9. ___A___
10. SANCTUARY	(A) religious music (C) school	(B) museum (D) holy place	10. ___D___

11. CLERGY	(A) secretaries (C) choir members	(B) church officials (D) religious books	11. B
12. TRILOGY	(A) third part (C) travel journal	(B) a three-part series (D) eating utensils	12. B
13. PROMPTED	(A) released (C) concealed	(B) encouraged (D) delivered	13. B
14. MULLAH	(A) religious teacher (C) altar	(B) farm animal (D) holy water	14. A
15. DISDAIN	(A) remove (C) relive	(B) repeat (D) reject	15. D

Part 2 Matching Words and Meaning

Match the definition in Column B with the word in Column A.
Write the letter of the correct definition on the line provided.

Column A	Column B	
16. Koran	a. unified; held together	16. d
17. ambivalent	b. in keeping with Jewish food laws	17. h
18. mecca	c. able to speak two languages	18. f
19. bilingual	d. sacred book of Islam	19. c
20. cohesive	e. one who frequently changes his mind	20. a
21. disintegrate	f. a center for people with a particular interest	21. g
22. laity	g. fall apart	22. i
23. kosher	h. having conflicting thoughts	23. b
24. fickle	i. members of a faith who are not officials	24. e
25. mosque	j. Muslim house of worship	25. j

Lesson 13 Part A

Name ______________________________

Giving Gifts

Today people travel farther and faster than at any time in history. While travel provides many opportunities to encounter new peoples and new cultures, it also has certain **pitfalls**. For example, many people attempt to show their goodwill toward others by offering gifts. Although giving gifts to show friendship is an almost **universal** practice, gift-giving customs are not the same the world over.

Each country has its own set of rules. If you give a gift to someone from another country or culture, it is important to know the **etiquette** of that country. Otherwise, an act meant to show friendship might have the **potential** to upset both the giver and the receiver. The wrong gift can insult or **antagonize** the person who receives it. It can damage a friendship rather than strengthen it.

Flowers are popular gifts for many occasions. Yet not all flowers are a good choice. Yellow daisies given to a sick friend would be a serious **breach** of etiquette in certain areas. In some countries, yellow is a color you give an enemy, so giving yellow flowers to a friend would be quite **offensive**. White flowers, too, can be a poor choice. In China, white, not black, is the color of mourning, so white is linked with death.

You cannot **eliminate** gift-giving problems entirely simply by avoiding flowers. Other types of gifts can also be the source of embarrassment or even a direct insult. In some cultures, giving the gift of a clock could **alienate** the recipient rather then drawing him or her closer to you. This is because clocks or watches are seen as reminders of death. Since clocks measure life, each tick brings a person closer to life's end. In several countries, people avoid giving anything sharp, such as knives, because such objects are seen as signs that the giver wishes to cut the friendship short.

With so many **cultural** differences, you may wonder how international businesspeople can stay out of trouble. How do they learn the unspoken rules of the countries they visit? Many international businesses now hire experts to advise them on such matters. These people explain all the important customs of a country. They know how to choose gifts that make everyone smile.

Words

- **alienate**
- **antagonize**
- **breach**
- **cultural**
- **eliminate**
- **etiquette**
- **offensive**
- **pitfalls**
- **potential**
- **universal**

Unlocking Meaning

Each word in this lesson's word list appears in dark type in the selection you just read. Think about how the vocabulary word is used in the selection, then write the letter for the best answer to each question.

1. Which word could best replace *pitfalls* in line 3? — 1. C
   (A) tiny holes (B) foods
   (C) traps (D) jokes

2. A *universal* practice (line 5) is one that takes place _____. — 2. A
   (A) everywhere (B) in underdeveloped countries
   (C) in Europe (D) in school

3. Which word or words could best replace *etiquette* in line 9? — 3. B
   (A) location (B) accepted behavior
   (C) traditional songs (D) close friends

4. Another word for *potential* (line 10) is _____. — 4. D
   (A) authority (B) desire
   (C) demand (D) possibility

5. Which word could best replace *antagonize* in line 11? — 5. A
   (A) anger (B) please
   (C) tire (D) invite

6. A *breach* (line 15) is a(n) _____. — 6. C
   (A) act (B) increase
   (C) violation (D) reminder

7. An *offensive* (line 17) gift _____. — 7. A
   (A) upsets people (B) is small
   (C) smells sweet (D) is correct

8. If you *eliminate* (line 20) a problem, you — 8. D
   (A) make it worse (B) notice it
   (C) experience it (D) make it disappear

9. If you *alienate* people (line 23), you _____. — 9. C
   (A) make new friends (B) invite them home
   (C) lose their friendship (D) photograph them

10. *Cultural* (line 29) differences occur _____. — 10. D
    (A) only among educated people (B) among relatives in one family
    (C) only in business (D) between people with differing beliefs and customs

Name ______________________________

Lesson 13 Part B

Applying Meaning

Follow the directions below to write a sentence using a vocabulary word.

1. Use any form of the word *universal* to describe a friendly act.
   Sample Answer: A smile is universally understood as a sign of friendship.

2. Use the word *offensive* in an apology.
   Sample Answer: I'm sorry, but I didn't know that yellow flowers were considered offensive.

3. Use any form of the word *eliminate* to tell someone to stop a certain action.
   Sample Answer: You should eliminate those words from your vocabulary.

4. Use *etiquette* in a sentence about proper behavior.
   Sample Answer: It is considered proper etiquette to allow the host or hostess to take the first bite of food at a meal.

5. Use any form of the word *potential* to describe how you avoided a problem.
   Sample Answer: I check my tickets twice to avoid potential problems at the airport.

Read each sentence or short passage below. Write "correct" on the answer line if the vocabulary word has been used correctly or "incorrect" if it has been used incorrectly.

6. Julie hoped her friend would *antagonize* her so they could become even closer friends. 6. incorrect

7. Dishonesty in any form will *alienate* most people. 7. correct

8. The police arrived when they learned that there had been a *breach* of the peace. 8. correct

9. Ada is just a *cultural* friend, but Chad and I are really close. 9. incorrect

10. If you're lucky, you will be able to experience some of the *pitfalls* of modern travel. 10. incorrect

For each word used incorrectly, write a sentence using the word properly.

Answers will vary.

Mastering Meaning

Imagine you are writing a letter to a friend in a foreign country who is about to visit your school. You want to help your friend adjust to life in school in your country. Write two or three paragraphs explaining local manners, customs, or clothing. Use some of the words you studied in this lesson.

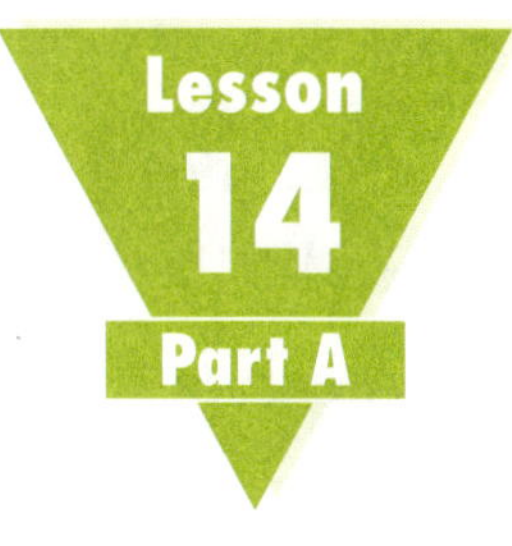

Name ______________________________

Words that look and sound alike but have different meanings can be the source of confusion for many writers. To avoid sending the wrong message and causing yourself great embarrassment, it is important to know the difference between similar words. In this lesson, you will learn five pairs of words that can be easily confused. Although they look and sound very much alike, these words have different meanings.

Words

biannual
biennial

human
humane

marital
martial

meddle
mettle

moral
morale

Unlocking Meaning

Read the sentences or short passages below. Write the letter for the correct definition of the italicized vocabulary word.

1. The Constitution calls for *biennial* elections to the House of Representatives.
   (A) occurring every two years (B) occurring twice a year
2. The *biannual* meetings of the recreation committee are held in June and December.
   (A) occurring every two years (B) occurring twice a year
3. The company replaced the answering machine with a live operator so customers could speak to a *human* being.
   (A) having the qualities of a living person (B) kind, merciful, or compassionate
4. Father Damien fought for the *humane* treatment of lepers at a time when they were treated as outcasts.
   (A) having the qualities of a living person (B) kind, merciful, or compassionate
5. The parade for the war hero began with a marching band playing rousing *martial* music.
   (A) related to marriage (B) related to war and the military
6. On their golden anniversary, my parents repeated their *marital* vows.
   (A) related to marriage (B) related to war and the military

1. A
2. B
3. A
4. B
5. B
6. A

7. President Monroe warned the European powers not to *meddle* in the affairs of the Americas. 7. A
   (A) to interfere with (B) daring and courage

8. The troops did well in training, but their *mettle* would be severely tested in actual combat. 8. B
   (A) to interfere with (B) daring and courage

9. The fable about the tortoise and the hare teaches the reader a *moral* about perseverance. 9. A
   (A) lesson or principle (B) the state of one's spirits or mental state

10. After the opposing team scored eight runs in the first inning, our *morale* reached its lowest point. 10. B
   (A) lesson or principle (B) the state of one's spirits or mental state

Name ______________________________

Applying Meaning

Decide which word in parentheses best completes the sentence. Then write the sentence, adding the missing word.

1. After reading the shocking reports of mistreatment, we demanded more _____ treatment of the prison population. (human; humane)

   humane

2. Property tax bills are sent to homeowners _____, usually in March and September. (biannually; biennially)

   biannually

3. Although Huang thought Bruce was making a mistake, he chose not to _____ in another person's affairs. (meddle, mettle)

   meddle

4. The _____ of the story was clear. (moral; morale)

   moral

5. In some cultures, it is a common _____ custom for the parents to choose spouses for their children. (marital; martial)

   marital

Read each sentence. Write "correct" on the answer line if the vocabulary word has been used correctly or "incorrect" if it has been used incorrectly.

6. Founded in 1630, Boston celebrated its *biennial* in 1830. — 6. incorrect

7. It is not wise to *meddle* in your sister's business. — 7. correct

8. The general raised the *morale* of the troops by telling them how proud he felt to be their commander. 8. correct

9. After months of intense study and practice in the *martial* arts, Sue was confident she could defend herself in any situation. 9. correct

10. The six-month trip to Mars will be a severe test of *human* endurance. 10. correct

For each word used incorrectly, write a sentence using the word properly.

Answers will vary.

The Dictionary

The dictionary provides information on the part of speech of each entry word. The example below shows how the word *moral* can be used as either an adjective or a noun.

mor·al (**môr'** əl or **mŏr'** əl) adj. 1. The judgment of an action as either good or bad: *Her decision is based on a moral principle.* 2. Teaching or expressing proper behavior. a moral act. —n. A lesson taught by a story: *the moral of a fable.*

Check the Dictionary: Look up the following words in a classroom dictionary. Write the parts of speech given for each word. Then write an original sentence using the word as each part of speech.

master	nurse	lance
knock	compound	exhaust

The Prefixes ante- *and* anti-

Lesson 15 Part A

Name ______________________________

Words

antebellum
antecedent
antedate
anteroom
anticlimax
antidote
antipathy
antiseptic
antisocial
antitoxin

The prefixes *ante-* and *anti-* look and sound very much alike, but their meanings are quite different. The prefix *ante-* comes from the Latin word *ante*, meaning "before." If one event *antedates* another, it comes before it. The prefix *anti-* , meaning "opposite" or "against," comes from the Greek word *anti*. Someone who is *antismoking* is against smoking.

Prefix	Meaning	English Word
ante-	before	antedate
anti-	opposite, against	antisocial

Unlocking Meaning

Write the vocabulary word that fits each clue below. Then say the word and write a short definition. Compare your definition with the one in the dictionary at the back of the book.

1. This word contains the Latin word *bellum* meaning "war." It describes the South before the Civil War.

   antebellum Definitions will vary.

2. Increasingly exciting events should build to a climax. This word describes what happens when things just come to an end, without a climax.

   anticlimax Definitions will vary.

3. A toxin is a poison. If you swallow some, you'll need to take this.

   antitoxin Definitions will vary.

4. This word contains the root *cedere*, meaning "to go." Every pronoun has one of these.

antecedent Definitions will vary.

5. This noun contains the root *pathos*, meaning "feeling." It is something you might have for an enemy.

antipathy Definitions will vary.

6. The Latin word *socius* means "companion." This word suggests that someone does not want or need a companion.

antisocial Definitions will vary.

7. A lobby or waiting room is a good example of this.

anteroom Definitions will vary.

8. The Greek word *septos* means "poisonous." You might use this to prevent a poisonous substance from entering your body.

antiseptic Definitions will vary.

9. If you wrote a rent check on July 15 but dated it July 1, this word describes what you did.

antedated Definitions will vary.

10. It could describe what laughter is to sadness, what food is to hunger, and what certain medication is for a snakebite.

antidote Definitions will vary.

Name ____________________

Applying Meaning

Decide which word in parentheses best completes the sentence. Then write the sentence, adding the missing word.

1. Potato crop failures in the 1840s were the _____ of Irish immigration to America in the 1850s. (antecedent; antidote)

   antecedent

2. Gwen had a strong _____ to air travel. (anticlimax; antipathy)

   antipathy

3. Jorge is not _____, but he had to work and couldn't spend the evening with his friends. (antiseptic; antisocial)

   antisocial

4. The antique dealer tried to _____ the historic document to make the buyer think it was much older. (antedate; antebellum)

   antedate

5. A weekend alone in the woods was the perfect _____ for the hectic week Julio spent in the office. (anticlimax; antidote)

   antidote

6. Because the risk of infection is so high, hospital rooms must always be kept in an _____ condition. (antecedent; antiseptic)

   antiseptic

Follow the directions below to write a sentence using a vocabulary word.

7. Describe some aspect of life in the South before the Civil War. Use the word *antebellum*.

   Sample Answer: The antebellum mansions in Mississippi reveal the aristocratic life of the plantation owners before the Civil War.

8. Use the word *anteroom* in a sentence about a public building such as a museum or courthouse.

   Sample Answer: Upon entering the museum, visitors find themselves in an anteroom where they must leave their cameras.

9. Tell about a vacation you looked forward to. Use the word *anticlimax*.

   Sample Answer: The anticlimax of my long-awaited week on the beach came in the form of flies, sunburn, and a hurricane.

10. Describe a life-threatening event or situation. Use the word *antitoxin*.

    Sample Answer: Without the antitoxin, death from the deadly spider bite could have occurred within hours.

Our Living Language

The prefix *anti-* is one of the most flexible prefixes in the English language. It is easily added to existing words to form new words that most people will understand immediately. During the 1960s the words *antiwar* and *antiestablishment* emerged. More recently, *antiabortion* and *antidumping* have become common.

Cooperative Learning: Work with a partner to write a dictionary definition and sample sentence for each of the following words: antibusiness, antibusing, antifeminist, antigun, antinuclear, antipollution, antismog, antitank

Assessment

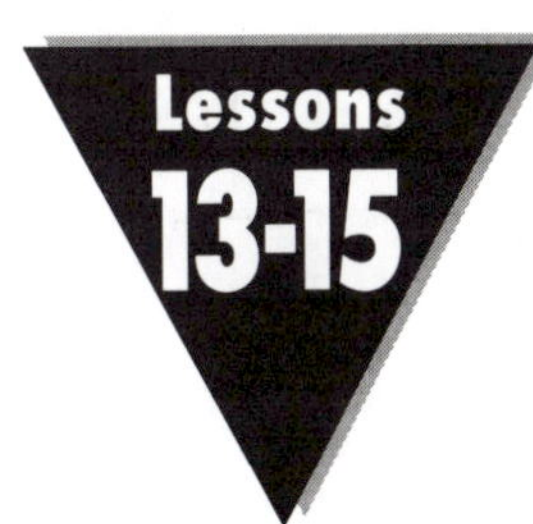

Name ______________________________

How well do you remember the words you studied in Lessons 13 through 15? Take the following test covering the words from the last three lessons.

Part 1 Antonyms

Each question below includes a word in capital letters, followed by four words or phrases. Choose the word or phrase that is most nearly opposite in meaning to the word in capital letters. Write the letter for your answer on the line provided.

Sample

S. SLOW	(A) lazy (C) fast	(B) simple (D) common	S. C
1. UNIVERSAL	(A) distant (C) educated	(B) limited (D) weak	1. B
2. HUMANE	(A) cruel (C) kind	(B) mechanical (D) intelligent	2. A
3. ANTISEPTIC	(A) ancient (C) clean	(B) safe (D) filthy	3. D
4. MARTIAL	(A) bright (C) earthly	(B) official (D) civilian	4. D
5. ANTEDATE	(A) follow (C) lead	(B) court (D) accompany	5. A
6. BREACH	(A) honor (C) provide	(B) divide (D) break	6. A
7. ANTIPATHY	(A) immortal (C) huge	(B) attraction (D) hatred	7. B
8. OFFENSIVE	(A) insulting (C) harmless	(B) odorous (D) clever	8. C
9. ANTISOCIAL	(A) rude (C) cute	(B) business-like (D) friendly	9. D
10. PITFALLS	(A) resting places (C) dangers	(B) advantages (D) challenges	10. B

11. ANTITOXIN	(A) warlike (C) type of leaf	(B) poison (D) electric	11. B
12. ELIMINATE	(A) keep (C) darken	(B) destroy (D) understand	12. A
13. ANTEBELLUM	(A) beautiful (C) historic	(B) awkward (D) postwar	13. D
14. ALIENATE	(A) befriend (C) discharge	(B) explore (D) renew	14. A
15. ANTAGONIZE	(A) protest (C) comfort	(B) identify (D) apply heat	15. C

Part 2 Matching Words and Meanings

Match the definition in Column B with the word in Column A. Write the letter of the correct definition on the line provided.

Column A	Column B	
16. meddle	a. related to customs and beliefs	16. i
17. etiquette	b. daring and courage	17. g
18. biennial	c. coming or happening before	18. j
19. morale	d. possibility or probability	19. h
20. antecedent	e. occurring twice a year	20. c
21. cultural	f. lesson or principle	21. a
22. mettle	g. rules of polite behavior	22. b
23. moral	h. spirit or mental state	23. f
24. potential	i. to interfere	24. d
25. biannual	j. occurring once every two years	25. e

Name ______________________________

Lesson 16 Part A

Autopsy

Regardless of one's beliefs about the spiritual life of the soul, the treatment of our earthly remains is a matter of considerable importance. In nearly all cultures, the **desecration** of a dead body, even the body of an enemy, is **abhorrent**. Extreme measures are taken to recover the victims of mining disasters, plane crashes, and other accidents in order that their bodies may be properly buried. The cremated remains of loved ones are usually handled with great reverence. They have been lovingly scattered over the sea, housed in shrines, and even shot into space.

It is little surprise then that the idea of cutting apart and studying a dead body is charged with deep emotions. The thought of cutting into the human body was deeply **repugnant** to the early Chinese and Muslims. In the Middle Ages, many Western civilizations prohibited such human **dissection**. Even today, authorizing an autopsy on the body of a loved one can be a heart-wrenching decision.

It was not until the Renaissance that the dissection and study of corpses became an acceptable scientific practice. Only then was it possible to **differentiate** between the normal and abnormal appearances of human organs and to begin to link certain **symptoms** of a disease with observable abnormalities.

Until the nineteenth century, autopsies were limited to observations that could be made with the naked eye. The microscope made it possible to study the changes in the cells and link their **mutations** with disease and death. Modern, scientifically **sophisticated** autopsies require **comprehensive** chemical analysis.

In addition to their scientific applications, modern autopsies have important legal significance. An autopsy can often determine whether death was the result of foul play or natural causes. The pathologist in such cases must be thorough and objective, listing all **lethal** and nonlethal facts uncovered during the examination of the body. Determining the cause of death requires a broad-based examination of the body, the scene of the death, and all related circumstances.

Words

abhorrent
comprehensive
desecration
differentiate
dissection
lethal
mutation
repugnant
sophisticated
symptom

Unlocking Meaning

Each word in this lesson's word list appears in dark print in the selection you just read. Think about how the vocabulary is used in the selection, then write the letter for the best answer to each question.

1. The best definition for *desecration* (line 3) is _____.
   (A) deep admiration
   (B) ridicule
   (C) the harming of something held sacred
   (D) removal from public view

1. C

2. If something is *abhorrent* (line 4), it _____.
   (A) causes disgust and hate
   (B) is a source of comfort
   (C) is highly admired
   (D) proves one's superiority

2. A

3. Another word for *repugnant* (line 12) is _____.
   (A) simple
   (B) clever
   (C) disgusting
   (D) alarming

3. C

4. The word *dissection* (line 14) means _____.
   (A) separating by size
   (B) violent argument
   (C) exploration
   (D) cutting apart

4. D

5. If you are able to *differentiate* (line 19) between two things, you can _____.
   (A) put them in order
   (B) tell the difference
   (C) place one on top of the other
   (D) ignore one and study the other

5. B

6. A *symptom* (line 21) is a _____.
   (A) part of the body
   (B) sign
   (C) scientific examination
   (D) careful experiment

6. B

7. Another word for *mutations* (line 24) is _____.
   (A) changes
   (B) colors
   (C) sounds
   (D) thickness

7. A

8. A *sophisticated* autopsy (line 25) is one that is _____.
   (A) rarely performed
   (B) required by law
   (C) scientifically complicated or complex
   (D) performed immediately after death

8. C

9. Another word for *comprehensive* (line 26) is _____.
   (A) thorough
   (B) careless
   (C) simple
   (D) brief

9. A

10. *Lethal* (line 31) means _____.
    (A) legal
    (B) able to cause death
    (C) experimental
    (D) microscopic

10. B

Name ______________________

Lesson 16 Part B

Applying Meaning

Follow the directions below to write a sentence using a vocabulary word.

1. Use *abhorrent* to describe something you observed, read about, or saw on television.
   Sample Answer: The abhorrent treatment of animals at the racetrack was reported in the newspaper.

2. Describe a report given by a classmate. Use the word *comprehensive*.
   Sample Answer: Reuben's report on the battle was so comprehensive that it included several graphs and illustrations.

3. Write a sentence about the uniforms players wear in a basketball game. Use the word *differentiate*.
   Sample Answer: Players on the home team wear white uniforms to differentiate them from the visitors, who wear a dark color.

4. Use *sophisticated* in a sentence about space exploration.
   Sample Answer: Samples were collected from Mars using a sophisticated device that could collect rocks and analyze their contents.

Each question below contains a vocabulary word from this lesson. Answer each question "yes" or "no" in the space provided.

5. Is each section of the country divided into smaller *dissections*? 5. **no**
6. Would a doctor order a *lethal* medication for a patient with a minor illness. 6. **no**
7. Is cancer a type of *mutation* in human cells? 7. **yes**
8. Does a game of chess or tennis require great *desecration* on the part of the players? 8. **no**
9. Is sneezing one *symptom* of a cold? 9. **yes**
10. Does rotting garbage give off a *repugnant* odor? 10. **yes**

For each question you answered "no," write a sentence explaining your reason.

Answers will vary.

Mastering Meaning

Experiments involving new drugs and surgical procedures are often performed first on animals. Such experiments undoubtedly cause great pain and suffering for the animals, but often lead to the development of medicines and surgical techniques that save human lives. Write a short essay defending or criticizing the practice of using animals for experiments. Use some of the words you have studied in this lesson.

Name ______________________

People's moods change, while their personalities are more constant. There are great varieties of moods and personalities, and the language that can be used to describe them is rich and colorful. In this lesson, you will learn ten words that describe different kinds of moods and personalities.

Words

- **egotistical**
- **indignant**
- **reluctant**
- **self-effacing**
- **skeptical**
- **snobbish**
- **sociable**
- **stolid**
- **sullen**
- **vindictive**

Unlocking Meaning

Read the sentences or short passages below. Write the letter for the correct definition of the italicized vocabulary word.

1. I can't believe that someone who was once such a show-off is now so *self-effacing*.
   (A) willing to take credit for everything (B) able to fix mechanical objects
   (C) modest; content to stay in the background (D) furious; filled with angry thoughts

2. Luckily, Theresa is not a person who is *vindictive*. She is usually willing to forgive and forget small injuries.
   (A) filled with a need to learn (B) forgetful
   (C) hard to understand (D) looking for revenge

3. People think of writers as lonely hermits, but Robert Benchley was a *sociable* sort, who enjoyed both people and parties.
   (A) friendly (B) foolish
   (C) sloppy (D) truthful

4. People who love animals become *indignant* when they see someone mistreat a helpless pet.
   (A) homeless (B) filled with joy
   (C) angry because of something unfair or mean (D) less able to remember things correctly

5. President Calvin Coolidge was said to be so *stolid* that when he died, writer Dorothy Parker asked, "How can they tell?"
   (A) filled with cheer and good humor (B) hard to excite; lacking in emotion
   (C) unwilling to serve his country (D) fearful of losing his money

1. ___C___

2. ___D___

3. ___A___

4. ___C___

5. ___B___

6. Let someone else give Carlos credit. He will seem *egotistical* if he says the project was his idea. 6. D

(A) concerned with numbers (B) aware of danger
(C) reckless or lacking in common sense (D) too self-centered

7. One child became *sullen* and uncooperative when the others decided to play a different game. 7. A

(A) sulky and silent; quiet because of a bad mood (B) eager to please someone else
(C) excited about the future; filled with joy (D) sorry about past behavior

8. Most scientists are *skeptical* of new theories until the ideas are proven by several people. 8. D

(A) full of smiles (B) innocent of wrongdoing
(C) not able to see clearly (D) filled with doubts

9. The horse was so *reluctant* to cross the bridge that Yani had to get off, cover the animal's eyes, and lead it across. 9. B

(A) glad (B) unwilling
(C) too stupid (D) proud

10. Neither candidate was *snobbish*. In spite of their money and power, they were both as polite to their drivers and household workers as they were to the mayor. 10. B

(A) able to forget a wrong that had been done to them (B) one who looks down on people with less money or rank
(C) quick to begin but slow to finish (D) strange in their clothing or actions

Name ______________________________

Lesson 17
Part B

Applying Meaning

Follow the directions below to write a sentence using a vocabulary word.

1. Tell how you would feed a cat that did not like the food you served. Use any form of the word *reluctant*.
   Sample Answer: My cat is a reluctant eater unless I offer her tuna fish.

2. Use any form of the word *sociable* to describe someone who is invited to many parties.
   Sample Answer: Lisa is very sociable, so everyone invites her to their parties.

3. Use any form of the word *snobbish* to describe a new student who is shy but looks unfriendly.
   Sample Answer: Because Todd never talked with anyone, everyone thought he was snobbish, but he was only shy.

4. Use any form of the word *egotistical* to describe how an unpopular person sounds to others.
   Sample Answer: This person is so egotistical that every other word is "I" or "me."

5. Describe a person you would not want to sit next to on a bus ride. Use any form of the word *sullen*.
   Sample Answer: The person wore dirty clothes and a sullen expression.

Read each sentence or short passage below. Answer each question "yes" or "no" in the space provided.

6. Is a *self-effacing* person likely to seek constant applause? 6. **no**

7. Is an *indignant* person likely to be smiling? 7. **no**

8. Would a *vindictive* person try to get even with someone who had played a mean trick? 8. yes

9. Is a *stolid* person very likely to be the one who has partygoers laughing constantly? 9. no

10. Would a *skeptical* person readily believe a story about alien invaders? 10. no

For each question you answered "no," write a sentence explaining your reason.

Answers will vary.

Our Living Language

During the sixteenth century, a popular new form of theater called the *commedia dell'arte* was developed in Italy. Traveling groups of actors went from town to town putting on funny performances. Although there were many different stories, all had the same group of characters. These often included a soldier and a delicate girl. One character was named Zanni, which is the short form of Giovanni. Zanni told jokes, engaged in low humor, and generally acted silly. From his name came the word *zany*, meaning "a clown" or "someone who acts foolish to make others laugh." The word also describes actions that cause laughter.

Write a List: Identify or create a character who is zany. List some of the things that person might do.

The Prefixes sub- *and* super-

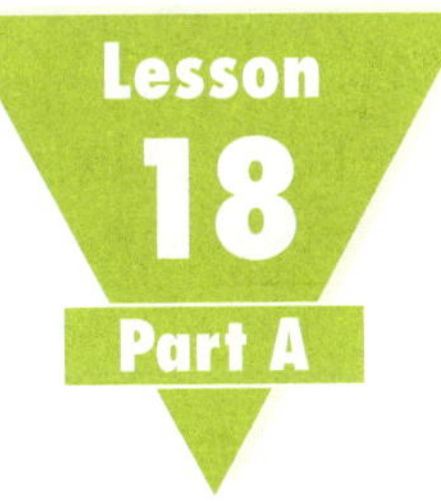

Name ______________________________

The Latin word *sub,* meaning "under" or "below," gives us the English prefix *sub-*. The *subconscious* is below the level of consciousness. The Latin word *super*, meaning "above" or "over," gives us the prefix *super-*. The *supernatural* world is above or outside of the natural world.

Prefix	Meaning	English Word
sub-	under, below	subconscious
super-	above, over	supernatural

Words

subconscious
subdue
submission
subordinate
subservient
subversion
superficial
superimpose
superlative
supernatural

Unlocking Meaning

A vocabulary word appears in italics in each passage below. The meaning of the root is given in parentheses. Write a definition for the vocabulary word. Compare your definition with the dictionary definition at the back of the book.

1. Even though I had tickets to the game, I had a *subconscious* wish to stay home. (Root word: *scire*, "to know")

   Definitions will vary.

2. It took hours for rescuers to *subdue* the wild moose that had strayed onto the highway. (Root word: *ducere*, "to lead")

   Definitions will vary.

3. Once the Union had forced the South into *submission*, a healing of the country's wounds began. (Root word: *mittere*, "to cause to go")

   Definitions will vary.

4. His assistant has a *subordinate* role. He offers advice, but the coach makes all decisions. (Root word: *ordinare*, "to set in order")

   Definitions will vary.

5. Alicia's *subservient* behavior toward the new boss is disgusting. Did you see how she ran to get his coffee? (Root word: *servire*, "to serve")

Definitions will vary.

6. The judge ruled that the police department's search was a *subversion* of the defendant's rights. (Root word: *vertere*, "to turn")

Definitions will vary.

7. The cut on her lip was quite *superficial*. It healed completely in two days. (Root word: *facies*, "face")

Definitions will vary.

8. The detective used a computer to *superimpose* possible disguises on a picture of the suspect. (Root word: *imponere*, "to place upon")

Definitions will vary.

9. A painter, inventor, and sculptor, Da Vinci is a *superlative* example of the Renaissance man. (Root word: *latus*, carried)

Definitions will vary.

10. Some ancient kings were also worshiped as *supernatural* beings. (Root word: *natura*, "nature")

Definitions will vary.

Name ______________________

Lesson 18 Part B

Applying Meaning

Write a vocabulary word to complete each statement.

1. Undivided is to *subdivided* as *unconscious* is to _____.
2. Revert is to *reversion* as *subvert* is to _____.
3. Market is to *supermarket* as *natural* is to _____.
4. Greater is to *comparative* as *greatest* is to _____.
5. Sad is to *happy* as *deep* is to _____.

1. subconscious
2. subversion
3. supernatural
4. superlative
5. superficial

Follow the directions below to write a sentence using a vocabulary word.

6. Describe a scene from a movie or television program involving the police. Use any form of the word *subdue*.

   Sample Answer: The movie ended when the police subdued the enemy agent and sent him to jail.

7. Use the word *superimpose* in a sentence about a trick someone plays on another person.

   Sample Answer: Helga tried to make us think she had won the lottery by superimposing today's date on an old ticket she had.

8. Describe the relationship between two people. Use the word *subordinate*.

   Sample Answer: The new plan requires the principal to create two subordinate positions: an assistant principal and a curriculum specialist.

9. Use *submission* in a sentence about an event in American history.

   Sample Answer: The Japanese submission in World War II came soon after the atomic bomb was dropped.

10. Complete the following statement: His *subservient* attitude was evident when he. . . .

Sample Answer: His subservient attitude was evident when he dusted off his chair and offered it to the new foreman.

Test-Taking Strategies

Analogy tests require you to think carefully about how two words relate to each other and then to find the word pair that best expresses a similar relationship. Remember, you are looking for the best match.

Practice: Each question below consists of a pair of related words, followed by four pairs of words or phrases. Select the pair that best expresses the same relationship as the original pair.

1. WIND:SAIL (A) rainbow:color (B) fish:water (C) brush:paint (D) gasoline:engine — 1. **D**

2. DOCTOR:ILLNESS (A) librarian:books (B) dentist:toothache (C) teacher:school (D) mechanic:tools — 2. **B**

3. RECIPE:COOK (A) uniform:soldier (B) word:sentence (C) map:driver (D) laboratory:chemist — 3. **C**

Assessment

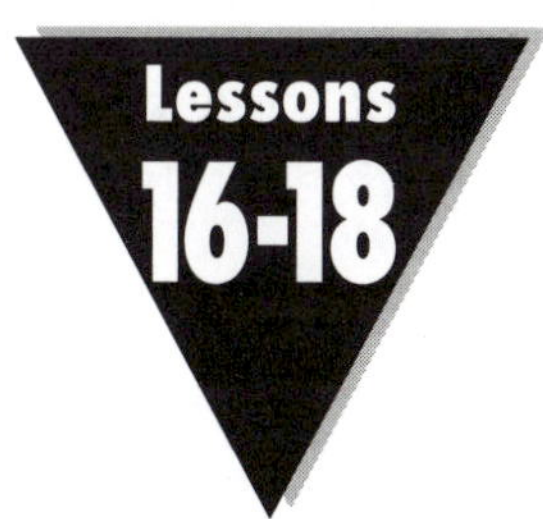

Name ______________________________

How well do you remember the words you studied in Lessons 16 through 18? Take the following test covering the words from the last three lessons.

Part 1 Choose the Correct Meaning

Each question below includes a word in capital letters, followed by four words or phrases. Choose the word or phrase that is closest in meaning to the word in capital letters. Write the letter for your answer on the line provided.

Sample

S. FINISH	(A) enjoy (C) destroy	(B) complete (D) enlarge	S. B
1. SULLEN	(A) glum (C) buried	(B) outnumbered (D) late	1. A
2. SUPERIMPOSE	(A) take advantage of (C) lay over	(B) accept (D) succeed	2. C
3. REPUGNANT	(A) inclined to fight (C) very useful	(B) overeager (D) strongly distasteful	3. D
4. SOCIABLE	(A) easily convinced (C) publicly funded	(B) friendly (D) anxious	4. B
5. EGOTISTICAL	(A) self-centered (C) experienced	(B) happy (D) talented	5. A
6. LETHAL	(A) sharp (C) level	(B) permissible (D) deadly	6. D
7. STOLID	(A) sentimental (C) foolish	(B) unemotional (D) huge	7. B
8. SUBORDINATE	(A) abnormal (C) unusual	(B) inferior (D) unseen	8. B
9. SUPERFICIAL	(A) shallow (C) likable	(B) excessive (D) particular	9. A
10. COMPREHENSIVE	(A) convincing (C) flattering	(B) intelligible (D) complete	10. D

11. SELF-EFFACING	(A) modest (C) careful	(B) weak (D) pompous	11. A
12. SUPERLATIVE	(A) skillful (C) productive	(B) excessive (D) the best	12. D
13. INDIGNANT	(A) concise (C) angry	(B) poor (D) tearful	13. C
14. SKEPTICAL	(A) ignorant (C) amused	(B) uncertain (D) noble	14. B
15. SUBMISSION	(A) obedience (C) separation	(B) classification (D) continuity	15. A

Part 2 Matching Words and Meanings

Match the definition in Column B with the word in Column A. Write the letter of the correct definition on the line provided.

Column A	Column B	
16. subversion	a. overly willing to serve	16. f
17. sophisticated	b. highly developed, advanced	17. b
18. vindictive	c. feeling or acting superior	18. g
19. symptom	d. a sign that something is present	19. d
20. reluctant	e. existing in the mind but not in conscious thought	20. j
21. dissection	f. overthrowing or destroying an authority	21. i
22. snobbish	g. wanting revenge	22. c
23. mutation	h. a change	23. h
24. subservient	i. taking apart	24. a
25. subconscious	j. unwilling	25. e

Name ______________________________

Lesson 19 Part A

Paul Bunyan and the Tall Tale

There must be something about campfires that **stimulates** the storyteller in us. It was around frontier campfires that boredom and a sense of competition combined to create a **proliferation** of tall tales. Here were born such characters as Pecos Bill and John Henry. Even the actions of real human beings like Davy Crockett were **enhanced** with carefully **contrived** tales of unbelievable strength and courage. Perhaps the best-known character is Paul Bunyan, the logger.

Stories of Paul Bunyan's size **abound**. One story claims that at birth a huge boat served as Paul's cradle. The river gently rocked baby Paul to sleep, but when he rolled around in his bed, he created waves so large that people had to climb on their roofs to escape them. Another story **recounts** how Paul created the Grand Canyon by dragging his ax behind him as he walked across the plains.

The **disparity** between Paul and his surroundings occasionally caused some problems. He had to be constantly reminded not to step on houses or put his foot on a mountain to tie his shoe.

In most of the stories of Paul Bunyan, he is accompanied by his famous blue ox named Babe. Like Paul, Babe was huge. Her size was a great advantage. Paul Bunyan could clear an entire forest in one morning. Before he had Babe, however, his work was **impaired** because he had no way to carry away the trees he cut down. Babe could carry all the trees in a forest on her back.

In one well-known tale, a serious water shortage occurred at a logging camp in North Dakota. Paul and Babe could not stand by **impassively** while men went thirsty, so Paul tied a big tank on Babe's back and set out to get water from the Great Lakes. On their return trip, Babe's hoofs made holes in the ground, and the water from the tank spilled into them. According to the story, this is how Minnesota came to have so many lakes. One **addendum** to the story concerns an accident that supposedly occurred midway through the journey. Babe tripped, and all of the water spilled out of the tank on her back. This spill was the start of the Mississippi River.

Words

abound
addendum
contrived
disparity
enhance
impair
impassive
proliferation
recount
stimulate

Unlocking Meaning

Each word in this lesson's word list appears in dark type in the selection you just read. Think about how the vocabulary word is used in the selection, then write the letter for the best answer to each question.

1. Which word could best replace *stimulates* in line 1? — 1. **B**
   (A) delays (B) arouses
   (C) explains (D) duplicates

2. A *proliferation* (line 3) is a _____. — 2. **C**
   (A) quiet pause (B) way of making money
   (C) rapid increase (D) promise

3. If you *enhance* (line 6) something, you _____. — 3. **B**
   (A) surround it in mystery (B) make it greater in size or value
   (C) force it into a small space (D) explain it to someone

4. A *contrived* (line 6) tale is one that is _____. — 4. **D**
   (A) true in every detail (B) full of surprises
   (C) about Paul Bunyan (D) cleverly planned

5. *Abound* (line 9) means _____. — 5. **A**
   (A) available in large numbers (B) go out of bounds
   (C) occurring with great certainty (D) disappear

6. If you *recount* (line 13) a story, you _____. — 6. **A**
   (A) tell it in detail (B) dismiss it from your memory
   (C) find it unbelievable (D) copy it into a notebook

7. Another word for *disparity* in line 15 is _____. — 7. **C**
   (A) mistrust (B) love
   (C) differences (D) similarity

8. Another word for *impaired* in line 22 is _____. — 8. **B**
   (A) strengthened (B) weakened
   (C) enjoyed (D) admired

9. If you sit around *impassively* (line 26), you _____. — 9. **D**
   (A) make rude remarks (B) stay alert and attentive
   (C) make many sudden movements (D) show no concern

10. An *addendum* (line 30) is _____. — 10. **A**
    (A) something added (B) anything that gets attention
    (C) an explanation (D) a mathematical term

Name ______________________________

Applying Meaning

Decide which word in parentheses best completes the sentence. Then write the sentence, adding the missing word.

1. His reputation as a war hero _____ the candidate's chances for winning the election. (enhanced; impaired)

   enhanced

2. Her _____ look suggested that she was bored. (contrived; impassive)

   impassive

3. The police were not sure about what happened because of the _____ in the accounts of the two witnesses. (disparity; proliferation)

   disparity

4. Without rain to _____ their growth, my tomato plants will simply wither and die. (impair; stimulate)

   stimulate

5. The mayor moved to include a(n) _____ to the treasurer's report to explain the loss in revenue. (addendum; proliferation)

   addendum

6. The assassins had a carefully _____ plot for taking over the government. (contrived; enhanced)

   contrived

Each question below contains a vocabulary word from this lesson. Answer each question "yes" or "no" in the space provided.

7. Would you expect joy and goodwill to *abound* at a holiday celebration? 7. yes

8. Is *proliferation* a type of air pollution? 8. no

9. Could a retired sea captain *recount* many stories about life at sea? 9. yes

10. Does it take an expert mechanic to *impair* modern jet engines? 10. no

For each question you answered "no," write a sentence explaining your reason.

Answers will vary.

Mastering Meaning

Think of some geographical feature of the United States. It might be a mountain, a peninsula, or a similar feature. Make up a tall tale about Paul Bunyan or another superhuman individual to explain how that feature came into being. Use some of the words you studied in this lesson.

Lesson 20 Part A

Name ______________________________

Imagine trying to describe the form or shape of an airplane to someone who had never seen one. Words like *big* and *long* are not specific enough. For this and other descriptions, we need words that define particular forms and shapes exactly, especially in science, mathematics, art, and architecture. In this lesson you will learn ten words that describe forms and shapes.

Words
- bilateral
- bulbous
- concave
- convex
- elliptical
- linear
- polygon
- serpentine
- statuesque
- symmetry

Unlocking Meaning

Read the sentences or short passages below. Write the letter for the correct definition of the italicized vocabulary word.

1. The two countries settled their differences. Leaders on both sides felt they could accept the terms of their *bilateral* agreement.
   (A) one-sided (B) two-sided
   (C) built of straight lines (D) triangular

   1. B

2. After the fighter's nose was broken several times, it began to take on a *bulbous* shape.
   (A) bulb-shaped (B) rectangular
   (C) long and narrow (D) egg-shaped

   2. A

3. Rainwater collected in the *concave* surface of the ditch.
   (A) bumpy (B) coiled
   (C) curved outward, like a dome (D) curved inward, like a bowl

   3. D

4. The children began the sand castle by creating a rounded hill of sand. Then, with a pointed stick, they etched details into this *convex* surface.
   (A) bumpy (B) coiled
   (C) curved outward, like a dome (D) curved inward, like a bowl

   4. C

5. The *elliptical* shape of a jelly bean may cause it to slip down one's throat and get caught there. This is not a good candy to give small children.
   (A) circular (B) oval
   (C) square (D) two-sided

   5. B

6. The *linear* dimensions of the court were 12 feet by 8 feet.
   (A) related to lines or length (B) made up of circles
   (C) triangular (D) long and narrow

   6. A

7. To make street signs easier to recognize, each one appears on a different *polygon*. *Stop* appears on a six-sided sign, and *Yield* appears on a triangle. 7. C

(A) any rough surface (B) a flat, red surface

(C) a geometric figure with three or more straight sides (D) a rectangle or square

8. The *serpentine* mountain road made all of us feel a little uneasy. More than once we narrowly missed one of the many sharp curves. 8. A

(A) having many bends and curves (B) straight and narrow

(C) wide (D) clearly marked

9. The diver struck a *statuesque* pose on the end of the board, then gracefully floated into the air and completed a perfect dive. 9. B

(A) short and round (B) tall, stately, and well-proportioned

(C) lean and thin (D) frightening

10. Greek architecture emphasized the need for *symmetry*. If one side of a building had four columns and twenty-four steps, the other side also had four columns and twenty-four steps. 10. C

(A) unevenness (B) long, narrow shapes

(C) perfectly balanced on two sides (D) a simple appearance

Name ____________________

Applying Meaning

Decide which word in parentheses best completes the sentence. Then write the sentence, adding the missing word.

1. The _____ shape of the egg made it difficult to stand it on end. (elliptical; linear)

   elliptical

2. The _____ honor guard stood at attention. (bulbous; statuesque)

   statuesque

3. Although it was ten miles long, the _____ river emptied into a lake just two miles from its source. (bilateral; serpentine)

   serpentine

4. Dali's painting *The Last Supper* is perfect in its _____. Its left side is a mirror image of the right. (polygon; symmetry)

   symmetry

5. The _____ satellite dish was designed to catch the signals from space and reflect them inward. (concave; convex)

   concave

6. Unless the negotiator could get a _____ agreement to the terms, the strike would surely continue. (bilateral; linear)

   bilateral

7. By comparing the building's shadow to the shadow of a ruler, we determined its _____ height. (linear; serpentine)

linear

Follow the directions to write a sentence using a vocabulary word.

8. Describe something using the word *bulbous*.

Sample Answer: The field was filled with the bulbous shapes of cauliflower and cabbage.

9. Complete this sentence: In math class we learned how to calculate the area of several *polygons*, including. . . .

Sample Answer: In math class we learned how to calculate the area of several polygons, including triangles, squares, and rectangles.

10. Use *convex* to describe the shape of something.

Sample Answer: The convex shape of the domed roof caused water and snow to roll off the roof easily.

Bonus Word

Quad-

The word *triangle* contains the prefix *tri-*, which means "three." Therefore, a triangle is a flat figure that contains three angles and three sides. The prefix *quad-* means "four." Words with this prefix have "four" as part of their meaning

Work with a Partner: Write a short definition for each of these words. Use a dictionary if you need help.

quadrant quadraphonic sound quadrennial quadruplicate

The Prefix ex-

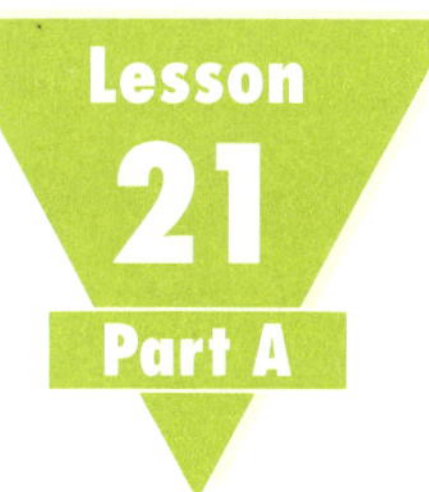

Name ____

The prefix *ex-* or *e-* comes from a Latin prefix meaning "out," "outside," or "away from." This prefix is usually combined with a root to form a word. Although the meaning of the root may not be well known, knowing the prefix and its meaning will help you unlock the meaning of an unfamiliar word.

Prefix/Meaning	Root/Meaning	Word
ex- out, outside	stinguere to quench	extinct
e- away from	rodere to gnaw	erosion

Words

eradicate
erosion
estrange
evolve
exacerbate
excel
expatriate
exterminate
extinct
extremity

Unlock Meaning

Write the vocabulary word that fits each clue below. Then say the word and write a short definition. Compare your definition and pronunciation with those given in the dictionary at the back of the book.

1. It is the verb form of *evolution*. It contains a root from the Latin word *volvere*, meaning "to roll."

   evolve Definitions will vary.

2. It comes from the same Latin word as *excellent*. In fact you can see this word in *excellent*.

   excel Definitions will vary.

3. This word is very similar to its Latin source, *exterminare*, meaning "to drive out."

   exterminate Definitions will vary.

4. This word is the noun form of the adjective *extreme*. Your foot is one of four that your body has.

   extremities Definitions will vary.

5. An antonym for *befriend*, the Latin source for this word means "to treat as a stranger."

estrange Definitions will vary.

6. This "gnawing away" word can literally describe what happens to soil or figuratively what happens to someone's confidence.

erosion Definitions will vary.

7. It describes something that is taken "away from" us forever, like the dinosaurs.

extinct Definitions will vary.

8. This word adds the prefix *e-* to the Latin root *radix*, meaning "root." Literally, it means to "eliminate the roots."

eradicate Definitions will vary.

9. The Latin word for one's native land is *patria*. One who prefers living in a foreign country is called this.

expatriate Definitions will vary.

10. This word combines the prefix *ex-* with the Latin root *acerbare* meaning "to make harsh." Rain does this to a flood.

exacerbate Definitions will vary.

Name ______________________________

Applying Meaning

Read each sentence below. Write "correct" on the answer line if the vocabulary word has been used correctly or "incorrect" if it has been used incorrectly.

1. The crowd was startled by the loud *erosion* when the supersonic jets flew overhead. — 1. incorrect
2. Miami is located at the southernmost *extremity* of Florida. — 2. correct
3. For a time, Hemingway joined a group of *expatriate* writers in Paris. — 3. correct
4. Upon entering the garage, we detected the *extinct* odor of gasoline. — 4. incorrect
5. The Salk and Sabin vaccines have nearly *eradicated* polio in the United States. — 5. correct
6. The moon *evolves* around the earth. — 6. incorrect

For each word used incorrectly, write a sentence using the word properly.

Answers will vary.

Follow the directions below to write a sentence using a vocabulary word.

7. Describe a relationship between two people. Use any form of the word *estrange*.

   Sample Answer: After Ellen learned that Julia had revealed their secret, the two became estranged.

8. Describe the effects of a political speech on a controversial topic. Use any form of the word *exacerbate*.

Sample Answer: The senator's demand for increasing the tax on social security payments only exacerbated the tension at the party's convention.

9. Use *exterminate* in a sentence about a pest.

Sample Answer: The pet shop suggested using mothballs to exterminate the fleas in Rover's favorite pile of blankets.

10. Describe an outstanding athlete. Use any form of the word *excel.*

Sample Answer: Gwen is very good in all track and field sports, but she excels in the high jump.

Using the Dictionary

A dictionary may give several meanings for a word. Sometimes a sample sentence or phrase using the word may also be provided in order to make the meaning clear. Study the sample dictionary entry below.

ex e cute (**ek'** si kyoot') *v.* **ex e cut ed, ex e cut ing, ex e cutes.**
1. To carry out: *For his final dive, Brad will attempt to execute a triple somersault.* 2. To put to death for a crime: *The state will execute the convicted murderer.*

Look up the following words in a classroom dictionary. Use each word in two sentences. The word should have a different meaning in each sentence.

deed prominent douse

Assessment

Name ______________________________

How well do you remember the words you studied in Lessons 19 through 21? Take the following test covering the words from the last three lessons.

Part 1 Antonyms

Each question below includes a word in capital letters, followed by four words or phrases. Choose the word or phrase that is most nearly opposite in meaning to the word in capital letters. Consider all choices before deciding on your answer. Write the letter for your answer on the line provided.

Sample

S. SLOW	(A) lazy (C) fast	(B) simple (D) common	S. C
1. PROLIFERATION	(A) array (C) expanse	(B) collection (D) reduction	1. D
2. EXTREMITY	(A) surface (C) part	(B) core (D) link	2. B
3. SERPENTINE	(A) oval (C) shapeless	(B) straight (D) snake-like	3. B
4. IMPASSIVE	(A) passionate (C) rude	(B) serious (D) active	4. A
5. EXACERBATE	(A) complicate (C) discuss	(B) consider (D) soothe	5. D
6. EXCEL	(A) difficult (C) deep	(B) flat (D) lag	6. D
7. SYMMETRY	(A) unevenness (C) color	(B) beauty (D) volume	7. A
8. ABOUND	(A) decrease (C) reverberate	(B) renew (D) flow	8. A
9. EXTERMINATE	(A) resolve (C) count	(B) kill (D) increase	9. D
10. DISPARITY	(A) happiness (C) improvement	(B) change (D) similarity	10. D

11. ESTRANGE	(A) invite (C) correspond with	(B) befriend (D) receive from	11. ___B___
12. IMPAIR	(A) couple (C) improve	(B) complete (D) solve	12. ___C___
13. ERADICATE	(A) liberate (C) dismiss	(B) create (D) clean	13. ___B___
14. STIMULATE	(A) copy (C) discourage	(B) return (D) move	14. ___C___
15. ENHANCE	(A) reduce (C) withdraw	(B) increase (D) unite	15. ___A___

Part 2 Matching Words and Meanings

Match the definition in Column B with the word in Column A. Write the letter of the correct definition on the line provided.

Column A	**Column B**	
16. extinct	a. on a line	16. ___g___
17. bilateral	b. carefully created	17. ___j___
18. elliptical	c. oval-shaped	18. ___c___
19. addendum	d. wearing away	19. ___f___
20. contrived	e. dignified, well-proportioned	20. ___b___
21. evolve	f. addition	21. ___i___
22. statuesque	g. no longer existing	22. ___e___
23. polygon	h. having three or more sides	23. ___h___
24. erosion	i. develop over time	24. ___d___
25. linear	j. involving two sides	25. ___a___

Lesson 22 Part A

Name ______________________________

The Siege of Vicksburg

Words

- asunder
- bastion
- citadel
- expedient
- formidable
- neutralize
- ration
- rebuff
- tactic
- untenable

The Union strategy in the midst of the Civil War was simple: gain control of the Mississippi River, and the Confederacy will be broken **asunder**. Severed from its important resources lying west of this great river, Lee's eastern armies would gradually collapse. There was, however, one **formidable** obstacle to this plan—Vicksburg. Called the Gibraltar[1] of the Confederacy, Vicksburg, Mississippi, offered the perfect **bastion** for the defenders. Entrenched on high bluffs overlooking a hairpin turn in the river, the forces at Vicksburg, commanded by the Union-born General John C. Pemberton, could sink any ship attempting to pass and **rebuff** any assault. The task of **neutralizing** this fortress fell to Ulysses S. Grant.

Grant tried a variety of **tactics** to unseat the rebel force. The simple **expedient** of crossing upriver and approaching Vicksburg from the east was defeated by an impassable swamp. Several attempts to sail down the river failed. At one point Grant even tried to dig a new channel in the river to bypass Vicksburg. Eventually he decided to march his armies south on the west bank of the river then to ferry them across below Vicksburg. Once across, he sent General W. T. Sherman east to block any efforts to reinforce the now-endangered **citadel**. Grant's huge siege guns began to bombard the isolated city with artillery.

Little by little the army and the civilian population of Vicksburg exhausted their supplies of food and ammunition. Instead of chicken or pork, small amounts of mule meat were **rationed** to the hungry defenders.

Finding his position **untenable**, Pemberton decided to surrender Vicksburg on July 4, 1863. By laying down his arms on this Union holiday, he hoped to gain more generous terms from Grant. It was eighty-five years before Vicksburg celebrated the Fourth of July.

[1] A three-mile peninsula dominated by a 1,396-foot cliff on the southern tip of Spain. It guards the entrance to the Mediterranean Sea.

Unlocking Meaning

Each word in this lesson's word list appears in dark type in the selection you just read. Think about how the vocabulary word is used in the selection, then write the letter for the best answer to each question.

1. Another word for **asunder** in line 3 is _____. 1. ___B___
   (A) together (B) apart
   (C) accidentally (D) slightly

2. A **formidable** (line 5) obstacle is one that is _____. 2. ___D___
   (A) oddly shaped (B) simple
   (C) quickly thrown together (D) difficult to defeat

3. A **bastion** (line 7) is a _____. 3. ___A___
   (A) heavily defended position (B) source of food
   (C) disagreeable person (D) deep valley

4. If you **rebuff** (line 10) something, you _____. 4. ___B___
   (A) polish it (B) drive it away
   (C) embrace it (D) examine it carefully

5. If you **neutralize** (line 11) a fortress, you _____. 5. ___C___
   (A) make an enemy of it (B) bargain with it
   (C) make it powerless (D) surrender to it

6. **Tactics** (line 12) can best be described as _____. 6. ___D___
   (A) systems for sending messages (B) a series of pauses to allow armies to regroup
   (C) offers of assistance (D) plans for meeting a goal

7. An **expedient** (line 13) is a(n) _____. 7. ___A___
   (A) way of achieving a desired result (B) areas that have been expanded
   (C) type of weapon used in naval combat (D) scouting party

8. A **citadel** (line 20) is a _____. 8. ___C___
   (A) source of water for a city (B) a small raiding party
   (C) a stronghold at or near a city (D) type of celebration

9. If food is **rationed**, (line 24) it is _____. 9. ___C___
   (A) allowed to become rotten (B) heavily seasoned
   (C) given out in limited amounts (D) hidden to avoid capture by an enemy

10. Another word for **untenable** (line 26) is _____. 10. ___B___
    (A) strengthened (B) indefensible
    (C) invisible (D) elevated

Name ______________________________

Applying Meaning

Read each sentence below. Write "correct" on the answer line if the vocabulary word has been used correctly or "incorrect" if it has been used incorrectly.

1. The lightning split *asunder* the trunk of the mighty oak tree. 1. correct
2. Hurricane Bob caused *untenable* damage to the homes of anyone living near the shore. 2. incorrect
3. The hero was awarded the nation's highest *citadel* in an impressive ceremony. 3. incorrect
4. Elderly residents were urged to drink lots of water to *neutralize* the effects of the heat wave. 4. correct
5. In history class we studied Richard Byrd's *expedient* to the polar regions of the Antarctic. 5. incorrect
6. The courts are the last *bastion* of hope for the powerless in a free and just society. 6. correct

For each word used incorrectly, write a sentence using the word properly.

Answers will vary.

Follow the directions below to write a sentence using a vocabulary word.

7. Describe a crisis or emergency. Use any form of the word *ration*.

   Sample Answer: During the flood, the Red Cross had to ration the limited amount of drinkable water on hand.

8. Use *formidable* in a sentence about a problem you or someone you know encountered.

   Sample Answer: My lack of experience as a goalie presented a formidable challenge when the coach told me to guard the net.

9. Write a sentence about how you approached a problem. Use any form of the word *tactic*.

   Sample Answer: My tactic for passing the test was to study an hour a night for a week.

10. Describe a real or imaginary battle. Use any form of the word *rebuff*.

    Sample Answer: Even after being bombed for days, the defenders were able to rebuff the attack of the invaders.

Mastering Meaning

Imagine that you are General Grant on July 5, 1863. Vicksburg has surrendered, and you now hold all of the Mississippi River. Write a report to your commander-in-chief, Abraham Lincoln, describing your success. Include some information on how you managed to achieve a victory and what it means for the war effort. Use some of the words you studied in this lesson.

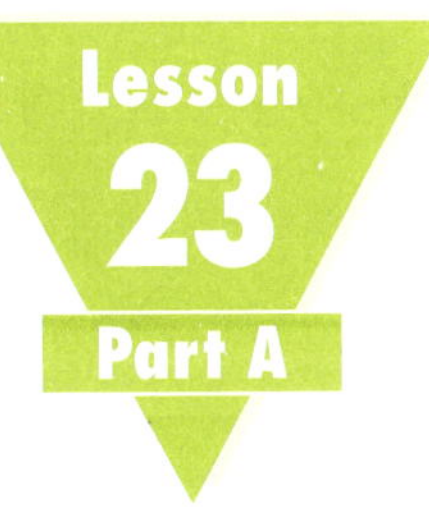

Name ______________________________

The English language sometimes uses the name of a person or place to describe something associated with that person or place. For example, an *atlas* is a book of maps. Its name comes from the Greek god Atlas. Because Atlas attempted to overthrow Zeus, the king of the gods, he was forced to spend the rest of his life holding the world on his shoulders. *Atlas* has come to mean "a book of the world's maps." In this lesson, you will learn ten words that have come from the names of people or places.

Words

babel
jovial
Lilliputian
limerick
narcissism
pandemonium
quisling
sadistic
tantalize
utopian

Unlocking Meaning

Read the sentences or short passages below. Write the letter for the correct definition of the italicized vocabulary word.

1. All of the children called out the answer at once. The kindergarten teacher could not make sense of such *babel*.
   (A) murmur
   (B) ringing, somewhat like a bell
   (C) confusing blend of many voices or sounds
   (D) crying or wailing

   1. C

2. His *jovial* laugh, ready smile, and desire to make learning fun made Mr. Ames my favorite teacher.
   (A) stern
   (B) highly educated; brilliant
   (C) silly or irresponsible
   (D) full of playful good humor

   2. D

3. In my dream, I landed in a village full of miniature houses owned by *Lilliputian* people.
   (A) cold
   (B) needy
   (C) tiny
   (D) suspicious

   3. C

4. Hannah's *limerick* began simply enough with the lines "I once saw a monkey named Phil, who slept on the side of a hill." By the time she finished, we were doubled up with laughter.
   (A) sad story
   (B) funny poem
   (C) opera
   (D) polite request

   4. B

5. My sister's *narcissism* is beginning to get on my nerves. She sits for hours in front of a mirror, admiring herself.
   (A) self-love
   (B) feelings of disappointment
   (C) envy or jealousy
   (D) cruelty or meanness

   5. A

6. When the rock star asked people to join him on stage, *pandemonium* broke out as scores of people ran down the aisles. 6. D

(A) agreement (B) disagreement
(C) laughter (D) wild disorder

7. Few citizens accepted the new governor general even though he was one of them. Instead they saw him as a *quisling* who followed the orders of the invaders. 7. B

(A) travel agent (B) traitor
(C) colleague (D) hero

8. Some thought she was a superb dog trainer, but to me the use of a whip and a choke collar seemed *sadistic*. 8. D

(A) successful (B) thought-provoking
(C) pleasant (D) extremely cruel

9. The smell of baking bread *tantalized* people as they walked past the bakery. Only the strongest could resist going inside and buying a loaf. 9. B

(A) surprised or delighted (B) teased
(C) misled (D) disgusted

10. The settlers hoped to create a *utopian* community in which everyone shared the work and the profits equally and fairly. 10. C

(A) impractical (B) fictional
(C) perfect (D) temporary

Name ______________________________

Applying Meaning

Each question below contains at least one vocabulary word from this lesson. Answer each question "yes" or "no" in the space provided.

1. Would it be wise to *tantalize* a hungry bear by holding up a nice, fresh salmon? — 1. no
2. Is Benedict Arnold an early example of a *quisling*? — 2. yes
3. Would you want a *Lilliputian* athlete in the starting lineup of your football team? — 3. no
4. Are movie stars more likely to suffer from *narcissism* than other people are? — 4. yes
5. In a *utopian* world, would all people get along with one another? — 5. yes
6. Is *pandemonium* a rare metal found only in mountains? — 6. no

For each question you answered "no," write a sentence explaining your reason.

Answers will vary.

Decide which word in parentheses best completes the sentence. Then write the sentence, adding the missing word.

7. To me the lyrics of the rock song were like poetry. To my father they were ______. (babel; sadistic)

babel

8. In some myths, Zeus is described as a harsh ruler, but other myths portray him as _____ and friendly. (jovial; utopian)

jovial

9. Have you heard the _____ that begins, "There was a young man from Mobile"? (quisling; limerick)

limerick

10. The activists pledged to put an end to the _____ metal traps used to catch wolves. (jovial; sadistic)

sadistic

Bonus Word

Donnybrook

Once a year a fair was held in Donnybrook, Ireland, a suburb of Dublin. This fair became well-known for the fights and large-scale brawls that broke out there. The town's name came to be associated with such brawls. Today *donnybrook* means "an uproar or large, free-for-all fight."

Cooperative Learning: Work with a partner to find the definitions and the word origins of these words: *saxophone, sideburns, cardigan, sandwich*.

The Prefix ab-

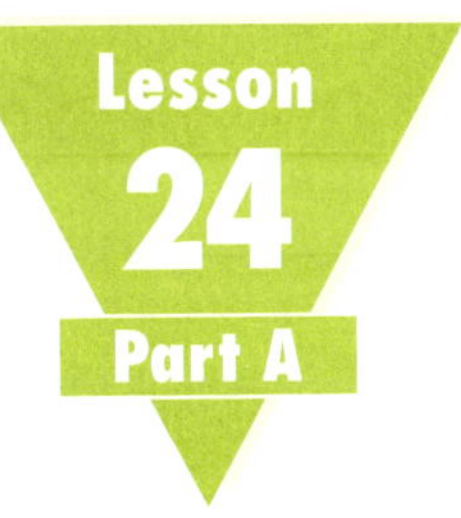

Name ______________________________

The Latin word *ab*, meaning "off" or "away" is the source of the English prefix *ab-*. In modern English this prefix may have a slightly broader, but similar, meaning. For example, in *abnormal* the *ab-* prefix means "not" normal. This differs slightly from "away from" the normal, which the prefix would suggest. Always use context clues as well as your knowledge of prefixes and roots to arrive at the meaning of an unfamiliar word.

Prefix	Root/Word	Word
ab-	normal	abnormal
ab-	tenere	abstain

Words

abdicate
abhor
abomination
aborigine
abort
abrasive
abrupt
absolute
abstain
abuse

Unlocking Meaning

A vocabulary word appears in italics in each passage below. The meaning of the root is given in parentheses. Look at the prefix and think about how the word is used in the passage. Then write a definition for the vocabulary word. Compare your definition with the dictionary definition at the back of the book.

1. In order to marry a divorcée, Edward VIII had to *abdicate* his throne and give up his royal title. (Root word: *dicare*, "to proclaim")

   Definitions will vary. ______________________________

2. The senator resigned because he had come to *abhor* the constant need to raise money for his campaigns. (Root word: *horrere*, "to shudder")

   Definitions will vary. ______________________________

3. The condition of the animals was an *abomination*. They lived in filth and most were sick. (Root word: *abominari*, "to disapprove of")

   Definitions will vary. ______________________________

4. The government realized that the *aborigine* people held an important link to the past. (Root word: *origo*, "beginning")

Definitions will vary.

5. The pilot could not confirm that the runway was clear, so she had to *abort* the landing. (Root word: *orini*, "to appear")

Definitions will vary.

6. Never use an *abrasive* cleaner on an automobile. It will leave small scratches. (Root word: *radere*, "to scrape")

Definitions will vary.

7. The storm caused an *abrupt* change in the temperature. It suddenly dropped 20 degrees.(Root word: *rumpere*, "to break")

Definitions will vary.

8. The man promised the *absolute* truth. He had no reason to lie or withhold information. (Root word: *solvere*, "to loosen")

Definitions will vary.

9. Both candidates pledged to *abstain* from personal attacks and discuss the issues. (Root word: *tenere*, "to hold")

Definitions will vary.

10. The principal warned students not to *abuse* their library privileges by talking or sleeping. (Root word: *uti*, "to use")

Definitions will vary.

Name ______________________________

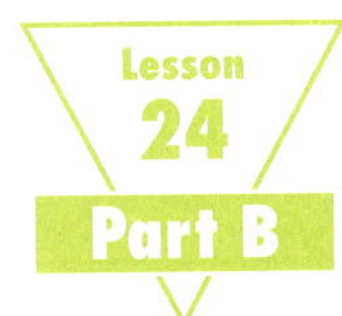

Applying Meaning

Read each sentence below. Write "correct" on the answer line if the vocabulary word has been used correctly or "incorrect" if it has been used incorrectly.

1. Upon hearing the verdict, the accused man became violent. It took several officers to *abstain* him. — 1. incorrect
2. Even though England still has a king or queen, these rulers long ago *abdicated* their unlimited powers. — 2. correct
3. The audience expected an entertaining speech, but instead the chairman *abhorred* his listeners with a financial report. — 3. incorrect
4. The astronauts had *absolute* trust in the project's director. They knew there was a good reason for his request. — 4. correct
5. The pottery held important clues about the *aborigines* who inhabited the area centuries ago. — 5. correct
6. Use a sponge or dry cloth to *abuse* the gasoline before it gets into the drain and becomes a danger. — 6. incorrect

For each word used incorrectly, write a sentence using the word properly.

Answers will vary.

Follow the directions below to write a sentence using a vocabulary word.

7. Describe a time when you changed your mind about something. Use any form of the word *abrupt*.

   Sample Answer: Just before turning in the test, I abruptly decided to change my answers to the last three questions.

8. Tell about something you saw or learned that shocked you. Use the word *abomination*.

Sample Answer: In history class we learned about the horrors and abomination of the holocaust.

9. Use the word *abrasive* in a sentence describing how to do something.

Sample Answer: To get a smooth surface on wood, rub it with an abrasive material like sandpaper.

10. Tell about an action you or someone else took. Use the word *abort*.

Sample Answer: At the last minute our class had to abort the planned field trip because of the teacher's illness.

Test-Taking Strategies

Some schools require students to take a test of standard English grammar, usage, and mechanics. This test is often used to place students in the appropriate English course. When taking such a test, always read the entire sentence before deciding on your answer. If you think you have found the error, ask yourself how you would correct it.

Practice: Write the letter for the underlined part of the sentence with an error. If there is no error, write E.

1. If you (A) get to the movies before Jenny and I (B), please save Jenny and me (C) a seat near the front (D). No Error (E) — 1. **B**

2. Jonathan, (A) one of our best athletes, (B) told the coach he would score (C) the touchdown all by hisself (D) if necessary. No Error (E) — 2. **D**

3. The committee to review (A) the new books will (B) be made up (C) of Jim, Olivia, and myself (D). No Error (E) — 3. **D**

Assessment

Name ______________________________

How well do you remember the words you studied in Lessons 22 through 24? Take the following test covering the words from the last three lessons.

Part 1 Choose the Correct Meaning

Each question below includes a word in capital letters, followed by four words or phrases. Choose the word or phrase that is closest in meaning to the word in capital letters. Write the letter for your answer on the line provided.

Sample

S. FINISH	(A) enjoy (C) destroy	(B) complete (D) enlarge	S. ___B___
1. ABHOR	(A) hate (C) support	(B) renounce (D) question	1. ___A___
2. PANDEMONIUM	(A) all-knowing (C) lengthy	(B) restrained (D) confusion	2. ___D___
3. RATION	(A) reason (C) earn	(B) measure out (D) supply	3. ___B___
4. ABDICATE	(A) appoint (C) retrieve	(B) give up (D) sell	4. ___B___
5. UNTENABLE	(A) forgivable (C) indefensible	(B) uncertain (D) forgotten	5. ___C___
6. ASUNDER	(A) sincerely (C) partially	(B) quickly (D) apart	6. ___D___
7. UTOPIAN	(A) ideal (C) new	(B) democratic (D) simple	7. ___A___
8. ABSOLUTE	(A) undeniable (C) complete	(B) unbelievable (D) incomprehensible	8. ___C___
9. BASTION	(A) fortification (C) training ground	(B) commissary (D) supply house	9. ___A___
10. ABRUPT	(A) sudden (C) desired	(B) useful (D) expected	10. ___A___

11. ABRASIVE (A) new (B) weak (C) cheap (D) harsh 11. D

12. QUISLING (A) cheapskate (B) traitor (C) coward (D) clever 12. B

13. LILLIPUTIAN (A) beautiful (B) tricky (C) tiny (D) numerous 13. C

14. REBUFF (A) reject (B) polish (C) alter (D) defeat 14. A

15. JOVIAL (A) drunken (B) obese (C) silly (D) jolly 15. D

Part 2 Matching Words and Meanings

Match the definition in Column B with the word in Column A. Write the letter of the correct definition on the line provided.

Column A	Column B	
16. neutralize	a. tease	16. f
17. abstain	b. refrain from	17. b
18. narcissism	c. horror	18. e
19. sadistic	d. fortress	19. j
20. abort	e. self-love	20. h
21. tantalize	f. offset	21. a
22. tactic	g. hard to defeat	22. i
23. citadel	h. to stop	23. d
24. abomination	i. plan	24. c
25. formidable	j. cruel	25. g

Lesson 25 Part A

Name ______________________________

Tropical Rain Forests

Rain forests were once thought to be little more than bothersome **encumbrances** to exploration and civilized development. This is no longer the case. Today people throughout the world are beginning to realize that a rich variety of plants and animals are sheltered in the rain forests. Like a desert, a tropical rain forest is a **biome** with its own unique climate, plants, and animals.

Trees that grow up to 150 feet in height form a canopy that holds most of the food sources for the animals that live in them. Tropical mammals who live at these heights have learned a variety of ways to move about. Gibbons and spider monkeys swing from branch to branch while other animals make **stupendous** leaps from one tree to another. For extra **stability**, tropical porcupines and monkeys wrap their tails around branches.

Sandwiched between the forest floor and the treetops is a layer of natural growth called the *understory*. The dim light at this level has been filtered through the forest's canopy. Here thin-trunked trees sprout leaves that look like partially closed umbrellas which have been bent to catch the scarce sunlight. Leaf-eating animals **forage** on these lush, leafy trees. The trees also attract insect-eating birds that travel the tree trunks and **ferret** out the insects that are dining on the rotting wood.

The cool, **dank** forest floor is blanketed with moss and wet leaves. Only 1 percent of the sunlight shining on the canopy reaches the ground. The **luxuriant** vegetation includes rare and strange flowers and other plants, many of which have medicinal value. Two-thirds of the medicines used today were first made from rain forest plants.

Many animals lay hidden among the layers of leaves and moss. A close look reveals the natural **camouflage** that helps conceal them. A leopard's **dappled** coat keeps it well hidden in the shadows, while the leafy-looking shell of a matamata turtle blends in with dead leaves floating down a stream.

Words

biome
camouflage
dank
dappled
encumbrance
ferret
forage
luxuriant
stability
stupendous

Unlocking Meaning

Each word in this lesson's word list appears in dark type in the selection you just read. Think about how the vocabulary word is used in the selection, then write the letter for the best answer to each question.

1. An *encumbrance* (line 2) can best be described as _____.   1. ___B___
   (A) a type of jungle plant
   (B) something that stands in the way
   (C) a plan for developing a resource
   (D) a form of assistance

2. A *biome* (line 5) is a _____.   2. ___D___
   (A) type of medicine
   (B) native tribe
   (C) explanation
   (D) natural community

3. A *stupendous* (line 11) performance is one that is _____.   3. ___A___
   (A) tremendous
   (B) terrible
   (C) terrifying
   (D) rare

4. Another word for *stability* (line 12) would be _____.   4. ___C___
   (A) shelter
   (B) money
   (C) firmness
   (D) amusement

5. When animals *forage* (line 19) they _____.   5. ___D___
   (A) destroy forest lands
   (B) hide
   (C) attack viciously
   (D) search for food

6. To *ferret* (line 20) is _____.   6. ___A___
   (A) to uncover
   (B) to frighten
   (C) to cover
   (D) to help

7. Another word for *dank* in line 22 is _____.   7. ___C___
   (A) dry
   (B) colorful
   (C) damp
   (D) dangerous

8. *Luxuriant* (line 24) vegetation is ____.   8. ___B___
   (A) expensive
   (B) thick and abundant
   (C) thin and yellowed
   (D) in need of water

9. *Camouflage* (line 29) helps animals _____.   9. ___A___
   (A) remain hidden from other animals
   (B) find their dens
   (C) sense changes in the weather
   (D) digest their food

10. A *dappled* (line 30) egg is _____.   10. ___B___
   (A) cracked
   (B) speckled
   (C) cooked
   (D) oddly shaped

Name ______________________________

Lesson 25 Part B

Applying Meaning

Read each sentence below. Write "correct" on the answer line if the vocabulary word has been used correctly or "incorrect" if it has been used incorrectly.

1. The *dappled* coat of a Dalmatian makes it easy to pick out in a crowd of other dogs. 1. correct
2. It took a great deal of *encumbrance* from his wife before FDR decided to run for president. 2. incorrect
3. Cactus, rattlesnakes, and intense heat are all part of the desert *biome*. 3. correct
4. Mushrooms grow best in a *dank* environment. That is why I raise mine in our basement. 4. correct
5. Without a compass or map, the child soon became lost in the dark *forage*. 5. incorrect
6. The rafting trip through the Rockies involved *stupendous* danger for the inexperienced traveler. 6. correct

For each word used incorrectly, write a sentence using the word properly.

Answers will vary.

Follow the directions below to write a sentence using a vocabulary word.

7. Use any form of the word *stability* in a sentence about a table.

Sample Answer: Our kitchen table lacked stability because one leg was shorter than the others.

8. Use *luxuriant* in a sentence to describe something that grows.

Sample Answer: Never before had the flower garden produced such thick and luxuriant roses and petunias.

9. Use any form of the word *camouflage* in a sentence about something you cannot find.

Sample Answer: It took hours to find my wallet because it lay camouflaged among the dead leaves in the yard.

10. Use any form of the word *ferret* in a sentence about a problem you solved.

Sample Answer: It took two hours and a calculator to ferret out all the possible answers to the math problem.

Mastering Meaning

Suppose you decided to take action on the problem of the destruction of the rain forests. Write a school newspaper reporting about the problems and suggest ways people at your school can work together to solve the problem. Write a headline and use some of the words you studied in this lesson in your newspaper article.

Vocabulary of Banking

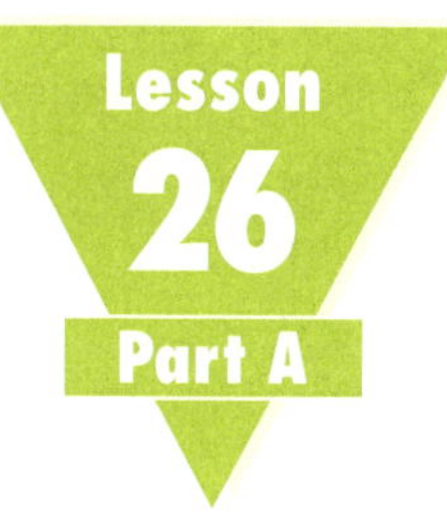

Name ____________________

Like the fields of law and government, the field of banking has its own vocabulary. When opening an account, applying for a loan, or reading your monthly statement, you will need to understand this vocabulary. In this lesson you will learn ten useful banking terms.

Unlocking Meaning

Read the sentences or short passages below. Write the letter for the correct definition of the italicized vocabulary word.

1. Before agreeing to loan Ms. Amico money to buy a new house, the bank wanted to *appraise* it. This way, the bank would be assured that the house was worth the money they were lending for it.
   (A) visit (B) judge the value of
   (C) measure (D) repair

2. Before drawing up his will, Mr. Donato reviewed his *assets*. They included his house, a savings account, and a new car.
   (A) things of value (B) expenses
   (C) items bought with borrowed money (D) desirable gifts

3. To make the most of a savings account, get one that pays *compound interest*. Such an account pays more than one with just simple interest.
   (A) fee based on the cost of living (B) charge for using a bank's services
   (C) money paid on money previously earned in a savings account (D) penalty for a late payment

4. When Hilda applied for a car loan, the bank was concerned that she might not be able to make her monthly payments. Therefore, they requested that she have a *cosigner* to share the responsibility for the loan.
   (A) legal advisor (B) close friend or relative
   (C) bank official who processes loan applications (D) someone whose signature guarantees that a loan will be paid

Words

appraise
assets
compound interest
cosigner
creditor
debit
default
foreclose
liability
lien

1. B
2. A
3. C
4. D

5. As your *creditor,* I am extremely pleased that you have never been late with your monthly payments. 5. A
(A) one to whom money is owed (B) someone with a poor credit history
(C) a person who owes someone money (D) a bank teller

6. Martin withdrew $50 from his savings account, so his next bank statement showed a *debit* of $50. 6. B
(A) error in a bank statement (B) deduction from an account
(C) money deposited into one's bank account (D) deposit into a savings account

7. A sudden drop in sales at his shop caused Mr. Jenkins to *default* on his bank loan. 7. A
(A) fail to pay money owed (B) offer to pay money owed
(C) increase in an amount (D) request that the terms of a loan be changed

8. The bank officer warned the owners of the neglected property that unless the overdue payments were received, she would be forced to *foreclose*. 8. C
(A) cancel a loan (B) increase the amount owed
(C) take a property to satisfy a loan (D) sell the loan to another bank

9. Ms. Talston was able to pay off the loans on her car and her refrigerator. Now she had just one remaining *liability*—the money she still owed on her home loan. 9. A
(A) an obligation to pay a debt (B) the total value of everything one owns
(C) a bill that another person has agreed to pay (D) a mistake or problem

10. Mr. Rowe owed the heating-oil company several hundred dollars. Because the company feared that he might never pay the debt, its treasurer decided to put a *lien* on Mr. Rowe's house. 10. D
(A) service charge (B) meter that measures the amount of oil used monthly
(C) type of lock (D) right to hold something to ensure payment of a loan debt

Name ______________________________

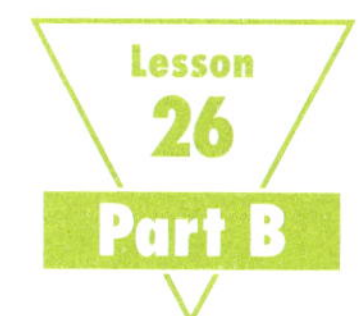

Applying Meaning

Each question below contains a vocabulary word from this lesson. Answer each question "yes" or "no" in the space provided.

1. Could a bank *foreclose* on a loan that has been paid faithfully? 1. no
2. Would most people like to have many *creditors?* 2. no
3. Would a bank be more willing to lend you money if you had a *cosigner?* 3. yes
4. Is it preferable to have more *assets* than *liabilities?* 4. yes
5. Could a homeowner put a *lien* on his or her own property? 5. no
6. Would a bank encourage a borrower to *default?* 6. no

For each question you answered "no," write a sentence explaining your reason.

Answers will vary.

Decide which word in parentheses best completes the sentence. Then write the sentence adding the missing word.

7. The bank inspectors _____ the property at approximately $100,000. (defaulted; appraised)

   appraised

8. Banks require a business to have enough real estate or other _____ to guarantee repayment of a loan. (assets; liabilities)

assets

9. Jamie was quite pleased to learn that the bank paid _____ on savings accounts. (debit; compound interest)

compound interest

10. The charge for preprinted checks will appear as a _____ on your monthly statement.(debit; lien)

debit

Bonus Words

ATM

Sometimes we use just the initials in place of long words. We say the letters ATM instead of the more cumbersome "automatic teller machine." If the initials are pronounced like a word, the name is called an *acronym*. For example, the initials of the North Atlantic Treaty Alliance make the acronym NATO, pronounced **nā′tō**.

Match the Terms: Match the initials or acronym in the first column with a name in the second column. Circle the term that is an acronym.

ETA	revolutions per minute
PA	bacon, lettuce, and tomato sandwich
OPEC	estimated time of arrival
RPM	Organization of Petroleum Exporting Countries
BLT	physician's assistant

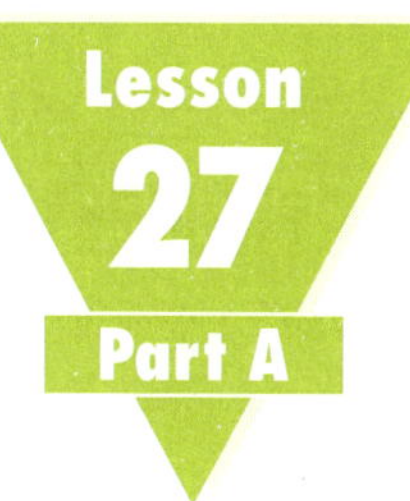

Name ______________________________

The Latin prefix *in-,* meaning "not" is one of the most common prefixes in English. It is often combined with a word to reverse the meaning of the word. *Inconspicuous* means the opposite of *conspicuous.* If the word to which the prefix is attached begins with the letter *r,* however, the prefix is said to be absorbed and its spelling changes to *ir-.*

Prefix	Word	New Word
in-	conspicuous	inconspicuous
in-	rational	irrational

Words

- **inarticulate**
- **inclement**
- **inconspicuous**
- **indiscreet**
- **invulnerable**
- **irrational**
- **irredeemable**
- **irrefutable**
- **irrelevant**
- **irretrievable**

Unlocking Meaning

A vocabulary word appears in italics in each sentence or short passage below. Find the prefix in the vocabulary word and think about how the word is used in the passage. Then write a definition for the vocabulary word. Compare your definition with the definition in the dictionary at the back of the book.

1. After seeing the evidence, the talkative defendant became *inarticulate,* making sounds but saying nothing.

   Definitions will vary.

2. The launch of the space shuttle was delayed for days by the *inclement* weather at the launch site.

   Definitions will vary.

3. The famous actress put on dark glasses and carried a camera in an effort to be *inconspicuous* in the crowd.

   Definitions will vary.

4. Most members felt Phil's *indiscreet* comments about the chairman's wife had ruined an otherwise cordial meeting.

Definitions will vary.

5. The Confederate position behind the stone wall atop a steep hill made it *invulnerable* to General Burnsides's attack.

Definitions will vary.

6. His *irrational* fear of spiders may have had its beginnings in some childhood event.

Definitions will vary.

7. The minister believes there is no such a thing as an *irredeemable* sinner. He feels that everyone is basically good.

Definitions will vary.

8. Even though certain *irrefutable* evidence pointed to the defendant's guilt, the lawyer promised an energetic defense.

Definitions will vary.

9. Emily felt the employer's questions about her family were *irrelevant*. They had nothing to do with the job.

Definitions will vary.

10. The keys were *irretrievable* because they fell over the side of the boat.

Definitions will vary.

Name ______________________________

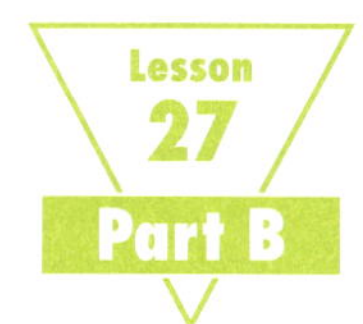

Applying Meaning

Each question below contains a vocabulary word from this lesson. Answer each question "yes" or "no" in the space provided.

1. Would a political party want an *inarticulate* candidate for president? 1. **no**
2. Is an *irrational* cook one that has run out of food? 2. **no**
3. Are coupons *irredeemable* if they were to be used before December 31, 1997? 3. **yes**
4. If you are accused of a crime, would you welcome *irrefutable* evidence of your guilt? 4. **no**

For each question you answered "no," write a sentence explaining your reason.

Answers will vary.

Decide which word in parentheses best completes the sentence. Then write the sentence, adding the missing word.

5. The spy learned the customs of the enemy so she would be _____ as she moved among them. (inconspicuous; irrelevant)

   inconspicuous

6. Hal's _____ remark about women in politics could cost him the election. (inclement; indiscreet)

   indiscreet

7. The cost of the yacht was _____. The wealthy sheik wanted the finest boat that money could buy. (invulnerable; irrelevant)

irrelevant

8. The hard shell of the armadillo makes it nearly _____, even to larger and stronger animals. (invulnerable; inconspicuous)

invulnerable

9. The _____ weather lasted for ten days. (inclement; indiscreet)

inclement

10. The condition of the sunken battleship made the bodies of the lost sailors _____. (invulnerable; irretrievable)

irretrievable

Our Living Language

in-, im-, il-

The prefix *in-* appears in more words than you may realize. You have seen how the spelling changes to *ir-* when the prefix is added to words or roots beginning with the letter *r*. The spelling changes to *im-* when *in-* is added to words or roots beginning with *b*, *m*, or *p* and to *il-* before words or roots beginning with *l*.

Build New Words: Add a form of the prefix *in-* to each of these words to create a new word that means the opposite of the original word.

in- + pure =	in- + legitimate =	in- + mobile =
in- + legal =	in- + mature =	in- + personal =
in- + potent =	in- + balance =	in- + prudent =

Assessment

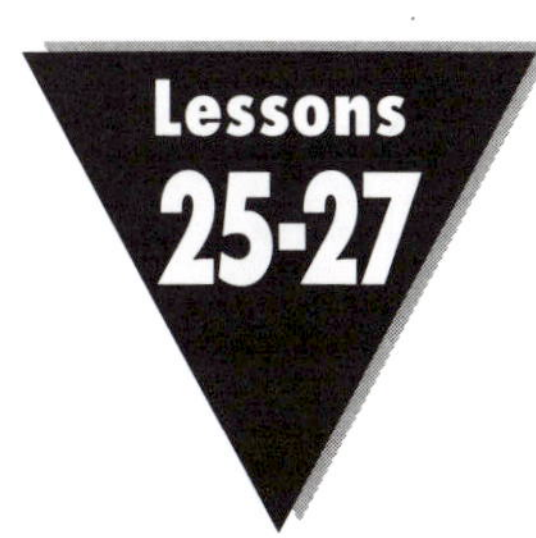

Name ______________________________

How well do you remember the words you studied in Lessons 25 through 27? Take the following test covering the words from the last three lessons.

Part 1 Antonyms

Each question below includes a word in capital letters, followed by four words or phrases. Choose the word or phrase that is most nearly opposite in meaning to the word in capital letters. Write the letter for your answer on the line provided.

Sample

S. SLOW	(A) lazy (C) fast	(B) simple (D) common	S. ___C___
1. INDISCREET	(A) careful (C) secretive	(B) slow (D) late	1. ___A___
2. DANK	(A) self-contained (C) dirty	(B) noisy (D) dry	2. ___D___
3. COMPOUND INTEREST	(A) low interest (C) simple interest	(B) variable interest (D) high interest	3. ___C___
4. INARTICULATE	(A) silent (C) well-spoken	(B) musical (D) creative	4. ___C___
5. INCLEMENT	(A) unexpected (C) hazy	(B) balmy (D) unpredictable	5. ___B___
6. STUPENDOUS	(A) bright (C) complex	(B) ordinary (D) colorful	6. ___B___
7. IRRELEVANT	(A) fitting (C) calm	(B) respectful (D) forgetful	7. ___A___
8. IRRETRIEVABLE	(A) shallow (C) new	(B) valuable (D) recoverable	8. ___D___
9. ASSETS	(A) hopes (C) debts	(B) skills (D) accounts	9. ___C___
10. INCONSPICUOUS	(A) easy to use (C) noticeable	(B) left behind (D) hidden from view	10. ___C___

11. IRRATIONAL	(A) excited (C) mature	(B) complicated (D) logical	11. D
12. ENCUMBRANCE	(A) hurdle (C) goal	(B) assistance (D) tool	12. B
13. INVULNERABLE	(A) defenseless (C) ready	(B) hospitable (D) without merit	13. A
14. IRREFUTABLE	(A) complete (C) questionable	(B) expected (D) usual	14. C
15. DEBIT	(A) deduction (C) balance	(B) credit (D) fee	15. B

Part 2 Matching Words and Meanings

Match the definition in Column B with the word in Column A. Write the letter of the correct definition on the line provided.

Column A	Column B	
16. camouflage	a. lush, abundant	16. b
17. foreclose	b. disguise	17. g
18. lien	c. failure to pay a debt	18. d
19. forage	d. property held to pay a loan	19. e
20. luxuriant	e. hunt	20. a
21. appraise	f. assess the value of	21. f
22. biome	g. take to satisfy a debt	22. i
23. liability	h. spotted	23. j
24. default	i. natural community	24. c
25. dappled	j. obligation	25. h

Lesson 28 Part A

Name ______________________________

Mark Twain's First Appearance

Besides being an **eminent** author, Mark Twain was also a talented speaker, who told stories to audiences with the same **shrewd** humor he showed in his fiction. On one occasion, Twain related a personal **anecdote** about stage fright. It seems he was attending his daughter's first singing performance, when the audience **cajoled** him into speaking. With no prepared speech in mind, Twain gave an **impromptu** talk about the steps he took to **ensure** success during his own first appearance on stage. Here is a portion of that talk:

> I had got a number of friends of mine, stalwart men, to sprinkle themselves through the audience armed with big clubs. Every time I said anything they could possibly guess I intended to be funny, they were to pound those clubs on the floor. Then there was a kind lady in a box up there, also a good friend of mine, the wife of the governor. She was to watch me **intently**, and whenever I glanced toward her she was going to deliver a gubernatorial laugh that would lead the whole audience into applause.
>
> At last I began. I had the **manuscript** tucked under a United States flag in front of me where I could get at it in case of need. But I managed to get started without it. I walked up and down—I was young in those days and needed the exercise—and talked and talked.
>
> Right in the middle of the speech I had placed a gem. I had put in a moving, pathetic part which was to get at the hearts and souls of my hearers. When I delivered it, they did just what I hoped and expected. They sat silent and **awed**. I had touched them. Then I happened to look up at the box where the governor's wife was—you know what happened.
>
> Well, after the first **agonizing** five minutes, my stage fright left me, never to return. . . . But I shall never forget my feelings before the agony left me, and I got up here to thank you for helping my daughter, by your kindness, to live through her first appearance. And I want to thank you for your appreciation of her singing, which is, by the way, hereditary.

Words

agonize
anecdote
awe
cajole
eminent
ensure
impromptu
intently
manuscript
shrewd

Unlocking Meaning

Each word in this lesson's word list appears in dark type in the selection you just read. Think about how the vocabulary word is used in the selection, then write the letter for the best answer to each question.

1. Which word could best replace *eminent* in line 1? — 1. C
   (A) humorous (B) old
   (C) famous (D) unknown

2. Which word could best replace *shrewd* in line 2? — 2. B
   (A) rapid (B) quick-witted
   (C) shy (D) quick-tempered

3. An *anecdote* (line 4) is best described as _____. — 3. A
   (A) an account of an event (B) a prepared speech
   (C) joke (D) commercial

4. To *cajole* (line 5) is to _____. — 4. A
   (A) urge gently (B) demand
   (C) applaud (D) ridicule

5. An *impromptu* (line 7) speech is one that is _____. — 5. C
   (A) filled with slanderous language (B) meant for a presidential candidate
   (C) not prepared in advance (D) prepared in advance

6. In line 7 *ensure* means _____. — 6. C
   (A) boast (B) deny
   (C) make certain (D) make worse

7. When a person looks *intently* (line 15), he or she looks _____. — 7. D
   (A) casually (B) questioningly
   (C) with concern (D) with close attention

8. A *manuscript* (line 18) is a _____. — 8. A
   (A) handwritten document or book (B) envelope
   (C) machine (D) container of money

9. Another word for *awed* (line 26) is _____. — 9. D
   (A) dreaded (B) ashamed
   (C) chilled (D) astounded

10. *Agonizing* (line 29) is best described as _____. — 10. C
   (A) binding (B) moving
   (C) painful (D) noticeable

Name ______________________________

Lesson 28 Part B

Applying Meaning

Follow the directions below to write a sentence using a vocabulary word.

1. Use the word *eminent* to describe someone.
   Sample Answer: The eminent poet, Maya Angelou, inspired me to write poetry.

2. Use *awed* in a sentence about something you saw in a theater.
   Sample Answer: I was awed by the magician's ability to make a live rabbit disappear.

3. Describe a speech you heard. Use the word *anecdote* in your sentence.
   Sample Answer: The graduation speaker began with an anecdote about something that happened at his graduation ten years ago.

4. Use *impromptu* in a sentence about something a friend did.
   Sample Answer: Marge did not expect the teacher to ask her such a question, but her impromptu answer was very good.

5. Describe something you did. Use *intently* in your sentence.
   Sample Answer: I did not want to lose sight of the child, so I watched her intently as she crossed the crowded room.

6. Use any form of the word *agonize* in a sentence about a problem you or someone you know encountered.
   Sample Answer: Standing in front of the class unprepared for the oral test was an agonizing experience.

Each question below contains a vocabulary word from this lesson. Answer each question "yes" or "no" in the space provided.

7. If you tear up some newspapers, do you leave it in *shrewds*? 7. **no**

8. Could a music group be *cajoled* by an audience into playing certain songs? 8. **yes**

9. Can you *ensure* the weather will be sunny next week? 9. **no**

10. Would you use an old *manuscript* to wash your car? 10. **no**

For each question you answered "no," write a sentence explaining your reason.

Answers will vary.

Mastering Meaning

Describe a personal experience about a time when you had to perform before a group. Tell how you felt and what preparations you made to make the performance successful. Use some of the words you studied in this lesson.

Name ____________________

Lesson 29 Part A

Unlocking Meaning

Words

capillary
esophagus
larynx
lesion
ligament
marrow
metabolism
orthopedic
pulmonary
sinew

The human body is filled with thousands of mechanisms and mysteries. There are words to describe each of these. Because the Greeks were the first to study anatomy systematically, many of the words for parts of the body come from their language. In this lesson, you will learn ten terms related to human anatomy.

Read the sentences or short passages below. Write the letter for the correct definition of the italicized vocabulary word.

1. Jonas pricked the tip of his finger on a thumbtack. When the wound bled a little, he knew that he had punctured a *capillary*.
   (A) knuckle (B) tiny blood vessel
   (C) major blood vessel (D) wrist bone

2. The emergency crew was trained in the proper way to dislodge food caught in someone's *esophagus*.
   (A) facial muscles (B) mouth
   (C) tube connecting throat and stomach (D) tube connecting intestines and stomach

3. Because Kim had a minor infection of the *larynx*, her voice sounded husky.
   (A) lining of the stomach (B) part of the small intestine
   (C) chamber of the heart (D) part of the windpipe

4. When he fell off his bicycle, Ken suffered a serious *lesion* on his leg. At the hospital, a doctor cleaned and bandaged the wound.
   (A) lung disease (B) injury or abnormal change to tissues or organs
   (C) heart attack (D) tumor or other growth

5. During the soccer game, Jan extended her leg too far and strained a *ligament*. A tight bandage was needed to avoid further injury.
   (A) tough tissue that connects bones (B) soft tissue that lines the heart
   (C) one of several bones in the ankle (D) one of two major bones in the lower leg

1. B
2. C
3. D
4. B
5. A

6. The magnetic resonance imaging allowed the doctor to look beyond the bone and into the *marrow*. 6. C

(A) muscles and nerves
(B) tough tissue that connects bones
(C) soft tissue that fills the cavities of most bones
(D) soft tissue that connects blood vessels

7. As his *metabolism* slowly increased, Julian began to lose weight. The doctor advised him that such changes were normal at his age. 7. D

(A) thoughts and feelings
(B) social behavior
(C) electrical currents that stimulate the heart
(D) the body's process of turning food into energy

8. Kwan's fracture was more complicated than it first appeared. His family doctor referred him to an *orthopedic* surgeon. 8. C

(A) related to muscles
(B) related to the eyes
(C) related to bones
(D) related to feet

9. Suddenly, Pierre's father had great difficulty breathing. At the hospital, he was diagnosed as having a *pulmonary* problem. 9. B

(A) related to the heart
(B) related to the lungs
(C) related to the ears
(D) related to the pancreas

10. The runner had trained for months and it showed. As she leaned into the starting block, the *sinews* in her legs pulled her muscles so tightly that it reminded me of a rubber band stretched to the breaking point. 10. C

(A) blood vessels
(B) glands that produce perspiration
(C) tough tissues that connect muscles to bones
(D) chemicals that aid in digestion

Name ______________________________

Lesson 29 Part B

Applying Meaning

Rewrite each sentence. Replace the underlined word or words with a vocabulary word or a form of a vocabulary word.

1. When Anna fell, she skinned her knee and broke a few small blood vessels.

   capillaries

2. The first thing the emergency room doctor did was to press on my tissue between bone and muscle.

   sinew

3. The doctor used a small light inside a magnifying glass to examine the tube leading from my mouth to my stomach.

   esophagus

4. Often one of the first signs of an allergy is the appearance of abnormal changes on the skin.

   lesions

5. The air pollution was so severe that people with lung conditions were advised to stay indoors.

   pulmonary

Each question below contains a vocabulary word from this lesson. Answer each question "yes" or "no" in the space provided.

6. Would you be wise to see an *orthopedic* doctor if you had a dislocated shoulder? 6. yes

7. If you injure your *larynx*, will eyeglasses help you? 7. no

8. If your *metabolism* slows, are you likely to gain weight? 8. yes

9. Could a doctor examine your *marrow* with a magnifying glass? 9. no

10. Could vigorous exercise strain a *ligament*? 10. yes

For each question you answered "no," write a sentence explaining your reason.

Answers will vary.

Our Living Language

The shapes and functions of the human body have been used as figures of speech to clarify or explain things that occur around us. The edge of a road is called the *shoulder* because its shape and position are similar to that of a human shoulder.

Explain the Figures of Speech: To what do each of the following figures of speech refer? Why is the human anatomy a good comparison?

eye of the storm nose of the spacecraft a neck of land

hairline fracture lip of a pitcher

The Prefix ad-

Name ______________________________

The Latin prefix *ad-* meaning "to" or "toward" appears in many forms. It is easy to see in a word like *admonish*, where *ad-* is added to the Latin root *monere*, meaning "to warn." However, when *ad-* appears before a word or root beginning with *c*, its spelling changes to *ac-*, and when it is used with a word beginning with *f*, its spelling changes to *af-*. Even so, the "to" or "toward" meaning is still part of the word in which it is found.

Prefix	Meaning	Word
ad-	to, toward	admonish
ad-	to, toward	accentuate
ad-	to, toward	affix

Words

accentuate
acquiescence
acquisition
admonish
advent
adversary
affiliate
affirm
affix
affliction

Unlocking Meaning

A vocabulary word appears in italics in each passage below. The meaning of the root is given in parentheses. Look at the prefix and think about how the word is used in the passage. Then write a definition for the vocabulary word. Compare your definition with the dictionary definition at the back of the book.

1. The cab drivers hoped their strike would *accentuate* the need to raise fares. (Root word: *cantus*, "song")

   Definitions will vary.

2. The general signaled his *acquiescence* to the terms of surrender with a nod of his head. (Root word: *quiescere*, "to rest")

   Definitions will vary.

3. The Rembrandt painting was the museum's most important *acquisition*. (Root word: *quaerere*, "to seek")

   Definitions will vary.

4. The counselor felt it necessary to *admonish* all campers to avoid eating any wild berries. (Root word: *monere*, "to warn")

Definitions will vary.

5. Before the *advent* of the computer, it took hours to prepare bank statements. (Root word: *vinire*, "to come")

Definitions will vary.

6. Because of his traitorous acts, Benedict Arnold became Washington's *adversary*. (Root word: *vertere*. "to turn")

Definitions will vary.

7. The minor league team hopes to *affiliate* with the New York Mets, a major league team. (Root word: *filius*, "son")

Definitions will vary.

8. I need a letter from the librarian to *affirm* that the fine has been paid. (Root word: *firmare*, "to strengthen")

Definitions will vary.

9. We were told to *affix* the beach sticker to the left corner of the windshield. (Root word: *figere*, "to fasten")

Definitions will vary.

10. The blind pianist was determined that his *affliction* would not halt his career. (Root word: *fligere*, "to strike")

Definitions will vary.

Name ______________________________

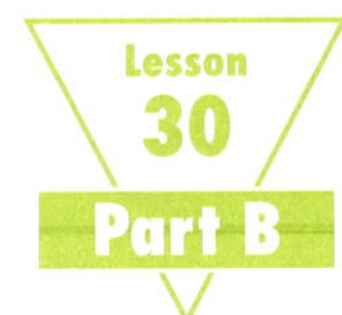

Applying Meaning

Follow the directions below to write a sentence using a vocabulary word.

1. Describe an important turning point in history. Use the word *advent*.

   Sample Answer: The advent of air travel brought the era of the luxury ocean liner to an end.

2. Tell about something a parent or a teacher told you to do. Use any form of the word *admonish*.

   Sample Answer: Ms. Chin admonished us to study the last two chapters before the test next Wednesday.

3. Use any form of the word *affiliate* in a sentence about a club.

   Sample Answer: Even though the club met in the school library, it was in no way affiliated with the school.

4. Use any form of the word *accentuate* in a sentence about an accident or a planned event.

   Sample Answer: The automobile accident served to accentuate the need for reducing the speed limit on that road and posting a warning sign.

Decide which word in parentheses best completes the sentence. Then write the sentence, adding the missing word.

5. The senator's opponent proved to be a fierce _____ in the first debate. (adversary; affliction)

   adversary

6. After the luggage had been searched, a guard _____ tape to the lock and placed it on the plane. (affirmed; affixed)

   affixed

7. Dad refused to take the job in Texas without the _____ of our entire family. (acquiescence; acquisition)

acquiescence

8. Before the Salk vaccine, polio was a dreaded _____ for every family with children. (acquiescence; affliction)

affliction

9. Don argued that the _____ of more weapons would not make the world safer. (acquiescence: acquisition)

acquisition

10. The courts have repeatedly _____ the right of every defendant to an attorney. (affirmed; affixed)

affirmed

Test Taking Strategies

Tests of vocabulary sometimes ask you to choose a synonym for the word being tested. A synonym is a word with the same or nearly the same meaning. For example, *request* is a synonym for *ask*. When taking this type of test, you should study each choice and eliminate any answers that are clearly wrong.

Practice: Choose the synonym for the italicized word in each sentence. Write your choice on the answer line.

1. The senator's *scurrilous* attack on his opponent at the end of the debate came as a shock to everyone. 1. C
   (A) effective (B) scholarly (C) vulgar (D) unreasonable

2. A general *apathy* exists about recycling in many communities around this state. 2. B
   (A) hostility (B) indifference (C) sincerity (D) confusion

Assessment

Lessons 28-30

Name ______________________________

How well do you remember the words you studied in Lessons 28 through 30? Take the following test covering the words from the last three lessons.

Part 1 Choose the Correct Meaning

Each question below includes a word in capital letters, followed by four words or phrases. Choose the word or phrase that is closest in meaning to the word in capital letters. Write the letter for your answer on the line provided.

Sample

S. FINISH	(A) enjoy (C) destroy	(B) complete (D) enlarge	S. B

1. ENSURE	(A) guarantee (C) reply	(B) question (D) approve	1. A
2. AFFILIATE	(A) make sick (C) associate with	(B) break from (D) surpass	2. C
3. LESION	(A) severe pain (C) wound	(B) obstacle (D) bandage	3. C
4. ADVERSARY	(A) supporter (C) teammate	(B) teacher (D) enemy	4. D
5. IMPROMPTU	(A) heated (C) unrehearsed	(B) clever (D) brilliant	5. C
6. CAPILLARY	(A) brain cell (C) organ	(B) nerve (D) blood vessel	6. D
7. AFFIRM	(A) prove (C) order	(B) ask (D) debate	7. A
8. EMINENT	(A) first (C) lucky	(B) well known (D) wealthy	8. B
9. ADMONISH	(A) publicize (C) warn	(B) congratulate (D) forgive	9. C
10. INTENTLY	(A) usually (C) secretly	(B) without interest (D) purposefully	10. D

11. AFFLICTION (A) habit (B) hardship (C) good fortune (D) requirement 11. B

12. CAJOLE (A) release (B) demand (C) coax (D) bribe 12. C

13. ACQUIESCENCE (A) consent (B) response (C) dissent (D) recognition 13. A

14. SHREWD (A) forceful (B) ineffective (C) experienced (D) clever 14. D

15. AFFIX (A) repair (B) attach (C) remove (D) glue 15. B

Part 2 Matching Words and Meanings

Match the definition in Column B with the word in Column A. Write the letter of the correct definition on the line provided.

Column A	Column B	
16. metabolism	a. coming, arrival	16. h
17. agonize	b. related to bones and joints	17. e
18. pulmonary	c. soft tissue inside bones	18. d
19. orthopedic	d. related to the lungs	19. b
20. advent	e. suffer, struggle	20. a
21. anecdote	f. a tale	21. f
22. larynx	g. tissue that connects bones	22. j
23. acquisition	h. the process of turning food into energy	23. i
24. ligament	i. something gained or obtained	24. g
25. marrow	j. part of the windpipe	25. c

Name ______________________________

Lesson 31 Part A

The Statue of Liberty's Roots

On an island in New York Harbor stands a **prominent** symbol of the United States: the Statue of Liberty. This magnificent monument did not **originate** in the United States, however. The Statue of Liberty was a gift from the people of France to mark the one-hundred-year anniversary of American independence. In 1869, sculptor Frédéric Auguste Bartholdi began to **execute** his concept for the monument.

Bartholdi chose the look of **classic** Greek and Roman figures. He envisioned Liberty as a strong and proud figure, one who **personified** not only the majestic Greek goddesses of the past, but also the working men and women of the present. Liberty's mountainous **proportions** made it necessary for Bartholdi to first build a small plaster model of the huge statue that eventually would rise over 111 feet. The index finger alone had a span of 7 feet 11 inches.

Finally, in 1884, the work was finished, and Liberty was packed into 214 crates and sent to New York City. Only one problem stood in the way. While the French had raised $400,000 to build the statue, New York had not secured the funds to build its foundation. It was not until a New York newspaper **implored** people for donations that money became available. Boys and girls sent spare change. Small donations by the thousands began to pour in. Finally, there was enough money to build the foundation, and on October 28, 1886, Americans celebrated the unveiling of the Statue of Liberty.

In the years that followed, the Statue of Liberty welcomed thousands of immigrants. In the 1980s, when the statue was found to have serious structural problems, people again rallied to restore the weak structure and **refurbish** the tarnished monument. During a full-scale **restoration**, the iron skeleton was reinforced with 300,000 additional rivets and painted a bright **vermilion** red to preserve the finish. Then Liberty was once again covered with copper. Today, the Statue of Liberty continues to stand as a symbol of freedom for those arriving on the United States' shores.

Words

classic
execute
implore
originate
personified
prominent
proportion
refurbish
restoration
vermilion

Unlocking Meaning

Each word in this lesson's word list appears in dark type in the selection you just read. Think about how the vocabulary word is used in the selection, then write the letter for the best answer to each question.

1. Another word for *prominent* in line 1 is _____.   1. ___B___
   (A) victorious   (B) noticeable
   (C) wholesome   (D) secluded

2. Which word or words could best replace *originate* in line 3?   2. ___D___
   (A) become rejected   (B) lose its way
   (C) expand   (D) come into being

3. If you *execute* (line 6) a plan, you _____.   3. ___A___
   (A) carry it out   (B) assign it to others
   (C) destroy it completely   (D) revise it

4. A *classic* (line 7) figure is _____.   4. ___C___
   (A) expensive   (B) difficult to understand
   (C) a model example   (D) simple

5. If something is *personified* (line 9), it is _____.   5. ___B___
   (A) falsely taken   (B) used as an example
   (C) never realized   (D) hopeless

6. *Proportions* (line 11) refers to _____.   6. ___C___
   (A) color and length   (B) artistic impression
   (C) dimension and size   (D) weight and texture

7. Another word for *implored* (line 19) is _____.   7. ___A___
   (A) begged   (B) taxed
   (C) threatened   (D) gestured

8. If you *refurbish* (line 28)something, you _____.   8. ___C___
   (A) build an addition to it   (B) take its measurements
   (C) make it fresh and bright again   (D) replace it

9. *Restoration* in line 29 is _____.   9. ___D___
   (A) the act of paying for a project   (B) a type of dedication
   (C) the act of creating a duplicate   (D) the act of bringing back to original condition

10. When something is given a coat of *vermilion* paint (line 30), it becomes _____.   10. ___A___
   (A) bright red   (B) black
   (C) warm   (D) rusted

Name ______________________________

Lesson 31 Part B

Applying Meaning

Read each sentence below. Write "correct" on the answer line if the vocabulary word has been used correctly or "incorrect" if it has been used incorrectly.

1. The large fountain was the most *prominent* feature of the garden. 1. correct
2. Since it was Josh's birthday, the biggest *proportion* of the cake was given to him. 2. incorrect
3. For her second dive, Lil planned to *execute* a twisting two-and-a-half somersault. 3. correct
4. The candidate *implored* his supporters to donate their time and money. 4. correct
5. Jazz is said to have *originated* in New Orleans, but other cities also claim it. 5. correct
6. We were told that any scraps of food left lying around would attract *vermilion*. 6. incorrect

For each word used incorrectly, write a sentence using the word properly.

Answers will vary.

Follow the directions below to write a sentence using a vocabulary word.

7. Describe a car or a piece of music. Use the word *classic* in your sentence.

Sample Answer: The 1957 Chevrolet is a classic example of the chrome and tail fins style popular at the time.

8. Write a sentence about an old building. Use any form of the word *restoration*.

Sample Answer: Unless work is begun immediately on our crumbling town hall, restoration will be impossible.

9. Use *personified* in a sentence about a quality such as honesty or self-sacrifice.

Sample Answer: George Washington personified the courage and commitment to liberty of patriotic Americans in 1776.

10. Use *refurbish* in a sentence about a project you or someone you know undertook recently.

Sample Answer: Mother decided to refurbish the furniture in our living room with some new slipcovers.

Mastering Meaning

Twenty-five hundred people stood on Bedloe's Island in New York City on October 28, 1886, as the Statue of Liberty was unveiled. President Cleveland was the last of several speakers to address the audience. Write a short speech you would have liked to deliver on this occasion. Use some of the words you studied in this lesson.

Lesson 32 Part A

Name ______________________________

Unlocking Meaning

Words
- blighted
- comely
- decrepit
- drab
- lackluster
- mundane
- pallid
- radiant
- resplendent
- slovenly

In describing the appearance or condition of something, words like *good*, *bad*, *nice*, and *pretty* do not tell you very much. In this lesson, you will learn ten adjectives that give a more exact description of the physical appearance or condition of people, places, or objects

Read the sentences or short passages below. Write the letter for the correct definition of the italicized vocabulary word.

1. Because of the heat spell and a lack of rain, the lettuce in the garden had a *blighted* appearance.
   (A) ripe (B) soggy or wet
   (C) withered and ruined (D) light green

1. ___C___

2. Everyone at the party complimented Janet on her new, *comely* hairstyle.
   (A) unattractive (B) attractive
   (C) stringy (D) difficult to manage

2. ___B___

3. Ms. Talarvan's friends were concerned when she bought the old, *decrepit* house. A year later, they were impressed when they saw the improvements she had made.
   (A) wooden (B) stone or brick
   (C) inexpensive (D) broken down or worn-out

3. ___D___

4. Sherry and her father repainted the walls of her bedroom. Once *drab* and dark, the room now seemed bright and cheerful.
   (A) dull and faded (B) hidden
   (C) small and insignificant (D) untidy

4. ___A___

5. Herb's *lackluster* speech and monotonous tone of voice put most of the audience to sleep.
   (A) interesting and fun (B) easy
   (C) boring or unimaginative (D) too difficult

5. ___C___

6. We had hoped the business course would address the obligations of employer and employee. Instead, it was the same *mundane* study of inventory, finance, and marketing.
   (A) longer (B) noisy
   (C) restful (D) ordinary or common

6. ___D___

7. Although he was not injured, Pete had a *pallid* appearance after the accident. The doctor decided to keep him under observation until the blood returned to his face.
   (A) pale (B) untidy
   (C) bruised (D) scratched

7. A

8. I felt strange and lonely in the new school until Beth introduced herself and flashed her *radiant,* friendly smile.
   (A) shy (B) bright and shiny
   (C) sly or clever (D) humorous

8. B

9. The parade float was a *resplendent* display of yellow and red flowers, colorful streamers, and costumed performers.
   (A) dazzling; beautiful (B) ordinary; common
   (C) interesting (D) creative

9. A

10. When I crossed out several lines in my composition, I tore the corner of the paper. The teacher refused to accept such *slovenly* work, so I had to make a clean copy.
   (A) unfashionable (B) tired and disappointed
   (C) sloppy or careless (D) filled with light

10. C

Name ______________________________

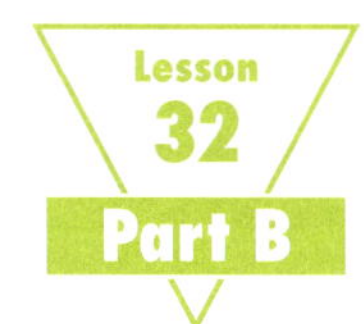

Applying Meaning

Each question below contains a vocabulary word from this lesson. Answer each question "yes" or "no" in the space provided.

1. Would a person with a *slovenly* appearance make a good impression in a job interview? — 1. no
2. Would a neighborhood organization work to achieve a *blighted* community? — 2. no
3. Are *drab* colors appropriate for funerals and other sad occasions? — 3. yes
4. Would a day in the sun leave you with a *pallid* appearance? — 4. no
5. Would yellow walls and numerous windows make a room *radiant* on a sunny day? — 5. yes

For each question you answered "no," write a sentence explaining your reason.

Answers will vary.

Decide which word in parentheses best completes the sentence. Then write the sentence, adding the missing word.

6. The store's Christmas tree was _____ with twinkling lights and silver ornaments. (lackluster; resplendent)

   resplendent

7. Fred planned the banquet, but left the _____ task of addressing the envelopes to his assistant. (comely; mundane)

   mundane

8. After paying $500 to rent the cottage, we were unhappy with its _____ appearance when we saw it. (decrepit; pallid)

decrepit

9. The little girl's _____ smile delighted her grandfather. (comely; drab)

comely

10. In spite of the _____ appearance of the table, Freida knew it was a valuable antique. (lackluster; resplendent)

lackluster

Spelling and Meaning

the boy's hat   the workers' uniforms   the mice's food

The possessive form of a noun shows ownership. A singular noun like *boy* requires an apostrophe (') and *s*: the boy's hat. Plural nouns ending in *s* require only an apostrophe: the workers' uniforms. Other plural nouns, like *mice* and *women* require both an apostrophe and *s*: the mice's food, the women's locker.

Change each of these nouns into a possessive noun. Then write a sentence using each possessive noun correctly.

Jess   children   Tony   girls   bus   geese   wolves

Jess's, children's, Tony's, girls', bus's, geese's, wolves'

Noun Suffixes

Name ______________________________

The *-ion, -tion* and *-sion* suffixes are used to change verbs into nouns. Sometimes the suffix is simply added to the verb, but often the spelling is also changed in other ways. Study the examples below.

Verb	Suffix	Noun
ignite	-ion	ignition
emit	-sion	emission
reform	-tion	reformation

Words

designation
emission
ignition
induction
inversion
liberation
provision
recession
recuperation
reformation

Unlocking Meaning

A vocabulary word appears in italics in each sentence or short passage below. Think about the verb and noun forms of the word. Then write a definition for the vocabulary word. Compare your definition with the definition in the dictionary at the back of the book.

1. The coach will designate the starting quarterback today. His *designation* will be watched anxiously by all the players.

   Definitions will vary.

2. The factory emits pollution into the air. The governor insisted that these *emissions* stop.

   Definitions will vary.

3. The astronauts must ignite their rockets. This *ignition* positions the craft for a safe return to earth.

   Definitions will vary.

4. The club will induct its new members at the next meeting. The *induction* ceremony will be held in the hotel ballroom.

   Definitions will vary.

5. I inverted the vase to see if it had been signed by its maker. The *inversion* caused a piece of paper to fall out.

Definitions will vary.

6. The victorious army liberated the prisoners. The *liberation* was a cause for great celebration.

Definitions will vary.

7. The outfitters will provide maps and flashlights for our hike in the cave. These *provisions* are essential for safety.

Definitions will vary.

8. It took weeks for the floodwaters to recede. Even after the waters' *recession*, it took months to clean up the mud.

Definitions will vary.

9. The doctor felt Floyd should recuperate in the hospital. Without this *recuperation*, the illness might return.

Definitions will vary.

10. The prisoner promised he would reform his behavior. The judge doubted that such a *reformation* was possible.

Definitions will vary.

Name ______________________________

Lesson 33 Part B

Applying Meaning

Follow the directions below to write a sentence using a vocabulary word.

1. Tell about a hiking trip you might take. Use any form of the word *provision*.

   Sample Answer: I packed food, water, extra clothes, and other provisions for the two-day hike.

2. Describe an important change an individual or a group made. Use the word *reformation*.

   Sample Answer: A complete reformation of the school's curriculum would require several years.

3. Write a sentence about a historic event. Use the word *liberation*.

   Sample Answer: The liberation of Paris in World War II marked an important turning point in the war.

4. Describe an important decision. Use the word *designation*.

   Sample Answer: The designation of the valedictorian was the responsibility of the graduation committee.

5. Use the word *ignition* in a sentence about an accident.

   Sample Answer: The accidental ignition of forest fires was a clear possibility because of all the dry grass and dead trees.

Decide which word in parentheses best completes the sentence. Then write the sentence, adding the missing word.

6. The injured player's _____ was slow and painful because of his earlier injuries. (recession; recuperation)

   recuperation

7. The trick mirror turned everything upside down. This _____ both confused and amused the guests. (inversion; recession)

inversion

8. The chemical plant's high _____ levels of sulfur fumes caused its neighbors to complain. (emission; induction)

emission

9. The mayor's _____ into office was applauded by his supporters, who had worked diligently to get him elected. (induction; inversion)

induction

10. The _____ in economic activity soon resulted in the loss of jobs. (recession; provision)

recession

Cultural Literacy Note

One of the oddities of English is the palindrome—a word, phrase, or sentence that reads the same backward or forward. The simplest palindromes are words in a consonant-vowel-consonant pattern like *dad* or *pop,* but there are many longer words that work as well, such as *radar* and *level.* Some sentence palindromes can be several words long, such as "A man, a plan, a canal, Panama!"

Cooperative Learning: With a partner, brainstorm a list of word and sentence palindromes.

Word Palindromes: Mom, peep, did, Anna, noon, deed, eve, toot, madam, level, dud, did, Bob, Hannah

Sentence Palindromes: Step on no pets. Never odd or even. Madam I'm Adam. Able was I ere I saw Elba.

Assessment

Name ________________________________

How well do you remember the words you studied in Lessons 31 through 33? Take the following test covering the words from the last three lessons.

Part 1 Choose the Correct Meaning

Each question below includes a word in capital letters, followed by four words or phrases. Choose the word or phrase that is closest in meaning to the word in capital letters. Write the letter for your answer on the line provided.

Sample

S. FINISH	(A) enjoy (C) destroy	(B) complete (D) enlarge	S. ___B___

1. PROVISIONS	(A) food (C) tools	(B) camping gear (D) supplies	1. ___D___
2. ORIGINATE	(A) verify the origin (C) cultivate	(B) grow (D) begin	2. ___D___
3. PALLID	(A) unpleasant (C) yellow	(B) colorless (D) ruddy	3. ___B___
4. DESIGNATION	(A) intention (C) selection	(B) substitute (D) subordinate	4. ___C___
5. IMPLORE	(A) beg (C) order	(B) investigate (D) forbid	5. ___A___
6. RECUPERATION	(A) recovery (C) advise	(B) attention (D) medication	6. ___A___
7. SLOVENLY	(A) hasty (C) poor	(B) sloppy (D) illegible	7. ___B___
8. PROMINENT	(A) noticeable (C) unchanging	(B) promising (D) solid	8. ___A___
9. RESPLENDENT	(A) expensive (C) dazzling	(B) complicated (D) detailed	9. ___C___
10. PERSONIFIED	(A) maligned (C) celebrated	(B) embodied (D) copied	10. ___B___

11. INDUCTION	(A) lessening (C) preface	(B) conclusion (D) initiation	11. D
12. DECREPIT	(A) run-down (C) dirty	(B) old (D) colonial	12. A
13. MUNDANE	(A) ordinary (C) difficult	(B) stupid (D) old-fashioned	13. A
14. REFORMATION	(A) change (C) religious belief	(B) improvement (D) promise	14. B
15. EXECUTE	(A) modify (C) carry out	(B) supervise (D) review	15. C

Part 2 Matching Words and Meanings

Match the definition in Column B with the word in Column A. Write the letter of the correct definition on the line provided.

Column A	Column B	
16. proportion	a. brilliant	16. b
17. emission	b. size and dimension	17. f
18. recession	c. unimaginative	18. h
19. blighted	d. pretty	19. e
20. vermilion	e. ruined	20. i
21. radiant	f. output	21. a
22. liberation	g. start	22. j
23. ignition	h. withdrawing	23. g
24. lackluster	i. bright red	24. c
25. comely	j. freeing	25. d

Lesson 34 Part A

Name ______________________________

Fossils Trapped in Tar

Not far from the **congestion** of the Los Angeles freeways, saber-tooth cats, mastodons, and giant ground sloths once roamed the land. During the Ice Age, which **encompassed** a period of time some 10,000 to 40,000 years ago, over 400 different kinds of animals lived on the grassy plain that is now Los Angeles.

Then, as now, large deposits of oil lay beneath the earth in California. When these deposits seeped through the cracks in the surface, the oil evaporated, leaving pools of sticky tar that would catch leaves and other forms of ground cover. During colder weather, these pools **congealed**, trapping the leaves in the hardened tar. Then in the summer heat the tar pools beneath the leaves softened into an ooze similar to molasses. Unsuspecting animals walked into the ooze and sank. Once these beasts became **immersed** in the tar, it was nearly impossible for them to escape. These oily tar pits caused the **demise** of thousands of animals. The animals' remains did not vanish, however. The same tar that caused their deaths also **pervaded** their bones and preserved them as fossils.

Until 1906, the tar from Rancho La Brea was **excavated** for use as a glue. It was then that Dr. John C. Merriam, at the University of California, realized the importance of the fossils that were being dug up along with the tar. After that, scientists began the **fervid** excavation of these revealing fossils. Evidence of mammoths, mastodons, saber-tooth cats, lions, wolves, sloths, camels, horses, and other animals was uncovered.

In 1977 the fossils were placed in a museum and research center. There paleontologists study bone fossils, which tell of events that took place thousands of years ago, and try to explain why the animals became extinct. One theory is that they were overhunted by early humans. While it is difficult to **confute** this theory, some scientists question why the bones of only one human have been found in the Rancho La Brea tar pits. As scientists continue to **probe** for answers, their discoveries about the past may help us glimpse the future.

Words

confute
congeal
congestion
demise
encompass
excavate
fervid
immerse
pervade
probe

Unlocking Meaning

Each word in this lesson's word list appears in dark type in the selection you just read. Think about how the vocabulary word is used in the selection, then write the letter for the best answer to each question.

1. *Congestion* (line 1) means _____. 1. A
   (A) overcrowding (B) disharmony
   (C) danger (D) scenic views

2. If you *encompass* something, (line 3) you _____. 2. C
   (A) explain it (B) ignore it
   (C) include it (D) change it

3. To *congeal* (line 10) is to _____. 3. A
   (A) thicken (B) pass over
   (C) reverse direction (D) guard

4. Which word or words could best replace *immersed* in line 14? 4. B
   (A) thirsty (B) completely covered
   (C) broken (D) displayed

5. Another word for *demise* in line 15 is _____. 5. D
   (A) sickness (B) burden
   (C) difficulty (D) death

6. *Pervaded* in line 17 means _____. 6. B
   (A) released (B) spread throughout
   (C) cured (D) destroyed

7. Which words could best replace *excavated* in line 19? 7. B
   (A) upset the natural balance (B) uncovered by digging
   (C) tore up the landscape (D) buried by digging

8. Another word for *fervid* (line 22) is _____. 8. B
   (A) casual (B) enthusiastic
   (C) humorous (D) unscientific

9. If you *confute* (line 30) a theory, you _____. 9. A
   (A) disprove it (B) prove it conclusively
   (C) explain it (D) ridicule it

10. Another word for *probe* (line 33) is _____. 10. D
   (A) pitch (B) mention
   (C) test (D) explore

Name ______________________________

Applying Meaning

Decide which word in parentheses best completes the sentence. Then write the sentence, adding the missing word.

1. The photographer _____ the film in a liquid developing fluid. (probed; immersed)

   immersed

2. The reckless driver caused the _____ of four innocent victims. (congestion: demise)

   demise

3. To complete the road, engineers had to _____ a tunnel through a mountain. (encompass: excavate)

   excavate

4. Overnight the melted ice cream on the kitchen floor began to _____ (confute; congeal)

   congeal

5. After the final count was announced, a stunned silence _____ the losing candidate's headquarters. (pervaded; probed)

   pervaded

Follow the directions below to write a sentence using a vocabulary word.

6. Describe an argument. Use any form of the word *confute*.

Sample Answer: Unless Sarah could confute Ben's many statistics on unemployment, she would certainly lose the debate.

7. Write a sentence about an investigation. Use the word *probe*.

Sample Answer: The fire department investigator assured the residents that he would probe the cause of the blaze.

8. Write a sentence about something you want. Use any form of the word *fervid*.

Sample Answer: It is my fervid desire to get the top grade on the next test in math class.

9. Use *congestion* in a sentence about your school.

Sample Answer: Between class periods, the halls are a mass of congestion.

10. Use any form of the word *encompass* in a sentence about a report.

Sample Answer: My report on drugs will encompass both legal drugs like alcohol and illegal drugs like heroin.

Mastering Meaning

Imagine that you are a paleontologist applying for a job at the museum that houses the Rancho La Brea fossils. Write a letter expressing why you think the museum's research is important and what contribution you could make to the work being done there. Use some of the words you studied in this lesson.

Name ______________________________

Lesson 35 Part A

Unlocking Meaning

There are probably hundreds of ways to say simple words like *yes* and *no*. Your tone of voice, gestures, or facial expressions flavor the words you say. In this lesson, you will learn ten words that flavor the many ways we speak and communicate our individual feelings to others.

Words

banter
beseech
bicker
blasphemy
coerce
lampoon
reiterate
scathing
scoff
scorn

Read the sentences or short passages below. Write the letter for the correct definition of the italicized vocabulary word.

1. On my favorite comedy show, the host often engages his guests in some entertaining, good-natured *banter* to get a few laughs.
   (A) conversation involving questions
   (B) conversation involving critical analysis
   (C) discussion of current events
   (D) playful conversation

2. When the citizens realized their town was surrounded by enemy troops, they decided to *beseech* friendly countries for assistance.
   (A) demand loudly
   (B) plead or request in a serious way
   (C) shyly suggest
   (D) ask in a casual or leisurely way

3. My two little brothers sometimes tire me out! They *bicker* about really silly things, such as whose turn it is to turn off their bedside lamp.
   (A) to talk quietly, watching one's words and tone of voice
   (B) to make jokes about; ridicule
   (C) to quarrel or squabble over unimportant matters
   (D) to suggest compromises

4. The vandals defaced and destroyed many of the monuments in the veterans' cemetery. Such *blasphemy* should not go unpunished.
   (A) show of respect
   (B) falsehood that is repeated many times
   (C) attempt to express one's self
   (D) act of disrespect toward something sacred

5. By threatening to move the team to another city, the owners were just trying to *coerce* the city into building a new stadium.
   (A) humor someone into agreeing with you
   (B) persuade though power or threats
   (C) prevent by law
   (D) suggest gently

1. D
2. B
3. 
4. D
5. B

6. The movie's script was a *lampoon* of all the so-called action movies. The audience roared at the unbelievable events and pointless explosions that unfolded in slow motion on the screen. 6. A

(A) type of humor based on exaggeration
(B) writing based on careful thought and analysis
(C) type of compliment
(D) writing that attempts to persuade people

7. Because several students were having difficulty deciding what to do, the teacher decided to *reiterate* the directions. 7. B

(A) change
(B) repeat
(C) shout or chant
(D) murmur

8. The committee members issued a *scathing* report blaming the supervisor for the accident that injured several workers. 8. C

(A) complimentary
(B) ridiculous
(C) severely critical
(D) complicated

9. The boaters were foolish to *scoff* at the Coast Guard's warning about the oncoming storm. 9. A

(A) dismiss or mock as unimportant
(B) believe completely
(C) persuade others to listen
(D) attack forcefully

10. His friends ridiculed Ed's decision to start his own business, so he was right to *scorn* their efforts to make up to him when he became successful. 10. D

(A) respect
(B) confuse and puzzle
(C) show sympathy or concern
(D) reject or refuse

Name ______________________________

Applying Meaning

Decide which word in parentheses best completes the sentence. Then write the sentence, adding the missing word.

1. After listening to the children _____ over who got the larger dessert, I decided to leave the table. (bicker; scoff)

   bicker

2. The police felt it was important to _____ the warning about the escaped prisoner. (beseech; reiterate)

   reiterate

3. The president made a _____ speech accusing the terrorists of attacking innocent people. (coercing; scathing)

   scathing

4. Even though Barbara was anxious to sell the car, she _____ at the amount we offered for it. (lampooned; scoffed)

   scoffed

5. By threatening to fire them, the director hoped to _____ the strikers into returning to their jobs. (banter; coerce)

   coerce

6. The tearful woman _____ the person who took her dog to return it. (beseeched; coerced)

   beseeched

7. Criticizing the local baseball team is almost considered a form of _____ in this sports-crazy town. (blasphemy; lampoon)

blasphemy

8. Some of the silly _____ between comics like Abbott and Costello is considered classic. (banter; scorn)

banter

9. The editor of the humor magazine included a _____ of a local politician in every issue. (blasphemy; lampoon)

lampoon

10. In the fairy tale, the evil king treated his subjects with _____, refusing even to meet with them. (scorn; lampoon)

scorn

Using the Dictionary

Homographs

Two or more words that are spelled the same way, but have different meanings and origins are called *homographs*. Each homograph has its own numbered entry in a dictionary. Even though the words look and sound the same, they are, in fact, different words.

bay[1] (bā) *n.* a body of water partly enclosed by land.

bay[2] (bā) *n.* a type of window.

bay[3] (bā) *n.* a reddish-brown horse.

bay[4] (bā) *n.* a long howl or bark.

Use a classroom dictionary to find the definitions for these homograohs: chord; maroon; converse; ear

Adjective Suffixes

Lesson 36 Part A

Name ____________________

Certain endings are used to change the way a word is used in a sentence. One such ending is the adjective suffix. An adjective suffix is used to change a word from a naming word, or noun, to a describing word, or adjective. Note how the suffixes below change the way the words are used in sentences.

Noun	Adjective Suffix	Adjective
geometry	-ic	geometric
influence	-ial	influential
larceny	-ous	larcenous
maniac	-al	maniacal

Words

geometric
influential
larcenous
lecherous
maniacal
medicinal
metallic
parasitic
strenuous
synonymous

Unlocking Meaning

A vocabulary word appears in italics in each sentence or short passage below. Choose the letter for the correct definition of the italicized word. Write the letter for your answer on the line provided.

1. Geometry is my favorite class. I love studying the various *geometric* shapes and the ways in which they are created.
   (A) related to the characteristics and measurements of lines and figures
   (B) having to do with rocks and minerals
   (C) invisible
   (D) formed in ancient times

2. The newspaper was very *influential* in the last election. Some even feel its influence changed the outcome of the vote.
   (A) well informed
   (B) having the ability to increase in size
   (C) not easily bent
   (D) having the power to change an event

3. The judge wondered if, after his third conviction, the thief's *larcenous* behavior could ever be changed.
   (A) characterized by rude behavior
   (B) involving theft
   (C) lacking truth
   (D) exceptional

4. The early settlers sometimes punished *lecherous* behavior by publicly humiliating the offenders.
   (A) talkative
   (B) lewd
   (C) reverent
   (D) revolutionary

1. A
2. D
3. B
4. B

5. The fullback charged into the line like a maniac, knocking down every player in his path. His *maniacal* behavior even frightened his coach. 5. A

(A) mad (B) clever
(C) heroic (D) pleasing

6. We rarely think of garlic as a medicine. However, some claim that garlic has a *medicinal* effect on high blood pressure and other illnesses. 6. C

(A) exotic or foreign in nature (B) spiritual
(C) having the ability to treat a disease (D) harmful

7. As the water passed through the metal pipes, it took on a rather bitter, *metallic* taste. 7. D

(A) having the characteristics of a disease (B) having a sweet flavor
(C) having to do with meteors (D) having the qualities of lead, copper, iron, and similar elements

8. Only a parasite would expect his parents to support him after he leaves school and gets a good job. I know my parents would never allow such *parasitic* behavior. 8. C

(A) generous (B) thoughtful about others
(C) tending to live off others (D) discourteous and selfish

9. It is important that I not strain the damaged muscles in my leg, so my doctor advised me to avoid all *strenuous* activity for a while. 9. A

(A) requiring great energy (B) disorganized
(C) carefully planned (D) unusual

10. The answer key to the test gave *stout* as a synonym for *fat*. Personally, I do not think they are at all *synonymous*. 10. B

(A) having the opposite meaning (B) having the same meaning
(C) correctly identified (D) rhythmical

Name ______________________________

Applying Meaning

Decide which word in parentheses best completes the sentence. Then write the sentence, adding the missing word.

1. After Benedict Arnold betrayed his country to the British, his name became _____ with *traitor*. (larcenous; synonymous)

   synonymous

2. The plastic had become so hard that it began to take on certain _____ properties. (medicinal; metallic)

   metallic

3. Many patterns in early quilts consist of circles, squares, and similar _____ figures. (geometric; parasitic)

   geometric

4. The police vowed to arrest those _____ drivers who race through town blowing their horns. (lecherous; maniacal)

   maniacal

5. Because the job was _____ and involved heavy lifting, all employees were required to pass a physical examination. (influential; strenuous)

   strenuous

6. The officer's behavior was _____. (lecherous; medicinal)

   lecherous

Follow the directions below to write a sentence using a vocabulary word.

7. Describe someone you know or have read about. Use the word *influential.*

   Sample Answer: As an influential member of the city council, Ed Stein was able to convince several members to vote for his resolution.

8. Describe the relationship between two people. Use the word *parasitic.*

   Sample Answer: Kim was tired of paying for Roger's movie ticket and lunch every Saturday, so she ended this parasitic relationship.

9. Use *larcenous* in a sentence about something you feel is wrong.

   Sample Answer: I consider charging $5.00 for a hot dog at the ball game absolutely larcenous.

10. Tell about something that you find refreshing. Use the word *medicinal.*

    Sample Answer: Sitting in a hot tub for 30 minutes has a medicinal effect on my body and my mind.

Test Taking Strategies

Tests of reading comprehension ask you to read one or two selections and answer some questions to test how well you understood what you read. The questions often ask you to draw inferences from the information. For example, if the selection described someone wiping sweat off his face, you would be expected to infer that he is hot.

Practice: Reread the selection "Tropical Rain Forests" on page 113. Write an X next to the statements that might be inferred from this essay.

1. It is dangerous to walk in tropical rain forests. — 1. ______
2. Animals in the rain forest have adapted to their surroundings. — 2. **X**
3. Human beings cannot survive in a tropical rain forest. — 3. ______
4. When rain forests are destroyed animals lose their natural habitat. — 4. **X**

Assessment

Name ______________________________

How well do you remember the words you studied in Lessons 33 through 36? Take the following test covering the words from the last three lessons.

Part 1 Choose the Correct Meaning

Each question below includes a word in capital letters, followed by four words or phrases. Choose the word or phrase that is closest in meaning to the word in capital letters. Write the letter for your answer on the line provided.

Sample

S. FINISH	(A) enjoy (C) destroy	(B) complete (D) enlarge	S. B
1. EXCAVATE	(A) escape (C) explore	(B) dig out (D) study	1. B
2. LAMPOON	(A) type of weapon (C) insult	(B) part of a lamp (D) ridicule	2. D
3. INFLUENTIAL	(A) source of disease (C) corrupt	(B) powerful (D) pleasing	3. B
4. PARASITIC	(A) living off others (C) generous	(B) spiritual (D) tending to spoil easily	4. A
5. STRENUOUS	(A) heroic (C) energetic	(B) strict (D) eager	5. C
6. SCOFF	(A) scrape (C) mock	(B) raise up (D) prove	6. C
7. FERVID	(A) heated (C) reverent	(B) unusual (D) eager	7. D
8. DEMISE	(A) death (C) type of tool	(B) device (D) unit of measurement	8. A
9. BANTER	(A) argument (C) facial expression	(B) chatter (D) religious belief	9. B
10. MANIACAL	(A) entertaining (C) insane	(B) illegal (D) manly	10. C

11. SYNONYMOUS	(A) spicy (C) having the opposite meaning	(B) simple (D) having the same meaning	11. D
12. COERCE	(A) join together (C) destroy	(B) compel (D) beg	12. B
13. IMMERSE	(A) cover (C) copy	(B) enlarge (D) doubt	13. A
14. PERVADE	(A) persuade (C) attack	(B) delay (D) sink in	14. D
15. REITERATE	(A) engrave (C) restate	(B) identify (D) ignore	15. C

Part 2 Matching Words and Meaning

Match the definition in Column B with the word in Column A. Write the letter of the correct definition on the answer line.

Column A	Column B	
16. confute	a. involving theft	16. d
17. beseech	b. extremely critical	17. f
18. larcenous	c. thickness	18. a
19. scorn	d. prove to be wrong	19. j
20. congeal	e. healing	20. h
21. medicinal	f. plead	21. e
22. bicker	g. encircle	22. i
23. scathing	h. harden	23. b
24. congestion	i. squabble	24. c
25. encompass	j. reject	25. g

Dictionary

Pronunciation Guide

Symbol	Example	Symbol	Example
ă	**p**a**t**	oi	b**oy**
ā	p**ay**	ou	**ou**t
âr	c**are**	o͝o	t**oo**k
ä	f**a**ther	o͞o	b**oo**t
ĕ	p**e**t	ŭ	c**u**t
ē	b**e**	ûr	**ur**ge
ĭ	p**i**t	th	**th**in
ī	p**ie**	*th*	**th**is
îr	p**ier**	hw	**wh**ich
ŏ	p**o**t	zh	vi**s**ion
ō	t**oe**	ə	**a**bout, it**e**m
ô	p**aw**		

Stress Marks: **′**(primary); ′(secondary), as in **dictionary** (**dĭk′**shə-nĕr′ē)

A

ab·di·cate (**ăb′** dĭ kāt′) *v.* **ab·di·cat·ed, ab·di·cat·ing, ab·di·cates.** To formally give up (power, responsibility, or rights): *The elderly queen abdicated her throne to her son.*

ab·hor (ăb **hôr′**) *v.* **ab·horred, ab·hor·ring, ab·hors.** To feel hatred or disgust for; detest; loathe: *I abhor ticks and mosquitoes.*

ab·hor·rent (ăb **hôr′** ənt *or* ăb **hŏr′** ənt) *adj.* Causing disgust or hatred; horrible; detestable: *The abhorrent crime shocked us.*

a·bom·i·na·tion (ə bŏm′ə **nā′** shən) *n.* **1.** A feeling of disgust or hatred. **2.** Something that is disgusting or hateful: *Deliberately setting a forest fire is an abomination.*

ab·o·rig·i·ne (ăb′ə **rĭj′** ə nē) *n.* One of the first known people to have lived in a region or country: *The aborigines were able to survive without modern conveniences.*

a·bort (ə **bôrt′**) *v.* To end something before it is completed: *The scientists aborted the rocket launch because of bad weather.*

a·bound (ə **bound′**) *v.* To exist or be available in large numbers; plentiful: *Wildlife abounds in the national forests.*

ab·ra·sive (ə **brā′** sĭv *or* ə **brā′** zĭv) *adj.* **1.** Causing a wearing away or rubbing off: *The abrasive cleanser harmed the wood table.* **2.** Irritating in manner. —*n.* A substance such as sandpaper used for polishing, cleaning, or grinding. **—a·bra′sive·ly** *adv.* **—a·bra′sive·ness** *n.*

a·brupt (ə **brŭpt′**) *adj.* **1.** Happening suddenly or unexpectedly: *The abrupt change in the flight schedule upset the travelers.* **2.** Steep. **3.** Blunt; impolite. **—a·brupt′ly** *adv.* **—a·brupt′ness** *n.*

ab·so·lute (**ăb′** sə lo͞ot′) *adj.* **1.** Complete or perfect: *The witness told the absolute truth.* **2.** Not restricted or limited: *The government was based on absolute freedom for the citizens.* **3.** Not doubted; utter: *The mother's love was absolute.*

ab·stain (ăb **stān′**) *v.* To voluntarily keep oneself from doing something: *I abstain from eating foods that are high in fat.*

a·buse (ə **byo͞oz′**) *v.* **a·bused, a·bus·ing, a·bus·es.** **1.** To use improperly or wrongly; misuse: *The mother told her children not to abuse their telephone privileges.* **2.** Mistreat; injure: *The dog owner was arrested for abusing the dog.* **3.** To attack or insult with harsh words. —*n.* (ə **byo͞os′**) Misuse: *Drug abuse is illegal.*

ac·cen·tu·ate (ăk **sĕn′** cho͞o āt′) *v.* **ac·cen·tu·at·ed, ac·cen·tu·at·ing, ac·cen·tu·ates.** To emphasize; stress: *The earrings accentuate the woman's blue eyes.*

ac·co·lade (**ăk′** ə lād′ *or* **ăk′** ə läd′) *n.* An expression of approval such as praise, an award, or honor: *The astronaut was given accolades for his work in space.*

ac·com·plished (ə **kŏm′** plĭsht) *adj.* Skilled; expert: *The lifeguard is an accomplished swimmer.* *v.* Successfully carried out; completed: *The girl accomplished her reading goal.*

ac·qui·es·cence (ăk′wē **ĕs′**əns) *n.* Quiet agreement without protest: *The teacher was surprised by the students' acquiescence to the new rules.*

ac·qui·si·tion (ăk′wĭ **zĭsh′**ən) *n.* **1.** The act of obtaining or getting: *The students were thrilled about the school's acquisition of new computers.* **2.** Something acquired: *The rare bird is the zoo's newest acquisition.*

ad·den·dum (ə **dĕn′**dəm) *n., pl.* **ad·den·da.** Something that is added; addition: *Movies about real people often have an addendum at the end to explain what became of the people.*

ad·mon·ish (ăd **mŏn′**ĭsh) *v.* **1.** To warn or caution against something: *The health department admonished consumers not to eat raw meat.* **2.** To scold or criticize in a mild way: *The teacher admonished us for whispering during the assembly.* **—ad·mon′ish·ment** *n.*

ad·vent (**ăd′**vĕnt′) *n.* The arrival or coming into being of a new thing or person: *The advent of cellular telephones allowed people to make calls from almost anywhere.*

ad·ver·sar·y (**ăd′**vər sĕr′ē) *n., pl.* **ad·ver·sar·ies.** An opponent, enemy, or foe: *Although the two countries had been adversaries in the past, they worked together on space exploration.*

af·fil·i·ate (ə **fĭl′**ē āt′) *v.* **af·fil·i·at·ed, af·fil·i·at·ing, af·fil·i·ates. 1.** To be joined or connected in close association: *Some voters are not affiliated with a political party.* **2.** To associate (oneself) with a larger group: *A local radio station hopes to affiliate with a national network.* —*n.* A person, group, or organization that is closely joined or connected with a larger or more important body or organization.

af·firm (ə **fûrm′**) *v.* To declare positively or firmly: *The Supreme Court affirmed that the Bill of Rights guarantees the rights of all citizens.*

af·fix (ə **fĭks′**) *v.* To fasten; attach: *I almost forgot to affix a stamp to the letter.*

af·flic·tion (ə **flĭk′**shən) *n.* A state or condition of pain, suffering, or distress: *Beethoven's affliction of deafness did not keep him from composing great symphonies.*

ag·o·nize (**ăg′**ə nīz′) *v.* **ag·o·nized, ag·o·niz·ing, ag·o·niz·es.** To feel or cause to feel great pain or distress: *I agonized over the decision of what to give my mother for her birthday.*

ag·o·niz·ing (**ăg′**ə nī′zĭng) *adj.* Causing great pain or distress: *Speaking to a group is an agonizing experience for many people.*

al·ien·ate (**āl′**yə nāt′ *or* **ā′**lē ə nāt′) *v.* **al·ien·at·ed, al·ien·at·ing, al·ien·ates.** To cause the loss of friendship or support: *Being rude to friends may alienate them.*

am·bi·dex·trous (ăm′bĭ **dĕk′**strəs) *adj.* Able to use both hands equally well: *The surgeon was ambidextrous.* **—am′bi·dex′trous·ly** *adv.*

am·biv·a·lent (ăm **bĭv′**ə lənt) *adj.* Having or showing conflicting feelings about someone, something, or an idea: *The boy is ambivalent about whether he wants to be a doctor or a lawyer.* **—am·biv′a·lent·ly** *adv.*

am·i·ca·ble (**ăm′**ĭ kə bəl) *adj.* Friendly; peaceable; showing good will: *The two rival teams were amicable toward each other after the game.* **—am′i·ca·bil′i·ty, am′i·ca·ble·ness** *n.* **—am′i·ca·bly** *adv.*

am·o·rous (**ăm′**ər əs) *adj.* **1.** Relating to, feeling, showing, or expressing love: *Mark wrote an amorous letter to his new wife.* **2.** Attracted to love: *The main character in the movie is an amorous girl.* **—am′or·ous·ly** *adv.*

an·ec·dote (**ăn′**ĭk dōt′) *n.* A short entertaining account of an interesting incident or event: *My grandfather often entertains us with anecdotes about his childhood.* **—an′ec·dot′al** *adj.*

an·tag·o·nize (ăn **tăg′**ə nīz′) *v.* **an·tag·o·nized, an·tag·o·niz·ing, an·tag·o·niz·es.** To cause dislike or anger; to make unfriendly: *People should not antagonize their neighbors' dogs by teasing them.*

an·te·bel·lum (ăn′tē **bĕl′**əm) *adj.* Existing before a war, especially the American Civil War: *Tourists may visit antebellum houses in the South.*

an·te·ce·dent (ăn tĭ **sēd′**ənt) *n.* **1.** A person, thing, or event that comes before another: *Studying should be an antecedent to a test.* **2.** A noun, phrase, or clause to which a pronoun refers. In the sentence *My dog was hungry, so I fed her,* the noun *dog* is the antecedent of the pronoun *her.*

an·te·date (**ăn′**tĭ dāt′) *v.* **an·te·dat·ed, an·te·dat·ing, an·te·dates. 1.** To come before in time; to be of an earlier date: *The invention of the television antedates the invention of the personal computer.* **2.** To put a date on something that is earlier than the actual date: *People should not antedate their checks when paying their bills.*

an·te·room (**ăn′**tē ro͞om′ *or* **ăn′**tē ro͝om′) *n.* A waiting room or entrance to a larger room: *The anteroom to the ballroom was filled with guests.*

an·ti·cli·max (ăn′tē **klī′**măks′) *n.* **1.** Anything that is viewed as a disappointing letdown to what has come before it: *Because it rained, the picnic was an anticlimax to all the preparations for it.* **2.** Something less important or interesting that follows more important or dignified events.

an·ti·dote (**ăn′**tĭ dōt′) *n.* **1.** A medicine, substance, or remedy that counteracts the effects of poison: *There was an antidote for wasp stings in the first* *aid kit.* **2.** Something that acts as a remedy: *Walking can be an antidote to stress.*

an·tip·a·thy (ăn **tĭp′**ə thē) *n., pl.* **an·tip·a·thies. 1.** A strong feeling of dislike: *The man had an antipathy to flying.* **2.** A person or object that arouses such dislike.

an·ti·sep·tic (ăn′tĭ **sĕp′**tĭk) *adj.* **1.** Free from germs; very clean: *An operating room should be antiseptic.* **2.** Preventing infection or rot by stopping the growth of germs. —*n.* A substance that kills or stops the growth of germs, such as alcohol: *Doctors rub the arm with an antiseptic before giving a shot.*

an·ti·so·cial (ăn′tē **sō′**shəl) *adj.* **1.** Not liking companionship; unwilling to associate with others; unsociable: *The antisocial woman never attended any parties.* **2.** Harmful to the general good of society: *Terrorism is an antisocial act.*

an·ti·tox·in (ăn′tē **tŏk′**sĭn) *n.* **1.** A substance formed in the body that acts against a specific toxin or poison produced by bacteria: *Because his body produced antitoxins against the bacteria, he didn't get ill.* **2.** A serum containing such an antibody obtained from the blood of an animal that has had a particular disease or that has been injected with a toxin.

ap·peal (ə **pēl′**) *n.* **1.** An earnest request or plea, as for help: *The storm was so strong that the captain of the small boat sent an appeal for help.* **2.** A request for someone to decide in one's favor. —*v.* To make a request: *During the flood, the city appealed for people to fill sandbags.*

ap·praise (ə **prāz′**) *v.* **ap·praised, ap·prais·ing, ap·prais·es.** To determine, judge, or estimate the value of: *The buyers wanted their bank to appraise the house.*

ap·pren·tice (ə **prĕn′**tĭs) *n.* **1.** A person who works for another skilled worker in order to learn a trade or craft: *An apprentice learns the work by doing what the boss says to do.* **2.** A student or beginner.

ap·ti·tude (**ăp′**tĭ to͞od′ *or* **ăp′**tĭ tyo͞od′) *n.* **1.** A natural ability, talent, or tendency: *The child showed an aptitude for music.* **2.** Quickness to learn or understand: *The teacher was amazed by the child's aptitude in math.*

as·sets (**ăs′**ĕts′) *n.* All the property and resources owned by a person or business that have a cash value and may be used to pay debts: *Before approving the loan, the bank wanted to know what assets the borrower had.*

a·sun·der (ə **sŭn′**dər) *adv.* **1.** Into separate parts or pieces: *The seaside restaurant was torn asunder by the hurricane.* **2.** Apart from each other: *The papers were blown asunder by the high wind.*

au·to·ma·tion (ô′tə **mā′**shən) *n.* The development and use of machines, electronic devices, computers, or robots that do the work rather than people: *Automation of factories has caused some people to lose their jobs.*

awe (ô) *v.* **awed, aw·ing, awes.** To inspire or fill with wonder, fear, and great respect: *The tourists were awed by the Grand Canyon.* —*n.* A feeling of wonder, fear, great respect: *I am filled with awe when I think of the size of the universe.*

B

ba·bel (**băb′**əl *or* **bā′**bəl) *n.* A confused mixture of many sounds, voices, or languages: *The babel in the crowded room made it impossible for me to have an intelligent conversation.*

badg·er (**băj′**ər) *n.* A mammal with a heavy body, short legs, long claws, and a thick short tail that lives in holes that it has burrowed. It usually feeds at night on insects and smaller animals.—*v.* To continuously annoy, pester, or nag: *The child badgered her mother to buy her a toy.*

ban·ter (**băn′**tər) *n.* Playful, good-natured conversation; joking, or teasing: *The whole class enjoyed the banter between the teacher and the coach.*

ba·sil·i·ca (bə **sĭl′**ĭ kə) *n.* A type of church having two rows of columns on either side and a central hall with two side aisles, ending in a semicircular area: *The wedding was held in a basilica.*

bas·tion (**băs′**chən *or* **băs′**tē ən) *n.* **1.** A part projecting from the main fortification that allows the defenders a wider range of fire. **2.** Anything regarded as firmly protecting some position, place, quality, or condition; stronghold: *Education is the bastion for freedom.*

beast·ly (**bēst′**lē) *adj.* **beast·li·er, beast·li·est. 1.** Like a beast. **2.** Unpleasant; terrible; disagreeable: *The five-mile hike in the cold rain was beastly.*

be·deck (bĭ **dĕk′**) *v.* To cover with decorations or ornaments; adorn: *The wedding cake was bedecked with flowers.*

ber·serk (bər **sûrk′** *or* bər **zûrk′**) *adj. & adv.* In or into a wild, violent, or crazed rage: *A symptom of rabies is berserk behavior.*

be·seech (bĭ **sēch′**) *v.* **be·sought** (bĭ **sôt′**) or **be·seeched, be·seech·ing, be·seech·es.** To ask (for) seriously; plead; beg: *The administrator of the shelter for homeless people beseeched the public for donations of food.*

bi·an·nu·al (bī **ăn′**yo͞o əl) *adj.* Happening twice a year: semiannual: *The store has biannual sales in January and July.* **—bi·an′nu·al·ly** *adv.*

bi·cen·ten·ni·al (bī′sĕn **tĕn′**ē əl) *adj.* Happening once every 200 years: *The bicentennial appearance of the comet was a newsworthy event.* —*n.* A 200th anniversary or its celebration: *The city celebrated the bicentennial of its founding.*

bick·er (**bĭk′**ər) *v.* To argue or quarrel over unimportant matters: *The children bickered about where they would sit in the car.*

bi·en·ni·al (bī **ĕn′**ē əl) *adj.* **1.** Happening once every two years: *The biennial elections are held in even years such as 1998 and 2000.* **2.** Lasting for two years: *The flower garden has quite a few biennial plants.* —*n.* A plant that lives for two years, blooming and producing seed in the second year. **—bi·en′ni·al·ly** *adv.*

bi·lat·er·al (bī **lăt′**ər əl) *adj.* **1.** Of, involving, or affecting two sides: *The bilateral treaty was signed by the presidents of both countries.* **2.** Having two sides. **—bi·lat′er·al·ly** *adv.*

bi·lin·gual (bī **lĭng′**gwəl) *adj.* **1.** Able to speak two languages equally well: *The Spanish teacher is bilingual.* **2.** Expressed or written in two languages: *The bilingual book is written in both English and French.*

bi·ome (**bī′**ōm′) *n.* A natural community made up of plants and animals that live in a particular geographical area with a particular climate: *Prairies are a type of biome.*

blas·phe·my (**blăs′**fə mē) *n., pl.* **blas·phe·mies.** A disrespectful remark or act against God or something sacred: *Writing disrespectful words on the walls of a temple is considered blasphemy.*

blight·ed (**blīt′**əd) *adj.* Withered, ruined, or destroyed: *The blighted plants were evidence of the extremely dry summer.*

bo·vine (**bō′**vīn′ *or* **bō′**vēn′) *adj.* **1.** Resembling an ox or cow. **2.** Dull, slow, or stupid: *The teacher gave the class a break when she noticed that the students all had bovine stares on their faces.*

brawn·y (**brô′**nē) *adj.* **brawn·i·er, brawn·i·est.** Muscular and strong; robust: *The brawny weight lifter works out every day.* **—brawn′i·ness** *n.*

breach (brēch) *n.* **1.** A violation of a law, promise, or obligation: *Driving faster than the posted speed limit is a breach of the law.* **2.** A hole, break, or gap made in something solid: *Water came in through the breach in the foundation of the house.*

bul·bous (**bŭl′**bəs) *adj.* **1.** Growing from bulbs: *Daffodils are bulbous plants.* **2.** Shaped like a bulb: *The clown's bulbous nose was not real.*

C

ca·jole (kə **jōl′**) *v.* **ca·joled, ca·jol·ing, ca·joles.** To persuade by flattery, insincere talk, or false promises: *I cajoled my mother into buying me a new violin by promising I would practice an hour every day.*

cam·ou·flage (**kăm′**ə fläzh′ *or* **kăm′**ə fläj′) *n.* **1.** A method used by the military to disguise or conceal troops or equipment to make them blend into the surroundings. **2.** A disguise or appearance that conceals or deceives: *The snake's camouflage made it look like a stick.* —*v.* **cam·ou·flaged, cam·ou·flag·ing, cam·ou·flag·es.** To hide by means of a camouflage: *The troops camouflaged the gun with tree branches and leaves.*

cap·il·lar·y (**kăp′**ə lĕr′ē) *n., pl.* **cap·il·lar·ies.** Any of the tiny blood vessels that connect the arteries with the veins: *The capillary bled for a long time.*

cit·a·del (**sĭt′**ə dəl) *n.* **1.** A fortress or stronghold built to overlook a city: *The citadel was built to protect the city from raiders.* **2.** A stronghold, safe place, or refuge.

clas·sic (**klăs′**ĭk) *adj.* **1.** Serving as a model or outstanding example: *The automobile is a classic example of man's search for faster transportation.* **2.** Typical: *Barking and a wagging tail are classic signs of a dog's excitement.*

cleave (klēv) *v.* **cleft** or **cleaved** or **clove, cleft** or **cleaved** or **cloven, cleaving, cleaves.** To divide or split as by force: *A tornado is able to cleave a building.*

cler·gy (**klûr′**jē) *n., pl.* **cler·gies.** People authorized to conduct religious services, such as ministers, priests, rabbis, or mullahs: *A member of the clergy is authorized to perform weddings.*

co·erce (kō **ûrs′**) *v.* **co·erced, co·erc·ing, co·erc·es.** To persuade or force by threats, pressure, or violence: *The child tried to coerce her sister to play with her by threatening to hide a favorite doll.*

co·he·sive (kō **hē′**sĭ v) *adj.* Capable of or tending to stick or hold together: *Even though our family is large, we are cohesive.* **—co·he′sive·ly** *adv.* **—co·he′sive·ness** *n.*

col·league (**kŏl′**ēg′) *n.* A fellow member of a profession, staff, or organization; coworker; associate: *My colleagues and I like to discuss our projects during lunch.*

come·ly (**kŭm′**lē) *adj.* **come·li·er, come·li·est.** Attractive; fair; good-looking: *Romeo thought that Juliet had a comely appearance.*

com·pel (kəm **pĕl′**) *v.* **com·pelled, compelling, com·pels.** To make people do something necessary by force or demand: *The state compels dri-*

vers to take an eye test when they renew their licenses.

compound interest *n.* Money paid on the original sum of money and the interest previously earned in a savings account: *Since the savings account earned compound interest, the balance grew rapidly.*

com·pre·hen·sive (kŏm′ prĭ **hĕn′** sĭv) *adj.* Covering a great deal; thorough; complete: *The comprehensive investigation led to the solution of the crime.* **—com′ pre·hen′ sive·ly** *adv.*

con·cave (kŏn **kāv′** *or* **kŏn′** kāv′) *adj.* Curved inward like the inside of a circle or bowl: *Children liked to play in the concave structure at the park.* **—con·cave′ ly** *adv.* **—con·cave′ ness** *n.*

con·fute (kən **fyōōt′**) *v.* **con·fut·ed, con·fut·ing, con·futes.** To prove to be wrong or false; disprove: *Despite efforts to confute the findings of the study, scientists have not found any evidence that the conclusions are wrong.*

con·geal (kən **jēl′**) *v.* To thicken or change from a liquid to a solid by cooling or freezing: *The gelatin congealed in the refrigerator.*

con·ges·tion (kən **jĕs′** chən) *n.* A condition of overcrowding: *It took a long time to get lunch because of the congestion in the cafeteria.*

con·trived (kən **trīvd′**) *adj.* Obviously or carefully planned: *The author worked for days on the contrived ending of the book.*

con·vex (**kŏn′** vĕks′ *or* kən **vĕks′**) *adj.* Curved outward like the outside of a circle or dome: *The convex shape of the domed stadium was easy to see in the pictures taken from the blimp.* **—con·vex′ ly** *adv.* **—con·vex′ ness** *n.*

co·sign·er (kō **sīn′** ər) *n.* A person who adds his or her signature to (a legal document, such as a contract) and accepts responsibility to fulfill the terms if the other person fails to do so: *His mother was the cosigner for the loan on the house.*

cred·i·tor (**krĕd′** ĭ tər) *n.* A person to whom money is owed: *The creditor sent a bill every month.*

cul·tur·al (**kŭl′** chər əl) *adj.* Of or relating to the way of life, customs, beliefs, and arts of a particular group of people: *It is interesting to learn the cultural differences of people from different countries.* **—cul′ tur·al·ly** *adv.*

D

dank (dăngk) *adj.* **dank·er, dank·est.** Unpleasantly damp; cold and wet: *The inside of the cave was dank.* **—dank ly** *adv.* **—dank ness** *n.*

dap·pled (**dăp′** əld) *adj.* Having spots, streaks, or patches of different colors or shade; spotted: *The grass was dappled with shade from the sun shining through the large trees.*

deb·it (**dĕb′** ĭt) *n.* The money deducted and recorded in an account: *My bank statement showed a debit of $10 for new checks.*

de·crep·it (dĭ **krĕp′** ĭt) *adj.* Broken down, weakened, or worn out because of old age or overuse: *We were afraid that the decrepit car would not make it to our destination.*

de·fault (dĭ **fôlt′**) *v.* **1.** To fail to pay money owed: *After losing his job, Sam had to default on his bank loan.* **2.** To fail to do what is required. —*n.* A failure to do what is required, especially to pay money owed. **—de·fault′ er** *n.*

de·fi·ant (dĭ **fī′** ənt) *adj.* Showing open or bold resistance or contempt to authority or an opponent: *The girl was grounded because of her defiant behavior.* **—de·fi′ ant·ly** *adv.*

de·mise (dĭ **mīz′**) *n.* **1.** Death: *The demise of the famous actor saddened his fans.* **2.** End: *The demise of the company forced many people out of work.*

des·e·cra·tion (dĕs′ ĭ **krā′** shən) *n.* The harming, violation, or destruction of something sacred: *The desecration of the tombstones shocked the townspeople.*

des·ig·na·tion (dĕz′ ĭg **nā′** shən) *n.* **1.** Selection for a particular duty, assignment, or purpose: *The designation of the Valentine's Day king and queen is made by a committee.* **2.** The act of indicating, pointing out, or specifying something: *The designation of the snow-removal route is shown on the city map.*

de·spise (dĭ **spīz′**) *v.* **de·spised, de·spis·ing, de·spis·es.** To hate or show scorn toward: *Even though I despise housework, I know I have to do it.*

de·spon·dent (dĭ **spŏn′** dənt) *adj.* Having lost hope; discouraged; depressed: *The actor was despondent when his movie was unsuccessful at the box offices.* **—de·spon′ dence, de·spon′ den·cy** *n.*

dev·as·tate (**dĕv′** ə stāt′) *v.* **dev·as·tat·ed, dev·as·tat·ing, dev·as·tates.** To lay waste; destroy: *A hurricane can devastate a beach as well as any buildings in its path.* **—dev′ as·tat′ ing·ly** *adv.* **—dev′ as·ta′ tor** *n.*

dif·fer·en·ti·ate (dĭf′ ə **rĕn′** shē āt′) *v.* **dif·fer·en·ti·at·ed, dif·fer·en·ti·at·ing, dif·fer·en·ti·ates. 1.** To tell the difference between; distinguish between: *Sometimes it is difficult to differentiate between expensive clothes and inexpensive ones.* **2.** To make up the difference: *Hard work can differentiate good grades from bad ones.*

dis·dain (dĭs **dān′**) *v.* To consider or treat as though low or worthless; to scorn: *The rude girl disdained the friendliness of her classmates.* —*n.* A feeling of dislike or scorn for something that is thought to be unworthy or lowly: *The woman's disdain for the simple meal hurt the host's feelings.*

dis·grun·tle (dĭs **grŭn′**tl) *v.* **dis·grun·tled, dis·grun·tling, dis·grun·tles.** To anger: make dissatisfied, disgusted, or displeased: *The poor service disgruntled the customers.* —*adj.* **dis·grun·tled** (dĭs **grŭn′**tld) Dissatisfied; disgusted; angry: *After the fifth loss in a row, the disgruntled football fans booed the team.*

dis·guise (dĭs **gīz′**) *v.* **dis·guised, dis·guis·ing, dis·guis·es.** To hide the real appearance or nature of: *The girl disguised her sadness by smiling.* —*n.* Something that hides.

dis·in·te·grate (dĭs **ĭn′**tĭ grāt′) *v.* **dis·in·te·grat·ed, dis·in·te·grat·ing, dis·in·te·grates.** To separate into small parts; to break up: *When the tide came in, the sand castle disintegrated.*

dis·par·i·ty (dĭ **spăr′**ĭ tē) *n., pl.* **dis·par·i·ties.** Lack of similarity or agreement; inequality; difference: *The mother knew the children were lying because of the disparity in their stories.*

dis·sec·tion (dĭ **sĕk′**shən *or* dī **sĕk′**shən) *n.* **1.** The act of cutting apart for study or scientific examination: *The dissection of the animal was necessary to determine if it had rabies.* **2.** A detailed analysis or examination: *The accountant conducted a dissection of the new tax law.*

dog·ged (**dô′**gĭd *or* **dŏg′**ĭd) *adj.* Not giving up; persistent; stubborn: *The girl's dogged determination to be a doctor paid off when she got her degree.* **—dog′ged·ly** *adv.* **—dog′ged·ness** *n.*

dom·i·nate (**dŏm′**ə nāt′) *v.* **dom·i·nat·ed, dom·i·nat·ing, dom·i·nates.** To have the main influence or control; to rule over: *Talk shows dominate daytime television.*

drab (drăb) *adj.* **drab·ber, drab·best.** Lacking brightness; dull; dreary; faded: *The drab carpet did not match the bright walls.* —*n.* A dull, grayish or yellowish brown. **—drab′ly** *adv.* **—drab′ness** *n.*

drudg·er·y (**drŭj′**ə rē) *n., pl.* **drudg·er·ies.** Boring, tiresome, or unpleasant work: *Weeding the garden in the hot sun may seem like drudgery.*

E

e·go·tis·ti·cal (ē′gə **tĭs′**tĭ kəl) *adj.* Conceited; self-centered: *I get tired of hearing egotistical people boast about themselves.* **—e′go·tis′ti·cal·ly** *adv.*

e·lim·i·nate (ĭ **lĭm′**ə nāt′) *v.* **e·lim·i·nat·ed, e·lim·i·nat·ing, e·lim·i·nates. 1.** To get rid of; remove: *It is difficult to eliminate all bad habits.* **2.** To leave out of consideration: *After the first race all but the two fastest runners were eliminated.*

el·lip·ti·cal (ĭ **lĭp′**tĭ kəl) *adj.* Of, relating to, or shaped like an oval with both ends alike: *Although the elliptical window was unusual, it was beautiful.* **—el·lip′ti·cal·ly** *adv.*

em·i·nent (**ĕm′**ə nənt) *adj.* Above all others, as in power, rank, position; famous; distinguished: *The eminent writer was gracious when she accepted the award for her latest book.* **—em′i·nent·ly** *adv.*

e·mis·sion (ĭ **mĭsh′**ən) *n.* **1.** Something that is released, discharged, or sent out: *Many states require that car exhaust systems be tested for dangerous emissions.* **2.** The act or process of releasing, discharging, or sending out.

en·chant (ĕn **chănt′**) *v.* **1.** To place under a spell; bewitch: *Merlin was able to enchant people.* **2.** To charm: *The music enchanted the audience.* **3.** To be under a spell or bewitched: *Hansel and Gretel were enchanted by the witch.*

en·com·pass (ĕn **kŭm′**pəs) *v.* **en·com·passed, en·com·pass·ing, en·com·pass·es. 1.** To include; contain: *Although the historical novel is fiction, it encompasses real events from the l800s.* **2.** To surround; encircle: *A fence encompasses the ranch.*

en·cum·brance (ĕn **kŭm′**brəns) *n.* A person or thing that stands in the way; something that burdens or hinders: *Not knowing how to type was an encumbrance to getting the job.*

en·hance (ĕn **hăns′**) *v.* **en·hanced, en·hanc·ing, en·hanc·es.** To make greater or better, as in value, reputation, or quality: *The actress's beauty was enhanced by her makeup.* **—en·hance′ment** *n.*

en·sure (ĕn **shŏŏr′**) *v.* **en·sured, en·sur·ing, en·sures.** To make sure; guarantee: *Consistently doing one's homework helps to ensure good grades in school.*

e·rad·i·cate (ĭ **rad′**ĭ kāt′) *v.* **e·rad·i·cat·ed, e·rad·i·cat·ing, e·rad·i·cates.** To get rid of; remove; destroy completely: *Scientists hopeto eradicate many diseases through the use of vaccinations.* **e·rad′i·ca′tion** *n.*

e·ro·sion (ĭ **rō′**zhən) *n.* The gradual wearing, washing, or eating away, especially of rock or soil, by wind, water, or glaciers: *The erosion of fertile soil is a problem for farmers.*

e·soph·a·gus (ĭ **sŏf′**ə gəs) *n., pl.* **e·soph·a·gi.** The tube or passageway connecting the throat and the stomach: *Food passes from the throat through the esophagus to the stomach.*

es·trange (ĭ **strānj'**) *v.* **es·tranged, es·trang·ing, es·trang·es.** To cause (someone) to change from friendly or kind feelings to unfriendly or unkind feelings: *I do not want to estrange my friends by telling lies about them.* **—es·trange' ment** *n.*

et·i·quette (**ĕt'** ĭ kĕt' *or* **ĕt'** ĭ kĭt) *n.* The rules and forms of proper behavior required in society or business: *People often take classes in etiquette so that they will know how to act in formal situations.*

e·volve (ĭ **vŏlv'**) *v.* **e·volved, e·volv·ing, e·volves. 1.** To develop gradually: *The idea for the book evolved over several years.* **2.** *Biology.* To undergo the development or change of organisms or species from their original state to their present state.

ex·ac·er·bate (ĭg **zăs'** ər **bāt'**) *v.* **ex·ac·er·bat·ed, ex·ac·er·bat·ing, ex·ac·er·bates.** To make worse, more intense or severe; aggravate: *The second ice storm in a week exacerbated the icy condition of the roads.*

ex·ca·vate (**ĕk'** skə vāt') *v.* **ex·ca·vat·ed, ex·ca·vat·ing, ex·ca·vates. 1.** To uncover by digging: *Archaeologists excavated the ancient city of Pompeii.* **2.** To make a hole in; hollow out: *The workers excavated under the English Channel to build the Chunnel.* **3.** To remove by digging: *A shovel was used to excavate the dirt.*

ex·cel (ĭk **sĕl'**) *v.* **ex·celled, ex·cel·ling, ex·cels.** To be better or greater than, as in ability; outdo; surpass: *The Hall of Fame baseball player excels in pitching.*

ex·e·cute (**ĕk'** sĭ kyo͞ot') *v.* **ex·e·cut·ed, ex·e·cut·ing, ex·e·cutes. 1.** To carry out; to put into effect: *Schools execute the law that students must have up-to-date immunizations to attend classes.* **2.** To do; perform: *The ice skater executed a very complicated jump.* **3.** To create or produce something, such as a work of art, according to a plan or design: *The sculptor executed a lifelike statue.*

ex·pan·sion (ĭk **spăn'** shən) *n.* The act of growing in size, number, volume, or scope: *The expansion of the use of computers will continue into the next century.*

ex·pa·tri·ate (ĕk **spā'** trē āt') *v.* **ex·pa·tri·at·ed, ex·pa·tri·at·ing, ex·pa·tri·ates. 1.** To remove someone from his or her native country. **2.** To voluntarily remove oneself from living in one's native country. —*n.* (ek **spa'** trē ĭt) A person who voluntarily lives in a foreign country: *During the French Revolution many French noblemen became expatriates in other European countries.* **—ex·pa' tri·a' tion** *n.*

ex·pe·di·ent (ĭk **spē'** dē ənt) *n.* A way to achieve the desired result: *Calling 911 is a quick expedient for getting emergency help.* —*adj.* Suitable or convenient for a particular purpose: *Using the microwave oven is an expedient way to prepare a meal quickly.*

ex·pel (ĭk **spĕl'**) *v.* **ex·pelled, ex·pel·ling, ex·pels. 1.** To force to leave: *A student may be expelled for bringing a weapon to school.* **2.** To force out, drive out, eject: *Take a deep breath and expel the air slowly.*

ex·ten·sive (ĭk **stĕn'** sĭv) *adj.* Widespread; large in amount; vast; far-reaching: *Extensive research is done to determine if a new medicine is safe for people to use.*

ex·ter·mi·nate (ĭk **stûr'** mə nāt') *v.* **ex·ter·mi·nat·ed, ex·ter·mi·nat·ing, ex·ter·mi·nates.** To destroy completely; to wipe out: *We had to exterminate the termites before we could move into the house.* **—ex·ter' mi·na' tion** *n.*

ex·tinct (ĭk **stĭngkt'**) *adj.* No longer living or in existence: *There are many theories about why dinosaurs became extinct.*

ex·trem·i·ty (ĭk **strĕm'** ĭ tē) *n., pl.* **ex·trem·i·ties. 1.** The farthest or outermost part: *The tip of Cape Cod is the extremity of Massachusetts.* **2.** The hands and feet: *The extremities need protection from frostbite.*

ex·u·ber·ant (ĭg **zo͞o'** bər ənt) *adj.* Overflowing with joy, high spirits, or unrestrained enthusiasm: *The fans were exuberant when their team won the state championship.* **—ex·u' ber·ant·ly** *adv.*

F

fer·ret (**fĕr'** ĭt) *v.* To find out by searching; uncover: *The baseball card collector ferreted out old cards at garage sales.* —*n.* An animal from the polecat family that is sometimes trained to hunt rats, mice, and rabbits.

fer·vid (**fûr'** vĭd) *adj.* Having or showing great emotion or warmth of feeling; enthusiastic: *The Olympic swimmer had a fervid desire to win a gold medal.* **—fer' vid·ly** *adv.* **—fer' vid·ness** *n.*

fick·le (**fĭk'** əl) *adj.* Changeable, especially with one's affections for others: *The fickle boy had a different girlfriend every day.* **—fick' le·ness** *n.*

flex·i·ble (**flĕk'** sə bəl) *adj.* **1.** Capable of adjusting to change: *A teacher must be flexible since students have different learning styles.* **2.** Able to be bent: *The hose is flexible.* **—flex' i·bil' i·ty** *n.* **—flex' i·bly** *adv.*

for·age (**fôr'** ĭj *or* **fŏr'** ĭj) *v.* **for·aged, for·ag·ing, for·ag·es. 1,** To search or hunt for food: *The raccoon foraged in the forest.* **2.** To search for something. *n.* **1.** Food for horses or cattle. **2.** The search for food. **—for' ag·er** *n.*

fore·close (fôr **klōz′**) *v.* **fore·closed, fore·clos·ing, fore·clos·es.** To take away the right to pay off (a mortgage) usually by taking the property, especially after failure to make payments on the loan: *The bank foreclosed on the house because no mortgage payments had been made for six months.*

for·mi·da·ble (**fôr′** mĭ də bəl) *adj.* **1.** Difficult to defeat, deal with, or do: *Climbing Mt. Everest is a formidable challenge.* **2.** Causing fear, dread, or awe. **—for′ mi·da·bil′ i·ty** *n.* **—for′ mi·da·bly** *adv.*

fu·ry (**fyo͝or′** ē) *n., pl.* **fu·ries. 1.** Violent anger; rage: *The man's fury frightened everyone in the room.* **2.** Violence; fierceness: *Beware of a mother bear's fury when she is protecting her cubs.*

G

gar·ner (**gär′** nər) *v.* **1.** To earn or collect: *The new symphony conductor garnered praise from the music critics.* **2.** To gather and store: *Squirrels garner acorns for the winter.*

gen·er·a·tion (jĕn′ ə **rā′** shən) *n.* **1.** A group of people born and living about the same time: *The younger generation often likes different music than older generations enjoy.* **2.** One step in the line of natural descent: *There were three generations at the family reunion—grandparents, parents, and children.*

ge·net·ic (jə **nĕt′** ĭk) *adj.* Of or relating to inherited characteristics found in similar or related organisms: *Sisters have the same genetic makeup.* **—ge·net′ i·cal·ly** *adv.*

gen·ial (**jēn′** yəl) *adj.* **1.** Pleasant; cheerful; friendly: *The genial neighbors invited everyone on the block to a barbecue.* **2.** Good for life and growth; comfortably warm and mild. *People like to live in a genial climate.* **—ge′ ni·al′ i·ty** *n.* **gen′ ial·ly** *adv.*

gen·try (**jĕn′** trē) *n., pl.* **gen·tries.** People of high social standing and good family: *Most of the local gentry belong to an exclusive club.*

ge·o·met·ric (jē′ ə **mĕt′** rĭk) *adj.* **1.** Of or relating to the characteristics, measurements, and relationships of lines, surfaces, and figures. **2.** Made of or using straight lines, angles, or circles: *The geometric design drawn on the computer was very interesting.* **—ge′ o·met′ ri·cal·ly** *adv.*

ger·mi·nate (**jûr′** mə nāt′) *v.* **ger·mi·nat·ed, ger·mi·nat·ing, ger·mi·nates.** To start or cause to start to grow or develop; sprout: *The flower seeds began to germinate a week after they were planted.* **—ger′ mi·na′ tion** *n.* **—ger′ mi·na tor′** *n.*

H

hu·man (**hyo͞o′** mən) *adj.* Having the qualities of a living person: *Scientists are constantly studying the human body.* —*n.* A person.

hu·mane (hyo͞o **mān′**) *adj.* Having or showing kindness, mercy, compassion, or sympathy: *The animal shelter was known for its humane treatment of lost pets.* **—hu·mane′ ly** *adv.*

hy·per·ac·tive (hī′ pər **ăk′** tĭv) *adj.* Highly or overly active: *The hyperactive child had difficulty sitting still for even a few minutes.*

hy·per·bo·le (hī **pûr′** bə lē) *n.* An intentional exaggeration that is not meant to be taken literally: *Everyone laughed at the hyperbole about how hot it was outside.*

hy·per·ex·ten·sion (hī′ pər ĭk **stĕn′** shən) *n.* The act of straightening or extending a bodily joint beyond its normal range of motion: *A hyperextension of the knee is very painful.*

hy·per·son·ic (hī′ pər **sŏn′** ĭk) *adj.* Moving at a rate of at least five times the speed of sound: *We heard the sound of the hypersonic jet quite a few seconds after we saw it.*

hy·per·ten·sion (hī′ pər **tĕn′** shən) *n.* High blood pressure: *People with hypertension should see their doctors regularly.*

hy·po·chon·dri·ac (hī′ pə **kŏn′** drē ăk′) *n.* A person who worries excessively that he or she is ill or is becoming ill: *The hypochondriac talked only about his poor health.*

hy·poc·ri·sy (hĭ **pŏk′** rĭ sē) *n., pl.* **hy·poc·ri·sies.** The practice of showing or stating feelings, beliefs, or qualities that one does not possess: *The hypocrisy of the candidate became evident after she was elected.*

hy·po·der·mic (hī pə **dûr′** mĭk) *adj.* **1.** Beneath the skin. **2.** Injected or used to inject under the skin: *The shot was given with a long hypodermic needle.* —*n.* An injection given under the skin with a needle.

hy·pot·e·nuse (hī **pŏt′** n o͞os′ *or* hī **pŏt′** n yo͞os′) *n.* The side of a right triangle opposite the right angle: *The teacher told the students to find the hypotenuse of the triangle.*

hy·po·thet·i·cal (hī′ pə **thĕt′** ĭ kəl) *adj.* Based on a theory; theoretical: *The hypothetical explanation sounded logical even though it had not been proven.* **—hy′ po·thet′ i·cal·ly** *adj.*

I

ig·ni·tion (ĭg **nĭsh′** ən) *n.* The act or process of setting on fire, burning, or catching on fire: *The ignition of the gasoline caused a terrible fire.*

im·merse (ĭ **mûrs′**) *v.* **im·mersed, im·mers·ing, im·mers·es. 1.** To completely cover with water or other liquid; submerge: *When it is very hot, it is refreshing to immerse oneself in a swimming pool.* **2.** To involve deeply; absorb: *A wonderful way to spend a rainy afternoon is to immerse oneself in a good book.*

im·mor·tal (ĭ **môr′** tl) *adj.* **1.** Living forever; never dying: *Human beings are not immortal.* **2.** Remembered or having eternal fame: *The words of the Declaration of Independence are immortal.*

im·pair (ĭm **pâr′**) *v.* To weaken or make worse the quality, strength, or quantity of; damage: *After I was hit in the eye by a ball, my eyesight was impaired.* **—im·pair′ ment** *n.*

im·pas·sive (ĭm **păs′** ĭv) *adj.* Not showing or feeling emotion: *The accused burglar was impassive as the verdict was read.* **—im·pas′ sive·ly** *adv.* **—im·pas′ sive·ness** *n.*

im·plore (ĭm **plôr′**) *v.* **im·plored, im·plor·ing, im·plores. 1.** To plead with; earnestly ask: *The child implored her mother for the new toy.* **2.** To plead, beg, or ask earnestly for: *He implored understanding from his friend.*

im·promp·tu (ĭm **prŏmp′** to͞o *or* ĭm **prŏmp′** tyo͞o) *adj.* Spoken, made, or done without previous preparation; offhand: *I planned to be only a spectator at the dedication, but instead I gave an impromptu speech.*

im·pulse (**ĭm′** pŭls′) *n.* **1.** A sudden urge or force that makes a person act without thinking: *I was so happy that I had an impulse to laugh out loud.* **2.** A driving force that causes motion.

in·ar·tic·u·late (ĭn′ är **tĭk′** yə lĭt) *adj.* **1.** Not clearly pronounced or spoken: *The inarticulate speech was impossible to understand.* **2.** Unable to express oneself clearly or meaningfully: *The contestant was so nervous that she was inarticulate.* **—in′ ar·tic′ u·late·ly** *adv.* **in′ ar·tic′ u·late·ness** *n.*

in·car·cer·a·tion (ĭn kär′ sər **ā′** shən) *n.* Imprisonment: *The incarceration of the convicted criminal lasted for ten years.*

in·clem·ent (ĭn **klĕm′** ənt) *adj.* Stormy; rough; severe: *The inclement weather forced the closing of many schools.* **—in·clem′ en·cy** *n.*

in·con·spic·u·ous (ĭn′ kən **spĭk′** yo͞o əs) *adj.* Attracting little attention; not noticeable; not easily seen: *The shy boy wanted to be inconspicuous in the crowded room.*

in·dig·nant (ĭn **dĭg′** nənt) *adj.* Angry because of something unfair, cruel, evil, or unworthy: *Many people were indignant about the abuse of the dog.* **—in·dig′ nant·ly** *adv.*

in·dis·creet (ĭn dĭ **skrēt′**) *adj.* Not showing good judgment or tact; unwise: *Leon lost his job because he made indiscreet statements.* **—in′ dis·creet′ ly** *adv.* **—in′ dis·creet′ ness** *n.*

in·duc·tion (ĭn **dŭk′** shən) *n.* The process or ceremony of being formally installed in office or brought into a group: *The induction of class officers is held at the beginning of the school year.*

in·flu·en·tial (ĭn′ flo͞o **ĕn′** shəl) *adj.* Having or exercising the power to produce an effect on or change an event: *Many people think that television programs have become too influential in the lives of young people.* **—in′ flu·en′ tial·ly** *adv.*

in·sig·nif·i·cant (ĭn sĭg **nĭf′** ĭ kənt) *adj.* **1.** Of little or no importance or meaning: *The babbling of the baby was insignificant.* **2.** Small in size, amount, or value: *The number of people at the meeting was insignificant.* **—in′ sig·nif′ i·cance** *n.* **—in′ sig·nif′ i·cant·ly** *adv.*

in·tent·ly (ĭn **tĕnt′** lē) *adv.* With close attention: *The baby intently watched his mother's every move.*

in·var·i·a·bly (ĭn **vâr′** ē ə blē) *adv.* Goes on constantly without change: *The teacher invariably will call on me when I don't know the answer to the question.*

in·ver·sion (ĭn **vûr′** zhən *or* ĭn **vûr′** shən) *n.* **1.** The act of turning upside down or the state of being turned upside down: *The inversion of the hummingbird feeder allowed the liquid to slowly drip into the bowl.* **2.** Something that is turned upside down.

in·vul·ner·a·ble (ĭn **vŭl′** nər ə bəl) *adj.* Impossible to harm, injure, or attack: *The castle was invulnerable because of the moat around it.* **—in·vul′ ner·a·bil′ i·ty** *n.*

ir·ra·tion·al (ĭ **răsh′** ə nəl) *adj.* **1.** Not able to reason or think clearly: *The survivors of the plane crash were irrational for several hours.* **2.** Not based on reason; senseless; absurd: *The child had an irrational fear of the dark.* **—ir·ra′ tion·al·ly** *adv.*

ir·re·deem·a·ble (ĭr′ ĭ **dē′** mə bəl) *adj.* **1.** Not able to be changed or reformed; hopeless: *The irredeemable shopper went to the malls every Saturday.* **2.** That cannot be brought back or paid off: *The expired coupon is irredeemable.*

ir·ref·u·ta·ble (ĭ **rĕf′** yə tə bəl *or* ĭr ĭ **fyo͞o′** tə bəl) *adj.* Impossible to prove wrong or false: *The astronomer claimed that the discovery of the comet was irrefutable.* **—ir·ref′ u·ta·bly** *adv.*

ir·rel·e·vant (ĭ **rĕl′** ə vənt) *adj.* Not having any connection with the matter at hand; beside the point: *The question about the movie was irrelevant to our discussion of sports.* **—ir·rel′ e·vance** *n.* **—ir·rel′ e·vant·ly** *adv.*

ir·re·triev·a·ble (ĭr ī **trē**′və bəl) *adj.* Difficult or impossible to get back or recover: *The family pictures were irretrievable after the fire.*

J

jour·ney·man (**jûr**′nē mən) *n.* A person who has completed training, is skilled in a trade or craft, and works for another person: *It was obvious that the carpenter was a journeyman because his work was excellent.*

jo·vi·al (**jō**′vē əl) *adj.* Full of fun and playful good humor; jolly: *The jovial speaker soon had her audience laughing.* **—jo′vi·al′i·ty** *n.* **jo′vi·al·ly** *adv.*

K

Ko·ran (kə **răn′** *or* kə **rän′**) *n.* The sacred book of Islam, containing the religious and moral code: *The Muslims study the Koran.*

ko·sher (**kō**′shər) *adj.* Conforming to or prepared according to Jewish dietary laws: *The woman bought kosher meat at the market.*

L

la·bo·ri·ous (lə **bôr**′ē əs) *adj.* Difficult and demanding; requiring hard work: *Building the scenery for the play was laborious work.* **la·bo′ri·ous·ly** *adv.* **—la·bo′ri·ous·ness** *n.*

lack·ey (**lăk**′ē) *n., pl.* **lack·eys.** A person who takes or follows orders in the manner of a servant: *The woman wanted a job where she could make decisions and not just be a lackey.*

lack·lus·ter (**lăk**′lŭs′tər) *adj.* Lacking brightness, brilliance, or interest; dull; boring: *The new movie did poorly at the box-office because of the actors' lackluster performance.*

lag·gard (**lăg**′ərd) *n.* A person who falls behind and does not keep up: *The track team lost the meet because the laggard lost his race.* —*adj.* Falling behind; slow: *The laggard hiker got lost.*

la·i·ty (**lā**′ĭ tē) *n.* Members of a religious group that are not the officials: *The laity of the church met to choose a new pastor.*

lame duck (**lām** dŭk) *n.* **1.** An elected official who has not been reelected but continues to hold office until the successor takes over: *Because he was a lame duck, the governor did not introduce any new legislation.* **2.** A weak or useless person: *After I announced my retirement I felt like a lame duck.*

lam·poon (lăm **pōōn′**) *n.* A piece of writing that uses humor, irony, or exaggeration to make fun of or attack someone or something: *Even though the lampoon of the city council meeting was funny, it upset some people.* —*v.* To make fun of with a lampoon.

lar·ce·nous (**lär**′sə nəs) *adj.* Of, relating to, or involving the theft of another person's property: *The criminal was sentenced to five years in prison for larcenous crimes.*

lar·ynx (**lăr**′ĭngks) *n., pl.* **la·ryn·ges** (lə **rin**′jez) or **lar·ynx·es.** The structure at the upper end of the windpipe, containing the vocal cords: *Because of an injury to my larynx, I couldn't talk.*

las·civ·i·ous (lə **sĭv**′ē əs) *adj.* Feeling or showing strong sexual desire; containing sexual material; obscene; indecent: *The lascivious movie was rated R.* **—las·civ′i·ous·ly** *adv.*

lech·er·ous (**lĕch**′ər əs) *adj.* Given to, characterized by, or showing excessive sexual desire or activity; lewd: *The woman sued the man for his lecherous behavior.*

le·sion (**lē**′zhən) *n.* A wound, injury, or abnormal change of an organ or tissue: *The lesion on the toddler's head was caused when he fell and hit his head on the sidewalk.*

le·thal (**lē**′thəl) *adj.* Causing or capable of causing death; deadly: *A lethal injection of poison was the cause of death.*

li·a·bil·i·ty (lī′ə **bĭl**′ĭ tē) *n., pl.* **li·a·bil·i·ties.** Something for which one is legally responsible, especially an obligation to pay a debt: *When planning a budget, one needs to know what liabilities one has.*

lib·er·a·tion (lĭb′ə **rā**′shən) *n.* The act of setting free or the state of being set free: *The liberation of the prisoners from the Bastille in Paris, France, marked the beginning of the French Revolution.*

lien (lēn *or* **lē**′ən) *n.* A legal claim on another's property for payment of a debt: *The remodeling company placed a lien on the house because the homeowner refused to pay the bill.*

lig·a·ment (**lĭg**′ə mənt) *n.* A band of strong tissue that connects two bones or holds organs in place: *The athlete needed knee surgery to repair the torn ligaments.*

Lil·li·pu·tian (lĭl′ə **pyōō**′shən) *adj.* Tiny: *The Lilliputian dolls were so small that they fit in the palm of the baby's hand.*

lim·er·ick (**lĭm**′ər ĭk) *n.* A humorous five-line poem with the rhyme scheme of *aabba*: *The limericks were such funny poems that we couldn't stop laughing.*

lin·e·ar (**lĭn**′ē ər) *adj.* **1.** Of, relating to, made, or using a line or lines: *The linear drawing of the house was done in ink.* **2.** Relating to length: *The linear measurement of the room is fifteen feet.*

li·on·ize (lī′ə nīz′) *v.* **li·on·ized, li·on·iz·ing, li·on·iz·es.** To treat as a very important person: *People lionize Olympic athletes.*

loath·some (**lōth**′səm *or* **lōth**′səm) *adj.* Extremely hateful or disgusting; detestable: *Being cruel to pets is loathsome.*

lux·u·ri·ant (lŭg **zhŏŏr**′ē ənt *or* lŭk **shŏŏr**′ē ənt) *adj.* Growing vigorously and abundantly: *The luxuriant flower garden has dozens of healthy plants.*

M

mam·moth (**măm**′əth) *n.* A very large extinct prehistoric elephant that had long tusks and thick shaggy hair. —*adj.* Huge; giganic: *It took a month to complete the mammoth research project.*

ma·ni·a·cal (mə **nī**′ə kəl) *adj.* Mentally ill; insane; mad: *The maniacal behavior was the result of a reaction to a drug.*

man·u·script (**măn**′yə skrĭpt′) *n.* **1.** A book or document written or copied by hand: *The original manuscript of the Declaration of Independence is carefully preserved.* **2.** The handwritten, typewritten, or computer-produced version of a book or article that is submitted for publication.

mar·i·tal (**măr**′ĭ tl) *adj.* Relating to marriage: *The husband and wife attended a class on marital happiness.*

mar·row (**măr**′ō) *n.* The soft, fatty tissue that fills the cavities inside most bones and that produces blood cells: *The doctor recommended a bone marrow transplant in order to cure the disease.*

mar·tial (**mär**′shəl) *adj.* **1.** Related to war, the armed forces, or the military life: *The cadet took martial training for six months.* **2.** Warlike; like a warrior.

mec·ca (**mĕk**′ə) *n.* A place that is the center of important activity or interest: *The space center is a mecca for those who want to be astronauts.*

med·dle (**mĕd**′l) *v.* **med·dled, med·dling, med·dles.** To interfere in the business or affairs of other people: *A good friend will not meddle in her friend's business.*

med·dle·some (**mĕd**′l səm) *adj.* Tending to interfere in the business or affairs of other people: *The girl told her meddlesome friend to mind her own business.*

me·dic·i·nal (mĭ **dĭs**′ə nəl) *adj.* Having the ability to act like a medicine: *Native Americans knew the medicinal qualities of many plants.*

mel·an·chol·y (**mĕl**′ən kŏl′e) *adj.* **1.** Sad; depressed; gloomy: *The people were melancholy as they left the funeral.* **2.** Causing sadness: *The melancholy poem made the reader cry.* —*n.* Sadness; depression.

me·ni·al (**mē**′nē əl *or* **mēn**′yəl) *adj.* Lowly; degrading: *The teenager did menial jobs like sweeping the floors and emptying the trash.*

me·no·rah (mə **nôr**′ə) *n.* A candleholder, traditionally with seven or nine branches, used in Jewish religious ceremonies: *The lighting of the menorah is an important part of the Hanukkah celebration.*

me·tab·o·lism (mĭ **tăb**′ə lĭz′əm) *n.* The chemical and physical processes by which a living thing maintains life. Metabolism is the body's process by which food is changed into the energy necessary to carry on all basic life processes.

me·tal·lic (mə **tăl**′ĭk) *adj.* Of, relating to, or having the qualities of metals, such as lead, copper, iron, and similar elements: *The fall leaves sometimes have a metallic gleam.*

met·tle (**mĕt**′l) *n.* **1.** Courage; daring; spirit: *The mettle of the movie's hero was an inspiration to all the characters.* **2.** The basic character or quality of a person: *A test of a person's mettle is how he or she deals with problems.*

mold (mōld) *v.* To work into a particular shape or form: *The sculptor began to mold the clay into a vase.* —*n.* **1.** A hollow form used for shaping something. **2.** Something made in a mold.

mor·al (**môr**′əl *or* **mŏr**′əl) *n.* A lesson or principle taught by a fable, event, or story: *The moral of the story is that winning takes hard work.* —*adj.* Relating to a standard of right and wrong: *The class discussed whether or not the actions of the story's main character were moral.*

mo·rale (mə **răl**′) *n.* The state of a person's or group's spirit, attitude, or mental state with respect to qualities like cheerfulness, courage, or confidence: *After winning three games in a row, the team's morale was very high.*

mor·tal·i·ty (môr **tăl**′ĭ tē) *n., pl.* **mor·tal·i·ties.** The condition or state of being subject to death: *Daredevils seem not to worry about their mortality.*

mor·ti·cian (môr **tĭsh**′ən) *n.* Someone who arranges funerals and prepares dead people for burial; funeral director; undertaker: *The mortician arranged the funeral for my grandmother.*

mosque (mŏsk) *n.* A Muslim place, house, or temple of worship: *The mosque was filled with worshipers.*

mul·lah (**mŭl**′ə *or* **mŏŏl**′ə) *n.* A male religious teacher or leader: *The mullah interpreted the religious law for the people.*

mun·dane (mŭn **dān**′ *or* **mŭn**′dān′) *adj.* Common; ordinary: *Sometimes doing mundane tasks like weeding the garden will help relieve stress.*

mu·ta·tion (myo͞o **tā**′shən) *n.* **1.** A change in genes or chromosomes of living things that can be inherited by their offspring: *The mutation of the gene was responsible for the disease.* **2.** A change: *Mutation of languages happens slowly.*

N

nar·cis·sism (**när**′sĭ sĭz′əm) *n.* Too much love or admiration for oneself; self-love: *The boy's narcissism was annoying because he constantly bragged about himself.*

nep·o·tism (**nĕp**′ə tĭz′əm) *n.* The giving of favors or jobs to relatives by someone in an official or high office: *When the senator gave his son a job, he was accused of nepotism.*

neu·tral·ize (**no͞o**′trə līz′ *or* **nyo͞o**′trə līz′) *v.* **neu·tral·ized, neu·tral·iz·ing, neu·tral·iz·es.** To make powerless or counteract the effect or force of: *The medicine was able to neutralize the effects of the wasp sting.*

O

of·fen·sive (ə **fĕn**′sĭv) *adj.* **1.** Causing resentment, anger, or displeasure; insulting: *The offensive remark was inexcusable.* **2.** Unpleasant or disagreeable to the senses: *The smell of the rotten eggs was offensive.* **—of·fen′sive·ly** *adv.*

o·rig·i·nate (ə **rĭj**′ə nāt′) *v.* **o·rig·i·nat·ed, o·rig·i·nat·ing, o·rig·i·nates.** To start, bring, or come into being: *Many everyday products were originated for the space program.*

or·tho·pe·dic (ôr′thə **pē**′dĭk) *adj.* Of, relating, or used in the branch of medicine that corrects or treats disorders, diseases, or injuries of the bones, tendons, ligaments, muscles, and joints: *An orthopedic doctor often treats athletes who injure their bones, ligaments, or muscles.*

P

pal·lid (**păl**′ĭd) *adj.* Lacking color; pale: *The roller coaster ride was so frightening that many riders were pallid when they got off of it.*

pan·de·mo·ni·um (păn′də **mō**′nē əm) *n.* Wild disorder, confusion, and noise; uproar: *After the football team won the championship, there was pandemonium in the stadium.*

par·a·sit·ic (păr′ə **sĭt**′ĭk) *adj.* Of or like a parasite, which is an animal or plant that lives on or in another animal or plant from which it gets its food: *A parasitic person takes advantage of another person for his or her own good.*

peal (pēl) *n.* **1.** A loud ringing of bells: *The peal of the church bells announced that the wedding was about to begin.* **2.** A loud burst of sound or noise: *A peal of laughter followed the comedian's joke.*

per·il·ous (**pĕr**′ə ləs) *adj.* Dangerous; hazardous: *The canoe trip over the steep falls was perilous.*

per·son·i·fied (pər **sŏn**′ə fīd′) *v.* Past tense of **personify.**

per·son·i·fy (pər **sŏn**′ə fī′) *v.* **per·son·i·fied, per·son·i·fy·ing, per·son·i·fies. 1.** To typify or be the perfect example of something, such as a quality or idea. *The child's laughter personified everyone's enjoyment of the fair.* **2.** To give human qualities to an idea or thing: *Some people personify their plants by talking to them.*

per·vade (pər **vād**′) *v.* **per·vad·ed, per·vad·ing, per·vades.** To spread or be present throughout: *The odor from the barbecue pervaded the park.*

phy·sique (fĭ **zēk**′) *n.* The form, development, and appearance of the body: *Hercules had a muscular physique.*

pit·fall (**pĭt**′fôl′) *n., pl.* **pit·falls. 1.** Hidden or unsuspected danger or difficulty: *Without careful planning, a traveler can run into many pitfalls.* **2.** A hidden hole dug into to the ground to trap animals.

pol·y·gon (**pŏl**′ē gŏn′) *n.* A closed geometric figure having three or more straight lines: *A rectangle is a polygon, but not all polygons are rectangles.*

post·mor·tem (pōst **môr**′təm) *n.* A medical examination of a dead body to find out the cause of death; autopsy: *After the man died suddenly, a postmortem was done.* —*adj.* Happening or done after death: *The postmortem examination revealed he died of a heart attack.*

po·ten·tial (pə **tĕn**′shəl) *n.* Possibility: *The potential for thunderstorms was increased by very hot humid weather.* —*adj.* Capable of being but not yet actual: *The talented actor is a potential star.*

pre·pon·der·ance (prĭ **pŏn**′dər əns) *n.* Superiority in number, weight, force, importance, influence, or power: *The preponderance of evidence showed that the accused person was guilty.*

pri·mar·i·ly (prī **mâr**′ə lē *or* prī **mĕr**′ə lē) *adv.* Mainly; chiefly; principally: *The radio station primarily plays classical music.*

probe (prōb) *v.* **probed, prob·ing, probes.** To investigate, explore, or examine thoroughly: *The aviation experts probed the cause of the airline crash.* —*n.* **1.** A thorough investigation: *The probe of the crime ended in an arrest.* **2.** A device, exploratory action, or expedition used for exploration or investigation: *The space probe on Mars was a huge success.*

pro·lif·er·a·tion (prə lĭf′ ə **rā′**shən) *n.* A rapid increase in number or growth: *In the past few years there has been a proliferation of people interested in the Internet.*

prom·i·nent (**prŏm′**ə nənt) *adj.* **1.** Very noticeable; conspicuous: *The Arch is a prominent feature of the St. Louis riverfront.* **2.** Well-known; distinguished: *The Chief Justice is a prominent member of the Supreme Court.* **prom′i·nent·ly** *adv.*

prompt (prŏmpt) *v.* To encourage, urge, or inspire to action: *My success in the local contest prompted me to enter the state contest.* —*adj.* Being on time: *I am always prompt for an appointment.* —**prompt′ly** *adv.* —**prompt′ness** *n.*

pro·pel (prə **pĕl′**) *v.* **pro·pelled, pro·pel·ling, pro·pels.** To cause to move forward or to keep in motion: *Wind in the sails propels a sailboat.*

pro·por·tion (prə **pôr′**shən) *n.* **1.** The relationship in size, amount, or degree of one thing to another: *The proportion of girls to boys in the class is the same.* **2. proportions.** Size; dimensions: *The number of hungry people in the world is of huge proportions.*

pro·pul·sion (prə **pŭl′**shən) *n.* **1.** A force that drives forward: *A strong push was the propulsion that the go-cart needed.* **2.** The act of driving forward.

pro·trude (prō **trōōd′**) *v.* **pro·trud·ed, pro·trud·ing, pro·trudes.** To stick out or cause to stick out: *The jogger hit his head on a branch that protruded from a tree.*

pro·vi·sion (prə **vĭzh′**ən) *n.* **1.** The act of giving, providing, or supplying: *The students appreciated the provision of computers in all classrooms by the parent organization.* **2.** Something that is provided. **3. provisions.** Supplies of food and other necessities: *The astronauts had enough provisions for a ten-day space trip.*

pul·mo·nar·y (**pōōl′**mə nĕr′ ē *or* **pŭl′**mə nĕr′ ē) *adj.* Of, relating to, or affecting the lungs: *The pulmonary disease caused difficulty in breathing.*

pulse (pŭls) *n.* **1.** The regular expansion and contraction of the arteries caused by the beating of the heart as it pumps blood through them: *My pulse was rapid after the race.* **2.** A regular beating. —*v.* **pulsed, puls·ing, puls·es.** To beat regularly.

Q

quench (kwĕnch) *v.* **quenched, quench·ing, quench·es. 1.** To satisfy: *The canoe trip over the rapids did not quench my desire for adventure.* **2.** To put out; extinguish: *The rain quenched the forest fire.*

quis·ling (**kwĭz′**lĭng) *n.* A person who aids an invading enemy; traitor: *After the war the quisling was found guilty of treason.*

R

ra·di·ant (**rā′**dē ənt) *adj.* **1.** Giving off light or heat; shining brightly: *The radiant sunlight cheered the patients in the hospital.* **2.** Showing or filled with joy, happiness, pleasure, or brightness: *My brother's radiant smile indicated that he had been accepted to the summer camp.* **ra′di·ant·ly** *adv.*

ran·sack (**răn′**săk′) *v.* To search through, damage, and leave in disorder in order to rob of valuables: *The thieves ransacked the jewelry store.*

rash·ly (**răsh′**lē) *adv.* Recklessly; hastily: *The mountain climbers acted rashly and did not take the necessary safety precautions.*

ra·tion (**răsh′**ən *or* **rā′**shən) *v.* To give out in fixed portions: *Water was rationed because of the severe drought.* —*n.* A fixed amount or share: *The refugee's ration of food was just enough.*

re·buff (rĭ **bŭf′**) *v.* To reject or drive away: *The army was able to rebuff the enemy.* —*n.* A blunt or sudden rejection or response: *My classmate's rebuff hurt my feelings.*

re·ces·sion (rĭ **sĕsh′**ən) *n.* **1.** The act of going back or away; withdrawal: *The recession of the glaciers at the end of the Ice Age took thousands of years.* **2.** An extended period of economic decline.

re·count (rĭ **kount′**) *v.* To tell in detail; relate; narrate: *The swimmer recounted her adventure of swimming across the English Channel.*

re·cu·per·a·tion (rĭ kōō′ pə **rā′**shən) *n.* The act of gaining back health or strength; recovery: *My recuperation after the accident took a long time.*

ref·or·ma·tion (rĕf′ ər **mā′**shən) *n.* The act of changing, improving, or correcting by giving up harmful ways or defects: *The judge was amazed by the reformation of the criminal.*

re·fur·bish (rē **fûr′**bĭsh) *v.* **re·fur·bished, re·fur·bish·ing, re·fur·bish·es.** To make fresh and bright again; renovate: *Even though the old car runs well, the body needs to be refurbished.*

re·gen·er·ate (rĭ **jĕn′**ə rāt′) *v.* **re·gen·er·at·ed, re·gen·er·at·ing, re·gen·er·ates. 1.** To give new life, strength, or energy to; revive: *A vacation helps to regenerate a person's enthusiasm for work.* **2.** To grow again or replace: *Some animals are able to regenerate parts of their bodies.*

re·it·er·ate (rē **ĭt′**ə rāt′) *v.* **re·it·er·at·ed, re·it·er·at·ing, re·it·er·ates.** To say or do over again or repeatedly; repeat: *The teacher reiterated the instructions for the test.*

re·luc·tant (rĭ **lŭk′**tənt) *adj.* Unwilling: *The dog is reluctant to go down the stairs.* **—re·luc′tance** *n.* **—re·luc′tant·ly** *adv.*

re·peal (rĭ **pēl′**) *v.* To cancel or withdraw officially: *The judge ruled that the law violated the First Amendment and should be repealed.*

re·pug·nant (rĭ **pŭg′**nənt) *adj.* Causing dislike or disgust; offensive; distasteful: *The smell of the rotten oranges was repugnant.*

re·pulse (rĭ **pŭls′**) *v.* **re·pulsed, re·puls·ing, re·puls·es. 1.** To drive back: *The offensive line of the football team was able to repulse the rival team on the third down.* **2.** To refuse to accept with rudeness: *The unfriendly girl repulsed her classmates' offer to join them at lunch.* —*n.* A rejection.

re·splen·dent (rĭ **splĕn′**dənt) *adj.* Dazzling; brilliant; beautiful; splendid: *The fireworks display was resplendent.*

res·to·ra·tion (rĕs′tə **rā′**shən) *n.* **1.** The act of bringing back to an original or former condition or state: *The restoration of the Sistine Chapel has taken years.* **2.** Something that is or has been brought back to an original condition: *We visited a restoration of a one-room schoolhouse.*

re·tail (**rē′**tāl′) *n.* The sale of goods in small amounts or individually directly to the public: *The retail of back-to-school items is profitable in August.*

S

sa·dis·tic (sə **dĭs′**tĭk) *adj.* Relating to or showing pleasure in being cruel: *The sadistic child likes to tease the hungry dog with food.*

sanc·tu·ar·y (**săngk′**cho͞o ĕr′ē) *n., pl.* **sanc·tu·ar·ies. 1.** A holy or sacred place, such as a church, temple, or mosque: *The worshipers were very quiet in the sanctuary.* **2.** A safe place: *The basement is a sanctuary during a tornado.* **3.** An area where animals are protected by law: *Animals are safe in the sanctuary because no hunting is allowed.*

scape·goat (**skāp′**gōt′) *n.* A person, group, or thing that unjustly bears the blame for the mistakes or wrongdoings of others: *The older brother was the scapegoat for the damage done by the younger brother.*

scath·ing (**skā′***thĭng*) *adj.* Severely or harshly critical: *The scathing editorial criticized the mayor for closing the city hospital.*

scoff (skŏf *or* skôf) *v.* To express contempt for or make fun of as unimportant; ridicule; mock: *Some students scoff at the importance of good grades until they apply to colleges.* —*n.* A mocking expression.

scorn (skôrn) *v.* To refuse or reject because of a feeling that a person or thing is inferior or unworthy: *The girl scorned help from people she didn't respect.* —*n.* A strong feeling of dislike or contempt for a person or thing considered low, bad, or unworthy: *The man felt scorn for the person who lied to him.*

self-ef·fac·ing (sĕlf′ĭ **fā′**sĭng) *adj.* Keeping oneself in the background; modest: *Even though the actress won an Oscar, she was self-effacing.*

sen·ior·i·ty (sēn **yôr′**ĭ tē *or* sēn **yŏr′**ĭ tē) *n.* The state of being more advanced than others in age, rank, or length of service: *The teacher who had taught ten years had more seniority than the beginning teacher.*

ser·pen·tine (**sûr′**pən tēn′ *or* **sûr′**pən tīn′) *adj.* Having many bends and curves; winding like a snake's body: *We had to drive very slowly on the serpentine mountain road.*

sheep·ish (**shē′**pĭsh) *adj.* **1.** Embarrassed: *When Lisa realized her silly mistake, she gave a sheepish grin.* **2.** Shy; timid: *Nobody noticed his sheepish entrance into the room.* **—sheep′ish·ly** *adv.*

shrewd (shro͞od) *adj.* Clever, sharp, or quick-witted, especially in practical matters: *The shrewd politician was able to convince the voters that the popular law was her idea.* **—shrewd′ly** *adv.* **—shrewd′ness** *n.*

sin·ew (**sĭn′**yo͞o) *n.* A tough tissue that connects a muscle to a bone; tendon: *By exercising regularly I was able to improve the sinews in my upper arms.*

skep·ti·cal (**skĕp′**tĭ kəl) *adj.* Doubting; disbelieving: *The mother was skeptical of her daughter's excuse for being late.* **—skep′ti·cal·ly** *adv.*

slov·en·ly (**slŭv′**ən lē) *adj.* Untidy, sloppy, or careless, especially in dress or manner: *The child's slovenly appearance was an indication that something was wrong.*

slug·gish (**slŭg′**ĭsh) *adj.* **1.** Without energy, alertness, or vigor: *Sometimes too much sleep can make a person feel sluggish.* **2.** Slow: *The water is sluggish to drain from the sink.* **—slug′gish·ly** *adv.* **—slug′gish·ness** *n.*

snob·bish (**snŏb′**ĭsh) *adj.* Characteristic of a person who looks down on people that he or she considers as inferior in intelligence, wealth, achievement, or taste: *The snobbish girl made fun of her classmate's clothes.*

so·cia·ble (**sō′**shə bəl) *adj.* Liking to be with others; friendly: *By the end of the party, the sociable man knew all the other guests.* **—so′cia·bil′i·ty** *n.*

so·phis·ti·cat·ed (sə **fĭs′** tĭ kā′ tĭd) *adj.* **1.** Highly complex; elaborate; complicated: *The sophisticated surgery was done with lasers.* **2.** Experienced and worldly-wise: *The sophisticated travelers ate at the best restaurants.*

sta·bil·i·ty (stə **bĭl′** ĭ tē) *n., pl.* **sta·bil·i·ties.** The condition or state of being firm; steadiness: *The highway department is concerned about the stability of old bridges.*

stat·u·esque (stăch′ o͞o **ĕsk′**) *adj.* Like a statue, as in size, dignity, and grace: *The statuesque pose of the model was very impressive.*

stim·u·late (**stĭm′** yə lāt′) *v.* **stim·u·lat·ed, stim·u·lat·ing, stim·u·lates.** To rouse or stir to greater action or effort: *The smell of my favorite food stimulates my appetite.*

stol·id (**stŏl′** ĭd) *adj.* **stol·id·er, stol·id·est.** Having or showing little or no emotion; unexcitable; impassive: *The defendant was stolid when the verdict was announced.*

stren·u·ous (**strĕn′** yo͞o əs) *adj.* Requiring or characterized by great effort or energy: *Everyone in the fitness class was tired after the strenuous workout.* **—stren′u·ous·ly** *adv.*

stu·pen·dous (sto͞o **pĕn′** dəs *or* styo͞o **pĕn′** dəs) *adj.* Of amazing excellence, force, volume, or degree; marvelous; tremendous; overwhelming: *The fans were awed by the stupendous distance of the homerun.* **—stu·pen′dous·ly** *adv.*

sub·con·scious (sŭb **kŏn′** shəs) *adj.* **1.** Existing in the mind, but the person is only partially aware that it is there: *Even though I had a lot to do, I had a subconscious wish to play.* **2.** Not completely conscious. *—n.* The part of the mind that keeps experiences and feelings below the conscious level. **—sub·con′scious·ly** *adv.*

sub·due (səb **do͞o′** *or* səb **dyo͞o′**) *v.* **sub·dued, sub·du·ing, sub·dues. 1.** To bring under control: *The zookeepers subdued the angry elephant.* **2.** To conquer: *The army troops subdued the enemy.* **3.** To lessen the intensity; tone down: *The parents asked their children to subdue their noise.*

sub·mis·sion (səb **mĭsh′** ən) *n.* The act of yielding or surrendering to the power or authority of another: *Germany's submission at the end of World War II ended the war in Europe.*

sub·or·di·nate (sə **bôr′** dn ĭt) *adj.* Lower in rank, importance, or order: *The salesman took a subordinate job because he needed money.* *—n.* A person or thing that is less in rank, importance or order. *—v.* (sə **bor′** dn āt) To put in a place of lower rank, importance, or order.

sub·ser·vi·ent (səb **sûr′** vē ənt) *adj.* Overly willing to obey or yield to others: *The boss wanted the employees to express themselves rather than be subservient.* **—sub·ser′vi·ence** *n.*

sub·ver·sion (səb **vûr′** zhən *or* səb **vûr′** shən) *n.* The act of overthrowing or destroying something: *The traitors were arrested before they could carry out their planned subversion of the government.*

sul·len (**sŭl′** ən) *adj.* Sulky, withdrawn, or gloomy because of anger or a bad mood; glum: *Whenever the child didn't get his way, he became sullen.* **—sul′len·ly** adv. **—sul′len·ness** *n.*

su·per·fi·cial (so͞o′ pər **fĭsh′** əl) *adj.* **1.** Being near the surface: *The superficial cut healed quickly.* **2.** Not thorough; shallow: *The audience was disappointed by the superficial interview with the mayor.* **—su′ per·fi′ ci·al′ i·ty** *n.*

su·per·im·pose (so͞o′ pər ĭm **pōz′**) *v.* **su·per·im·posed, su·per·im·pos·ing, su·per·im·pos·es.** To lay or place (something) over or on top of something else: *To show the correct answers, the teacher superimposed the answer key over the questions.*

su·per·la·tive (so͞o **pûr′** lə tĭv) *adj.* Superior to all others; of the highest degree: *Some gardeners think that roses are superlative flowers.*

su·per·nat·u·ral (so͞o′ pər **năch′** ər əl) *adj.* Relating to existence beyond the power of the natural world, specifically involving something spiritual or divine: *Since there was not a scientific explanation for the bright light in the sky, the author gave a supernatural explanation.*

sym·me·try (**sĭm′** ĭ trē) *n., pl.* **sym·me·tries.** An exact arrangement so that parts are matching and balanced on either side of a central line: *The symmetry of the paintings is pleasing to the eye.*

symp·tom (**sĭm′** təm *or* **sĭmp′** təm) *n.* **1.** A sign or indication that a disease or disorder exists: *Weakness was the first symptom of the illness.* **2.** A sign or indication that something exists: *The big brown spot was a symptom that something was wrong with the lawn.*

syn·on·y·mous (sĭ **nŏn′** ə məs) *adj.* Having the same or very similar meaning: *The words* investigate *and* examine *are synonymous.*

T

tac·tic (**tăk′** tĭk) *n.* A plan for achieving a goal: *My tactic for getting into better shape is to walk two miles a day.*

tan·ta·lize (**tăn′** tə līz′) *v.* **tan·ta·lized, tan·ta·liz·ing, tan·ta·liz·es.** To tease by tempting with something desired but out of reach: *My friend likes to tantalize me by talking about food when I am hungry.*

tem·po·rar·y (**tĕm′** pə rĕr′ ē) *adj.* Lasting for a limited time; not permanent: *The job was temporary and would last only for the summer.*

ten·den·cy (**tĕn′** dən sē) *n., pl.* **ten·den·cies. 1.** A trend or direction: *The tendency to use more convenience foods is growing.* **2.** A natural or usual inclination to act or behave in a certain way: *Latasha has a tendency to copy her older sister.*

tol·er·ate (**tŏl′** ə rāt′) *v.* **tol·er·at·ed, tol·er·at·ing, tol·er·ates. 1.** To accept; to put up with: *People who work in unskilled jobs may have to tolerate low salaries.* **2.** To allow; permit: *Teachers often tolerate lots of noise during recess.*

tran·si·to·ry (**trăn′** sĭ tôr′ ē *or* **trăn′** zĭ tôr′ ē) *adj.* Lasting only a short time; brief: *Even though the vacation was transitory, it was enjoyable.*

tril·o·gy (**trĭl′** ə jē) *n., pl.* **tril·o·gies.** A group of three related plays, operas, novels, or other dramatic or literary works that make up a series: *The author wrote a trilogy of mystery novels.*

tri·pod (**trī′** pŏd′) *n.* An adjustable three-legged stand or support: *I put the camera on a tripod so it would be stable.*

tri·um·vi·rate (trī **ŭm′** vər ĭt) *n.* Government by three persons who share authority, as in ancient Rome: *The triumvirate did not last because the three rulers did not trust each other.*

U

u·ni·fi·ca·tion (yo͞o′ nə fĭ **kā′** shən) *n.* A joining together into a single unit: *The destruction of the Berlin Wall marked the unification of Germany.*

u·ni·lat·er·al (yo͞o′ nə **lăt′** ər əl) *adj.* Of, affecting, or done by only one side: *The unilateral withdrawal of troops ended the conflict.* **—u′ ni·lat′ er·al·ly** *adv.*

u·nique (yo͞o **nēk′**) *adj.* **1.** One of a kind: *Each snowflake is unique.* **2.** Without an equal: *Shakespeare's plays and poems are unique.* **—u·nique′ ly** *adv.* **—u·nique′ ness** *n.*

u·ni·ver·sal (yo͞o′ nə **vûr′** səl) *adj.* Present or existing everywhere: *Universal peace is a worthy goal.* **—u′ ni·ver·sal′ i·ty** *n.* **—u′ ni·ver′ sal·ly** *adv.*

un·ten·a·ble (ŭn **tĕn′** ə bəl) *adj.* Not capable of being supported or defended: *The girl realized that her argument was untenable.*

u·to·pi·an (yo͞o **tō′** pē ən) *adj.* **1.** Of, relating to, or like a perfect place where people live together in peace and happiness: *People would like to live in a utopian neighborhood.* **2.** Excellent or fine in theory but not possible or practical in reality.

V

ver·mil·ion (vər **mĭl′** yən) *n.* A bright red to reddish-orange color: *The beautiful bird had vermilion feathers.*

vin·dic·tive (vĭn **dĭk′** tĭv) *adj.* Showing or wanting revenge: *After the candidate lost the election, she was vindictive and said mean things about her opponent.* **—vin·dic′ tive·ly** *adv.* **— vin·dic′ tive·ness** *n.*

Word	Lesson
abdicate	24
abhor	24
abhorrent	16
abomination	24
aborigines	24
abort	24
abound	19
abrasive	24
abrupt	24
absolute	24
abstain	24
abuse	24
accentuate	30
accolade	7
accomplished	1
acquiescence	30
acquisition	30
addendum	19
admonish	30
advent	30
adversary	30
affiliate	30
affirm	30
affix	30
affliction	30
agonize	28
alienate	13
ambidextrous	12
ambivalent	12
amicable	2
amorous	1
anecdote	28
antagonize	13
antebellum	15
antecedent	15
antedate	15
anteroom	15
anticlimax	15
antidote	15
antipathy	15
antiseptic	15
antisocial	15
antitoxin	15
appeal	3
appraise	26
apprentice	5
aptitude	5
assets	26
asunder	22
automation	4
awe	28
babel	23
badger	8
banter	35
basilica	11
bastion	22
beastly	8
bedeck	1
berserk	2
beseech	35
biannual	14
bicentennial	12
bicker	35
biennial	14
bilateral	20
bilingual	12
biome	25
blasphemy	35
blighted	32
bovine	8
brawny	1
breach	13
bulbous	20
cajole	28
camouflage	25
capillary	29
citadel	22
classic	31
cleave	10
clergy	11
coerce	35
cohesive	10
colleague	7
comely	32
compel	3
compound interest	26
comprehensive	16
concave	20
confute	34
congeal	34
congestion	34
contrived	19
convex	20
cosigner	26
creditor	26
cultural	13
dank	25
dappled	25
debit	26
decrepit	32
default	26
defiant	2
demise	34
desecration	16
designation	33
despise	10
despondent	2
devastate	7
differentiate	16
disdain	10
disgruntled	2
disguise	1
disintegrate	10
disparity	19
dissection	16
dogged	8
dominate	4
drab	32
drudgery	5
egotistical	17
eliminate	13
elliptical	20
eminent	28
emission	33
enchanted	1
encompass	34
encumbrance	25
enhance	19
ensure	28
eradicate	21
erosion	21
esophagus	29
estrange	21
etiquette	13
evolve	21
exacerbate	21
excavate	34
excel	21
execute	31
expansion	4
expatriate	21
expedient	22
expel	3
extensive	7
exterminate	21
extinct	21
extremity	21
exuberant	2
ferret	25
fervid	34
fickle	10
flexible	4
forage	25
foreclose	26
formidable	22
fury	7
garner	7
generation	6
genetic	6
genial	6
gentry	6
geometric	36
germinate	6
human	14
humane	14
hyperactive	9
hyperbole	9
hyperextension	9
hypersonic	9
hypertension	9
hypochondriac	9
hypocrisy	9
hypodermic	9
hypotenuse	9
hypothetical	9
ignition	33
immerse	34
immortal	6
impair	19
impassive	19
implore	31
impromptu	28
impulse	3

Word List — Lime Book

Word	Lesson
inarticulate	27
incarceration	10
inclement	27
inconspicuous	27
indignant	17
indiscreet	27
induction	33
influential	36
insignificant	4
intently	28
invariably	1
inversion	33
invulnerable	27
irrational	27
irredeemable	27
irrefutable	27
irrelevant	27
irretrievable	27
journeyman	5
jovial	23
Koran	11
kosher	11
laborious	5
lackey	5
lackluster	32
laggard	5
laity	11
lame duck	8
lampoon	35
larcenous	36
larynx	29
lascivious	2
lecherous	36
lesion	29
lethal	16
liability	26
liberation	33
lien	26
ligament	29
Lilliputian	23
limerick	23
linear	20
lionize	8
loathsome	2
luxuriant	25
mammoth	8
maniacal	36
manuscript	28
marital	14
marrow	29
martial	14
mecca	11
meddle	14
meddlesome	2
medicinal	36
melancholy	2
menial	5
menorah	11
metabolism	29
metallic	36
mettle	14

Word	Lesson
mold	10
moral	14
morale	14
mortality	6
mortician	6
mosque	11
mullah	11
mundane	32
mutation	16
narcissism	23
nepotism	5
neutralize	22
offensive	13
originate	31
orthopedic	29
pallid	32
pandemonium	23
parasitic	36
peal	3
perilous	7
personified	31
pervade	34
physique	1
pitfalls	13
polygon	20
postmortem	6
potential	13
preponderance	4
primarily	7
probe	34
proliferation	19
prominent	31
prompt	10
propel	3
proportion	31
propulsion	3
protrude	1
provision	33
pulmonary	29
pulse	3
quench	10
quisling	23
radiant	32
ransack	1
rashly	7
ration	22
rebuff	22
recession	33
recount	19
recuperation	33
reformation	33
refurbish	31
regenerate	6
reiterate	35
reluctant	17
repeal	3
repugnant	16
repulse	3
resplendent	32
restoration	31
retail	4

Word	Lesson
sadistic	23
sanctuary	11
scapegoat	8
scathing	35
scoff	35
scorn	35
self-effacing	17
seniority	5
serpentine	20
sheepish	8
shrewd	28
sinew	29
skeptical	17
slovenly	32
sluggish	8
snobbish	17
sociable	17
sophisticated	16
stability	25
statuesque	20
stimulate	19
stolid	17
strenuous	36
stupendous	25
subconscious	18
subdue	18
submission	18
subordinate	18
subservient	18
subversion	18
sullen	17
superficial	18
superimpose	18
superlative	18
supernatural	18
symmetry	20
symptom	16
synonymous	36
tactic	22
tantalize	23
temporary	4
tendency	4
tolerate	4
transaction	26
transitory	7
trilogy	12
tripod	12
triumvirate	12
unification	12
unilateral	12
unique	12
universal	13
untenable	22
utopian	23
vermilion	31
vindictive	17

Made in the USA
Lexington, KY
25 January 2017

A Rip of Realms

A Shade of Vampire, Book 39

Bella Forrest

Cover design inspired by Sarah Hansen, Okay Creations LLC
Formatting by Polgarus Studio

Also by Bella Forrest:

THE GENDER GAME

The Gender Game (Book 1)
The Gender Secret (Book 2)
The Gender Lie (Book 3)
The Gender War (Book 4)

A SHADE OF
VAMPIRE SERIES:

Series 1:
Derek & Sofia's story:

A Shade of Vampire (Book 1)
A Shade of Blood (Book 2)
A Castle of Sand (Book 3)
A Shadow of Light (Book 4)
A Blaze of Sun (Book 5)
A Gate of Night (Book 6)
A Break of Day (Book 7)

Series 2:
Rose & Caleb's story:

A Shade of Novak (Book 8)
A Bond of Blood (Book 9)
A Spell of Time (Book 10)
A Chase of Prey (Book 11)
A Shade of Doubt (Book 12)
A Turn of Tides (Book 13)
A Dawn of Strength (Book 14)
A Fall of Secrets (Book 15)
An End of Night (Book 16)

Series 3:
Ben & River's story:

A Wind of Change (Book 17)
A Trail of Echoes (Book 18)
A Soldier of Shadows (Book 19)
A Hero of Realms (Book 20)
A Vial of Life (Book 21)
A Fork Of Paths (Book 22)
A Flight of Souls (Book 23)
A Bridge of Stars (Book 24)

Series 4:
A Clan of Novaks

A Clan of Novaks (Book 25)
A World of New (Book 26)
A Web of Lies (Book 27)
A Touch of Truth (Book 28)
An Hour of Need (Book 29)
A Game of Risk (Book 30)
A Twist of Fates (Book 31)
A Day of Glory (Book 32)

Series 5:
A Dawn of Guardians

A Dawn of Guardians (Book 33)
A Sword of Chance (Book 34)

A Race of Trials (Book 35)
A King of Shadow (Book 36)
An Empire of Stones (Book 37)
A Power of Old (Book 38)

A SHADE OF DRAGON:

A Shade of Dragon 1
A Shade of Dragon 2
A Shade of Dragon 3

A SHADE OF KIEV TRILOGY:

A Shade of Kiev 1
A Shade of Kiev 2
A Shade of Kiev 3

BEAUTIFUL MONSTER DUOLOGY:

Beautiful Monster 1
Beautiful Monster 2

DETECTIVE ERIN BOND

(Adult mystery/thriller)

Lights, Camera, GONE
Write, Edit, KILL

For an updated list of Bella's books, please visit her website:
www.bellaforrest.net

Join Bella's VIP email list and she'll personally send you an email reminder as soon as her next book is out! Visit here to sign up:
www.forrestbooks.com

Contents

The "New Generation" Names List

- **Arwen:** (daughter of Corrine and Ibrahim - witch)
- **Benedict:** (son of Rose and Caleb - human)
- **Brock:** (son of Kiev and Mona – half warlock)
- **Grace:** (daughter of Ben and River – half fae and half human)
- **Hazel:** (daughter of Rose and Caleb – human)
- **Heath:** (son of Jeriad and Sylvia – half dragon and half human)
- **Ruby:** (daughter of Claudia and Yuri – human)
- **Victoria:** (daughter of Vivienne and Xavier – human)

Benedict

I must have dozed off again, because when I woke Yelena was gone. At first I thought I was having another nightmare; the floor was rumbling and the bed was vibrating so violently, I was almost shaken off. A loud crash made me jump up—the chest of drawers had fallen forward, and the wood had split in two from the force of the impact.

"Get up!" Ruby cried, slamming open the door to my room.

"What's going on?" I shouted, running after her.

Ruby yelled back a reply, but I didn't hear it. Bookcases,

chests and tapestries were crashing to the floor. The castle was being hit with shock after shock of what I could only assume was an earthquake—the gray stones of the room were shifting in the walls, and it didn't feel like it would be long until the entire castle came crashing down around us.

"It won't open!" Yelena yelled over at Ruby. Both girls were by the entrance doors to our quarters, furiously trying to shove them open.

"I think they're blocked." Ruby grunted with the effort of pushing open the heavy wood frame. She managed to press the door partly ajar. "There's a crack… I can see rubble. I think we're trapped!"

"Is anyone going to come help us?" another one of the kids cried out, waving their arms about in front of the windows. Ruby snorted with derision.

"Unlikely. We need to get ourselves out of here."

"Servants' entrance," Julian croaked from the small door where he was standing with Jenney, both of them holding onto the walls as the floor shifted wildly beneath them. "We can get out through the kitchen."

"Okay, kids!" Ruby barked at the cowering children. Some were hiding under coffee tables in the hope that the

wooden surfaces would save them, others followed Julian and Jenney's lead, backing up against the shifting, shaking walls. "We need to stick together, okay? Just follow me. Keep your eyes on one of us"—she pointed at me, Julian and Jenney—"at all times. Don't run off, no matter how scared you might get. We're all going to get out of here in one piece."

I started toward the door, letting Ruby lead the way.

"Do you think it's the entity?" Yelena asked me breathlessly as we ran down the stone staircase to the servant quarters.

"No idea," I replied, lying. Had it been anywhere other than Nevertide, I would have assumed that this was a regular earthquake. But this *was* Nevertide, and I was pretty certain that there would be some entity-shaped reason as to why this was happening. All around us I could hear the crashes of stone tumbling to the ground, the sounds of tearing, ripping, metals being crushed and annihilated under rock.

Up ahead, Ruby pushed open the door to the kitchen. I heard the thunderous blaze of fire erupting from the room even before the flames flickered out from the door.

"We need to find another way!" Ruby cried, both she

and Jenney forcing the door back as it lit up their faces and scorched the outside of the frame, instantly blistering the wood and leaving it charcoal black.

"I know a way!" Jenney called back, gesturing to us all to follow her. She ran forward, past the kitchen and into the labyrinth of the servant quarters. The ceilings were low here, and I was already starting to feel claustrophobic, like the walls were closing in on us with every step. Luckily, the stone remained intact, though I didn't think it would stay that way for long.

We moved further along the corridor. Now I couldn't see any light ahead, only the silhouettes of the kids, visible in the firelight that had now fully erupted through the kitchen door behind us, casting its light through the tunnels. I could feel the heat of it on my back as I ran, praying that the kids would move faster.

Yelena reached back to grab my hand, and my fingers closed around hers. I focused on the back of her head and the occasional glimpse of her profile as she glanced back to double-check I was okay.

The corridor started to open out a bit, and Jenney slammed her body against a small wooden door. I recognized it as the side-entrance to the castle, the one that

Ash had used to smuggle us in with the root cart. It felt like a lifetime ago.

"It's locked!" she cried out to Ruby. Julian rushed forward to help her push against it, but was clearly still too weak from his time spent in Queen Trina's castle. The door didn't budge. I looked around for something that we could use to force it open—something sharp and solid…

I let go of Yelena's hand, spying a bronze vulture head that had fallen to the ground.

"Julian, help me!" I called out, waving toward the fallen ornament. The skull was too heavy for me to pick up by myself, so I started to drag it across the floor. Julian hadn't heard me, but in a moment, Ruby was by my side, and together we heaved the ornament off the floor and staggered toward the door.

"Stand back," I yelled out, simultaneously swinging the vulture head, with Ruby holding the other side, into the door. The first hit reverberated up my arms painfully, but the second swing smashed the wooden paneling, creating a hole in the door. We swung again, and this time the vulture head went sailing through the door, splintering it completely.

"One by one—out you go!" Ruby ushered the kids

through as quickly as she could. They stumbled and practically fell over themselves trying to get out, each face appearing soot- and tear-stained in the daylight.

The last few disappeared out of sight, and I looked around.

“Where’s Yelena?” I asked. I hadn’t seen her go through the door.

“We’re missing two!” Jenney cried out, half out of the door as she counted the heads of the kids.

The inferno was getting closer, and Ruby looked worriedly back down the corridor.

“We need to leave now,” she replied, holding on to the sleeve of my robe.

“Not without her!” I yelled, pulling back my robe and twisting out of her grasp.

“That’s suicide!”

“I don’t *care*,” I retorted, running back the way we had come. I knew none of them would follow me—Ruby would want to, but Jenney and Julian wouldn’t let her. But there was no way I would leave Yelena on her own. I didn’t know why she’d run off, but I owed it to her to go after her—for everything she’d done for me—and everything I’d done to her. Yeah. I owed her. I owed her big time.

I ran back along the corridor, my body breaking out in a sweat as the heat from the blaze battered me, unrelenting and dry, my face feeling like it was going to melt off. My eyes started to water, the smoke irritating them and blocking off any oxygen so that my head swam.

"Yelena!" I called out, coughing and spluttering, knowing that it was probably useless to call her name. She wouldn't be able to hear me over the sound of the fire and falling stone.

The fire was only several feet ahead of me: a solid wall of flame, blocking my path…which meant she had to be in one of the rooms off this part of the corridor, or else she was dead.

"Yelena!" I roared again, kicking open the doors that I passed. Most of them were bedrooms, as small and cramped as Ash's had been. I bent low, trying to make out human forms in the billows of smoke that poured in from the blaze of the corridor. There wasn't time to give each of them more than a cursory look—there wouldn't be anywhere to hide anyway. I just had to keep searching rooms and hope that she was in one of them.

I was two more doors from the blaze when the door to the left flew open and Yelena came staggering out, carrying

the young Portuguese kid in her arms. His body lay limp, but Yelena was choking badly.

“He ran off…he didn’t understand,” she hacked out, before she started to sway on her feet. She stumbled forward, and I rushed forward to catch them both before they smacked into the ground.

‘Yelena!” I cried out, trying to shake her upright, whilst keeping one eye on the flames that were snaking closer by the second. “You need to stand up! Please—I can’t do this without you!”

The boy looked dead to the world, and I didn’t know if he was alive or not, but his expressionless face and closed eyes didn’t give me much hope. I took him out of her arms and flung him over my shoulder as best I could—he was small and light, but I wasn’t going to be able to carry them both.

“Wake UP!” I screamed at her. I pulled at her waist with my spare hand, pulling her upward so that her body was leaning against mine.

“Just let me rest here for a minute…” she murmured, disorientated and completely oblivious to the flames and, even more worrying, the sound of the ceiling starting to rumble and creak.

Without stopping to think, I started to move forward, grabbing Yelena more tightly. I staggered toward the dim light up ahead, just able to make out the cries of Ruby and Julian urging me forward.

I could practically feel the flames inches away from my bare neck.

We have to make it.

Don't stop…

The fumes were starting to get to me. The hint of daylight started to move about as my vision blurred, but I kept my grip on Yelena tight, putting one foot in front of the other.

The broken doorway was only about five feet in front of me when the ceiling started to cave in. I shoved Yelena in front of me, pushing her through the break in the door and into Ruby's outstretched hands. Without waiting to see whether or not the coast was clear, I launched myself through with the boy still over my shoulder.

I smacked into Yelena's back, breathing in a lungful of air before I slapped down, hard, onto the ground.

Dust and debris billowed out behind me. The servant quarters' foundation had collapsed completely; the sound was deafening, shaking the ground outside and shifting the

entire castle with a horrible, uneasy rumble.

"Thank God you're safe!" Ruby rasped, turning me over. "I thought we'd lost you – don't *ever* do that to me again!"

"Yelena?" I asked, my throat as dry as a desert.

"She's okay," Ruby reassured me, still looking half furious and half relieved, "you saved her life, Benedict."

I smiled.

Cool.

Hazel

"Put me down!" I cried, struggling once again in Tejus's arms. We had reached the edge of the exterior castle walls, along with a mass of other sentries who had poured out of the portcullis, all yelling and screaming, blindly following one another as they shoved and fought their way out of the grounds.

"Seriously, Tejus!" I screamed, "I can walk by myself!"

He grunted in anger, but his grip loosened and he let me slide down to the floor. As soon as my feet touched the ground, I slipped out of his grasp and started to run back the way we'd come, determined to find Benedict and my

friends and make sure they had escaped.

"What the HELL are you doing?"

Tejus bellowed after me, but I was soon swallowed up by the mass of ministers and I didn't bother to turn around. I would return to him when I found them but I had to know that they were safe. Tejus still didn't fully understand that when it came to Benedict and my friends, if they weren't okay, I wouldn't be okay. Much to his annoyance, my own safety would always come second place. I pushed and elbowed my way through to the portcullis. Most of the crowd didn't even notice me. I was too small compared to them to attract much attention: the only danger would be losing my footing and being trampled to death by the mob.

With one final shove, I broke free of the bottleneck of sentries that had formed at the gate and started to run toward the main entrance.

My strides seemed more powerful than normal, like I was running at twice my speed…and more than that, I could feel *strength* coursing through me, as if I could easily obliterate anything that stood in my path. I didn't know if it was the adrenaline, or my newfound sentry powers, but it felt good not to feel so powerless, even for just a

moment.

I reached the entrance in a matter of moments; when I got there, I skidded to a halt.

No!

There was a loud boom, like dynamite exploding, and I stared open-mouthed as the entrance arch split in two and collapsed, almost gracefully, in on itself. I heard the screams of the sentries who had been standing beneath it—and the ones behind who hadn't made it out yet. Then a brief silence, as all cries stopped.

"BENEDICT!" I yelled out, shattering the silence. A commotion broke out behind me as the ministers and guards realized what had happened, and within a few short moments it was total chaos.

Ignoring the sentries, I started to run around to the side entrance of the castle. My stomach was twisted in a tight knot, a sick lurching feeling accompanying every step I took.

Please be safe.

Racing ahead, I had to make a wide berth around the grounds of the castle. The rock and stone from the towers and buttresses rained down with heavy thuds and splintered off into lethal shards. I paused for a second as I

caught sight of the small door to the side entrance—I could see the familiar figures of humans gathered outside it, along with bright red flames pouring through, black smoke snaking into the sky.

"Ruby!" I called out, recognizing the blonde halo of my friend. The group of kids surrounding her moved out of the way to let me pass, and I raced up to Ruby. She and Julian were hunched over the body of my brother.

"He's okay," she asserted before I could say a word, still stomping out fire embers on Benedict's robe.

"I'm fine," Benedict agreed sleepily. His face was soot-stained and perspiring from the heat, but he was alive.

"We need to move him back," I replied. The flames erupting from the doorway were growing more intense by the second. Ruby and I started to drag him away from the door—I held onto a corner of his robe, trying to make sure that I touched him as little as possible. I noticed Yelena being carried off by Jenney and Julian, and the rest of the kids doing the same to a small dark-haired kid I'd almost syphoned from a few days ago. I hoped he was okay.

"Does it hurt anywhere?" I asked, turning my attention back to Benedict. Now that he was away from the fire, I placed my hands behind my back, careful not to come into

physical contact with any part of him as the hunger started to rear up inside the pit of my stomach.

"No," my brother murmured deliriously, "it was just *really* warm in there... It must be the entity doing this, right?"

"I think so," I replied. "Nevertide is split up the middle, like a huge landslide or something...and the sky, well, that's just *weird*."

Benedict looked at me in confusion, but before he could ask what I meant, one of the kids cried out.

"The tower! The tower's going to fall!"

I looked up. The north tower directly above us had started to sway, lurching like a drunk back and forth as more splits and tears and crashes emanated from within the castle.

"Everyone back!" I cried out, knowing already that we were too late...The first rock fell just a foot away from where Benedict's head lay. The kids screamed out. In the next moment, a familiar hand slammed into mine.

"Throw your energy out—now!" Tejus yelled down at me. He must have followed me as soon as I'd left his arms, and I was immensely grateful in that moment that Tejus refused to abandon me under any circumstances, no

matter if it threatened his own life.

"What do I do?" I cried back.

"A barrier!"

"*I don't know how to do that!*"

"Let your instinct take over, Hazel. Just trust me."

He clasped my hand tightly, and, trying to see into his head without syphoning his energy, I followed his lead, attempting to throw my energy outward so that it encircled all of us from the falling rocks. Tejus was still weak, I could tell, but somehow he still managed to start building the shimmering, bluish barrier.

"Don't hold back." Tejus yanked at my hand. "I'm syphoning off your friends—I'll be fine."

The entire process took only a few seconds; I poured the rage and fury, the power and the desperation I felt into a single channel outward. In my mind, it created the same thick rope of 'energy' that I used to bond with Tejus, but this time it was directed onto the ground—and where the energy came into contact with the ground, it spilled out, covering the ground and then rising up into a large bubble, merging with the wisps that Tejus had already started to create.

"You're doing it," Tejus whispered as the bubble

encased us.

Just in time. The rocks of the tower screamed, stone grinding against stone as the aged mortar crumbled away to dust. It collapsed, covering the barrier that we'd created, shutting out every ounce of light, and making the earth shudder on impact.

The moment rocks hit the barrier, I howled in pain. It was as if each stone had landed on my head—but *inside* my brain, ricocheting around my skull, knocking every nerve, muscle and bone in my body. The edges of my vision started to turn gray.

"Tejus…" I murmured, unable to get any more words out as the world felt like it was fluttering away to nothingness.

"It's all right, I've got it—I can hold it."

I heard his reassuring murmur like it was traveling down a long, long tunnel.

"Everyone's safe," he continued.

Everyone's safe.

We're all okay.

I let go of his hand, yearning for rest and hardly able to keep my eyes open for another second.

Benedict's startled expression was the last thing I saw;

he was looking up at me from the ground, his eyes wide and disbelieving as I smiled and then fell, gratefully, into unconsciousness.

ASH

As the bird continued on toward Hellswan castle, I looked down at the complete devastation below me. A large crack split Nevertide in two, like a gaping, smirking mouth across the landscape. Smaller cracks hair-lined off it, the roots of trees exposed by landslides, as if the forests and fields were sloping down into the center of the world. Villages lay in ruins, barns burning, and most homes looked as if they'd collapsed entirely, falling over as if they were made out of paper, not stone.

A cloud of smoke rushed up to meet us, momentarily blinding me in a thick fog, and when it passed, I got my

first look at Hellswan castle. Or what was left of it.

Ruby!

She was my one and only thought as I looked down at the annihilation of my home. The main fortress of the castle was just about still intact, but every other inch of it lay sprawling outward, nothing more than rubble, with the black dots of ministers swarming around the wreckage like confused ants.

Queen Trina groaned next to me. She was still out of it, her eyes closed and her body limp in the talons of the vulture.

This is your fault.

A large part of me wanted to drop her down to the land below—to watch her somersault through the air until she landed like a rag doll on the rocks or was swallowed up by fire. It would serve her right: this was her doing, every dead sentry, every crack and split in Nevertide on her hands—evidence of her betrayal of her own people. If Queen Trina lived and Ruby didn't, I would never forgive myself – or her.

As we drew closer to the castle, I realized that the tremors and the shifting of the ground had come to a halt. The crack in Nevertide wasn't widening any further, for

now, but I didn't know if this would be a brief reprieve or the end of the entity's destructive force on the land.

I need to get them to safety.

We dropped down just outside the portcullis where most of the ministers and guards were gathered, all flapping about like headless birds. I anxiously searched the crowd for a familiar blonde head, but I didn't see her.

"Ashbik!" one of the guards cried out, and my name was echoed across the waiting group. I shoved Queen Trina to the floor, and the bird took off in flight once again, no doubt to find a safer spot than here.

"Watch her! She's not to move—if she wakes, secure her to something," I instructed, pointing at five waiting guards who appeared to be only partly injured. "The rest of you wait here, by the entrance. Do not leave—you all wait for my command, is that clear?" I roared out.

I heard the resounding chorus of 'yes, your highness'. Had it been under other circumstances, the meek and mild response of the ministers would have made me laugh. As it was, I didn't care whether they stayed here or not, not really. I just wanted to find Ruby.

I looked at the other guards; there were three who weren't injured at all, and I beckoned them over.

"I'm going to search for the humans, you're to follow me."

"Your highness, no one will have gotten out alive—the towers, everything—it collapsed," stuttered one of them, avoiding meeting my eye.

"We'll find them," I repeated implacably.

The ministers stood aside hurriedly as I walked toward the portcullis. I didn't bother checking to see if the guards had followed my lead. I was going anyway. Using True Sight, I scanned the entrance of the castle while walking closer to the worst of the rubble. The sight made me sick. There were at least fifteen sentries—some ministers, some servants—who had been caught in the rock as it had fallen down, crushing all of them. The only mercy would have been that they would have died quickly.

Please don't let Ruby...

I couldn't even finish the thought. The idea that she had met the same fate was unimaginable.

Searching every single pile of rubble, including the interior of the blocked-off main fortress, I anxiously sought her out, looking for any sign of the rest of the humans, Tejus or Hazel.

"There are sentries trapped in there," I muttered to the

guards. Inside the main fortress I could see ministers who were still alive, trying to remove the rubble that blocked their paths. Already their movements were becoming slow and weak. "One of you go and fetch more who are able to help—we need to start trying to get them out. They're going to suffocate in there otherwise."

Where the collapsing building hadn't killed them, the fire shortly would. It seemed to be worse at the lower levels of the castle, but with the entrances and exits blocked, those left alive would soon suffocate or be burnt alive.

The guard hurried back to the portcullis. I continued my search with the two remaining guards, starting to edge around the right side of the castle where the damage was the worst. The towers had all collapsed, one leaving only the iron staircase jutting out of the foundation of the keep, burnt and twisted, but still standing.

I started to focus on the piles of rubble. The first two contained nothing, but as I moved closer toward the side entrance, a large, built-up pile caught my attention.

"Ruby!" I ran closer to the pile of rocks, seeing a group of humans trapped inside along with the distinct, hunched-over figure of Tejus.

"Help me move these!" I called to the guards. Then,

realizing that the three of us wouldn't move fast enough, I commanded, "One of you go back and get more help—anyone who's able-bodied!"

I could see that Tejus had built a barrier that was covering them all—but how long he could hold it up, I didn't know. He was obviously syphoning off the humans to keep it in place, and if any of them grew too weak…

I started to throw the rocks back, moving the top ones first. Shortly, footsteps hurried to my aid. Three more guards and two ministers launched themselves at the pile, helping me heave off the worst of the rubble.

As we moved a dented iron spike, three large gray stones tumbled off the barrier. Then Ruby peered out at me, dusty and soot-streaked, but smiling.

"Shortie!" I breathed, grinning at her weakly.

She waved, knowing I wouldn't be able to hear her through the protection of the barrier. I kept removing the stones, smiling at her reassuringly, but I felt sick. That had been too close for comfort—I had almost lost her again, and where I should have felt relief, instead a knot of anxiety twisted in my gut. The danger was getting worse, seemingly at the same rate that my feelings for Ruby were intensifying. The thought of losing her was becoming

more and more agonizing.

Most of the kids were huddled together on the ground, while Ruby was kneeling up against one of the fallen rocks, anxiously monitoring our progress as her energy was syphoned. Tejus kept still, focusing on keeping that barrier in place, with Hazel lying next to him. She wasn't moving.

We cleared off the top of the stones, creating a nest-shaped crater in the ground where nothing would be able to fall on the humans once the barrier was removed. Tejus checked it was safe, and then, with a sigh of relief, he let the barrier fall.

"Hazel needs help," Tejus barked the moment the barrier came down. I nodded, turning to one of the ministers, who reluctantly edged his way down into the pit and over to Hazel.

"Do I get more white knight points?" I joked feebly with Ruby as I put out an arm to help her up. Her fingers closed around my hand, and she grinned.

"Yeah, you get more points."

She looked back, watching the guards carry Benedict and then Yelena out.

"What happened?" I asked.

"Benedict decided to be a hero." She rolled her eyes. "I

think he feels like he's got a lot to make up for—especially when it comes to Yelena."

I nodded. In his position, I would feel the same way.

"I'm so glad you're safe," she breathed, turning her attention back to me. "Did the earthquake affect the Fells as well?"

"It did, but...well, some of us survived."

She nodded.

"Memenion?" she asked.

"Gone."

Ruby closed her eyes briefly, taking a moment. "He was a good man," she whispered. "Like Varga."

She flew against my chest, her arms wrapping around my waist. I returned the hug, resting my lips against the crown of her head. A small sliver of jealousy unfurled within me—I hated that she still thought of Varga, that it still caused her pain to think of him. It was irrational. He had rescued her from the ice fires, after all. If anything, I should be grateful to the sentry. I thought when he was revealed to be an Acolyte, it would have tainted her memories of him. Clearly not.

"What are we going to do now?" she murmured against me, and I could feel her warm breath heating up my chest.

“I don’t know exactly,” I replied. “I need to speak to Tejus. I don’t know how many kingdoms were destroyed, or how many villagers, ministers and guards are going to be homeless now. Perhaps we can find shelter somewhere else.”

The prospect was a gloomy one. I didn’t know which kingdoms would be truly safe for us—of those that were left. Or if we’d be welcome at any of them, if they were still standing.

“I need to stay with Benedict and Hazel.” Ruby released her grip, looking up at me with worried eyes.

“They’ll be moving everyone out of the castle grounds,” I replied, watching as the guards helped more of the kids out of the pit. Benedict and Hazel were being carried off toward the outskirts of the gates. “Go. I need to speak to Tejus.”

“Okay.”

Ruby leaned up toward me and I kissed her, sinking into the familiar sensation of her pliant lips. Instantly I felt drugged. Varga, the entity, the destruction of Nevertide all faded away to nothing.

Tejus

Since I was a child, Hellswan castle had invoked mixed feelings in me. It had been my home, the only one I had ever known. Although the gray walls and the strict, unyielding rule of my father had made me long for escape—even causing me to stay in the Seraq kingdom for an extended period of time—seeing it reduced to nothing but rubble and dust was physically painful.

I stood next to Ash, both of us gazing at the destruction, almost as if it would suddenly start to mend itself, a twist in the universe making the stones reassemble, turning back time till it was once again the oppressive, impenetrable

hulk that Hellswan castle had always been. The feelings of powerlessness I had been experiencing ever since I'd learnt of the entity's rise started to return; what could I do—what could the kitchen boy do to stop this? If the entity was capable of such mass devastation, how would two sentries—both riddled with faults and flaws that clouded their judgment, with a limited army behind them and no closer to finding answers regarding the true nature of the evil that faced them—ever hope to defeat it?

Ash cleared his throat.

"What do we do now?" he asked, quietly.

I looked up at the sky. It was mid-morning now, and as long as the sky didn't rip further to expose the night, we would have a decent amount of time before sundown.

"We need to get everyone somewhere safe—relatively safe," I muttered, thinking of the few options that we had available to us.

"Where do you suggest? I was thinking that we could send scouts out—find the kingdoms that are least destroyed, and hope that they're willing to take us in," Ash offered, his tone doubtful.

"Take in the Hellswans?" I smirked.

"The villagers, at least?"

They might have a chance of being accepted elsewhere, perhaps if the Memenion kingdom was still secure, but they would be unlikely to accept our ministers or our guards. For too long my father had alienated the surrounding kingdoms, and while he had been respected as emperor, he had been hated. I doubted that those long-standing feuds would be eradicated in the face of a disaster—even one as severe as this.

"There is the summer palace," I replied, ignoring his suggestion. "It is the only place I can think of. If it has survived the earthquake, then it will be habitable—sort of."

Ash raised his eyebrows. "I have never been."

"But you've heard of it?"

"Yeah, but I was never asked to work there."

"We didn't go after my mother's death. The palace belonged to her family, and was given as a gift to my mother for her dowry. It's located by the North Coast, far from the Acolytes' temple. If no one knows we are heading there, we may manage to stay out of their way until we can come up with a plan."

Ash nodded.

"But if you wish, we can take the villagers to

Memenion," I continued, thinking out loud. There wouldn't be much space for us all in the old palace—perhaps Ash was right, better to get the villagers somewhere safe, away from the harm that I suspected would follow us.

"He is dead." Ash's words were barely above a whisper.

"At the Fells?" I asked, my throat tightening.

"He dropped…into the ground. There was nothing I could do."

"Did he know about his son?" I asked, hoping that his dying moments weren't ones of regret and shame over his offspring's allegiance to Queen Trina and the Acolytes.

"Yes."

I swallowed, not wishing to discuss the matter any further. With Memenion gone, our kingdom was truly isolated, as were our efforts to battle the entity. My mind drifted to Hazel once again. She was my primary concern. Keeping her safe would be the one outcome that I would not compromise on. If she survived this, even at the expense of every other soul in Nevertide, including my own, then I would have accomplished my goal; the entity would not have taken everything from me—would not have succeeded in destroying the one thing that mattered.

"What of the Impartial Ministers?" I asked. "Did any of them survive?"

"I saw one of them die—I don't know what happened to the others. I wouldn't have thought that they would concern you?"

"They don't. You becoming emperor does," I retorted. "It will be the only way that we'll be able to read the book; I hope it has the answers we need."

Ash eyed the remains of the castle.

"The book is kept in Hellswan castle?" he asked despondently.

"We'll just have to pray it survived."

I hoped that the book was protected by the same magic that the Impartial Ministers seemed to have access to. I recalled the way, during the imperial trial, I had emerged from the hallucination with the bloodstained sword in my hand. Those ministers were obviously tapping into a greater power somehow. With any luck, the book had remained intact.

"Isn't there another way? Do we have to have the blessing of the Impartial Ministers?" Ash asked.

"I have a theory," I replied, telling Ash what I thought about the magic of the Impartial Ministers. "If the book is

in any way linked to them, if we appoint you emperor without their blessing, then I doubt that the book will be able to be read. We will have a hard time proving the credibility of your claim with the other kingdoms as well."

"Ruby once asked me if we had witches here. I laughed at her," he replied in astonishment.

"I'm not talking about witchcraft," I snapped. "Just power—old, ancient power that neither of us have a conception of."

"All right," he muttered stiffly. "I was just saying."

"My apologies," I replied curtly. "It irritates me that we were never told of this power—that it has been kept in the domain of the Impartial Ministers, those least worthy to wield it."

Ash shrugged off my apology, shuffling his feet in the dust.

"Perhaps it's a good thing that your father couldn't access it," he replied.

Touché.

"Perhaps."

"It sounds like heading out to the summer palace is our best plan," he continued. "Then we can search for the Impartial Ministers and get one of us crowned."

I raised my eyebrows in surprise at his assessment. "One of us?" I asked. "Ash, the emperor will be you, not I. You deserve it, and the people need you." I frowned. There was only one potential problem with our plan. "What of Queen Trina? Tell me we were lucky enough to be rid of her."

Ash grinned broadly. "Better than that, she's our prisoner."

I smiled.

That was good news—good news indeed.

Rose

After I'd received the radio call from Caleb, Mona and Corrine had transported us back to The Shade to meet with the rest of GASP. Caleb had told us Sherus's fears the moment the witches had ceased working on the portal, and now we were being called to the Great Dome to meet with the king of the fire fae himself.

Usually I would be intrigued, but right in this moment I was just plain furious. I stormed through the redwoods toward the council chamber, an irrational rage flooding every nerve.

"You're going to need to keep your cool in there, Rose,"

Caleb muttered as we approached the building. "You know your father isn't going to respond well if you fly off the handle—he'll have enough to deal with. Claudia's on the warpath too."

At the mention of Claudia, I faltered. None of us reacted well when her temper flared, and if I went in guns blazing, then Dad would be much less likely to hear me out.

"You're right, give me a minute."

I paused, standing next to Caleb, rubbing my temples and trying to collect myself. I needed to *breathe*—this meeting needed to be handled in the right way. I couldn't just dismiss the fears of the fae; I had to treat this like any other job. Of course, it was dangerous opening an unknown portal, especially considering the stone that had emerged from it, but…the kids. They were all that mattered to me. How *could* I think straight when their lives were riding on this?

"Did Dad seem like he was on Sherus's side with all this?" I asked.

"Your father seemed conflicted," Caleb replied evenly. "So did Ben—you know that both of them want the kids back as much as we do."

I groaned.

"Caleb, how are you being so level-headed about this?" I asked despairingly.

"Because I have to be. Trust me, if you were the one being level-headed, I would be flying off the handle."

His brown eyes betrayed a spark of something feral; my husband was doing his best to keep control, but I realized under the surface a storm was brewing. I knew he would be having a hard time trusting the fae king, and if he was managing to keep his cool, then so could I.

"Let's go," I replied, gripping his hand.

The Dome was packed; pretty much the whole of GASP's core was present. Corrine shuffled over in her seat so that Caleb and I could sit at the front. We would be the ones arguing most heavily in favor of opening the portal, but I knew we wouldn't be alone. Mom hurried in, coming to sit next to us. Her emerald-green eyes were flashing with determination.

"Rose, are you okay?" she asked, leaning forward on her seat.

"Pissed off, and getting pretty desperate," I replied candidly. "Where's Sherus?"

"I left him and your father arguing alone, 'round the

back of the building."

I stood up, wanting to join them. If there was going to be a discussion, then I wanted in on it.

"Sit down, Rose. They'll be through in a minute," she added. "Let your father try to persuade the fae before he hears our case."

"Sherus has no jurisdiction here!" I exploded. "This is a decision GASP should be making alone."

She nodded, her expression troubled. "We might need him, we don't know—better to have the fae on our side than not."

I slumped down in my seat, knowing that my mom was right. Yuri and Claudia entered the Dome, both nodding in our direction. Claudia looked like she was ready for a fight—her large brown eyes seemed to crackle with electricity, a sure sign that her more passionate nature was bubbling to the surface. Ashley and Landis followed behind, both of their faces etched with disappointment.

The group hushed, and I sensed that my dad was on his way in. Sure enough, he and Sherus entered through the side door, both stormy-faced. Perhaps the conversation hadn't gone very well. Following Sherus was a red-headed woman I presumed to be his sister — Ben had informed

me that she had also come to stay in The Shade — and behind her followed two other fae I didn't recognize.

"Thank you all for coming," my father started as the fae took a seat, his deep voice reverberating around the ancient meeting chamber. "As you all know, we're here to discuss the opening of the portal. We have good reason to believe that the children have been taken into an unknown dimension, and that the portal in question will lead us to them. However, Sherus and the rest of the fae believe that opening the portal is dangerous, perhaps fatally so—that the threat which has been foreseen will come from the very same portal."

The chamber was entirely silent. I looked over at the fae king. His copper hair and relatively youthful features gave no indication of his true age, but his eyes betrayed an old, weary soul. He turned his head, his gaze meeting mine for the briefest moment. In that look I saw compassion, and perhaps pity, but also resolve. I didn't think he would change his mind on this matter…I only hoped that he wouldn't manage to sway any of the other GASP members.

Sherus stood up. I heard the creak and groan of wood as every single person in the council turned to get a good

look at him.

"My concern is with the stones," he announced. "The jinn locked deadly creatures into those prisons so they would not escape. We have no way of knowing what is contained within that portal, but if it is a land full of these creatures, then giving them a way to access Earth could be fatal."

The GASP members started to mutter, and my mother leaned over and squeezed my hand. Whether it was in warning or reassurance, I wasn't sure.

"We don't even know what these creatures are," Claudia retorted. "Plus, it's our kids in there! How can we *not* open it?"

"Are you so willing to risk sacrificing all to save a few?" Sherus asked. Removing my hand from my mom's grasp, I clenched my fists. It was all very well for him to be so high-minded about it, and of course, if we were all thinking pure battle tactics with willing soldiers, I would have agreed with him. But we weren't. We were talking about *kids*. *Our* kids.

"How DARE you!" Claudia raged. "We can't treat it like that—"

"Enough, Claudia," my father scolded her. "We need

everyone's point of view shared, whether or not they differ from yours."

Sherus's sister shot Claudia an evil scowl. I suspected that perhaps the female fae was just as fiery as the blonde vampire. It was going to be interesting watching *that* relationship unravel if we had to spend more time with their kind.

Standing up, I addressed both my father and Sherus.

"I understand the concerns of the fae, but I also believe that if we were to gain access to the portal, we could lock it behind us, preventing what we find within from getting out. Once we've neutralized the threat, then we can reopen the portal."

Murmurs of agreement erupted from around the room.

"And what if you can't neutralize this threat?" Sherus glowered at me. "What then?"

"Then what chance do we have anyway?" I shot back. I realized as the words came out of my mouth it was true. We had no alternative other than to open the portal. If the danger that Sherus had been warned about in his visions *was* on the other side of the portal, then it was going to emerge anyway—with or without our help.

"Rose is right." My brother's voice came from the back

of the room. I hadn't seen him sitting with River—he normally took center stage with Dad at these proceedings. "We can't just leave it locked and wait for whatever's in there to escape. If we enter the portal, we might have the upper hand. We don't know who threw that stone out—it could be someone wanting our help, someone on our side..."

"Or it could be a trap!" Sherus countered.

"It could be a land where jinn reside," I argued. "Maybe some settlement other than The Dunes. They created the stones in the first place, it might be a group that we don't know about—but an enemy that could potentially be reasoned with, especially with the jinn we have on our side."

"I very much doubt I would have had an omen about a land of jinn," Sherus spluttered. "The threat that we're talking about is going to be much greater than that."

I sat down. I had said my part. Now it was up to my dad and Ben to decide what the right course of action was going to be.

"What's happening with the portal now?" My father directed his question at Mona.

"We have left a few witches and jinn watching it. They

will inform us if anything changes, but so far the portal has been left partway open. Nothing has emerged other than the stone," she replied. "But the lock is now weakened. If we do decide that we're not going to go and investigate, we need to shut it back up completely."

"Can you do that?" my father asked.

"We can, but I don't advise it. I agree with Rose—better to face the danger head on, rather than hoping it will go away if we keep it locked up."

"And what of the rest of the stones, the ones collected from the In-Between? Where are they now?"

The witch glanced over at Queen Nuriya, who nodded quickly from the back of the room.

"We will take them back to the planet, if they are no longer needed."

"All right," my father said, then fell silent for a moment, his sharp blue eyes scanning everyone in the room—no doubt contemplating our arguments. Eventually he sighed, rubbing his temple. From the familiar gesture, I realized that he hadn't come to a decision yet. My heart sank.

"I will take all points into account, and reach a decision this evening. In the meantime, I want everyone available

to research the nature of these stones—I want to know *exactly* what the jinn locked in them."

At his announcement, I looked over at Caleb. His expression was one of sheer frustration. I knew exactly how he felt – we'd gotten so close to opening the portal, and now we had to wait even longer for a final decision to be made. I could only hope that whatever we found out about the stones, Dad would still put his family first.

Hazel

Syphoning off the minister was strange. It felt weirdly intimate to me—I had never even had a conversation with the woman who offered up her energy, yet she had borne the pain of my unpracticed mind-suck without complaint. We sat side by side on the outskirts of the castle when I had finished, both looking out over the collapsed trees of the forest that faced the castle.

"I'm sorry," I muttered. "That must have been…unpleasant."

She turned to face me, her hair half-falling out of a bun and a large slash across her face that looked as if it had only

recently stopped bleeding.

"It doesn't matter. I've had children, it was much the same with them when they were first born. You will learn, in time, how to control it."

"Where are your children now?" I asked, hoping that they weren't among the sentries still trapped inside the castle.

"They moved to the kingdoms of Memenion and Hadalix long ago," she replied. "I hope they are safe now…I suppose I can only wait and see."

It seemed quite a measured, rational response from a mother, but then sentries—and especially ministers—had always seemed cold to me. Their parenting practices were more hands off than was the norm where I came from.

"I'm sure they're fine." I smiled weakly.

"As am I."

They felt like empty words to offer, but I didn't know what else to say. I leaned back against the rock behind me, grateful for the energy that I could feel coursing through me, but also trying to calm some of it down—I felt like I'd just drunk about ten espressos at once, and it made me kind of jittery. I started drumming my fingers against my legs.

The minister smirked.

"You will also learn how much you need to take. I suspect your body has a surplus right now…it will fade, eventually."

I grimaced at her, embarrassed that she'd noticed.

"Sorry again."

"Don't be." She shrugged. "Really. I suppose we will all need to be of service to one another in the days ahead. Perhaps it is time that we ministers were of genuine use." She lowered her head, staring at the ground.

"Excuse me," she continued after a moment, "I need to speak with someone."

The woman rose to her feet and smiled briefly at me. I watched her walk away in surprise. Perhaps the devastation of Nevertide was the one thing that might bring about its salvation. If all the ministers were like her, and had begun to realize the error of their ways, perhaps there was hope. Well, if the entity didn't finish what it had started, anyway.

Tejus approached from the portcullis. All the ministers, guards and servants were gathered there. Some lay in the grass in front of the castle, wounded and unable to stand, but most who had managed to escape seemed okay: bloodied, covered in soot and dust, but okay.

Without saying a word, he came and sat down a few feet from me, his body sinking gratefully to the ground with feline grace. He was no longer wearing his robes, just the habitual black uniform of silk pants and shirt, which had escaped relatively intact. His expression was pensive. Looking out at the destroyed forest, he sighed, rubbing at his temples.

"Did any more manage to escape?" I asked hopefully.

"Some."

Some wasn't enough.

"I'm sorry," I replied. He shrugged, stoic as ever.

"You survived. That's what matters," he muttered. "We're going to move out in a couple of moments, to another palace that belongs to the Hellswan family. Are you ready to travel?"

"What palace?" I asked. I hadn't been aware that he owned another home.

"One that belonged to my mother, not far from here."

"I'm ready." I smiled. "I actually feel quite good. The minister really…helped."

He nodded, smirking.

"You'll get used to it."

"I don't know if I will," I grumbled. "It wasn't a very

fair exchange."

"It will be, with me."

He moved closer, and then, turning toward me, he reached out his hand and traced the line of my jaw with his thumb—slowly drawing my face closer to his.

"Are you feeling better?" I swallowed.

"A bit." He smiled down at me hungrily and my breath caught in my throat. He studied my lips, either to drive me insane or to prolong his gratification—I didn't know which, but when he finally brushed his mouth against mine, I breathed him in like oxygen. As the kiss deepened, I clung to his frame, elated that I didn't feel the need to syphon off him, and overwhelmed by the feelings I *did* have rushing through me—acute lust and desire, more intense than I'd ever experienced them, even the night I'd spent in Tejus's bed.

He broke the kiss first, breathing heavily as he pushed me away.

"I can't continue this," he panted. I stared back at him incredulously – how could he have pulled away? The physical tremors of Nevertide hadn't managed to shake my world up as much as our kiss just had.

"What was that, Tejus?" I asked, referring to the

intensity of what we'd just shared—had it been me alone? Or did he share the same feelings? I could see from the color in his cheeks he had certainly felt *something*.

He rose to his feet, offering me his hand. I took it, launching myself upward, irritated at his silence.

"Well?" I asked again.

He started to walk forward, in the direction of the portcullis, but I kept pace with him, trying to match his strides.

"I think it is perhaps another effect of your transformation," he muttered eventually. "I can feel your energy when I kiss you—it's different, more…*intense*."

Is that a good thing?

"So why did you stop?" I asked, annoyed.

He came to an abrupt halt and swung to face me.

"Because we were in *public*, and I wanted you," he bit out.

Oh.

Idiot, Hazel.

"Sorry—I missed that," I stammered awkwardly, my cheeks hot.

"Don't be," he grunted. "Just know that whenever we're together, I want more of you than I can have."

Without waiting for me to reply, he stormed off toward Ash, who was waving him over. Ash stood at the rear of a large Hellswan-embossed carriage that had miraculously escaped being damaged, and was surrounded by stern-looking guards.

I thought about what he had said to me the night that Ash had officially become king. How he intended to marry me, when the time was right. I had been completely thrown by it — the simple way in which he'd said it, as if to him, it was an obvious conclusion. I hadn't even spoken to Ruby about it…I guessed I was still trying to process everything. There wasn't a single doubt in my mind that when the time came, I would say yes. I knew I wasn't exactly the most experienced when it came to love and romance — Tejus was my first boyfriend, if I could even call him that — it kind of felt like a weird label for what we had, but I was still sure. I didn't need to go out and kiss a million frogs to know that there was no one on Earth — in this dimension or any of the others — that would make me feel the way that Tejus did. On top of that, I didn't think there was a single soul that would ever try to understand me the way he did — or support and protect me, no matter what the consequences. His love was

humbling, and I didn't ever want to lose it.

"Hey!" Ruby appeared next to me as Ash and Tejus debated over something.

"Hey." I smiled at her, taking a step back. The instant I'd felt her energy, my thoughts had disappeared and the hunger had returned—clearly syphoning would only give me a short window of reprieve. *Great.* "What's going on there?" I asked, gesturing toward the carriage.

"Didn't Tejus tell you? Ash captured Queen Trina!" she replied, delighted.

I laughed at her Machiavellian smile. It was great news—hopefully we'd be able to get some answers out of Trina, and at the very least, the Acolytes would have lost their leader. She would also serve as a guilt-free energy buffet…

"Where's Benedict?" I asked. We'd been separated when he'd been taken to be tended to by a minister.

"He's fine. Come on, I'll show you." Ruby led me over to the other side of the gate, where the kids had gathered. Benedict was sitting up, back to back with Julian, chatting animatedly while Yelena hung onto his every word.

He looked up as I approached, breaking into a huge smile that mirrored my own. The last time I'd seen him properly was on the wet sand of the cove, barely alive after

the entity had left him.

"Can I hug you yet?" he asked, his eyes filled with amusement.

"I'm still an energy-sucker."

"This isn't going to go well for me when we fight over the remote, is it?" He smirked.

"Nope. I suggest you get Mom or Dad to turn you into a vampire, otherwise you're not going to stand a chance."

Yelena looked at me in confusion, but I just shrugged—she would know who we were eventually, no doubt, but right now I couldn't handle the ton of questions that would come with it...and I suspected Benedict would probably want to impart that news anyway.

"How are you feeling?" Benedict asked. "How come you passed out when you created the barrier?"

"I guess I'm not used to it, so stuff like that uses more energy...and I can't syphon properly without hurting anyone, not yet, anyway."

He nodded solemnly.

"I'm sorry, Hazel. That sucks."

"Yeah," I replied. "It does."

Ash approached the group, clearing his throat to get our attention. He looked like he'd aged since I last saw him.

Though I knew that Tejus hadn't abdicated responsibility for Hellswan by a long shot, I was glad that he was no longer king—I couldn't imagine how it must feel to be in charge of the kingdom right now, knowing that the care of the wounded and displaced fell entirely on his shoulders.

"How are you holding up, Ash?" I asked.

"All right. We're ready to move out. We're all going to travel by bull-horse while the guards and some of the ministers take the birds to see what state the rest of Nevertide is in. I want to take us via the village—see if we can pick up anyone on the way."

"Is Lieutenant Ragnhild leading them?" Ruby asked.

"Yes," Ash replied – surprised at the question.

Ruby nodded stiffly but stayed silent.

What was that about?

"Let's go," Ash instructed after Ruby didn't elaborate. "Hazel, are you okay to travel with Tejus?"

"Um, not really—not yet."

The hunger had resurfaced fully, and it was painful enough being surrounded by the humans. Being around Tejus would be intolerable until I could syphon again.

"All right, we'll get you your own bull-horse."

"That's not fair," Benedict objected.

I glared at him, half bemused and half irritated.

Seriously?

* * *

Ash and Ruby rode up front together, followed by Queen Trina in the Hellswan carriage. She was surrounded by guards, and the compartment was wrapped in heavy iron chains. Clearly, they weren't taking any chances. Tejus and I were bringing up the rear, herding the kids, who sat four each to a bull-horse, led by a few ministers on foot. Julian had flown on ahead with Jenney on one of the vultures—she had been hit quite badly by some of the falling rocks, and Julian had insisted that she didn't travel the journey on horseback. For someone who was usually quite shy and awkward, Julian had kicked up a massive fuss, arguing with the guards until Ash intervened.

As we approached the village, my heart sank. I'd be amazed if there were any survivors. The crack in the earth ran alongside the main road, and most of the land that lay to the north of it had fallen inward—up ahead I could see it starting to snake through the main thoroughfare of the village, and where once there had been cluttered rows of

small cottages, now the land looked almost entirely flat.

“Oh, my God,” I breathed as we passed the first set of homes, all completely destroyed. Farm animals roamed over the rubble, their hooves clamoring, breaking the oppressive silence that had settled over everything, along with the thick dust that hung heavy in the air. The place was starting to give me the creeps—the piles of wood and stone created dark shadows in the daylight, black crevices where I felt eyes watching me as I rode past.

“Hello! Anyone out there?” Ash called out from the front, his voice echoing on for miles. It seemed strange that there weren’t more sentries wandering about; the atmosphere at the castle had been crazy, ministers and guards rushing to and fro as they tended to the wounded, but here there was absolutely nothing, not a soul to be seen.

“Anyone?” Ash called again. The kids started to join in, but still nothing stirred in the piles of broken houses and farms.

I looked over at Tejus. His brows were furrowed—he was clearly finding the silence as odd as I did. We walked a bit further, the end of the village in the distance. My bull-horse was starting to get jumpy, not wanting to move

forward.

"Tejus, there's something wrong," I murmured. "I don't like this."

"Neither do I," he muttered. "Hang on—I'm going to ask that we turn back."

He reared his bull-horse, ready to gallop to the front, when a voice cried out from behind a part-crumbled stone wall.

"Ash?" It was a woman's voice. We all came to a standstill.

"Abelle?" Ash replied, jumping off the bull-horse.

I recognized the woman who emerged from behind the wall—she was large, even for a sentry, wearing brightly colored robes that were swathed about her as if she were a Grecian statue. I'd seen her last at Ash's coronation, talking to Ruby.

"I'm so glad you're safe!" she cried, embracing him.

Leaving the horses, Tejus and I followed Ash and Ruby over to the woman. I kept looking around to see if I could find any of the other villagers, but I couldn't see anyone.

"Are you alone?" I asked her as she extricated herself from Ash.

She shook her head, smiling. "Thankfully not. Some of

us made it out alive—they're in the barn." She pointed to one of the more stable-looking buildings further off in the field behind her. "We wanted to be careful. I was worried that with Hellswan destroyed, Queen Trina would be on the warpath, but I haven't seen her or any of her followers yet."

Ash smiled at this, and as he started to explain to Abelle who we had in the carriage, I caught Tejus's attention and cocked my head in the direction of the barn. He nodded and together we began to navigate our way over the debris.

"Hello?" I called. "It's safe to come out!"

I couldn't hear a sound other than the fragments of conversation Ash and Abelle were having. I looked at Tejus, who shook his head, perplexed. Maybe they were still frightened?

The barn was more or less in one piece, with the only obvious damage being to its doors, which were hanging lopsided off their hinges. I peered inside the gloom, careful not to move too far away from Tejus—seeing Abelle hadn't lessened the weirdness of the place, and I was still feeling a little jumpy.

As my eyes grew accustomed to the gloom, I saw twenty or so villagers, huddled together at the back of the room,

all totally silent, staring at us.

"Hello?" I called again, my voice breaking slightly.

"You're safe," Tejus barked at them, striding across the floorboards, clearly unaffected by their strange behavior.

One of the children started crying, and my shoulders slumped in relief. Suddenly it didn't seem as scary—it was *they* who were afraid, and no reason why I should have been.

"Why should we trust you?" an old man retorted.

"Abelle said we should remain here," another of the villagers replied, eyeing us suspiciously. "She told us we had to wait, and not leave."

"King Ashbik is outside," Tejus replied, already sounding bored. "Please follow us out—we're moving you all to a safe palace a few miles from here." He turned away from the wide-eyed villagers. "Come on, I'll get some of the guards to assist them."

I nodded, following him out. I took one last look at the villagers before stepping out into the sunlight—they hadn't moved from the back of the barn, and were still staring at us. I shivered, wrapping my arms around my frame, and hurried after Tejus.

Hazel

We had been riding for hours and the sun was starting to set, casting the ravaged land in a haze of fiery pinks and red. I felt like we were the only people left alive in Nevertide—I couldn't hear the sounds of wildlife in the forests, or birds overhead. Once we had left the village, there were no more sightings of stray farmyard animals – the villagers had caught what they could, tying up a couple of strange-looking pigs and sheep who now trailed along behind us, but even they were completely silent. The rip in the sky was now behind us, and every time I glanced back it seemed to taunt me, as if it was smiling down at us,

watching, waiting.

What is wrong with you? I scolded myself. First the village and now this—I was like a kid, afraid of the dark, waiting for monsters to come and jump out at me when there were more than enough real-life threats to be wary of. The villagers were walking up ahead with Ash, keeping their distance from Tejus and me. After the initial weirdo behavior, they seemed to be fine—muttering to one another and looking dazed, but nothing out of the ordinary given the circumstances.

"Only another mile to go," Tejus muttered at me. "The forest clears in a moment."

He had been quiet on the journey, and I wondered if the desolation of Nevertide was starting to get to him.

"Are you okay?" I asked softly.

"Fine."

"This place belongs to your family?" I prompted, wondering if our destination was the cause of his silence.

"My mother. It belonged to her family—I haven't been here since I was a boy. Hopefully it will still be intact. It was once beautiful, but my father didn't wish to visit after her death."

I nodded. Perhaps this was painful for him? I didn't

want to ask—I knew it would only make him tense up and remain taciturn. If he had any feelings about the place they would come out sooner or later, in his own time.

Soon the forest did clear, opening up into wild, unkempt grassland that came up to the bellies of the bull-horses. Ahead I could see the palace—a beautiful, ornate building with towers that reached up into the sky. Where the dying light shone on it, the white of the stone dazzled, making it look as if it was carved out of glass.

"It's incredible," I breathed.

Tejus just grunted.

"We're too far away to see the damage," he replied after a while. I shot him a bemused look, but his eyes were fixed on the building and he didn't notice. As we got closer, I saw that he was right—the palace was suffering from disuse. The ornately carved marble was stained yellow with age, and the sandstone was starting to crumble in places. But it was still beautiful, perhaps more so for its wear and tear – it made it look romantic, like something out of a fairy tale. The building was comprised of the main body of the palace, supported by four elegant towers, which I guessed were too narrow for much real use other than aesthetics. On either side of the main building were glass

houses, each containing long-dead botanical gardens, with only weeds breaking through some of the glass panes. The palace didn't have much in the way of defense—no outer wall guarded it, and only a large oak door would stand between us and intruders.

"Will we be safe here?" I asked Tejus.

"As safe as anywhere else." He shrugged. "Hellswan castle was the best defended in the kingdom, and that didn't make the slightest difference."

I could see his point. It wasn't like a moat was going to keep out the entity. I jumped off the bull-horse, eager to explore more.

"Wait for me," Tejus instructed as he disembarked, slowly scanning the surrounding forests as he did so.

I waited impatiently, watching as Ruby and Ash and the rest of the kids started clambering off their horses, all looking toward the palace with barely concealed delight. After the grim grayness of Hellswan, it felt like we'd entered a completely different world.

"Did you like this place as a child?" I asked Tejus, probing just a little.

"It was fine."

I wanted to laugh—was all of its charm really lost on

him?

"You're so strange." I smiled back at him, already drifting toward the entrance.

"What do you mean?"

"Oh, nothing," I said, knowing that I was irritating him. He started to stalk toward the palace and I joined him, idly running my hands along the grass and flowered weeds. When we reached the doorway, I paused, looking up at Tejus expectantly.

"Do you have a key?"

"At Hellswan, yes."

"Oh."

He smirked, walking along the columned patio. He stopped at one of the large glass windows, and started unbuttoning his shirt.

"Um, Tejus, what are you doing?" I asked, looking back at the fast-approaching group of my friends.

"Getting us in," he replied, staring at me as he reached the final button. I started to feel a hot flush running down my back—his eyes had become dark and hooded, his smile like a private challenge.

He removed his shirt, the taut muscles of his torso still ravaged by the scar from the ghoul during the imperial

trials. Twisting the material around his fist, he smashed it into the glass with one abrupt strike.

Oh.

The glass splintered with a loud crash, leaving the frame completely bare. It was large enough for Tejus to step through, and soon he'd disappeared from sight. Moments later I heard the door creak, and turned to see him standing in the entrance, still shirtless.

"Put it back on," I tutted.

He laughed, loudly, but did as I asked.

Stepping into the main hallway, I gasped. The place was magnificent. A huge chandelier dripped down from the ceiling, where the sunset fell on it. Shafts of bright light reflected off its glass surface and covered the room in diamond-shaped dots. The floor was polished marble, leading off into three other rooms, with a large staircase sweeping down from the mezzanine above.

"This place…"

"Is impressive," he finished, rolling his eyes.

"You're so…*dismissive* of it," I countered. "Why?"

I'd changed my mind about waiting for him to tell me in his own time—it was a puzzle I wanted an answer to, now, before I went off into more raptures of delight.

He sighed.

"Because it belongs to me, that's why. My mother left it to me in her will—it irritated me that she'd done so. I felt it was her way of saying that I should choose a different life other than becoming king."

"Because she left you a *palace*?"

Tejus shrugged. "It seemed that way to me. In her will she wished that I would live here with my family, far from the walls of Hellswan—far from the seat of power."

"Do you still feel the same way about it now?" I asked, wondering if it was a sore reminder that he was no longer king.

"I feel indifferent about it now," he replied curtly.

Liar.

Leaving Tejus to his brooding, I started to ascend the staircase, taking care to test the stairs before fully putting my weight behind each one. As I looked around, I noticed that there were dark patches on the walls—places where pictures had once hung. When I reached the mezzanine, only bare stone floors greeted me, and drafty rooms that opened off the main landing. Still, it was habitable—once we got some of the old fireplaces lit and found some bedding we'd be comfortable.

"How is it?" I heard Ruby's voice echoing from downstairs. I leaned over the banisters, smiling down at her blonde hair, uncharacteristically in complete disarray.

"Amazing," I called back.

"Like a fairytale palace, right?" she replied.

"Try telling that to Tejus," I laughed.

Ruby shrugged. "Ash keeps complaining that there's no outer wall, and no arsenal tower."

"Is there a dungeon for the evil queen?" I asked, coming back down the stairs.

"They've put her in a grain shed around the back, she's under heavy guard."

"As long as I can get in when I'm hungry." I smirked.

"I know you're joking, but please don't," Ruby replied earnestly. "We don't know how much power she has—I don't think it would be a good idea."

"But it's guilt-free," I whined, reluctantly realizing that she was right—it would be a mistake to go anywhere near the queen. Now that the entity had risen, we didn't know what she was capable of.

I motioned that I would come down and join her. I made my way back down the stairs, passing more empty rooms till I came to the kitchen. It was large and basically

equipped, but one wall had completely crumbled away, showing an uninterrupted view of the sprawling, unkempt garden. Ruby entered from behind one of the walls.

"Maybe they can put barriers up," Ruby suggested, "keep out the cold? Can barriers even do that?"

"Maybe I can try," I replied quietly.

"You should."

Ruby's reply surprised me—I still wasn't sure how she felt about me developing into a sentry.

"Don't look at me like that," she retorted. "Of course you should try. It's what you are now, there's no use trying to ignore it. And, plus, a lot of the sentry powers are amazing. Think about when we're back in The Shade. All that stuff, True Sight if you're lucky enough to have those skills, barriers—it might all come in handy."

"I guess so," I replied slowly. I hadn't really thought about any of the powers being a gift before—something that could help GASP in the future.

"Abelle still says that she can help you with one of her potions or whatever…you should take her up on it. It might make the transition easier for you? Hopefully it will stop being so difficult for you to be around us."

"Thanks, Ruby."

I was touched that she'd thought to discuss it with Abelle, and was being so positive about my transformation, especially considering it was probably hard for her to see…If she and Ash decided to go there, well—I wouldn't be the only one with new superpowers…

"Have you and Ash—"

"No," she replied quickly, "not exactly." She looked out toward the garden, avoiding catching my eye. "It's just…difficult right now, with everything going on. I can't decide what I want…"

I nodded in understanding. It wasn't like it was an easy decision—it was a life-changing one, and though I'd accepted my fate, I wasn't sure that it was something I'd be happy to watch Ruby going through.

"Whatever you decide…" I trailed off, shrugging.

"You'll be there for me. I know." She smiled.

"What are you two talking about?" Benedict asked, sauntering into the kitchen with a frown.

"Nothing," I replied quickly.

"This place is stupid," he continued, ignoring me. "There's no protection. I'm helping Ash assess the weak spots. This is obviously one!" He scoffed at the hole in the wall.

I glanced over at Ruby and she hid a smile. Were we the only ones that appreciated the palace?

"Right," I agreed sarcastically. "This place is a *dump*."

Ruby

"This isn't exactly the most kingly duty," I laughed, as Ash tried to air out a sheet with me. We'd found bedding, slightly damp and mildew-stained, in an old trunk, and in the absence of the kids—who had run off to explore the gardens—Ash and I were left to sort out the designated sleeping areas.

"Yeah, I didn't exactly envision this being number one priority on my Hellswan leadership agenda. Not that I'm complaining. It's certainly better than having to think about what we're actually going do now that we're all here."

"Has Tejus got any ideas?" I asked.

"Only that I need to become emperor as soon as possible," he replied with a sigh. "He believes it's the only way to stop the entity."

"Don't you?"

"Not sure. You know what the ministers are like. Do *you* think there's going to be anything helpful in that book?" Ash asked pointedly.

"I think it's worth a try. What other option do we have?"

Ash plumped up a cushion with ferocity, sending dust flying off it in huge plumes.

"I don't know," he muttered. "That's the problem. I don't know *anything*."

"Hmm…I think you need to start knowing," I replied, my gaze fixed on the doorway where I could see a group of villagers fast approaching along the corridor.

"What?" Ash turned around. "Oh, damn."

"I think they'll want some answers."

Ash put down the pillow, and I backed away from the door, allowing the villagers to have unrestricted access to their king.

"Don't go anywhere," Ash hissed at me as they arrived.

Six of them stood in the doorway. Abelle wasn't among them, which was a shame—she could have been a bit of a buffer—but I reminded myself that these were Ash's people. He didn't alienate them the way Tejus and his father had. Most of them looked like farmers, with ruddy faces and gnarled hands that were fisted at their sides, and a few bonneted women looking woebegone, one clutching the hand of a grumpy-looking toddler.

"King Ashbik? Can we have a moment of your time?" one of the farmers asked politely.

"Of course," Ash replied, adjusting his robes.

"We want to know what's going on," the farmer started. "It's madness, all this—the blood rain, ice fires, and now our entire village destroyed, half of it down a great crack in the ground…no one giving us any answers!" As the farmer talked, he got madder and madder, the rest of the villagers nodding furiously as he spat out each event. "The last emperor never listened to us, but at least we had a bit of peace. Now we've got nothing, no land, all our animals dead or scattered—how are we going to grow crops, make a living?"

"Families torn apart!" piped up one of the women. "I've lost everyone, and I just know that Tejus Hellswan is at

least partly responsible for all this. Ever since he got the crown there's been nothing but trouble! We hoped you'd put an end to it all, but nothing's changed, and then whenever we see you, that devil king isn't far away!"

"Stop!" Ash raised his hands.

I clutched the sheet tightly; the villagers were getting themselves agitated, and I realized this could escalate out of control if Ash didn't say the right thing.

"Listen to me." He spoke calmly, but I could see the slight shake of his hands that betrayed his nerves. "Tejus has nothing to do with this, I swear to you. All of this is out of our hands; there's something rising in Nevertide that's beyond our control. We're doing everything we can to stop it—"

"Lies!" roared the farmer. "We've heard the rumors! Do you take us for fools?"

"No!" Ash said quickly. "It's not lies, it's just unbelievable—but I wouldn't lie to you. A great evil has been locked up in Hellswan castle for centuries; the emperor unleashed it, and Tejus and I, and the rest of us, are trying to contain it again. If you want to blame anyone, it's Queen Trina!"

"Tejus's lover!" one of the women spat. "We know their

history—they're like a pair of snakes!"

Mentioning Queen Trina had been a mistake. I could see the villagers rousing themselves into a fury. In a quick flurry of movement, one of the farmers produced a thick-bladed hunting knife, holding it out toward Ash's face. I froze in horror.

"I don't want to do this," the farmer hissed, "but you're making desperate men, King Ashbik."

Ash stared at the tip of the blade.

"Take this as a warning. Neither you, nor any king, hold claim over us. We'll protect what's ours, and if there's any more of this funny business, we'll hold you to account. Got it?"

Ash rested his fingers on the blade, lowering it and then moving it away from his body. The farmer watched him with curiosity, not daring to actually follow through with his threat.

"You can turn your back on us if you wish." Ash spoke, his voice surprisingly level. "You're more than welcome to. But understand that you will be in danger wherever you go. At least here you have guards and ministers to protect you." The farmer opened his mouth to speak, but Ash silenced him with a look. "I know they haven't been of

help in the past. That is about to change. We *need* each other, more than ever before. Or we will all die."

The farmer lowered the knife completely, re-sheathing it.

"I want your word—as a man, not a king," he muttered, defeated.

"You have it," Ash replied.

The farmer nodded, slowly backing away from the room. He didn't remove his glare from Ash until he'd left the doorway, and then he and the rest of the villagers turned and left.

I exhaled, hardly aware that I'd been holding my breath throughout the entire exchange.

"Wow," I whispered. "Are you okay?"

Ash remained staring at the door, and I hovered where I was, not knowing what to say or do.

After a few moments, Ash's shoulders relaxed and he turned to face me, his face practically gray and his expression deeply concerned.

"I'm worried there's going to be an uprising…if it remains contained to the Hellswan villagers we should be able to manage it, but if it becomes wider spread than that…"

His voice trailed off.

We're in trouble.

He didn't need to say it out loud. If the villagers' opinion was shared throughout Nevertide, then there would be a lot of ruler-less sentries with no one to guide them—and one convenient target they could lash out at.

"I need to call a meeting," Ash muttered. He walked out of the room, and I followed him, not sure where I'd be most helpful, but not wanting Ash to feel like he was alone in all of this. *Where is Tejus?*

Ash looked over the banister of the mezzanine to the floor below, and called to two guards waiting by the door.

"Where's Lieutenant Ragnhild?" he asked.

"We don't know, your highness—he told us to guard the front doors," one of them replied. "Do you wish to meet with him?"

"With all of you. Find Ragnhild and gather everyone else in the ballroom."

Ash turned back to face me.

"I need the lieutenant's support," he muttered. "He's not as liked as Varga was, but he's respected."

"Ash..." I hesitated, not sure whether I was overreacting, but wanting to be honest with him

regardless. "Ragnhild lied to me, on the night that we went to the Viking graveyard. He said that you sent him, but you hadn't. I know it's a small thing, but it means that he wanted to be there—enough that he would lie about it. Don't you think that's strange?"

Ash looked uncomfortable, then shook his head. "I don't have much of a choice. I can't afford not to trust him, Ruby."

"Can you afford *to* trust him?"

"There's hardly anyone left. I need all the support I can get—and so far, he hasn't proved that he can't be trusted. Maybe he just wanted to make sure that you were protected—it's not that unreasonable. Varga *certainly* went to extensive lengths to ensure your safety."

"What's that supposed to mean?" I retorted, noting his snarky tone.

"Nothing."

I crossed my arms. "No, go on, you meant something by that. Was it the letter, or the fact that he saved my life that you're more pissed about?" I asked.

"This isn't really the time," he bit out.

"Ash, he was just a good guy. I didn't have feelings for him beyond that. I don't even know why this is an issue.

He's dead!" I was getting really mad now, angry that Ash would be so childish about this.

"I'm not the one making it an issue—you are," he replied. "I need to speak to the guards. Maybe we can talk about this when you've calmed down a bit."

"*Calmed down*?" I repeated.

"Yes, calmed down!"

"Whatever. I'll see you later."

I turned on my heel, leaving him standing by the banisters. I was furious with Ash…and with myself. How had that escalated into an argument so quickly? Maybe we were all a little tense and overtired. I was also worried that Ash was making another pig-headed mistake. He hadn't listened to me about Queen Trina—despite me telling him over and over again that she wasn't to be trusted—and now I was worried that the same thing was happening with the lieutenant.

I walked through into one of the smaller rooms of the palace, one I assumed had once been someone's bedroom. It had a small set of glass-paneled doors leading out onto a balcony that overlooked the glass greenhouses. I opened them up, showering myself in a cloud of dust and splintered paint. Stepping out onto the ledge, I inhaled the

fresh air. It felt good.

From here I could see the grain shed where Queen Trina was being kept. Five guards were stationed outside. I hoped they'd be excused from Ash's meeting. I didn't want her left alone for a single second, especially not when the kids were playing nearby. I sighed. Hazel had been making jokes about syphoning off her earlier today, and Ash was far too pleased with himself having her kept under lock and key. They were all treating her like she was some petty criminal. Didn't they realize how dangerous she was? I didn't believe for a second that we were safe from her while she was still alive. She was a monster—and we had no idea what she was capable of.

Tejus

Hazel was off somewhere with her brother, and Ash was having a meeting with the guards. Now was my chance to have a meeting with Queen Trina alone. I knew that if I could get her talking, she'd be more forthcoming with me than with the others present. I also knew that we wouldn't be able to keep the queen hostage for very long. The Acolytes would come – or someone else that wanted her free to rise to power and raise the entity… The sooner I could speak to her, the better. We needed to know more about what was coming, and I suspected that she would at least have some of the answers; deranged answers, perhaps,

but even that was something. I crossed the grounds, heading toward the grain shed. Guards stood outside the door and around the perimeter of the wooden shack, all heavily armed. If she tried to escape, no number of swords and daggers would make a blind bit of difference, but I supposed Ash still held out hope that he could contain and control her.

Fool.

I approached the guards, staring them down.

"Ki—Tejus." One of them recovered himself, stopping mid-bow. "How can we help you?"

"I wish to speak with Queen Trina, alone," I replied evenly.

"The king's orders are not to let anyone in or out of the shed."

"The king's orders don't apply to me." I smiled, wondering how much of a fight the guards would put up.

"I'm sorry, Tejus—"

"Stand aside," I barked, already bored of the game. They looked at one another, and then with their eyes lowered they started to shift sideways, allowing me access to the door.

"The key?" I prompted, observing the heavy chains that

had been wrapped around the shack.

One of the guards fumbled with the keys on his belt and clumsily handed it over to me. I thanked him with a nod, and released the padlock. The chains fell down to the floor. I yanked the door open, revealing Queen Trina's crumpled figure lying amidst the dust and grime of the floor. She was out cold.

Turning on my heel, I walked back to the palace.

"Tejus!" the guards called out after me in confusion.

Ignoring them, I strode to the wall-less kitchen, picking up an old swine-feed bucket as I went. I filled it up with ice-cold water from the sink and marched back. I wasn't in the mood to wait for her to come around.

The guards visibly relaxed as they saw me returning, but I ignored their stares as I sauntered back up to the door. Reopening it, I threw the icy contents of the bucket over the sleeping figure of Queen Trina.

"Arghhhh!" she screeched, sitting bolt upright and glaring at me with fiery rage. I threw the bucket on the floor, where it rolled into the corner of the shed.

"You're awake." I smirked. "Welcome back."

"*Animal,*" she hissed.

It was perversely pleasing to see her in such disarray for

once; her hair stood on end, and the heavy kohl coated around her eyes ran down either cheek. I wouldn't let her appearance catch me off guard though—behind the exterior of powerlessness, Trina's mind was always whirring and plotting.

"Do you know where you are?" I asked.

"Your new abode?" she replied cattily, looking around. "Did Ashbik downgrade you?"

I laughed, determined that she wouldn't get under my skin. Not this time.

"Hellswan has relocated—the castle has been destroyed, along with most of Nevertide...but then you knew that would happen, didn't you?"

She smiled up at me. "I don't know what you're talking about, Tejus."

"I think you do."

She started to run her hands through her hair, trying to get it under control, and then moved down to her robe, brushing off the dust that covered its royal blue velvet. She reminded me of a cat preening. I thought of my lost feline Lucifer, and I wanted to smack her.

"Do you mourn it that much?" she asked coyly. "Were you ever happy at Hellswan, Tejus? Did you ever believe

it to be truly your home—did you ever even consider Nevertide to be your home?"

"That is irrelevant," I replied, keeping my smile in place.

"Is it?"

"Trina, enough. Tell me what you know."

She burst into peals of laughter.

"Tejus, really, don't you know how to get information out of me yet? Let me tell you how I prefer to divulge my secrets…I like to operate on information exchange. You tell me something, and I shall repay the favor."

"I don't think you're in a position to bargain."

"Don't you?" she replied softly, and I heard the threat beneath her words. She had a plan. I started to feel uneasy.

"What do you want to know?" I asked, testing the waters.

"The human—I want to know if you've fallen in love with her."

What?

This time my laughter was genuine. We were in a life-or-death situation, and all Queen Trina was concerned about was petty jealousies and slights. She was *insane.*

"Yes," I replied simply.

A look passed over Queen Trina's face, so quickly I couldn't catch what it was, but when she looked back up at me, her smile was once again fixed and her eyes shone brightly.

"So you decided to be selfish and put yourself first – before the needs of your kingdom?"

I frowned, wondering what she was getting at.

"I did."

"Shame on you, Tejus of Hellswan. And what a pitiful fool you are. It's futile—she will die. She will die in Nevertide, and it will be all your fault."

I kept my hands at my sides, but my body was starting to shake with the effort of keeping my emotions in check.

"I doubt that will be the case," I replied quietly.

"My master is rising," she spat. "There is nothing that you can do—there is nowhere that you can hide. A new dawn will be brought to Nevertide, a future beyond your imagining, and that human soul will be torn to shreds—returning to ashes and dust, gone." She clicked her fingers, her eyes boring into mine. "What will your world be like without her, Tejus?"

"Are you so sure of this?" I snapped. "Because I don't see the entity here. I see a half-completed job, and a

wretched queen sitting in a grain shed, trying to bargain with me."

"He is coming," she repeated again, her smile returning.

"Tell me about the Acolytes," I said, trying a different tactic. "I know you lead them—what are you doing for the entity?"

"You know all you need to about us." She dismissed the subject with a wave of her hand. "We are his faithful servants, and I will benefit greatly from the new world order. If you're lucky"—she smirked—"I will keep you on as a personal slave, a position you are perhaps better fit for than you were king."

If Queen Trina believed that she would benefit so greatly, I wondered why she bothered to involve herself with the trials at all. What was the point?

"So why did you put yourself in the running for the imperial trials?" I asked through gritted teeth.

She shrugged. "It always helps to eliminate the competition. I honestly thought it would be quite fun."

"Fun? Ash says you almost died during the last trial."

Trina pursed her lips.

"That's enough questions for today," she purred. "Just know that I never wanted you to be hurt in all this, which

is incidentally why I was such a huge fan of Ashbik winning the trials...but, alas, you persevered, and you have interfered. And now it is too late."

"Too late for what?"

Her eyes rested on the door behind me, and I spun around. The door was how I'd left it, still closed, without a sound coming from outside. I turned back to face her, confused. The moment our eyes met, I heard the loud bang of wooden planks falling backward onto the earth. The door was ripped open—along with the rest of the shed wall. I spun around to see a group of hooded figures who could only be Acolytes standing, silent, in front of the exposed shed.

Before I could move, an agonizing pain ripped through my skull. Stunned at the immediacy of the effect, I stumbled forward. Through fast-graying vision, I watched as Queen Trina rose from the floor, her eyes alight with victory.

"You should have chosen me, Tejus," she murmured as she walked past.

"If you touch her—if you EVER touch her, I will end you," I hissed as my knees collapsed beneath me, sending me sprawling to the floor. The pain only intensified, and I

grunted in pain, writhing on the ground as the group of black-hooded Acolytes slowly backed away with their leader. The motionless bodies of the guards lay in the grass, as helpless as I was to stop them.

Queen Trina walked free.

Hazel

Abelle had somehow managed to cart what looked like an entire apothecary with her to the palace. She was sitting in the middle of hundreds of glass bottles, each filled with dried herbs, petals, unassuming-looking sticks, and some liquids that I wasn't too eager to look closely at.

"Come and sit, Hazel." She patted a cushion next to her. "Don't worry about the hunger—we'll soon get that fixed."

I glanced over at Ruby, who smiled reassuringly and sat down on the other side of Abelle.

"This all looks amazing." Ruby picked up one of the

bottles, holding it up to the fire that was blazing in the hearth. “What is this?”

Abelle glanced over. “Oh, that’s *Surdi Ossa*. You don’t want to touch that. It confuses the senses, hearing in particular…it’s not nice.” Ruby hastily placed the bottle back down, and shoved her hands under her thighs.

Abelle started opening more bottles and jars, dumping their contents into a small iron pot. It wasn’t a million miles away from what I’d seen Corrine do, and the familiarity of her actions encouraged me to take a seat next to the woman.

“Are you a…witch, Abelle?” I asked, stumbling over my words, worried that I might offend the woman.

“Oh, no, there’s no such thing here, dear,” she replied in an off-hand manner.

I shot Ruby a meaningful look, but she just shrugged. I presumed she’d had a similar conversation with the woman before, as Abelle’s answer didn’t seem to come as a surprise.

“Right. But you do, err, magic?”

Abelle laughed loudly. “Nonsense! I just work with herbs, with nature, I suppose, to make remedies.”

Right.

She seemed to be witch-like to me, but maybe Nevertide didn't really have a concept of magic—Tejus had thought that vampires were mythical creatures, and clearly this was a dimension that hadn't been exposed to this species.

"So, what is this?" I asked, moving back to the concoction that Abelle was creating.

"This is something that will dull the hunger—but I'm afraid it will dull everything else too, all the power you may be experiencing in your sentry form. But after a while, once you learn to control the hunger, you can take less and less of this."

I nodded, thinking that I didn't mind the exchange too much. Better that I could be around my family and friends without wanting to suck them dry, than remain a liability with powers that I still didn't know how to use.

"How will she learn to control the hunger?" Ruby asked.

"It will just come with time—time and repression of your instincts. Most sentries feel the hunger, especially around humans; it's such a pure form of mental power that it's hard to resist…but we manage, and we learn over time to keep it under control."

This was sounding more and more like vampirism; perhaps my condition wouldn't be too hard to deal with. I supposed it was somewhat similar to the future that I'd envisioned for myself anyway…just in a different form. I started thinking about Tejus. How hard it would have been for him not to syphon off me all those times we were together, especially in the beginning. How, for the most part, he did it gently, rarely causing me any pain. I had a lot to thank him for.

"It's almost ready," Abelle announced. "I just need to boil it for a short while."

Picking up the pot, she placed it on the side of the fire. Flames snaked up the side of the iron. Ruby shuddered.

"Bringing back memories?" I asked her quietly, observing her reaction to the flames.

"Yeah. Being in that castle—it just felt so claustrophobic, like we'd never get out…and then when Benedict rushed back toward it…" She shook her head. "It was horrible."

"You know, I have memory herbs. They can help you forget unpleasant things—things you'd rather not remember?" Abelle suggested. I hadn't thought that she was listening, and her offer took me by surprise.

"No," Ruby replied hastily. "I'm okay to remember it. I'll probably just become a fire alarm Nazi or something—it's a good lesson."

"Suit yourself," Abelle replied. "Just remember the offer is always here."

"Thanks," replied Ruby, sounding like she wasn't sure she meant it.

"The elixir's ready!" Abelle took the pot off the fire and started pouring it into yet another glass bottle. Its liquid was a dark, sludgy brown—not the most appetizing thing I'd ever seen. Abelle held it out to me.

"Just one sip, twice a day," she instructed, smiling at me.

"Okay, thanks."

I took the bottle. The liquid was still warm, and I clutched it in my fist, hesitating before drinking it. Something was holding me back—I didn't know if it was because I wasn't that well acquainted with Abelle, or that the loss of power she warned of was more troubling to me than I had first assumed, but something just didn't feel quite right.

"It doesn't taste as bad as it looks," Abelle said, observing my reluctance with a small smile.

"Maybe think about hugging Benedict? Or you know, someone else?" Ruby added with a wink.

I rolled my eyes at her, but her comments had the desired effect. I removed the lid and held the bottle to my lips. On the count of three, I took a small sip of the foul-smelling stuff.

"Ugh!"

It doesn't taste as bad as it looks? She had to be kidding me.

"Sorry." Abelle shrugged. "I didn't think you'd do it otherwise."

"Thanks for the warning," I muttered. It tasted like soil and boiled cabbage. I was sorely regretting my decision when I started to feel the potion taking effect. A warmth spread across my body, and the hunger that had been my constant companion over the past few days—with the exception of when I'd syphoned off the minister—started to vanish. I sighed with contentment.

"It works," I announced dreamily. "It actually works!"

It was such a relief to finally be free from my never-ending hunger that I sank back onto the stone floor, lying with my eyes closed and letting all the tension drain from my body.

"Hazel, are you okay?" Ruby asked, peering down at me.

"Better than okay," I replied. "Much, much better."

"Did she take too much?" Ruby asked Abelle. "She looks kind of weird."

"It's just because it's the first time," the sentry replied calmly. "The more potent effects will wear off—the absence of hunger is quite powerful if it's been a constant thorn for a while. Don't worry."

The two women fell silent, and someone cleared their throat.

"It looks like I'm interrupting something." A stern, very familiar voice seemed to float over from the doorway.

"Are you okay?" Ruby exclaimed, rushing to her feet. Dazedly I sat up—what was wrong with Tejus?

I looked over to the doorway, seeing him slumped against the frame, his face pale and perspiring. I tried to stand up, every bone in my body feeling like rubber, and the ground moving when it shouldn't have been.

"What's wrong with her?" Tejus demanded, striding over to me.

"An elixir to repress the hunger," Abelle snapped at him.

"I'm fine," I interjected, finally standing up. I clutched

onto Tejus's arms, trying to get him in focus.

"You're clearly not," he muttered.

"What happened to you?" I persisted, desperate for him to stop analyzing me for a second.

"Queen Trina happened to me," he replied with a deep scowl. "She's gone—the Acolytes attacked, they've taken out five guards. Ruby, will you go and tell Ash? I couldn't find him."

"Of course." She moved hastily toward the door. A moment later I could hear her footsteps running along the marble tiles.

Queen Trina had escaped. This didn't bode well at all.

"And I would like to be alone with Hazel," he said to Abelle, "so can you take all this with you?"

Abelle didn't reply, but I could tell by the brusque nature of her movements, the rattling of the glass bottles as she packed them up, that she wasn't happy about being ordered around by him.

"Let me know if you need anything, Hazel," she muttered, glaring at Tejus before she left.

I pulled at his arms, wanting him to sit down by the fire with me—I was still feeling woozy and standing was an effort. Tejus didn't look like he could hold out much

longer either. Why hadn't he asked Abelle to give him something?

"What were you doing with Queen Trina anyway?" I asked when we were both seated. I realized, happily, that I could be as close to him as I liked without any unwanted side effects.

"I was questioning her. I thought she'd be more inclined to give me answers than anyone else."

"Because of your history?" I asked quietly.

"Yes. Our *ancient* history."

"Did you find out anything useful?" I asked, trying to hide my smile at his emphasis on the word 'ancient'.

"No, not really. The entire exercise was futile—her master will rise, he will kill us all, etc. etc. And now she is gone. My only saving grace is that I believe it would have happened whether or not I had gone to speak with her. It might stop me from getting beheaded by King Kitchen, at the very least."

I leaned my head against his arm, disappointed that we didn't know more, but very glad that I could once again be close enough to Tejus, smell his distinct musk and feel the warmth of his body against mine.

"I love you, Tejus," I whispered.

"Is this the potion talking, or you?"

"Me."

"After everything, still?" he asked, uncertainty creeping into his tone.

"Still... Always."

He turned toward me, cupping my jaw in his hand. His lips grazed mine in a soft kiss. He moved away, leaning back down on the floor and motioning me to follow him. I slid into his outstretched arm, our bodies lying side by side in front of the fire. My hands ran across the hard muscles of his chest, and I was just grateful that I could be touching him like this, feeling nothing else but the hot prickles of desire flooding my body.

"Can I try to mind-meld with you—give you some of my energy?" I asked.

"You can try, but it doesn't seem that strong. What did that fool crone give you?"

I tutted at his mean assessment of Abelle—she was only trying to help. Without her, none of this would be possible.

"So, let's try," I encouraged.

Tejus smiled down at me, the tender, loving gaze quickly becoming something else entirely.

"I have a better idea." He smirked, running his thumb along my temples and down to my lips. I didn't argue. Moments later Tejus had locked the door and I was a million miles away, sinking into Tejus's soft caresses.

ASH

"Dammit!" I swore, kicking the chair.

"Are you angry at Tejus or the furniture?" Ruby replied, cocking an eyebrow at me, clearly unimpressed.

"Tejus," I snapped. "Tejus and Queen Trina and this entire situation. I think it warrants some chair-kicking."

I was beyond furious. Ruby had said that Tejus was overpowered by the Acolytes, but even so, the warning of Memenion rang in my ears. Had Tejus been lenient on her, let her escape because when it came down to it, he wasn't able to kill her? I couldn't afford for Tejus to have that kind of weakness—what I had in mind for him

wouldn't be possible if he couldn't protect us all, put Nevertide before his own feelings.

"I don't think he could have done much to stop it, Ash. Keeping Queen Trina hostage was a mistake. She was always going to get out eventually, surely you could see that?"

Great.

As if I didn't have enough worries, it now felt like Ruby was questioning my ability to make sound decisions.

"We needed the information," I said.

"I know." She sighed. "But we still need to read the book—we just need to find a way for you to become emperor. Maybe then we'll get some real answers."

She was right about that. I didn't want to delay the trip to seek out the Impartial Ministers a moment longer. At dawn tomorrow we'd leave to find them—I just hoped that Tejus had some idea as to where they might be. The ministers had kept their abode secret for centuries, and I didn't know of any non-minister who had ever visited them.

"All right. We'll leave tomorrow. In the meantime, I've asked the guards to take turns in keeping watch, and I've put barriers up around the palace. It will have to be enough

for now—hopefully Queen Trina will be busy recuperating and not planning a return."

Ruby nodded.

"You should get some rest," she replied.

"I know."

I was so short-tempered that even Ruby was irritating me. I let out another breath, looking around the empty ballroom. The meeting with the guards hadn't gone particularly well—if it hadn't been for Ragnhild, I doubted that a single one of them would have listened to what I had to say. It didn't exactly make me feel spectacular.

"So, where do we sleep?" I asked tetchily.

"Jenney and the kids are sleeping together in one of the upstairs rooms. We could join them, there are enough beds up there."

"Fine, let's do that."

We left the ballroom and walked up the main staircase. I felt like I hardly had the energy to reach the top—every single part of my body felt like it wanted to give up, to just slump on the marble floor and let someone else take over for a while.

When we reached the kids' room, I could hear laughter

coming from inside—the sound of the kids squealing, and Benedict arguing with Yelena.

I stopped at the door, holding it shut when Ruby tried to open it.

“I can’t,” I replied. “I need to be somewhere quiet. I’ll see you later.” I started walking off when Ruby grabbed my arm.

“Ash, wait. What’s wrong? I mean aside from Queen Trina escaping. Something else is bugging you. What is it?”

“I’m just in a bad mood, that’s all,” I replied, removing my arm from her grasp.

“Don’t be like this,” she said. “Just tell me what’s wrong—I can’t help otherwise.”

“You can’t help me anyway!” I exclaimed. “I feel completely useless—I have no idea what to do, everything feels like it’s totally and utterly out of my control, the guards have absolutely no faith in me, and right now it feels like you don’t either!”

She looked stung, her eyes widening with shock at my revelation.

“That’s totally not true!”

“Shortie, come on—what about Queen Trina?

Apparently, you *knew* she would escape, and I thought we had her secured till we could get some answers!"

"I didn't mean that the way it sounded," she replied sullenly. "I believe you can do this. You know I do—I always have."

I stayed silent, not knowing what else to say. I was handling this all wrong, and I knew it. Yet again, Ruby and I were arguing when I didn't want us to be, creating more distance between us, which, considering we couldn't get intimate, was an idiotic thing to do.

"Come on," Ruby announced, dragging me along the corridor by my robe.

"Where are we going?"

"Somewhere quiet. That's what you wanted, right?"

I followed her in silence, wondering where in Nevertide she was taking me. At the end of the corridor she pushed open one of the doors, revealing a small box-shaped room that was completely empty apart from a small window, a dilapidated-looking chair and a wood burner.

"Wait here," she instructed, storming back out again.

I leaned against the wall, not really seeing any other option.

She came back a moment later, carrying a blanket and

two pillows, all strongly smelling of damp.

"This is all I could find. It will have to do."

I nodded, watching as she laid the blanket on the floor and arranged the pillows at one end. Then she turned toward the wood burner, tapping her foot in agitation as she looked around for some wood.

I walked toward the chair and started to break it up best I could.

"I feel bad," Ruby said, watching me destroy the furniture.

"Don't," I replied. "Another year and it would have rotted away to nothing anyway." I shoved the wood into the stove and lit it by scraping a piece of flint up the side of the stove. Soon the wood caught light, and I sat back on the blanket, feeling mildly satisfied for the first time that day.

Ruby came and sat down next to me, just out of reach.

"I'm sorry," she stated, looking down at her fingers. "I didn't mean to doubt you. I'm just frightened, and I'm not handling it very well. Forgive me?"

"Already have." I smiled. "And you don't need to say sorry. I'm being an idiot. I'm just frustrated, about a million things, and one of those things is us…*you*—all the

things we can't do because…well, you know."

Ruby's cheeks turned bright pink, and I scratched the back of my head, feeling the same heat rising over my own face.

"This is awkward," I muttered. "I shouldn't have brought it up."

Ruby took a deep breath and exhaled. Her fingers reached across the blanket, entwining with mine.

"I actually had a thought about that," she breathed, "I thought we could try something…"

I looked at her quizzically, not understanding what she meant.

"I want you to mind-meld with me, syphon off me," she replied.

I grinned at her, understanding that she wanted intimacy, and if a mind-meld was all that was available to us, then I was more than happy to do as she asked. I reached out for her, delving into her mind and finding her energy bright and pure, waiting for me. I sighed, instantly drinking in its power and hazy comfort.

Just as I was enjoying the tingling, rushing sensations that were flooding my body, an image started to flicker into my mind. At first it was gray and fuzzy, like looking

through an unfocused telescope, but then it started to clear, and I could see Ruby, softly smiling at me.

This is different.

When I'd shared images with Ruby during a mind-meld before, they'd been accidental, our subconscious flittering along the bond we shared, but this time it felt like she was purposefully projecting the image toward me.

The image of Ruby laughed, and the picture shifted, showing me more; Ruby standing in the room that we were physically in, with the same fire and damp blanket. The only difference was that her vision was far cozier and inviting than the reality was.

Hey. Her voice drifted through my head.

Hi, I replied mentally. *Can you hear me?*

Yeah, I can hear you. Impressive, huh?

That's one thing to call it…

Are you weirded out? she asked, her smile faltering.

No, absolutely not—I'm just a bit blown away.

Her smile returned, and she knelt down in front of me.

It's an experiment, she whispered.

I like it.

Gently, half afraid of breaking our bond, I leaned forward and kissed her. I knew that it was only our shared

imagination, but I could feel the answering pressure of her lips, their warm moisture, the taste of her mouth, the smell of her hair that brushed against my face.

I can feel it, she exhaled, looking up at me in fragile surprise.

Me too.

I grabbed her more insistently this time, knowing that she was solid, whole. It was all real, amazingly real. Our kiss deepened, and a shudder ran through Ruby's body. Her hands curved up around my neck, and we fell backward onto the blanket, our bodies entwined.

Ash, she whispered, *I want tonight to be ours.*

I groaned, digging my hand in her hair, twisting its thick length in my hand, tugging her head backward, placing kisses down her neck and chest till I reached the top of her shirt. Her breaths shuddered, pulling me toward her as I undressed her, her fingers working just as urgently as mine to remove the clothing that separated us.

My heart was pounding, my throat tight as I looked down at Ruby's body in the firelight.

I've never done this before, I admitted.

Me neither.

Will you tell me to stop if it…

She nodded, her blue eyes large, meeting mine with openness and willingness.

I trust you, Ash.

They were the words I needed to hear.

I buried myself in her arms, pulling her to me tightly. I made love to her with every bone and muscle in my body on fire.

The night burnt itself on my mind for eternity: the soft moans that escaped her lips, the muted glow of our skin, golden hair entangled in my fingers, and always her blue eyes—endless pools that I drowned in time and time again.

I love you, she whispered, just before the dawn rose.

Stay here, I pleaded as I felt our bond starting to weaken. I tried to hold onto it, sending all the energy I had toward her.

I don't think I can.

She brushed her finger along my temple, her eyes sad and wistful. It was coming to an end. The bond broke. Ruby lay next to me, both of us fully clothed on the cold floor of the palace, the fire dead in the hearth.

"Ruby?" I croaked.

"That was…amazing." She sighed, curling up toward me, a small smile on her lips. I laughed, running my palm

across my forehead, grateful that my body still ached, that I could still feel the rushing after-effects of what we'd just shared.

"Yeah." I grinned up at the ceiling. "It really was."

Tejus

I woke just before dawn. The sky was an inky blue, the tear in it masked momentarily by the darkness. I left Hazel sleeping on the floor of the room for a few moments longer while I went off in search of Ash. We needed to leave to find the Impartial Ministers as soon as we could; with Queen Trina on the loose, we couldn't afford any further delays.

Closing the door quietly behind me, I entered the empty hallway. The light was dim—only two torches had been found in working order yesterday, and they flickered ineffectually in the gloom. I located the stairway, hoping

that Ash would already be up and ready. Two guards waited by the main door at the bottom of the stairs, nodding in greeting at my approach.

“King Ashbik?” I asked.

“The kitchen,” one replied.

I made my way there, finding Ash standing in front of the collapsed wall, looking out into the shadows of the garden.

“My apologies about Queen Trina,” I said, coming to stand by his side. He glanced over at me, nodding.

“I suppose it was only a matter of time.”

“That was the idea – to speak to her before she was rescued,” I muttered, uncomfortable with the idea of justifying my actions to Ash. It would take some getting used to.

He grunted.

“Just let me know next time.”

“Fine,” I said. “Are you ready to make a visit to the Ministers?”

“As ready as I can be. Do you know where we’ll need to go?” he asked.

“The Impartial Ministers are rumored to live at the foot of Ghouls’ Ridge—there’s a monastery built into the

mountain, accessible only from the ravine that runs at the foot of the mountains. I've never been there, but it's what I've heard."

"From a reliable source?"

I smirked; it was Queen Trina who had divulged the information to me long, long ago.

"Not remotely, but do you have any other ideas?" I replied.

"No, I suppose I don't."

We stood in silence for a while, both watching the sky rapidly changing color as the sun began its ascent. It seemed strange to me that only a day had passed since the entity's destruction had ravaged Nevertide. It felt like a lifetime ago; waking up in this palace had felt like a strange dream—it had taken me a few moments to recall why I wasn't in Hellswan tower.

"We should leave the guards here, for the protection of the villagers and the kids," Ash said.

"I will not leave Hazel," I asserted.

Ash nodded. "I won't leave Ruby either—they can come with us. I'm going to leave Jenney and Abelle in charge."

What?

"Are you mad?" I asked incredulously. "A child and a half-witted woman?"

Ash glared at me.

"I'm not mad—they're the only two I can trust. The guards will have their orders, but if there are decisions to be made I want one of those two making them."

"What about Lieutenant Ragnhild?" I snapped, wondering once again at the wisdom of leaving Ashbik to take my place as king.

"We can't trust him," Ash replied quietly. He began telling me about the night of the temple visit, how Ragnhild had lied to Ruby about his presence being dictated by Ash. I wasn't entirely sure that meant we couldn't trust him, but after Varga perhaps it *was* better that we didn't take the risk.

"Is every Hellswan subject going to be revealed as a traitor?" I grumbled, more bothered by the fact that I seemed to be such a terrible judge of character.

"We have your father to blame for that," Ash retorted.

I sneered at the kitchen boy. If Ash didn't rise to the challenges that faced him, my father would be a convenient scapegoat for him throughout his rule—whether that would be years or only a matter of days.

"Let's depart," I muttered. I had no desire to argue with Ash. He would learn soon enough the true burden of his crown.

* * *

I knelt on the ground in front of the palace entrance with Ash and the rest of the ministers. Our hands were outstretched, and I could feel the collective power running through my veins.

"Higher!" Ash commanded through gritted teeth. I expelled more energy, my muscles contorting with the effort. We were building a barrier for the humans and sentries we'd be leaving behind, and Ash wanted to leave nothing to chance.

The walls piled up, thick and high, and the tension and power slowly seeped away from my body. It was done.

"Ready?" I asked, turning to Ash.

"Ready."

We rose, and I turned my attention to Hazel, who was waiting by the bull-horses at the far end of the overgrown lawn. We had chosen to travel by land rather than using the vultures, in order not to attract undue attention. It meant the journey would take longer, but it would be

worth it to remain hidden.

“How are you feeling?” Hazel asked, her eyes flashing down to the scars on my chest—the wounds concealed from others by my shirt, but not her.

“Never better,” I muttered. She looked at me doubtfully, but it was the truth. The wound had healed, and even though I’d been drained aggressively by the Acolytes, this morning I hadn’t felt it.

“You?” I asked as I climbed onto the bull-horse.

“Fine, still no hunger, but…” She shrugged.

“Still weak?”

“It’s worth it,” she pointed out. “I’m not half crazy with the need to syphon off everyone in sight.”

It might be worth it within the confines of the palace, when she was around her family and friends, but taking her out into Nevertide suddenly didn’t seem like such a good idea.

“Fine,” I replied, not sharing my misgivings yet. She seemed more content this way, relaxed for the first time since she had acquired the powers. But today was the first time I couldn’t feel her energy, and that worried me. Normally it came off her in waves, unbelievably strong when she was a human, and stronger still since she became

a sentry. I could recall my brothers occasionally being weakened by potions when they were younger, to prevent them from syphoning mindlessly—but I couldn't remember them, or myself, losing the constant hum of energy that surrounded sentries. Perhaps it was because Hazel was an adult, and whatever herbs she needed to take were stronger than those given to children. I made a mental note to discuss the elixir with Abelle, to double check what she was feeding Hazel and the dosage…Was Hazel taking more than she should have been to ensure that her friends and family remained safe from her syphoning? I couldn't believe that she'd do something so foolish, so I dismissed it.

"Let me know if it gets worse," I added. "You need to be careful."

"I know, I will," she reassured me. "Maybe soon I can ask Abelle to lower the dosage or something – start weaning me off."

I nodded, privately relived that Hazel was willing to accept a future as a fully active sentry – not one that was constantly repressing her powers.

Once Ash was ready, we left the grounds of the palace at a rapid pace. Hazel rode beside me, with Ash and Ruby

following. I stuck mainly to the forests, though our trek would have been an easier one had we followed the main roads—but where there were roads, there would be sentries: lost, angry and eager for answers that neither Ash nor I could provide.

Ruby

"It's so quiet," I murmured to Ash, more to break the silence than anything. We'd been riding for about an hour, and the complete absence of any noise other than the cracks of twigs and dried leaves beneath the hooves of the bull-horses was starting to drive me crazy. We'd started the journey chatting among ourselves—well, Ash, Hazel and I had. Tejus had mostly remained his taciturn self. But as the journey progressed we'd grown quieter, the oppressive atmosphere sucking the conversation dry.

It was also difficult for me to even remotely try to focus on the task ahead. My mind was filled with images of last

night, moments replaying over and over again on loop, warming the pit of my stomach as I replayed every touch and sigh, every feeling that I'd experienced—from complete ecstasy to the bittersweet disappointment of returning to reality, knowing that none of it had been *physically* real. This morning I had woken to find Ash already gone, and I had felt like I'd been robbed of something—that we both had. I wanted so badly for it to be real, and the idea scared me. I had some tough decisions ahead of me, decisions I didn't feel like I was fully equipped to make. I was starting to realize that when it came to Ash I lost all sense of reason. Had the mind-meld broken at any point during the experience, I wouldn't have stopped. I would have abandoned myself completely to the consequences, just to remain in his arms.

Careful, Ruby.

I felt dizzy, bowled over by the stark reality of the situation, of how close I was to following in the same footsteps as Hazel.

"I don't get it," Ash muttered, breaking through my reverie. "It's weird. The birds at least should have survived."

"I know, the vultures did…but I can't hear a sound

from anything else," I replied, trying to bring myself back out of my head and focus on what Ash was saying.

Looking around, I was starting to get the feeling that we were being watched, that this silence was a pause before something *happened*—something terrible, waiting in the dark depths of the forests, where the morning sun couldn't get to it. We were also starting to get closer to Ghouls' Ridge—I could see the huge precipice towering ahead of us. I'd only seen it before from up above, where I could see the thick swirling mists that settled in the ravine. We were riding into the mists—a dense, heavy fog that made the air smell pungent and moldy.

"How far away are we?" Hazel asked Tejus. Our bull-horses had drawn closer together as we'd begun to enter the ravine, partly due to the narrowing of the path, and I thought partly because the animals seemed to be as spooked as we were. Their hooves took each step tentatively, and the great muscles on their bodies quivered, ready to cut and run at a moment's notice.

"We're not far. The monastery is built into the stone of the ridge, allegedly," Tejus replied.

"What do you mean 'allegedly?' Haven't you been here before?" I asked.

"No. No one other than ministers are permitted to enter the Impartial Ministers' home."

That news wasn't comforting.

"What if we can't get in—like it's protected, or something?" I asked anxiously.

Tejus turned to glance over at me with a slightly bemused expression, and shrugged.

"Then we'll face that problem when we come to it."

Okay.

I got the feeling that this wasn't an entirely well-thought-out plan. The ridge was getting closer, a sheer rock face that looked completely impenetrable, and, as far as I could see, showed no evidence of anything built within it.

We started riding single file as the path became narrower, and large, thorny bushes started to appear on either side of us, their spikes catching onto our robes and scratching at any uncovered skin as we passed.

"I can't see anything," I called to Tejus. "Are you sure this is the right place?"

"It's what I've been told," he replied drily.

Could you be more vague?

Tejus's relaxed demeanor was starting to irritate me. It

was as if the rest of us were on a world-saving apocalypse mission, while he was taking a nice stroll through a garden.

"She's got a point," Ash observed, looking up at the wall. "Where would the entrance be? There's nothing here. We should have brought a minister along with us."

Tejus pulled his horse to a stop; the sudden snort of the animal echoed loudly around the valley, making us all jump.

"We should get off here. I think we're going to need to walk the rest of the way—it's too narrow."

"Rest of the way to *where*?" Ash insisted. "I can't see a thing, Tejus, am I missing something?"

Tejus rolled his eyes, and then glared at Ash. "Maybe you want to try using True Sight, your highness?"

"What do you—" Ash started out sounding belligerent, and then fell silent. "Oh," he replied, a moment later. "I see what you mean." His eyes rolled back in head as he used his True Sight ability. Clearly, he was seeing *something* on the other side of the stone wall in front of us.

"Want to fill us in?" I prompted, irritated that I couldn't see what they clearly could.

"I can see the monastery," Ash replied sheepishly. "It's inside the wall of the ridge. Still don't understand how

we're going to get inside though."

"There's got to be an entrance around here somewhere," replied Tejus, scratching his jaw-line in contemplation.

"We should get closer," Hazel announced, leading the way forward. She was clearly as frustrated as I was at not being able to see anything, but I suspected her frustration came from her abilities being subdued by Abelle's potion.

We all followed her, Tejus frowning at her departing back. I could tell he wanted to yank her back so that she wasn't the one going first, but he managed to reject the impulse. I smiled as I followed my friend, wondering how one of the most independent women I knew managed to get involved with such a protective, over-cautious boyfriend.

"Here!" Hazel shouted out, so close to the wall that her nose was practically pushed against the stone, but her arm pointed sideways, toward the joint where the valley met the wall of the ravine on the left of the path. From a distance, it looked like they were joined together, but up close I could see there was a narrow gap between, just large enough for a sentry to fit through.

"Ash, lead the way," Tejus insisted, holding Hazel back.

"Seriously?" Hazel hissed at him.

"Seriously," he repeated, ignoring her answering glare. I stifled a giggle, and watched as Ash slipped between the two rock faces, vanishing into the gloom. After a moment, I followed, running my hands on the rock on each side to guide me. For a few seconds I couldn't see Ash at all, but then the passage was suddenly flooded with light—pure, white and almost painfully brilliant.

"Ash?" I called out, my voice timid.

I didn't hear a reply, and I blinked in the bright glare for a few moments, trying to see his figure up ahead.

"Ruby, what's going on?" Hazel asked, and I felt her hand brush against my back. I turned around, seeing both her and Tejus shading their eyes.

"Ash!" I tried again, moving forward.

"I'm here," he called back, stepping out in front of the light. "You've got to come and see this—it's incredible!"

I walked further along, finding Ash standing next to an opening in the rock. I stepped through its arch, and gasped.

What the heck?

The view before me was mind-boggling. Rationally, I knew we were inside the rock of the ridge, but it looked as if we'd entered a completely different world. The light was

actually sunlight—a huge, perfectly blue expanse of sky appeared over us, seeming to stretch on for miles into the distance. The glare I'd seen from the outside was the sunlight reflecting off the white stone that covered the ground. The only object breaking the endless expanse of the white stone and sky was a large pillared coliseum. Each column was at least seven yards high, circling a large marble basin.

We all looked at each other, our expressions stunned.

"What *is* this place?" Hazel whispered eventually, looking to Tejus for answers.

"I have no idea," he murmured. "I've never seen anything like this in my life..."

"Should we call out or something?" I asked.

"Hello?" Ash called. "Anybody out there?"

His call was unanswered—there wasn't a soul here. We waited for a few moments, standing awkwardly by the entrance, not entirely sure if we should venture forward or leave.

"We've come this far, let's look around," Tejus instructed, looking warily toward the coliseum. Together we approached the building, our footsteps echoing across the floor.

As we moved closer, I could see that the basin was filled with water, motionless and almost glowing, like there was a white light coming from within it.

"Well, looks like we found the ministers," Ash commented. He was the first to reach the edge, and was looking down into the basin. I hurried forward, wondering what he meant.

As I looked down, I saw five of the Impartial Ministers lying, completely submerged, in the water. Their long gray beards and hair floated like seaweed around them, their robes undulating as if being rocked by a current that wasn't visible from the surface.

"I don't understand," I whispered.

"That makes two of us," Ash replied in wonderment.

Julian

"Look what I found." Benedict stalked into the room, brandishing a crossbow in his arms, the bolts in a quiver slung across his back.

"That's cool." I grinned. "Where did you find it?"

"In those towers. They've got a bunch of old blankets and paintings in them, but there's a couple of old swords too. What shall we shoot?" he asked eagerly.

I jumped up, looking out of the window into the garden for a suitable target.

"The shed?" I suggested, looking at the remaining three walls of the grain house where Queen Trina had escaped.

Maybe after we'd used it as target practice we could set the whole thing on fire—I hated looking at it, knowing that she'd sat in there, her smug smile and twisted mind plotting against us all.

"Perfect." Benedict nodded. "Let's go out now before Jenney sees us. She's in the kitchen with the kids, we can go out the front."

"Okay," I agreed.

We left the room and peered over the mezzanine, making sure that the coast was clear. A couple of guards were pacing up and down by the door, but I doubted they would stop us—most of them were still terrified of Benedict and tended to keep out of his way.

"Let's go," I hissed.

We raced down the stairs, but stopped midway as the guards swung the front doors open. Shouts and jeers came from outside. I looked at Benedict, puzzled—were the villagers making that noise? We both hurried down the stairs, the crossbow cradled in Benedict's arms.

As we stepped onto the marble entrance hall, ministers and villagers started to emerge behind us, all looking equally baffled by the source of the noise. When I stepped outside through the main entrance, I froze.

"We're in *deep* trouble."

Behind the barriers, fighting to get through, stood a horde of very angry sentries—villagers mostly, with some ministers and guards. They created a sea of bodies as far back as I could see, all chanting Ash and Tejus's names, spitting, throwing rocks and battering their fists on the barrier.

"What do we do?" Benedict breathed, his eyes wide as he took in the crowd.

"Stand back," a guard commanded, shoving us back toward the door.

"Who are they?" I yelled, shoving him back.

"They're from the other kingdoms—they're not our lot," the guard replied. "Go and get the lieutenant—"

"I'm here." Lieutenant Ragnhild appeared behind me. "Go and get all the ministers we have. I don't know how long that barrier's going to hold."

He was right. The villagers started to part, letting their own ministers move through to the front of the crowd, ready to tear down the only thing standing between them and us.

I stood aside as Hellswan ministers started to pour out of the front door. There weren't enough—we had about

fifteen in total, and on the other side of the barrier there were hundreds.

"Oh, man," Benedict whispered. "This isn't going to go well."

He started to load up the crossbow.

"What are you doing?" I hissed. "Get back indoors!"

"You get back indoors," he argued. "At least I'm armed."

I ignored his objection and moved to stand in front of him. The other ministers were starting to work on the barrier. I could see the slight blue tint of the wall starting to ripple and stretch; it wouldn't be long till it collapsed.

"What are they doing?" Jenney gasped. She had run outside, a knife and chopping board still clutched in her hands.

"Getting revenge?" I suggested, glancing down at Lieutenant Ragnhild deploying the few guards and ministers we had in a protective semi-circle around the entrance. The small group was thinly spread out.

"Hold this." Jenney handed me her kitchen equipment, and I took it, staring at her as she marched down the front steps.

"Don't let the barriers fall!" she cried out to the guards

and ministers. "All of you, focus on supporting it. Benedict, run and get *our* villagers. We need everyone out here, including the kids – they'll need to be syphoned."

Benedict dropped his weapon and headed back indoors.

"The guards need to be ready to attack," Ragnhild snapped at Jenney.

"Only if the wall comes down," she retorted. "If they work on keeping it in place, we'll be okay."

It was too late.

The barriers started to rip and collapse.

"STAND BACK," Ragnhild screamed at the oncoming rioters. "Don't attack!"

"We want Tejus! The Hellswan swine, Tejus!" the crowd chanted, hurling insult after insult—some including Ash in their rage, some blaming Hazel. It was a deafening roar of hate and confusion, all of their faces contorted with rage. With Benedict at their helm, the Hellswan villagers started to emerge from inside the palace, pushing me further along the side of the patio as they poured out onto the front lawn.

"We warned you something like this would happen!" one of the Hellswan women cried. "You never listened!"

"Listen!" Ragnhild roared to the oncoming horde. "We

have women and children here. Don't attack! We are not your enemies."

The Hellswan ministers tried to fix more barriers in place, but each time a sliver of translucent blue appeared in the air, the opposing kingdoms would knock it down. The only blessing was that they still hadn't charged and attacked, keeping back as if there was an invisible line in the ground that they weren't willing to cross.

I ran forward to Jenney's side. "They just want to be heard," I panted. "Just listen to them. I don't think they're going to harm us, not if we listen."

"I don't think that's true," she replied quickly. "They don't look like they're going to be satisfied till they have Tejus's head on a plate."

The moment the words left her mouth, one of the villagers hurled something in our direction. Without thinking, I stepped in front of Jenney, knocking her out of the way. She fell sideways just as a sharp rock spun through the air, slamming into my forehead.

"Damn," I breathed, smarting at the pain, before I fell backward onto the grass.

Benedict

Julian's head jerked backward and his body tumbled to the ground.

"Julian!" I raced across the lawn. "Julian?"

Jenney was kneeling next to him. "I think he's unconscious."

There was a cut across his forehead, bleeding profusely. His spectacles, already broken a couple of times since we got here, lay crumpled by his side, both lenses smashed.

I didn't know if it was the glasses, the pale, unconscious face of Julian, or the fact that my friend had been knocked down yet *again,* but my temper snapped. My head rushed,

red spots dancing in front of my vision as I looked out at the screaming, hysterical crowd of sentries.

"Hey!" I roared. "HEY!"

Everyone from the palace glanced over at me, but the crowd was still paying me no attention.

"None of this is Tejus's fault. This is Queen Trina! Everything is *her* fault—and Tejus has done absolutely nothing but try to stop this from happening!"

At the mention of Queen Trina, I had managed to attract the attention of some of the crowd nearest the front.

"QUEEN TRINA!" I screamed at the top of my lungs. It worked. The sentries stopped yelling, and fixed their attention on me.

"She is our common enemy, not Tejus! And if you want to blame anyone, you can start with the last emperor, and the stupid entity that's been locked in the Hellswan castle for centuries, and is now free! He caused this mess! It's evil, and dark—and none of us are going to survive this if we're busy fighting each other."

"What are you talking about?" one of the villagers called out. "Queen Trina didn't start this!"

"She's the leader of the Acolytes. They want Nevertide completely destroyed, and the only people trying to stop

her are Tejus and Ash!" I yelled back. I didn't want to mention that I had suffered at the hands of the queen or the entity. I knew it would only make the crowd more suspicious – there was no way I could make them understand it, not in the short time I had to sway their opinion.

A boy, probably about my age, stumbled forward, his eyes dark and angry. He glanced warily over at the guards who had started to move toward me, but continued walking up to me, stopping a few feet away. His clothes were ragged, torn and mud-stained, his feet bare.

"Queen Trina is the one who told us that Hellswan was behind all this," he sneered. "And we believe the queen. We've lost everything, and yet all you people are living like royalty in another palace! Strange coincidence that a Hellswan palace remained intact when nothing else managed to, don't you think?"

I wanted to point out the obvious flaw in his logic, that Hellswan castle had been completely obliterated, but I didn't think he'd listen to reason. If Queen Trina had put them all up to this, then no one would be interested in anything I had to say—not until we had proof of her crimes.

“Please believe me,” I begged the boy, “she’s not to be trusted. She’s dangerous; she’s been lying to you—lying to us all.”

“Why should I listen to you? You’re just a kid, and a human one at that.” The boy crossed his arms, trying to stare me down.

“What kingdom do you come from?” I asked, not willing to back down until I got through to him. The crowd was listening to our exchange, and I felt that if I could persuade him to at least consider the possibility that Queen Trina wasn’t all she seemed, then we had a chance.

“Hadalix,” he retorted.

“Your king died in the trials, right?” I replied.

“What of it?”

“Do you know how he died?”

The boy frowned, impatient at my questioning. “Creatures in the forest.” He shrugged. “It happens—the trials are dangerous. Like I said, so what?”

I shook my head, divulging the information that Ash had passed on. “No. Not creatures. Queen Trina killed him, leaving his body in the forest to be eaten. Ash and Memenion saw it, but the Impartial Ministers didn’t believe them—or refused to believe them…just like you

are refusing now."

"You have no proof," he shot back.

"Why don't you wait—ask Ash when he returns?" I replied evenly. "He wouldn't lie to you."

"Don't listen to his lies!" a voice cried out from the back of the crowd. I couldn't see who it was, but it made no difference. The interruption caused the boy to falter. Whatever semblance of a connection we'd managed to create was broken, and his face grew stormy again, black eyes fixed on mine.

"Are you trying to trick me, human?" he hissed. "You want all of us dead? Swallowed up by the earth like my parents were?"

"It's not like that," I insisted.

He reached into the back of his robe, and before I could move, he'd whipped out a scythe, holding the blunted and rusted blade toward my throat. He moved closer, his breath hot and putrid on my face.

"Another word, and you'll be joining them."

"STOP!" Ragnhild cried.

I held my breath, staring into the eyes of the stranger who threatened me, wondering if today I was going to die.

ASH

We stared down at the bodies of the ministers, floating peacefully underwater.

"Are they dead?" Ruby asked.

"Only one way to find out," Tejus retorted, his expression murderous. He leaned into the water, grasping the nearest Impartial Minister by the lapels of his robe. He yanked the old sentry upward, laying him out on the side of the basin and shaking him awake.

"Ash, get another one out," he commanded, still preoccupied with trying to wake the first. I did as he'd asked, leaning in and submerging my arms in the warm

water till I could grab hold of another. I hauled him out, his clothing water-logged and heavy, and pulled him over the side. He didn't *look* alive.

Tejus's minister gasped, and then choked, shoving Tejus back.

"What in the name of Nevertide are you doing?" the minister roared.

"I could very well ask you the same question," Tejus snapped back, undeterred by the quivering rage of the Impartial Minister.

"This is the water of Lyis; it has healing properties—we were near dead!" the minister spluttered. "And you, son of Hellswan, have the audacity to rip us from our sacred ritual!"

Tejus pushed the minister back in disgust, leaning against one of the columns and crossing his arms as he looked down at the old sentry with as much disdain as he could muster.

"I want answers from you." Tejus spoke in a bored monotone, glancing over at me. Hastily, I shook the second minister awake. He coughed, spraying water over his already sodden clothing, and then stared around, wild-eyed and just as furious as the first.

"Answers from both of you," Tejus continued, before the second minister had time to condemn us for the rude awakening.

"Why should we speak to you?" the first one demanded. "You gave up your kingship, Tejus—you have no right to demand anything from us."

"Speak to *me* then," I interjected. "You've managed to eradicate most of the royalty in Nevertide, surely I will suffice?"

"Their deaths were not our responsibility!" the second minister objected, glancing at the first. They were starting to realize that we could potentially pose a threat—one look at Tejus's glare and they fell silent again.

"We want to know why you sided with Queen Trina, why you abandoned Nevertide to her," Tejus demanded. "What did you gain?"

"We d-didn't," the first stuttered. "We didn't!"

"You *did*," I shouted back. "You sided with her throughout the trials—you ignored Hadalix's death, and I'd be amazed if you didn't give her a heads up at every single trial!"

"She was the strongest contender," blustered one of them.

"We needed a strong emperor, one who could protect us from the entity, one who would be able to unite the kingdoms and repair the damage done by *your* father." The Impartial Minister pointed at Tejus, his old, gnarled finger trembling.

Tejus barked with laughter.

"You fools! Queen Trina is the head of the Acolytes—she's been aligning herself with the entity since this began. Had you no idea? Were you so arrogant that you couldn't see what was right in front of you?"

"Nonsense!" one of the ministers cried. "She was the only one worthy of the imperial title!"

Tejus sighed, rubbing his temples in frustration.

"Shall we pull out the rest?" I asked, hoping that at least one of the others might be more forthcoming and reasonable.

"No!" the first minister cried. "Let them heal. We'll tell you anything you want to know, but leave them to their peace. You are not the only ones who have suffered."

"But we seem to be the only ones not taking a nap," muttered Hazel. Tejus smirked.

"What do you know about the entity?" I asked. "We need to know more if we're going to put a stop to it." The

accusation on my tongue, that they were clearly not going to do a thing, remained unspoken.

"We don't know much," one of them replied.

"Just tell us what you do know. I'm running out of patience."

There was a long pause before one of them began in a shaking voice, "He has risen now. It was foretold…if one ever removed the stones that held him, he would rise—and he would end the reign of the sentries. He will awaken his army from the depths of the sea; they have lain there, waiting, for centuries—waiting for the day when they will be called on by their master to be reborn, and take back the land that was once theirs."

"What do you mean?" Hazel asked quickly. "An army of *what*, exactly?"

The old minister turned his rheumy eyes toward her, surprised that a mere girl would demand answers from him so directly.

"We don't know exactly," he replied after a moment. "But the entity and his army are the pure forms of sentries. When the first settlers landed here, human settlers, Nevertide—or the 'Lost Land', as it was known then—was already inhabited by deadly, vicious and powerful

creatures. In awe of these creatures, the humans begged for the powers of the 'pure' sentries—and their wishes were granted. Today, we are all the descendants of these human and sentry hybrids."

"We're really part human?" I asked in astonishment.

The minister nodded, looking shamefaced. Clearly it was something that brought them great distress, but it temporarily lifted my spirits. I glanced over at Ruby. Our eyes met and she gave me a small smile.

"When the hybrids grew in number and power, the 'pure' sentries were banished at the request of the emperor, locked into the stones for all eternity. They became known as the 'forbidden'—the true nature of them being long ago forgotten, and their mention erased from our history books. Well, most of them." He glared at Tejus and me, as if we were somehow at fault for knowing about the entity. Was their pride so great that it was more important to keep our enemy secret than to annihilate it? These ministers were insane if that was what they thought.

Still, the information was hard to digest. Tejus remained silent, evidently as stunned as I was. I couldn't believe that the entity we so feared was essentially our creator—that the shameful secret the Impartial Ministers

had tried to bury for so long was our own origin.

"Do you know how we defeat it?" Tejus asked after a few moments.

"We do not," the minister replied. "The book of the emperor, however, is rumored to have the answer to that question. We must, *must* progress with the trials if we are to contain the situation."

"Contain the situation?" Tejus repeated incredulously. "No. There will be no trial. We cannot risk Queen Trina being victorious. Ash is our only option; you will anoint him emperor today."

"How dare you make such demands of us!" one of the ministers blustered. "Who are you to change the ancient traditions, the sacred acts that were created long before your birth? The trials are a Nevertidian institution—we must preserve them."

"Even if it means the death of all Nevertide's people?" Ruby exploded. "You people are crazy! What is *wrong* with you? Are you so blind that you don't see what's happening here? Everyone's going to die!"

"You are hysterical," the old man shot back. "We will contain the entity, and Nevertide will resume as normal."

I wanted to laugh. I couldn't believe their complete and

utter ignorance. It blew my mind that Nevertide had survived this long with such foolish men at its helm. I looked over at Tejus, who hadn't reacted to the latest insanity. We all fell silent, and I realized that we were waiting for him to speak.

We didn't have long to wait.

He leaned down toward the minister who had just spoken, and smiled at him.

"Old man," he said, his voice low and caressing, "please believe me when I say that I am perfectly willing to end your existence—all of you, in fact—to get this done. Know that your life hangs in the balance."

"What of Memenion?" asked the minister. "Where is he? He should have a chance to compete."

Tejus let out a low growl, grabbing the minister by the robe. "He is *dead*," he snarled. "He lies at the bottom of the crevice that has torn its way across this land. Dig him up and see for yourself if you wish."

"I did not know," the old man whispered, clearly shaken by the news. "He was a good king."

"Yes, he was," Tejus bit back.

The ministers looked at one another, their glances frightened. We had won. In theory. I still had huge

reservations about this plan… Everything that I had been shown since I became king—the danger of my homeland, the gray areas between right and wrong, the true nature of Tejus, the underbelly of evil in the best of us, and most of all Ruby and my love for her—made me want to turn my back on this responsibility. The boy who had dreamed naively of ruling Nevertide, of righting wrongs, had died the day of the disk trial, and I was left with nothing but uncertainty and fear—nothing but self-doubt, and the knowledge that Tejus was the right sentry for the job, not I.

"Very well then," the minister muttered. "Ash, we will anoint you emperor. Please understand this is a great undertaking. I hope you show more dignity than this…*madman*." The minister directed his insult at Tejus. He rose slowly, painfully up from the floor, and then helped his friend to do the same.

"Move away from the basin," the minister commanded, gesturing to the stone floor. We all backed up, giving the ministers some space.

"Shall I wake the others?" one said to the other.

"No, we will do it. Let them rest—let them arise in another time, a happier one than this, perhaps."

I looked at Ruby, who shrugged.

How old are these sentries?

The ministers staggered toward us, stopping a few feet away. One of them bent down, placing his palm flat out on the stone. He closed his eyes, and as I watched, open-mouthed, his hand sank into the floor, disappearing from sight. A few moments later he pulled his arm back, holding the imperial staff, the crown, and a roll of parchment. He handed them to the second minister, who placed them carefully on the floor, the staff first.

"Are you ready, Ashbik of Hellswan, to do your duty for Nevertide?" the first minister asked.

"I am." I swallowed.

I am not. I am not—not in a million years.

Ruby's hand found mine, and our fingers entwined. I looked down at her and she gave me a reassuring smile. One of the ministers cleared his throat, and she let go of my hand, moving back to stand with Tejus and Hazel.

"This is the staff of Nevertide, a symbol of your leadership," the minister intoned. "It represents the promise you are making today to protect each sentry, to protect each kingdom, to treat all as equal."

I nodded, taking the staff in my hand. It was gold, and

felt impossibly heavy — even more so than the replica scepters we had retrieved from the forest.

"This is the crown of Nevertide. It represents your position as head of all six kingdoms. You are responsible for their unity. You are their leader."

The crown was placed on my head. It was heavy too…the staff and the crown felt like chains.

Am I losing Ruby?

The thought struck me suddenly, without warning.

The ministers continued speaking, informing me that the parchment was the irrefutable evidence of my decree. But all I could think about was her. Was this why Tejus had abandoned his crown? Had he chosen Hazel instead of this? I felt a million miles away from Ruby—the objects might have symbolized a lot to the ministers, but to me they just represented the divide between Ruby's world and mine. For some reason, I looked up toward Tejus. His eyes met mine for the briefest moment, and then he looked down at the floor, avoiding me. Hazel's hand was tightly clasped in his. Suddenly everything became blindingly obvious. He *had* chosen her. My heart broke into a million pieces. I hadn't realized—I hadn't thought this through. I hadn't understood the consequences.

I am a fool.

I have lost everything.

The staff, the crown, the parchment, they *were* chains tying me to Nevertide.

"Well done, Ash." Ruby turned to me. The crowning was obviously over, but I hadn't listened to a word they had said.

"How do you feel?" she prompted.

"Great," I replied, my throat tight.

"You'll get Nevertide back on its feet. I believe in you, Ash." She grinned, completely misunderstanding my demeanor.

"Yeah." I tried to smile.

"Let's go," Tejus muttered, looking uncomfortable. "Shall we take the ministers with us?" he asked, deferring the decision to me for the first time since I had been crowned king.

"Let's do it." I nodded.

I didn't care either way. I didn't care in the slightest.

Ruby

Hazel and I gave up our bull-horses to the Impartial Ministers. Even after everything they'd done, I kind of felt bad for them. It might have been because they looked like they were going to keel over and die at any moment, but I also felt that Tejus had been effective enough in making them come at least partway to their senses. They wouldn't be crossing us again in a hurry—accidentally or otherwise.

"Where to now?" I asked as we made our way back down the narrow path. I was riding on the back of Ash's bull-horse, and turned my head to see Tejus and Hazel behind me.

"We should get to Hellswan castle as swiftly as possible. Ash?" Tejus deferred again, and I gave Hazel a bemused look. It was the weirdest thing to see Tejus checking in with the man I'd previously heard him refer to as the 'Kitchen King.'

"I agree, though we should get more of us to help. Let's go via the palace and get help. I don't suppose finding it is going to be an easy task," Ash muttered.

"Absolutely," Tejus replied.

Ash pulled the bull-horse to a stop, turned around and glared at Tejus. "Stop it," he barked.

Stop what? Was Tejus's deferral making Ash uncomfortable?

Tejus nodded sullenly. "Fine. As we were, then."

What? I didn't really understand why Ash would have a problem with Tejus acknowledging his new position—if anything I'd thought he would have wanted it, would have reveled in Tejus bowing down to him. I frowned as Ash spurred on the bull-horse. He had been acting strange ever since he was crowned, and through the ceremony, like he wasn't listening to a word that the Impartial Ministers had been saying. This was what he'd always wanted, wasn't it?

"Ash," I said, leaning my head against his back, "are you

okay? You seem to be…distracted."

"I'm fine, Shortie, don't worry. It's just a bit strange, that's all."

"As long as that's all it is?"

"Yeah." He squeezed my hands that were clasped around his waist. "That's all it is."

I only felt half reassured. There was something in his tone that made me think his sentiments weren't exactly true. Then again, it wasn't like I'd ever been crowned emperor of a country—how the hell would I know how he felt? There must have been a million thoughts going through his head right now, and it wasn't as if Nevertide was in good shape. Ash would have hardships ahead of him. We all would.

The journey passed without incident. The Impartial Ministers didn't say a word. Ash asked them if they needed a break at one point, but they shook their heads, muttering something about not slowing us down. I realized that we didn't even know their names. It was something we would have to remedy later…especially if they were going to be staying at the palace with us.

The return journey felt a lot shorter, and soon the towers of the palace broke through the treetops in the

distance.

"What's that noise?" Hazel asked as we approached the muddy path that would lead to the grounds.

"Damn!" Ash hissed, spurring the bull-horse onward. Tejus's horse started to canter as well, coming to ride side by side with ours. A moment later, I could hear the thundering of hooves from the Impartial Ministers' mounts as well.

"What's going on?" I yelled.

"The other kingdoms," Ash yelled back.

I didn't get more of an answer than that, but I didn't need one. A few seconds later, we were on the lawn of the palace, which was completely covered with yelling, rowdy sentries.

Benedict and Julian!

Without a doubt, these sentries weren't gathered here for any purpose other than revenge and taking their frustrations out on someone they could hold accountable…

They were so intent on screaming toward the palace that none of them noticed our presence.

"Do something!" Tejus barked at the Impartial Ministers. "They need to know! We need to stop them

before this gets out of hand!"

The Impartial Ministers kicked their bull horses ahead of us, taking the lead. A few sentries fell silent at their approach, and the effect fell across the rest of the crowd—one by one, the villagers, ministers and guards stopped hurling insults and the crowd parted to let us through.

"Oh, my God!" I cried out as I saw Benedict standing, frozen, at the opposite end of the lawn, a mean-looking young sentry holding a scythe to his throat. The offender dropped his weapon as the Impartial Ministers approached. He stood back from Benedict, glaring at us.

"All silent for the emperor of Nevertide!" the ministers announced. "All silent for Emperor Ashbik!"

Absolute silence descended. Hazel clambered off her horse and rushed toward Benedict, holding him in a tight embrace. Her soft mutterings were the only sound that came from the lawn.

A moment later, I heard rustling coming from behind me—then next to us—then from every single part of the lawn as each soul gathered in front of the palace began to kneel.

"Oh, Ash," I whispered.

It was the most moving sight I'd ever seen. I could

hardly believe that the Ash I knew—the boy who had rescued me from a dank cellar with a cart of vegetables, who had slept in a makeshift bed buried deep within the Hellswan castle, who had faced defeat after defeat—was witnessing the survivors of all six kingdoms bowing down to him in reverence and respect.

Tingles ran throughout my body and I felt tears welling up in my eyes. I vowed I would remember this moment forever. Every time I thought something was impossible—when my *grandchildren* thought something was impossible—I would be reminded of this moment. The day a kitchen boy became an emperor.

"Rise!" Ash barked, following the Impartial Ministers in the direction of the palace. "Someone tell me what's going on here!"

The crowd did as they'd been commanded, and as we waited by the porch, a minister stumbled forward from the crowd.

"Your imperial highness." He bowed. "Forgive us, but we wanted answers. Our kingdoms have been destroyed, our rulers killed—the human boy tells us that Queen Trina is to blame, but many suspected Tejus…" He trailed off.

Ash disembarked from the horse and then turned to help me down.

"What kingdom are you from?" he asked the minister.

"Hadalix, your highness."

Ash nodded.

"The human boy is right—but we face a greater danger than Queen Trina; the entity, an unknown threat to us all, rises, and we will not survive if we do not unite."

Benedict sighed from behind me. "That's what I said," he muttered.

"Your highness, with all due respect," the minister continued, "we have not managed to unify in the whole of Nevertide's history—what makes you think we will be able to accomplish such a thing now?"

"He's right!" piped up another sentry from the crowd. "There's never been harmony between the kingdoms—and that's been mostly the fault of the Hellswans!"

Ash raised his arms, signifying silence.

"Tejus is not to blame for any of this. Today we will forgive the rulers who came before us." He glanced toward Tejus, who had come to stand at Hazel's side. "Forgive them their mistakes, so that we can save Nevertide from the entity—so we can build ourselves a better future. One

that isn't shrouded in lies and deceit, divided by rulers and their subjects; one where each sentry can choose their future. It will come at a price, but it will be the price of freedom. I urge you to join me, to join us."

"I will pay that price—I will fight for my freedom." A voice, distinctly female, came from the back of the lawn. I couldn't see who it belonged to, until the crowds parted and a familiar face appeared. It was Queen Memenion. She walked toward us, as radiantly beautiful as I remembered, flanked by her ministers, a soft smile on her face.

"Well said, Emperor Ashbik." She bowed low as she reached the palace. "The kingdom of Memenion pledges our allegiance to you—as my husband would have wanted it, so it shall be."

I glanced up at Ash. He swallowed, speechless, and then returned the bow.

"I see many of you are in need of medical assistance," she commented, looking around the groups of sentries from Hellswan and then those from the other kingdoms. "If you agree, your imperial highness, I can take those who are critically sick or injured back to my palace—we haven't incurred too much damage from the earthquake. Miraculously, we avoided the largest fissure through the

earth — my home and our grounds still stand."

"Thank you," Ash replied, "that would be a great help, your highness."

"Ruby." Queen Memenion turned to me. "It's a pleasure to see you again. I was very saddened to hear of Commander Varga." She lowered her eyes, and a look of physical pain flashed across her expression.

"And I am sorry to hear about your husband," I replied quietly. At this, the queen merely nodded, thanking me. I wondered why the news of Varga's death seemed to cause her more pain than that of King Memenion. Was it because she knew of her son's likely role in it? Or was it something more personal than that?

I wanted to ask Ash if he thought it was safe for the sentries to go to a palace where the queen's son was a known member of the Acolytes, but I couldn't ask with the queen present. She probably had no idea.

"I will take my leave, then. Please don't hesitate to contact me should you require further assistance."

"Your highness." Ash stopped her before she turned to leave. "Queen Trina—"

"We are on our guard," Queen Memenion replied before he said anything further. "I know what she is. Don't

concern yourself with that. We will be ready for her."

I heaved a sigh of relief. If Queen Memenion knew about Queen Trina, then she would also know about the Acolytes—the sentries in her care would be protected. I realized we were putting a lot of faith in the woman being more like her husband than her son…but it was a leap of faith that we would have to take. We couldn't look after everyone here; we just didn't have the space or the facilities.

Slowly the crowd started to disperse. I even saw the Hellswan guards helping those who were less able to walk, and the ministers offering their assistance to others from different kingdoms. It looked like Ash's plan was coming into effect already.

"I am so unbelievably impressed with you," I muttered as we turned to walk indoors. "The stuff you said in that speech…you were born for this, Ash. You were born to lead people."

"Thanks, Shortie." He grinned, a more genuine smile this time. "I'm going to speak to the guards about leaving for Hellswan. I'll come and find you when I'm finished?"

I nodded, remaining in the doorway.

It was only as I watched his retreating figure that I

realized that perhaps I needed to start getting used to the idea that the dream Ash and I had once shared—about him coming back to Earth with me when the time came—was probably over. It hurt.

It hurt a lot.

"Ruby?" Hazel came to stand next to me, glancing first at me and then at Ash as he went off into one of the rooms, followed by an assortment of guards.

"Are you all right?"

"No," I whispered, "I don't think so."

"It will work out. Somehow."

She held my hand tightly, knowing, without me having to explain a thing.

Hazel

By the time the commotion had died down, it was too late to head out to the castle. We would be leaving first thing tomorrow morning, and until then we just had to wait. Ruby and I had tried to keep ourselves busy by making sure everyone got fed. For the first hour or so, I tried to keep Ruby occupied with inane prattle, but it was difficult…it wasn't exactly a skill of mine, and too much had happened since we'd arrived in Nevertide to keep conversation light.

"I'm impressed with how the herbs are working," Ruby commented as we sorted through more damp sheets.

"How is it feeling? Have you been hungry?"

"No—it's been amazing, actually. I didn't expect it to work so well…I mean, my powers are next to useless, and I feel a bit like I'm floating around in a medicated bubble—but other than that, it's great!"

Ruby laughed. "I don't know how much I'd mind a medicated bubble about now."

"It has its plus points," I agreed.

"What about that water the Impartial Ministers were floating in?" Ruby commented. "Do you think it has healing properties…like keeping them alive for centuries or something?"

"I think so—I've never come across anything like that before."

The conversation prompted me to revisit a thought I'd had when we were at the ridge, and I put the sheets down, reaching for the dagger that Tejus had given me. I kept it sheathed in a belt around my waist, and now I pulled it out, studying it, in particular the white stone on the ornate handle.

"Don't you think this looks similar?" I asked, showing the dagger to Ruby.

She peered over at the dagger, her eyebrows rising. "The

stone? I wouldn't say similar," she replied, taking the dagger to inspect it more closely, "I would say exactly the same. The white glow…"

I nodded as she handed it back to me. It looked just like the light that had come from the water the ministers had been submerged in.

"Impressive weapon." Ruby smiled. "Did Tejus give you that?"

"Who else?" I grinned. "It's his idea of a romantic gesture."

"Figures."

"I should probably mention this to him, he might know what it is," I replied, realizing that I hadn't seen so much as a glimpse of Tejus for a while.

"I'm almost finished here anyway. Go." Ruby pushed me gently toward the door. I left, looking down from the mezzanine to see if Tejus was downstairs. I couldn't see him, so I checked a couple of rooms on the floor I was on. Finding them empty, I rushed down to the ground floor.

"Have you seen Tejus?" I asked Benedict, when I peered around the door of the kitchen.

He and Julian turned to me from the table with blank looks.

"Not seen him," Benedict replied. "He's probably with Ash somewhere—I haven't seen him either."

"Thanks," I muttered, slightly concerned that Julian's head looked like it was coming up with a monster bruise. Poor kid. I left them to it, not wanting to fuss, and walked through to the front entrance.

"Have you seen Tejus?" I asked one of the guards.

"In the garden," he replied. "He and the emperor have been out there for a while."

I frowned. Why were they outside now? It was almost dusk…I stepped out onto the lawn, looking around for them. Not seeing anyone, I went around the back, coming to a halt when I saw a small group of guards, Tejus, Ash and the Impartial Ministers, hidden by a cluster of trees to the right of the palace.

Not wanting to disturb them, I crept closer, chastising myself for trying to eavesdrop again. Would I ever learn? It was a strange scene though, and the fact that they were doing it far away from the palace, at dusk, made me curious.

Ash and the Impartial Ministers were standing directly in front of Tejus, who was kneeling on the grass, his chest bare. I watched for a few moments, my mouth drying as I

became transfixed by the beauty of his skin and physique, at once lit up and heavily shadowed by the dying sun. His profile was solemn, looking up at Ash and the ministers. He looked like a fallen angel, the light making his skin appear marble-white and his otherworldly beauty contrasting with his long jet-black hair and impregnable lines of his face.

One of the ministers recited something, his voice low and methodical. After a few moments, Ash leant down, holding his fist out. He held a sharpened rock, and I watched in astonishment as he began to carve something into Tejus's left pectoral. Tejus inhaled ever so slightly. It must have stung, but his body remained completely still.

When Ash was finished, Tejus rose, bowing before Ash. Then the three guards who had been standing behind Tejus knelt down on their knees.

"We pledge our service to the commander of the six kingdoms," they chanted. "His sword leads us, his command we follow in faith. We are the sons of Nevertide, sworn to protect our brethren, sworn to protect our land."

The guards rose, and a silence fell upon them. Ash handed Tejus a sword with both hands, his head lowered in reverence.

Commander of the six kingdoms?

I realized that I had truly intruded on a private moment, something that I wasn't meant to see, and wasn't meant to know about until Tejus chose to tell me. As quietly as I could, I made my way back to the entrance of the palace. I would just have to stay silent on the matter until Tejus was ready to talk to me about it.

As soon as I entered the palace, I rushed back upstairs, finding an empty room and shutting the door behind me. I needed a moment to myself. I leaned against its wood, my heart thumping in my chest, my legs feeling like jelly, as if they were going to give way at any moment. I couldn't get out of my mind the image of Tejus's face, serene and solemn, as he surrendered himself to Ash. It reminded me of the night that I'd overheard him telling the council that he was resigning as king. I felt the same overwhelming rush as I had that night, love and admiration feeling like it was going to burst out of my body. He *was* a soldier—a protector, a leader, capable of making the decisions that the rest of us couldn't, the choices that none of us wanted to—and I loved him for it.

Tejus

My shirt stuck to the blood that trickled down from the carving on my chest; it stung lightly, a reminder of what I had promised to Nevertide, and to Ash. Walking ahead of the group that had been present at the small, makeshift ceremony—all the more meaningful to me without the pomp and extravagance of my coronation—I reflected on the task that lay ahead. It wasn't a position I took lightly. I felt honored and humbled that I had been chosen to unite the guards of the six kingdoms. How that would actually be achieved, I had no idea; the guards, like the populations of the kingdoms, were scattered—some would

be residing with Queen Memenion, but not all. Another problematic aspect was the fact that this position had only just been created; the commanders of the kingdoms had never before had someone appointed over them. Telling them would require diplomacy. A skill I had never grasped.

"Tejus, wait a moment," Ash called out, hastening to catch up with me as I headed in the direction of the summer palace. I came to a halt, noticing that Ash had left the Impartial Ministers and the guards back by the trees in order to join me.

"What is it?" I asked.

"I want to talk to you about Queen Trina," he replied, continuing to walk and indicating that I should do the same.

"Go on."

"Before he died, King Memenion told me he was worried that you wouldn't be able to kill the queen, if given the chance…that because of your history, you might…hesitate."

It was dark, but I knew that color would be rising in the emperor's cheeks. He was clearly uncomfortable bringing the subject up, but that didn't make me feel any better—the insult was severe.

"That is absolute *nonsense,*" I hissed back at him. "I've sworn to end that woman's life, and I shall do so—happily."

I could barely contain my fury. How *dare* he question me? More insultingly, mere seconds after he had sworn me in to command his armies, to protect the sentries of Nevertide.

"Ash, have you ever killed another?" I asked, when he fell silent.

He hesitated for a moment.

"No, I don't think so."

"Are you thinking about my father?" I asked him wryly.

Ash came to an abrupt halt – staring up at me, his eyes wild. As much as I was enjoying his discomfort, I decided to let him out of his misery.

"I know you poisoned the soup, but I also know that it wouldn't have been enough to kill my father – someone finished off what you started."

Ash looked down at the floor, and I could see a violent blush appearing at the back of his neck.

"My deepest apologies, Tejus. It was only to distract everyone while I retrieved Ruby and the others…" He trailed off.

"I know. No apologies necessary – he had it coming I suppose."

We walked on in silence for a while, until Ash cleared his throat.

"Do you know who it was that actually killed him?" he asked quietly.

I didn't have any firm evidence, but there were obvious candidates – more than a few, but I had only one true suspect.

"My first guess is Queen Trina."

Ash nodded, "makes sense – she wouldn't have wanted him to return the stone after the trials. Did she admit it, when you questioned her?"

"I didn't even ask." It hadn't actually occurred to me to do so — there were so many other pressing matters at hand, and I wasn't sure whether or not I even cared if she had killed my father. Her crimes were extensive — I didn't need any further reasons to end her existence.

"So your answer is no," I stated, returning to our original conversation. "If you haven't ever killed anyone, then you have no idea what you're talking about. It is never easy—no matter if it's a stranger or someone you know. But you do it because it needs to be done, because taking

that one life might prevent a handful of others from meeting their maker. I will not hesitate, and I will not *fail.*"

"I'm sorry I doubted you," he mumbled. "I should have known better."

"It's fine," I replied curtly, dismissing him.

"I'll see you tomorrow morning."

He left, heading through the entrance doors to the palace. I decided to wait a while to calm down before I went in search of Hazel. I walked further along the moonlit lawn, avoiding bumping into the Impartial Ministers and guards as they retired for the night. My fury hadn't dissipated at his apology, and a part of me wondered if it was so offensive because it was true.

The truth was, I had shown Queen Trina leniency that I wouldn't show another. Had it been anyone else who had attempted to kidnap Hazel, they wouldn't have gotten away with it. Was it because I couldn't bear to end the life of someone I had known so intimately? Or was it because she was more valuable alive, for the moment? I hoped that it was the latter, but I could no longer be sure. Damn Ash for making me question myself. Before our conversation, I had never once doubted my ability to kill her, and now I feared that the doubt itself would be what made me falter

when the time came.

* * *

"You're back." Hazel smiled at me, color staining the tops of her cheekbones. Ah. I suspected she'd seen the ceremony—I'd thought I'd felt her presence, but I'd assumed it was because I was still in close proximity to the palace.

"I am." I smirked. "What have you been doing?"

The blush intensified. "Nothing much…helping Ruby with the rooms and…stuff."

I nodded, waiting for her to come clean.

"Did you do much?" she asked brightly.

"No. Not much."

Her face fell, and she pushed a falling strand of her hair behind her ear. "Oh, okay."

Before I lost the last vestiges of my self-control and wrapped her up in my arms, I decided to let her out of her misery.

"So, you saw the ceremony, then?" I asked dryly.

"It was an accident!" she protested. "I was looking for you in the garden, and then I saw…"

"It doesn't matter. I was on my way to tell you anyway."

I pulled her toward me, making sure she knew I didn't mean any of it seriously—I had decided to stop keeping secrets from Hazel after the harm my silence had done in causing her transformation. Her fingers tentatively snaked up to my left pectoral, finding the warm damp of the wound beneath my shirt.

"Does it hurt?"

"Not badly."

"What is it?" she asked, trying to pry open my shirt as her curiosity was piqued. I unbuttoned the collar, exposing the mark so she could see. It was difficult to make out the symbol—it was smudged with drying blood, but it was three short lines, crossed with another three lines the same length, representing the six kingdoms, and then a circle around the cross to represent their unity.

"Will it scar?" she asked, her fingers tracing the lines.

"Yes, it's supposed to."

I grabbed her hand, kissing the tips of her fingers. I could taste the bitter iron of my own blood, and Hazel squirmed as my tongue flickered against the sensitive pads.

"How do you feel about it—the position, I mean?" she asked softly.

"Nevertide needs it; we can't accomplish anything with

kingdom-less guards and commanders."

She was silent for a moment, then looked up at me, her eyes troubled.

"Is it permanent?" she asked.

"I don't know."

She nodded. I could tell she was a million miles away, thinking into the future.

"I can't answer any of those questions, Hazel."

I didn't know what was going to happen if we survived the entity and Queen Trina, and knew even less about what would happen when the borders opened and the humans were finally free to return home. I knew what I *wanted* to happen, but I was fast learning that it didn't make a blind bit of difference.

"I know you can't." She sighed, taking her hand out of mine, but wrapping it around my waist instead as she leaned her head against me.

"I think we should start practicing—develop your new powers, what do you think?" I asked, partly to distract her, partly because it needed to be done—Hazel would be better able to protect herself if she had some concept of what she was capable of.

"Yes!" she answered instantly, then hesitated. "I don't

know if I can though—the potion that Abelle gave me…"

"You should still be able to practice. I'd be amazed if it neutralized your powers completely."

Amazed and *furious.*

"Okay, good. Where do we start then?" she asked, breaking away from me, her eyes sparkling in anticipation.

"True Sight," I replied. "It would be interesting to see if you have the ability."

"Really?" she asked doubtfully. "I thought True Sight was rare? What about barriers instead?"

"I have True Sight – all the Hellswans have been blessed with the ability," I said. "If your sentry powers are the result of our bodies and souls joining, then I wouldn't be surprised if you had the ability as well. Additionally – you know you can create barriers."

"In an emergency," she objected, "with your help. I want to be able to do them by myself. What if I need to protect Benedict or Julian?"

"After True Sight. Trust me, the effort it takes will help sharpen your mind."

"I honestly didn't realize till today that you had the ability." She looked impressed.

"Well," I replied reluctantly, "It's not actually as

advanced as Ash's ability – as much as it pains me to say it."

Hazel hid a snicker behind her hand, and then agreed to progress with the lesson.

We sat down at one end of the room, facing the wall that adjoined the room we were in with the humans' sleeping quarters. I sat a few feet away from her, giving her some space so she wouldn't be tempted to syphon by mistake. I wanted Hazel to be able to use her powers without drawing off others' energy; it was harder, but would be necessary.

"I can only see *wall*," she announced glumly after a few moments. I suppressed a laugh at her impatience.

"Try imagining what's beyond it—and don't stare at a fixed point, try to see the larger picture, almost as if the wall isn't really there."

"Oh, that simple, huh?"

"That simple."

She rolled her eyes, then closed them briefly before starting again. I waited patiently next to her, unbothered by the time passing. It was a rare pleasure to have time with Hazel when we weren't in immediate danger, and under circumstances where I could just sit and stare at her,

without her becoming aware of me and therefore embarrassed.

I could see the muscles of her entire body tensing, her small frame trying to expel as much energy as she could. A small, delicately blue vein on her forehead started to pulse with the effort, and I clenched my hands by my sides, restraining myself from leaning forward and pressing my lips against it.

"I got it! Well, a bit, the outline of some of the kids. It's still a bit blurry, but in black and white—do you see it in color?" she asked excitedly.

"Color will come, keep trying," I murmured.

She turned her attention back to the wall with renewed energy, a small smile playing on the edges of her lips.

After a few moments, she slumped back, sighing.

"It's still black and white."

"It takes time, don't worry. You just need to keep practicing."

"I want to stop taking the potion. I think that will help. My energy feels almost non-existent, it's really frustrating," she implored, turning toward me.

I was tempted to agree with her. I didn't like the idea of her taking an unknown potion concocted by Abelle, a

woman who had always struck me as hare-brained and foolish. However, Hazel was happier being able to spend time around her friends, and less alienated. Selfishly, I didn't want her transformation and first experiences of being a sentry to be more painful than they needed to.

"I don't think that's a good idea," I replied eventually.

"But I think I can control the hunger—now that I know what it is, what it feels like…I'm more prepared."

I raised an eyebrow at her.

"Are you sure this isn't wishful thinking?"

Hazel was silent.

"Maybe." She leaned her head back against the wall, dejected. "I just don't want you worrying about me, worrying that I can't protect myself, now that you've got this new position. You'll need to look after *everyone*, not just me—and I don't want to be in the way."

I laughed out loud. "Hazel, you could have powers beyond my imagining—superhuman strength, the skills of a deadly assassin—and I'd still worry about you. I'd still want to protect you above all else."

She sighed. "Okay then… I'll keep taking the potion."

I nodded, satisfied.

"Thank you," I replied.

"What for?"

"Allowing me to continue to do this."

I dragged her toward me, pulling her up onto my lap and wrapping myself around her. Her head nestled into the crook of my neck, and I sighed at the warmth emanating from her body.

"Get some rest," I murmured. She nodded, yawning as if on cue, and snuggled deeper against my chest. I watched her sleep, feeling content, until the first streaks of dawn broke through the night's sky.

Julian

"You would have thought that Ash and Tejus would have learnt by now. Seriously, I almost *died*, for like the fifteenth time—obviously, it's not a good idea. I should come, I can help look!"

I waited for Benedict to finish his rant while I tried to find a clean sock.

"Speak to Ash, not me," I replied, distracted.

"Fine—I will."

The door banged shut just as I found my sock. It wasn't exactly clean, but it would do. It wasn't like my mom was around to disapprove.

“Are you ready?” Ruby poked her head around the door.

“Yeah,” I replied. I felt like I was still half asleep. The sky was still mostly dark. It was going to be hard enough looking for a single book in the pile of stones that had once been Hellswan castle without doing it in the dark.

“Why are we leaving so early again?” I asked as I followed her down the stairs.

“Because it’s kind of a big deal?”

“Oh, yeah, right.”

Ruby snorted with derision.

“Why are you so tired anyway? Didn’t you get any sleep?” she asked, now looking concerned.

“I’m fine. It’s just that some of the kids snore. And Benedict. Benedict is the worst of them all.”

Ruby laughed. “Yeah—I remember that from the castle.”

I was about to ask her where she was sleeping now, but then thought better of it—I didn’t want to know. No doubt she and Ash had bagged the best room, one that probably had an actual bed, rather than a dusty floorboard.

We made our way out onto the lawn in silence. Ash, Tejus, Hazel and a small group of guards and ministers were gathered at the far end, standing by bull-horses and

three vultures.

"Hurry up," Tejus snapped, busying himself with helping Hazel up on one of the bull-horses. I bit my tongue, wondering if I'd be permitted to ride with one of the sentries who would be traveling with a vulture.

"Come on, kid." One of the guards looked me up and down. He didn't look impressed, and no wonder. I knew I had a bruise the size of a walnut on my face, I was squinting like a new-born mole thanks to my broken glasses, and my robe was too big. I felt like an idiot. The guard had obviously decided to take pity on me.

"I'm flying—you'll be all right with that?" he continued, the same skeptical look on his face.

"That's great."

I suddenly didn't mind what he thought of me—I'd be flying, and that was all I cared about. We'd probably be able to chase the dawn as it rose. I climbed up on the vulture, feeling the soft feathers run beneath my hands. The guard sat himself in front and a moment later we were off, soaring high above the palace.

"Thanks for letting me come," I yelled to the guard over the wind that rushed past us. He turned his head sideways.

"No problem. I saw you protect Jenney yesterday. It was

brave."

His compliment surprised me. Maybe I didn't need to be as embarrassed of my bruise as I thought.

"You looked funny falling down though—ha!" He guffawed.

Thanks…

Ignoring him, I looked down at the landscape below us. I could see the crack that ran through Nevertide clearly from this perspective. The damage was extensive. Around the crack, landslides had appeared, tipping the forests downward like waterfalls, and large rock formations had exploded out of the earth like jagged teeth. Soon, what was left of the castle appeared on the horizon. My gut clenched. I had hated the place, but seeing the ruins of something that had always looked so foreboding and indestructible was an unwelcome reminder of the awesome power the entity had. If we didn't find this book, we wouldn't have a chance.

We landed inside the ring of rubble that had once been the outer wall of the main castle. I jumped off the vulture, my legs wobbly from the adrenaline of the flight. The guard and I looked around, both of us silent as we digested the enormity of the task.

"Guess we better get on with it," muttered the guard. "Mind you, I'll be blown over if this book has survived all this—see the black of the stone?" he asked, pointing at the main part of the castle. Only half-towers and broken walls suggested what the building had once been, and as the guard had observed, the stone was mostly charred black.

"Fires have done that," he continued, "they must have been burning for a long while for them to have caused damage like that. And the emperor thinks a book would have survived? Pah!"

I was inclined to agree with him. What were the chances that paper would have remained intact when the stones themselves were practically burnt to cinders? This was starting to look like an idiot's errand.

The two other vultures had been flown by a pair of ministers, and Ash and Ruby. I heard the approach of the birds, and soon the guard and I were joined by Ruby, while Ash discussed the likely location of the book with the ministers.

"I guess we just start looking," Ruby said, looking despondently at the ruins.

"Okay," I agreed, walking toward the nearest pile, which I suspected had been one of the four towers. I

clambered over the larger stones, pulling out anything that looked like it wasn't just plaster and crumbling rock.

It was tiring work. I had to keep hauling stones about, only to find an assortment of burnt objects, none of which resembled a book. I envied the ministers and guards—they all had double our strength, and a few were using True Sight, standing in front of rocks, seeing right through them without having to do a thing. Hazel had joined our search party and kept trying to do the same, swearing that she'd accomplished it last night, but unable to achieve it today.

"Old Viking coin, anyone?" I asked, holding it up to the light. I'd found a pile of them wedged in between some rocks and an iron pipe. "I think this could make us pretty rich once we got back home."

"Julian, can you focus?" Ruby snapped.

"Sorry."

She turned back toward me, her face scrunched in remorse. "I'm sorry. I'm a bit moody. This feels kind of hopeless." She chucked a bent cooking pot back where she'd found it with a frustrated sigh. I'd noticed that for most of the morning Ruby had seemed a bit distracted and glum—maybe we all were, but because she was normally

upbeat, it was more obvious that something was bothering her.

"What's up, Ruby?" I stopped rifling through the rubbish and went for the direct approach. "I mean, besides looking for a needle in this crappy haystack. Something's bugging you."

"It's nothing really."

She glanced over to where Ash and Tejus were standing, a few yards off to our left. I followed her stare. It was something to do with Ash.

"How's it feel being the girlfriend of an emperor?" I asked, pretending to turn my attention back to moving rocks so she might feel more comfortable opening up.

She groaned. "Difficult. We had all these plans…I don't know, it's just difficult. There's always something standing between me and Ash. If it's not Queen Trina, it's Nevertide politics—and I guess now, as emperor, he has this massive responsibility that I can't even begin to understand…it makes me feel separate from him, you know?"

Uh… Not really.

"Sure," I murmured. "That must be difficult."

"Anyway, ignore me. I'll snap out of it." She forced a

grin, and I returned it.

Privately, I thought that Ruby might have been better off without Ash. I didn't understand how they could have a future together—he would always be needed in Nevertide, and Ruby couldn't just turn her back on her home and her friends, and GASP. She had a whole life back at The Shade, one that Ash just wouldn't understand. I didn't really understand Ruby or Hazel's interest in dating sentries—to me it seemed plain weird. They were so old-fashioned and strangely unemotional, and *tall.* They were really, really tall. Nobody needed to be that tall! Ruby would have an amazing future ahead of her—dating someone from back home would be way better for her. Someone who could fight by her side when they joined GASP…

"I think I can see it!"

The guard I'd traveled with shouted out from one of the rock heaps up ahead. All three of us started to clamber toward him. I could hardly bear to hope that this long and boring search would finally be over.

"Under there!" The guard was standing above the shell of a room that would have originally come off the main hallway. The rubble from one of the towers had

surrounded it, creating a pile that we could climb up, giving us a bird's-eye view of the room. Most of it was covered in gray stone, but I could see the golden glint of a lavish headboard.

"Is this the old emperor's room?" I asked.

"Think so." The guard nodded. "The book's in a box, down under those rocks."

"You're right," Ash announced, climbing up behind us. Tejus joined us a second later, and we all peered down at the room.

"Let's get on with it then," I prompted. I wanted this over and done with already.

Hazel smirked at me.

"Volunteering, are you?"

The remaining construction of the room didn't look all that stable, but if I could find another way in, by going down and around, it would be safer.

"Yep," I replied stoutly.

"I'm joking—I'll join you." Hazel laughed.

"No, you won't," Tejus barked.

Surprise, surprise.

"Tejus, I'm going. It's fine. We're all smaller than you guys—we can get in more easily," Hazel reasoned, as she

and Ruby started to make their way back down the slope of rocks. I hurried to join them, not wanting to be left dealing with the brunt of Tejus's wrath.

I slowed my pace as I neared the bottom of the stone pile, the ground becoming more perilous as I jumped from one stone to another to keep up with Ruby and Hazel. We started to climb over the old entrance to the castle. The stench of rotting flesh grew in intensity, and I felt nauseated.

"I think this is where most of them were killed," Hazel said sadly. "They all flocked here, trying to escape."

I tried not to look down. At one point, clambering over one of the stones that made up the arch, I stepped on something soft. I leapt forward, not looking behind me, but the stink that emerged filled my nostrils and I vomited—quickly and quietly, trying not to draw attention to myself.

"Are you okay?" Ruby's voice was muffled by the sleeve of her robe.

I could only nod, not wanting to breathe.

As we traveled along the hallway, the smell started to fade, to be replaced by the much more palatable stench of burnt fabric.

As I climbed over a pile of broken rocks, I heard a faint yowl. Pausing, I looked back in the direction of the sound.

"Guys — I hear something." I waved for them to come back, and made my way to where a half-burnt doorframe had fallen against an old chest. Hazel and Ruby followed, and the sound grew louder and more insistent.

Was it… a cat?

I lifted the wood, sending debris scattering off its surface and clattering to the ground. A dark shape leapt out from the gap I'd uncovered, knocking me sideways.

"Lucifer!" Hazel gasped, running toward the creature – which I now recognized as a lynx. It started to hiss around her legs, covering her in black soot.

"You poor thing." Hazel picked up the animal and cradled it, while its yellow eyes gleamed at me with undeniable malevolence. It looked like it would claw us to shreds given half the chance. I also remembered where I'd seen it — the lynx belonged to Tejus.

Ruby glanced at it with misgiving.

"Are you sure it's…*domesticated*?" she asked warily, taking a step back.

"He's all right," Hazel replied, cooing at the devil-cat, "he's never been this friendly to me before, though…I

guess I must smell like Tejus. We'll get you home, buddy." She returned her attentions to the lynx, while I motioned to Ruby that we should get going.

"Come on," Ruby announced, "you think it will follow us?"

Hazel placed it gently on the ground. It moved away gracefully – not bothering to glance back in our direction as we started to climb back the way we'd just come.

"I'm sure he'll find Tejus now that he's not trapped," Hazel declared, watching him saunter off.

Great.

Another welcome addition to the palace.

We continued our way along the hallway, clambering over more broken rock till we came to what would have been the Emperor's room – the recognizable gilded gold wallpaper still hanging in some places – though ripped and burnt.

"Here," announced Hazel, coming to a half-broken wall. I looked up to see the rest of the sentries peering down from above.

"Hazel, be careful," Tejus shouted down. I rolled my eyes at Ruby, but she didn't share in the joke. Maybe she was starting to dig overly protective men?

Whatever.

We started exploring the room, being directed by the guard who shouted down instructions.

"It's under here," Ruby muttered, shifting a large stone away from the headboard. Hazel and I joined her, moving the debris until we uncovered a heavy metal box. Ruby picked it up with difficulty, and then gave it a shake. It sounded hollow, with a single, heavy object hitting the sides.

"How do we open it?" Hazel asked.

There was no lock—the box appeared to be completely smooth, without any kinks in the metalwork that would suggest an opening.

"We could just try chucking it on the floor?" I suggested.

Both of them turned to look at me as if I was stupid. I shrugged. "It's worth a try… anyone got any better ideas?"

"I guess not," Ruby admitted. She slammed the box down as hard as she could. It made an awful sound, high and screeching, but the lid popped open.

"Told you," I said, feeling more than a little bit smug.

Both of them ignored me, staring down at the large, gold-plated book that had been contained within the box.

Hazel bent down and picked it up, holding it aloft for the others above to see.

"It's so *cold,*" she whispered. "And it weighs a ton."

"Well, what does it say? Is it the right one?" I asked impatiently.

There was nothing written on the cover, just a blank sheen of gold, with an equally plain spine. It looked old though—and like it hadn't been removed from the box in over a millennium.

Unable to wait another moment, I took the book from Hazel, opening it to the first page. My heart sank. I flicked through quickly, looking at more pages, my hands starting to grow clammy as I reached the end of the book.

Every single page was the same.

Completely blank.

Jenus

The power is yours…

Yours alone, son of Hellswan…

Release me.

Release me.

The voices came, over and over again—tantalizing, calling to me, whispering the deepest desires of my heart. Offering me all the power and the glory I had ever dreamed of. Not just the kingdoms of Nevertide, but realms far out in the ether, humans, supernaturals, all kneeling down to me. All quaking with fear at my name. I was a god, an omnipotent thing, beyond the body of man

or sentry, beyond all…

"Busy?"

Queen Trina stood in the doorway, a sly smile on her face. She reminded me of a viper, snaking through long grass, poised for a moment of stillness before darting forward to claim its prey.

I lowered myself deeper into the black tar, letting its thickness pull at my shoulder blades, slowly starting to snake up around my neck like some living thing. She couldn't touch me while I was so close to our master.

"Be careful not to submerge yourself, Jenus. It's hungry."

She smirked, coming to seat herself on the edge of the pool. She dipped her long nails into the liquid, her pupils dilating as the waters called to her.

"What do you want?" I asked sharply. I was in no mood for her games today—or her interruptions.

"I had a vision last night," she announced.

Now she had my attention. The visions were the way our master communicated with Queen Trina, and she had been anxiously waiting for another one since the night before the earthquake.

"Well?"

"The plan to use the unexpected visitors our master sensed at the mouth of the portal has failed – the boy's stone did little use. Someone on the other side of the portal interfered, keeping it closed."

"What does that mean?"

"It means we go back to the original plan. Nevertide's purest energy needs to be collected, and then drained to generate enough power to reopen the portal."

"And you've seen this?" I asked.

"I've seen it." Queen Trina's eyes flashed at the suggestion I might doubt her. I returned her glare, not willing to back down, not anymore—not since the master had started to communicate with me, too.

"He wishes you to perform this task." She smiled. "It is what I saw, and so is what shall be."

"And if I don't?"

"Then you will not have proved your worth—to him, or to me."

I remained silent, contemplating my response. Sometimes I doubted whether these 'visions' Queen Trina received were accurately communicated to me, they differed so greatly to the ones that I had been receiving. The dark dreams that came to me in the middle of the

night were only glimpses of images—faces of strangers contorted in pain and misery, screams so loud they would wake me, thinking that there was either human or animal at the end of my bed in unimaginable pain. I also saw death; I saw the bodies of the sentries crushed beneath the arch at Hellswan, souls trapped in stones, frozen in their horror for eternity, children bleeding, their crimson blood falling on an ocean.

When Queen Trina told me of her visions, she spoke of a benevolent spirit whispering to her, weaving tales of things which were to come and things which had passed.

Did the entity favor her above me?

Perhaps that was why her visions were of love and guidance, and mine were nightmares—dark, unforgettable nightmares.

"I will do it, gladly," I replied.

She smiled at me, and this time it was almost genuine.

"I am pleased to hear it. We shall make an Acolyte out of you yet, Jenus."

"I want assistance," I interjected hastily before she could leave. I was suddenly wary that this could be a ploy of hers to be rid of me. "I will need a distraction, and time to formulate a plan."

“And you shall have them,” she replied, “as much as you like. We will not abandon you, not while you faithfully follow the cause.”

I nodded, only half reassured. She wasn’t to be trusted, and until the task was completed, I wouldn’t know for sure whether or not her promise was a genuine one. She knew I didn’t trust her either—the smirk she gave me as she rose from the side of the pool made me grit my teeth.

She was a malicious, calculating monster.

I watched her retreating figure as she sauntered out the door, shutting it behind her.

I settled back into the black tar, waiting to hear the soft, soothing whispers of the voices once again. I didn’t have to wait long.

Lord…King…Master…

We are waiting for you…

The world, and all other worlds are waiting for you…

ASH

We clambered down to join Julian, Ruby and Hazel back on the ground. When they reached us, their faces were downcast.

"There's nothing in it," Julian panted as he stumbled toward us, the book held out for me to take.

"It's for the emperor's eyes only," corrected one of the ministers, "of course you wouldn't be able to see it."

I took the book from Julian's hands. As soon as my fingers touched the cold, gold metal of the cover, the book started to hum with energy. A white light burnt brilliantly across it. I turned my face to shield my eyes from the glare

for a moment, and when I turned back, the book had changed.

The blank cover was now filled with elaborate carvings: runes, flowers and patterns all etched into the gold. The book had no title, no name, but I had no doubt that this was the book I was meant to see: the book that would save us from the entity and the Acolytes and restore Nevertide.

"Open it!" Julian exclaimed, his face marked with relief.

I turned to the first page in the book, my hands trembling slightly—partly because of the extreme weight of it, and partly with the adrenaline that was pumping through every single nerve in my body.

The pages were devoid of text, but as soon as I placed my finger on the page, words started to appear—written by hand in navy ink, the handwriting a careful calligraphy that I hadn't seen used since I was a small child, and only then on official documents of the ministers.

I started to read.

The book started with a written account of Nevertide's history, how humans had sailed to the land, only to find it was overrun by creatures that they'd never come across before—evil, malevolent and bent on destroying the human race. The visitors were taken as slaves by the

creatures, but after generations of servitude the humans led an uprising with the help of a magical creature who saved them, locking the creatures into stones.

"Ash," Tejus barked at me, "what does it say?"

"Nothing yet. It's just an account of the history we already know."

I sat down on the nearest rock, irritated that everyone was hovering over me—I'd never been the world's quickest reader as I'd never had much use for it in the kitchens.

"Just give me some time," I snapped at Tejus and the ministers. They took a few steps back, and started murmuring amongst themselves. Tejus grunted with irritation, and then proceeded to pet and pamper his moody lynx – both he and Hazel murmuring over it like proud parents.

The more I read, the more disheartened I became. A lot of this stuff was already known to us, most of it pieced together by Tejus and Hazel when they'd read the old ministerial accounts.

The author, whoever it was, wrote about a creature – a 'jinni' relinquishing the stones and the entity's lock to the emperor, and that henceforth, over time, whoever was emperor would be responsible for keeping the land safe

from the scourge of the entity and its followers—the 'forbidden'. Beginning to skim-read in haste, I tried to look for a contingency plan…what happened if the lock was opened?

Finally, I found something.

"Listen to this." I called the group back. "It says that if the entity is released, the forbidden will rise again—the entity will open the portal, and the forbidden will seep into all the dimensions, and once again reclaim Nevertide as their home…" I trailed off. That wasn't as helpful as I'd thought it would be.

"The portal is closed?" Tejus asked.

"Apparently…" I re-read some of the pages I'd just gone past – finding the part about the jinni's warnings; the ice-fires, pestilence of silence and red rains.

"So, it also says that once the entity breaks free of the stones, the portal to Nevertide will close – 'keeping in the evil, lest it spread about the lands and populate itself across dimensions.' So yes – the portal must have closed, and the entity is going to try and open it again."

"Huh," Julian replied, looking thoughtful. "We would never have gotten home anyway, even if the borders hadn't been up."

"But what about *stopping* the entity?" Ruby interrupted. "What does it say about that?"

I flicked through the pages again—the words started to blur and shift on the page, and I began to feel panicked.

"It… It doesn't say anything…It just talks about guarding the locks as the primary duty of the emperor—about not succumbing to their power, or using the stones for one's own selfish needs."

"That has already come to pass," Tejus hissed.

"What about the Acolytes? Does it say anything about them?" Hazel pressed.

"Hang on," I muttered, flicking through the pages once more. Eventually I found an extract that mentioned them, and once again I started to read out loud.

"Since the uprising of the humans, there have been *friends of the forbidden.* They called themselves the Acolytes, and claimed that they were able to communicate with the entity through visions, and are dedicated to bringing about their master's rule. They took to regularly sacrificing humans and animals to their master in order to feed him energy…'

"So, nothing remotely helpful once again?" Tejus questioned sarcastically.

"No, nothing helpful," I retorted. I was just as angry about this as he was, and I didn't like his accusatory tone—it wasn't my fault that the book didn't hold anything of use.

The only information that I hadn't heard before was the inclusion of the 'jinni'—I'd never heard Tejus mention it when he'd passed on the information he and Hazel had gathered.

"What's a jinni?" I asked.

"A kind of supernatural creature, really powerful—it's rare to hear of one on their own though, they tend to live in tribes," Hazel replied, pacing up and down on the debris and rubble.

"They live on Earth?" I asked.

"Well… some. But they originate from the supernatural dimension."

I nodded slowly, wondering how Hazel knew about a dimension different to hers. Before I could ask, Tejus interrupted.

"Does it mention at all what these 'forbidden' are? What the entity is? How the jinni managed to trap them in the first place?" He shot the questions at me, one after the other, but I could only shake my head wearily. The book

didn't disclose anything that might answer those questions.

"So this is a dead end." Tejus sighed.

"Not necessarily," Hazel said. We all looked at her in astonishment, wondering what she could have possibly understood from what I'd read out that might lead her to believe that there was a way out of this.

"Listen, it said that the 'forbidden' are going to open the *portal*—that's good news. If we can get all the sentries out of Nevertide before it's destroyed, then GASP has a chance of either shutting the portal, or battling whatever these creatures are in both Earth and the supernatural dimensions. It's a risky strategy, but it might be the only chance we have."

"That's not a bad idea," Ruby murmured, deep in thought. "These creatures can't be much worse than what we've faced before…and at least we'd have an entire army of jinn to help out, not just one."

What?

"What's GASP?" I asked.

Hazel stopped pacing, and looked over at Ruby with a guilty expression on her face. Ruby glared at her for a split second, and then turned to me.

"Um…I guess I have a couple of things to tell you…"

Benedict

We surveyed the kitchen in the summer palace, the dirty plates and leftover food, and winced as a globule of oat paste slipped off the kitchen counter with a heavy slop.

"This is gross," I remarked to Jenney.

"This is nothing. Try cleaning up after a banquet of over one hundred ministers."

I sighed. My friends were off searching for a way to save Nevertide from the entity, and I was here babysitting. Even Julian had gone, declaring that he'd made a full recovery from his time in Queen Trina's dungeons. I didn't believe him for a moment.

"You'd think, after being the entity's puppet for weeks, they'd let me join them," I muttered.

"Haven't you had enough excitement to last you a lifetime?" Jenney countered. "I'd have thought you'd be happy to take it easy for a while."

"This isn't taking it easy." I gestured at the mess. The kitchen looked like a bomb had hit it. I could hear the kids next door as well, sounding like a horde of elephants running rampant around the room.

"You can go and join them, try to keep them under control while I clean up here?" Jenney offered.

"No, thanks," I replied hurriedly. "I'll clean."

Jenney gave me a knowing smile and then handed me a grease-encrusted cooking pot.

"Get to it then."

I started washing up, using mostly cold water—the plumbing wasn't great here, and for baths we'd had to heat up water on the stove. Since arriving here, Hellswan had started to feel like a luxury. At least we'd had beds there and a constant supply of hot water. Still, it beat the temple, and at least I was getting some sleep, not wandering around hallways trying to collect stones.

"Cut the water a second," Jenney said. I did as she

requested, waiting for her to explain why.

"Can you hear anything?" she asked.

I stopped clashing the pots around and stood still for a moment.

"Not a thing." I shrugged. The palace was silent.

"Don't you think that's a bit odd?" she replied, wiping her hands on her apron, and moving toward the door.

Where are the kids?

I couldn't hear a sound coming from next door, and immediately started to feel a bit tense. It was pretty rare that Yelena stayed silent for longer than a couple of seconds…I hurried out behind Jenney.

She flung open the door to the next room and tried to walk through—only to be bounced back.

"Barrier!" she shouted. "It's the Acolytes!"

The floor of the ballroom was almost entirely obscured by the fallen bodies of the kids. Six black-cloaked Acolytes moved around them, gathering them up in their arms and piling them up by Jenus. He was clean-shaven and dressed in the same black robes as the rest of them, but hadn't bothered to put his hood up. Clearly he didn't care that he might be recognized. He turned toward the door as we opened it, smiling at me.

Asshole.

I dragged Jenney off by the arm, heading back toward the kitchen.

"What are you doing?" She tried to resist my pull, but I held on fast.

"He'll have a getaway—vultures, carriages or something," I hissed back at her, leading her out through the busted wall in the kitchen and into the gardens.

I looked around for some form of transportation method, but couldn't see anything.

"Around the side," I panted. Setting off at a run, we turned the corner of the palace just in time to see the exterior wall of the ballroom explode outward. Shards of sandstone and rock flew across the lawn.

"Go and get any villagers you can find!" I yelled at Jenney. I suspected that for the Acolytes to get access in the first place, they would have syphoned off the guards so heavily they'd be useless now.

Up ahead, I saw a row of carriages, all embossed with the Seraq kingdom's coat of arms. Clearly Queen Trina also no longer cared about keeping her name clear of all this, and the thought frightened me. It meant we were running out of time.

I ran toward the last carriage, the one closest to me. Just as I reached the back of the buggy, Jenus started to lead the children out. They were all standing upright now, each one of them tied to a thick cord of rope. None of them were fighting or calling out, so either Jenus was able to control them somehow, or they just didn't have the energy to do anything other than follow one another.

Fight, damn it!

There were Acolytes guarding either side of the procession. If the kids didn't try to fight back, then there would be no commotion that I could use as a distraction…I just had to hope that the rest of the Hellswan sentries would come running before they left the palace.

Then I saw Yelena.

She was the last kid tied to the rope, her red hair standing out starkly against the Acolytes robes. No way would they be taking her.

Over my dead body.

If that was what it came to, then fine. I was about to be stupidly reckless and rush forward, when I heard the cries of the stampeding villagers rushing around the corner of the palace from the kitchen.

I held on a few seconds longer, waiting till I saw the first furious face breaking through the trees—it was Jenney's. Behind her were about ten or so other sentries—some villagers, and a few guards and ministers. They all held weapons aloft – some swords, some carrying whatever they'd found in the kitchen as they rushed to the aid of the kids.

The Acolytes were quick to respond.

The first few went down instantly, Jenney among them, screaming out as they were syphoned. Their bodies writhed on the floor, and they clutched at their heads as if they wanted to tear their own brains out.

Focus!

Ignoring the distraction, and the plight of the Hellswan sentries, I picked up a rock from the ground and ran forward into the fray. I headed directly for Yelena, only partly hearing Jenus's screams for the Acolytes to stop me, but nothing happened. The sentries were performing their own syphoning. Some of the Acolytes left their posts at the rope, bellowing in agony as they got a taste of their own medicine.

The Acolyte guarding Yelena was facing the oncoming horde. Before he had a chance to turn around and stop me,

I leaped toward him, slamming the rock into the back of his head, embedding it in his skull.

He screamed out in pain while I started working on the knots that were tying Yelena's hands to the rope. It kept slipping out of my hands, I fumbled too much in my hurry, and before I knew it, the Acolyte was slowly raising himself up off the ground.

Hurry, hurry, hurry!

The knot came loose just as another Acolyte reached out and grabbed hold of Yelena's arm.

"No!" I cried out, tugging her away from him. For a few seconds, we tugged at Yelena's body like she was a rag doll. I was about to let go before one of us dislocated her arm, when the Acolyte yelled out. He released Yelena as he fell backward onto the ground. His body twisted sideways on impact, revealing the handle of a chopping knife sticking out of his back. I looked up to see a villager smile in satisfaction at the dead Acolyte on the floor.

Nice save.

Thanking him briefly with a nod, I picked Yelena up, throwing her over my shoulder with some difficulty—for all her wiry and small appearance, she was kind of heavy. I didn't wait around to see the outcome of the fight. I could

hear from the sound of Jenus's victorious yells and the screams of the villagers that the Acolytes were winning, and not us.

I ran in the opposite direction of the kitchen, where the coast was relatively clear, praying with every step I took that we wouldn't be attacked from behind. I imagined Jenus gaining on us, his cloaked figure clamping a hand on my shoulder…I couldn't turn around to find out, so I just ran all the harder—panting, feeling like my legs were going to collapse beneath me till I reached the main entrance to the palace. Stepping over the bodies of two guards by the door, I pushed it open and slammed it behind me.

After the bright light of the afternoon, the hallway of the palace was complete darkness. Unable to go any further, I dropped Yelena to the marble floor as gently as I could, then sank against the door, catching my breath—and wondering why the hell Ash and the rest of them continually thought it was a good idea to leave us alone in the palace.

Hazel

Tejus and I held back as we journeyed by road to the summer palace. The rest of the ministers, guards and Julian had traveled by vulture. Ash and Ruby rode ahead, choosing to return on bull-horse rather than travel by air. I heard a few mentions of GASP floating over to us, along with some raised voices and stilted replies. I didn't think the conversation was going that well. No wonder. I didn't understand why my friend had held the truth about herself back from Ash for so long. It seemed weird, but I knew Ruby well enough to know that she would have a logical reason for it...even if the reason made no sense to anyone

else but her.

Night was falling, and the forests on either side of the road looked as creepy as they had in the morning light. I still had the feeling that I was being watched, and wondered if it was the power of the entity. If he was non-corporeal, then could he be everywhere at once, watching us? Waiting for us to fall into a trap? Waiting for the entity to make his next move was doing my head in—the suspense almost felt more torturous than the actual event might be. I nestled myself back into Tejus's chest, feeling his arms tighten around me. The simple gesture was a reminder that I was safe, at least for now, and at least while he was near me.

"Tejus, did you see many you knew today – in the ruins?" I asked quietly. I couldn't get the smell or the sight of crushed sentries out of my head. It had been complete carnage.

He was silent for a few moments, and then sighed heavily.

"I looked for Zerus, but I didn't see him. Perhaps he escaped, I don't know. He was always very solitary…I rarely saw him during the trials. He might have left Hellswan long before the earthquake. I hope so."

I registered the name of Tejus's brother with surprise. Since the night of the old Emperor's trials, I hadn't seen Zerus and Tejus had never brought him up. I knew that the brothers' weren't close – but I imagined that Zerus's 'missing' status bothered Tejus more than he would like to admit.

"I'm so sorry, Tejus. I hope he got out. If you didn't see him, maybe he did leave."

"Maybe."

"We'll find him," I whispered. "Don't give up on him yet."

We rode on in silence. I started to ignore my surroundings and my mind drifted to thoughts of the jinni who had locked up the entity in the first place. It was strange for them to be alone—like I'd explained to Ash, they were tribal creatures, and to just have one jinni mentioned struck me as weird. Also, if there were more, there was the possibility that there still might be jinn living in Nevertide somewhere all these centuries later.

"Do you think the jinni, or jinn, could still be in Nevertide?" I asked Tejus.

"If it or they were, someone would have seen it, surely. How long do they live for, anyway?" he asked.

"I don't know, exactly, but a *long* time, far longer than humans. There's a possibility that the jinni who locked up the entity in the first place could still be alive—if not here, then somewhere else."

"Then we should start looking for it," Tejus replied. "I'll ask Ash to speak to the Impartial Ministers when we return to the castle. Perhaps they'll know something."

"Because they've been such fountains of wisdom so far?"

Tejus smirked darkly. "It baffles me why all this has been shrouded in such secrecy for so long…I can't help but wonder if it was to avoid the discovery that sentries are descended from humans, a shameful secret they wanted to keep hidden."

"I think you're right, but honestly, I've never heard anything so stupid in all my life. This could have all been avoided if the Impartial Ministers had been a bit more open."

"It seems like a lot of unpleasant things could have been avoided if some of us had been a bit more open," he remarked, nodding his head in the direction of Ruby and Ash.

"Seriously?" I laughed. "And you don't think that applies to *you*?"

“Good point,” he grunted.

I’d never known someone to struggle so much with honesty. It was almost like he thought the world would be turned upside down if he told the truth—that any kind of openness would make me turn away from him in disgust. I’d never known anyone like that before, and if it hadn’t been for Ash I would have wondered if it was a trait specific to sentries, but he had always seemed pretty upfront with Ruby. Which probably made her hiding GASP from him all the harder for him to take. As for the rest of them, the Impartial Ministers, Tejus, all the other ministers and Tejus’s father had pretty much operated in a shroud of secrecy that I doubted we’d ever be able to fully remove and get to the truth.

“Tejus,” I asked after a moment, “why do you think your father risked taking the stone? I mean, I know he wanted Jenus to win the trials…but if he’d read that book, he would have had to be insane to risk it.”

“I’ve been wondering the same thing, but I’m at a total loss.”

We rode on in silence.

“I doubt he hated you or your brothers *that* much,” I continued after a few moments. I assumed that Tejus

would have thought that would be the only possible reason the emperor would have been so reckless and stupid.

"I don't know about that," he replied calmly. "Perhaps he was just determined that the Hellswans would continue to rule—and he was right to doubt me. I became king for only a few days, and then handed the crown to Ash."

"He wasn't to know that!" I corrected. "How could he?"

I felt Tejus shrug. "He knew me. As much as I hate that fact, it's true. Maybe he could see I wasn't as power-hungry as Jenus, and wouldn't hang on to the crown till the last, dying breath in my body. Jenus would."

"Do you think Ash will?" I asked.

"I do."

I agreed with him.

Ruby would have some difficult choices to make.

* * *

We trotted up the pathway to the palace gardens, gaining on Ash and Ruby till we were riding side by side. They were both silent, but the tension between them was gone—from the way Ruby was relaxing forward against Ash's back, I presumed that the argument was over.

Before we entered the clearing of the lawn, Julian ran

toward us with Benedict in tow.

"The Acolytes," Julian panted, "they came—they've taken the kids."

I jumped off the bull-horse instantly, looking Benedict up and down to check he wasn't hurt.

"What happened?" I asked.

Benedict told us the story, his face pale and contorted with fury.

"Why did you leave us?" he demanded when he'd finished. "That's the second time something's gone wrong—and now all the kids are missing, probably being locked up by Queen Trina so she can bathe in their blood or something equally sick and gross."

"I'm sorry, Benedict," Ash muttered. "I thought that the danger would follow us, not the other way around."

"Yeah, well, you should have thought a bit harder. Obviously, they knew you'd be gone, so someone is telling them what we're up to—or they're watching us. Jenus wouldn't have tried it otherwise."

"He's right," I replied, feeling sick. "This was premeditated. They must have known somehow."

We all started walking back toward the palace. Now that there was a chance we really were being watched, I

couldn't help glancing over at the dense thickets of trees that surrounded the gardens—seeing things that weren't there, feeling the hairs on my neck prickle.

"Get inside." Ash hurried us along.

"The threat might also be in the palace," Tejus replied curtly. "I suggest we have a word with Lieutenant Ragnhild—he's the likely suspect so far."

"Agreed," Ash replied.

Ruby gave a short, indignant snort—I recalled that she'd been the one to warn Ash about the lieutenant. *Why didn't he listen to her?*

"Yelena's the only one they didn't take," Benedict announced, walking beside me. "She's the only one I was able to get free."

"You went up against Jenus?" I replied, my voice semi-hysterical at the danger my brother had put himself in.

"He was distracted by the villagers," he mumbled. "And it was worth it—at least they didn't take them all."

I put my arm around Benedict, so relieved that he was safe. If Tejus or Ash thought I'd be leaving him alone in the palace ever again, they were sorely mistaken. From now on, we'd be sticking together no matter what happened.

"How is Yelena?" I asked. "Is she okay?"

"She's okay. I think she's just a bit pissed off she got syphoned *again,* and she's worried about the other kids. Jenney's with her now—she got hurt as well. The Acolytes are powerful. Jenney says they syphon harder than other sentries. She's had to borrow energy off two other ministers just to be back to normal, and to me, she still doesn't look that great."

I nodded. It didn't surprise me. If the book was right, then the Acolytes seemed to be linked to the entity—if they shared visions, then it wouldn't surprise me if they could somehow tap into its energy as well now that it had risen, and all those animal sacrifices probably helped…

Sacrifices.

I stopped walking, a cold, sick feeling in the pit of my stomach.

"The kids—they're a sacrifice!"

Everyone turned around to look at me. Ruby's face drained almost entirely of color, while Ash and Tejus looked at one another, both expressions contorted with rage.

"What do you mean?" Benedict asked quietly. "They're going to be killed? I thought that Jenus would just want them for their energy — like in the trials."

"We'll get them before anything can happen," I reassured him.

I hope we can.

"We will march on Queen Trina's kingdom at dawn," Ash stated.

"That will be too late."

Both Ruby and I looked at him, imploring Ash to do something sooner—not only were the kids in grave danger, but so were the rest of us if the entity took their collective power.

"They're right," Tejus agreed. "We should move out in a couple of hours."

"With what army?" Ash snapped. "We need a proper force, and most of our men are in the Memenion kingdom—we'll only get one shot at this."

"I'll send word out; they can join us as we travel."

Ash nodded reluctantly.

"All right then. We depart in two hours."

We all hurried inside. Tejus went to speak with the guards to send messengers off to the rest of the kingdoms, and Ash disappeared with the ministers.

"I'm coming this time, by the way," Benedict announced stoutly.

"You are," I agreed.

He looked surprised at how easily I'd given in, but there was no way I was leaving him on his own again. We would be stronger together, and somehow we would just have to survive this. With any luck, it would be the last hurdle we faced before freedom from Nevertide.

"I need to go and speak to Abelle." I turned to Ruby. "Make sure Julian and Benedict are ready?"

"I will. But Hazel, be careful. It might not be the best idea."

I hadn't had to mention why I wanted to see the herbal apothecary—Ruby had instantly guessed that I wanted to regain my powers for the fight ahead. It was risky to have them, I knew that, but it was riskier *not* to have them. And it was the only way I had a hope in hell of protecting Benedict and my friends.

"I know, but I need to do this, Ruby."

She bit her bottom lip, her eyes concerned.

"Trust me," I replied. "It's the only way."

I left them, going off in search of Abelle. I hoped that she would have something to reverse the effect of the potion—I wasn't sure that I had time for it to wear off on its own. I quickly searched all the rooms on the upper

mezzanine. When I found no trace of her, I tried the rooms downstairs, finally finding a large room where all the syphoned ministers, guards and villagers were recovering.

I scanned the room, looking for Abelle, but could see no sign of her. I turned to one of the villagers who was propped up against the wall, looking tired and dazed, but not too badly injured.

"Have you seen Abelle at all?" I asked.

The woman thought about it for a few moments, and then nodded slowly.

"I did," she replied after a while, her voice drawling and soft. "I think she went to get more herbs from the garden…she's been such a help."

"Thanks!" I darted back out of the room before the woman could reply, and made my way through to the kitchen and out onto the lawn through the busted wall.

I peered out into the darkness, wondering where the sentry had gotten to. Impatience and frustration were starting to get the better of me, and I stalked out toward the surrounding forest.

Hazel

Low mists wrapped themselves around the tree trunks, making it harder to see what might lie beyond. I was reluctant to travel too deeply into the forests. Their eerie silence still made me feel as if I was being watched, and the dark, unfathomable shapes created by twisting roots and rock formations made my body tense.

I wondered if Abelle would have even bothered to go so far into the woods—what herbs would grow in the constant shade of the dense trees? But she was nowhere else. She had to be around here somewhere.

"Abelle?" I called out into the night.

No reply. I tried a couple more times, but felt like my voice was being drowned by the heavy clusters of trees and dank mists. The only other option I had was to try to use my faulty True Sight skills to see into the forest.

I leaned against the trunk of a tree, closing my eyes briefly to calm myself and summon the energy I needed. I took a few deep breaths, determined to make this work, and reopened my eyes. Trying to follow Tejus's instructions, I fixed my gaze way ahead in the distance—acting as if the shroud of the forest wasn't really there, like a curtain I could part and reveal what lay behind it.

It took a while. I could feel perspiration beading on my forehead, and my breaths becoming heavier and more labored as the mental energy took its toll. Even my eyes started to ache, growing dry and uncomfortable. Eventually I was rewarded with a slight wavering of the scene before me, and my sight extended to see past the first cluster of trees, then the second, and then on beyond that. The outlines of objects grew more blurry the further my sight reached, but still just about distinguishable.

Slowly I started to move my head, taking in more of the forest.

Where are you?

I couldn't see anything other than trees, rocks and thick clusters of undergrowth, none of it stirring. The complete absence of wildlife, and the strange trance-like state that using True Sight created, made me feel totally isolated, like I was the only person left alive in a dead world.

Just when I was about to give up and return to the palace, I saw a movement out of the corner of my eye. Turning, I could see the blurry outlines of two figures. I still couldn't see in color, which made it harder for me to make out who they were. I started to move closer, not wanting to call out just yet—there was something shifty about the way they were moving through the forest, slow and warily, as if they didn't *want* to be seen.

Trying not to make a sound, I reached a point where I could make out one of the figures—it was definitely Abelle, the large and slightly rotund silhouette was unmistakable. The second figure was just as tall as Abelle, and dressed in a black robe with the hood entirely covering the sentry's face.

Acolyte?

They were the only sentries I knew who dressed that way…

I moved even closer, straining to hear their

conversation.

"He'll know!" Abelle was saying to the black hooded figure. "If I give her anymore, or make the dosage stronger, they'll guess—one of the kitchen workers is already suspicious."

The hooded figure was silent, his concealed face turning toward Abelle as she seemed to tremble in fear.

Are they talking about me?

Abelle was meant to be helping all the Acolyte-syphoning victims, but as far as I was aware, I was the only one that Abelle was giving remedies to on a regular basis.

"This isn't a request, Abelle," the cloaked figure replied. "If you don't continue to weaken the girl, we will expose you—there will be no doubt as to what you truly are, and who you've been working for. I imagine Ashbik would be so *very* disappointed."

"Please don't," Abelle replied. "I've done all that you have asked so far—"

"It is not enough!" the figure hissed.

I now had no doubt whatsoever that the figure was an Acolyte, and presumably Abelle had been working for them all this time—right under our noses.

"Fine! Fine…I will increase the dosage. They are leaving

soon—I will slip something in her drink, something more potent." Abelle hastened to reassure the Acolyte, clutching her robe around her as she started to slowly back away. Clearly she wanted out of the conversation, to be a million miles away from the cloaked figure.

"Make sure you do," the Acolyte replied. "This is a personal vendetta of Queen Trina's—if anything were to go wrong, the consequences would be severe."

"What if Tejus questions me? What do I say?"

"That is not my concern. Say anything you want. It is too late for them all anyway, the entity will rise and their end shall come."

"Then…then why am I doing this? What difference does it make?" Abelle trembled more obviously now, as if afraid of the wrath her questioning might elicit.

There was a long pause before the Acolyte replied. When he did, it was not with anger, but instead a satisfied purr.

"Queen Trina has particular plans for Hazel."

My heart seemed to stop beating as my name rolled off the Acolyte's tongue.

What plans?

Whatever they were, I wasn't sure I wanted to know.

Backing away silently, I obscured myself behind a thick-trunked tree, no longer able to hear their conversation clearly. A few moments later, the Acolyte took his leave from Abelle.

She hurried back in the direction of the lawn and the palace, moving swiftly for a woman of her size. I started to move toward her, intending to cut her off before she reached the palace.

Pure fury rushed, unchecked, through the veins in my body. Abelle was a traitorous coward, deceiving Ash so completely that he thought of her as a mother-like figure, and fooling the rest of us into thinking she was a kind, saving grace when we needed help the most.

Abelle halted mid-stride, hearing my approach. She glanced over in my direction, her face frozen in shock. I could see her wondering how much, if any, of the conversation I'd heard—not knowing whether to keep running, or stand and face me.

I didn't give her the opportunity to run.

As soon as I was close enough, I let my hunger consume me, syphoning off Abelle as aggressively as I could. She yelled out in pain, clutching her head, and tried to reverse the effect. I gritted my teeth, knowing that my hunger was

stronger—that my power was stronger. The more I sucked her energy, drinking thirstily of what she had to offer, the more she screamed.

Her knees buckled beneath her, and she fell onto the forest floor. I closed the gap between us, grabbing her arm so that I could completely eradicate any energy that might remain. I couldn't let her get away and return to the Acolytes—better that when I faced Queen Trina she thought I was weak and powerless.

Soon she was a motionless heap, her breathing faint and labored.

I felt sick.

The image before me, Abelle's crumpled body, reminded me of the nightmares I'd had when I first transformed into a sentry: helpless bodies lying at my feet while I felt all-powerful, bloated with their energy.

Shaking the recollections of the visions away, I hurried back to the palace. I wouldn't be able to move Abelle on my own—guards would be needed to lift her, and then we could lock her up somewhere, preventing her from having any further contact with the Acolytes.

As I ran toward the kitchen, the first person I saw was Ruby. She watched me, looking surprised to see me

running from the direction of the forest. She stopped what she was doing, stepping out into the garden.

"What's happened?" she asked.

"Abelle…sh-she's an Acolyte," I panted, stopping short of entering the kitchen and lowering my head down to my knees to catch my breath.

"What?"

"I heard her in the forest. She was trying to weaken me with the potions—some personal vendetta of Queen Trina's, apparently."

Ruby groaned.

"Oh, God, this is all my fault…"

"It's not—not at all. How were we to know? I trusted her as well, so did Ash. We all did!"

Regaining my breath, I stood upright, feeling Abelle's energy starting to take effect. I felt *good*—unstoppable and ready for whatever lay ahead. I felt the last vestiges of the dulling effect from the potion start to weaken. About now I would usually be taking my second dose, which meant in a few hours, whatever Abelle had been feeding me would start to drain from my system…hopefully without any withdrawal affects.

"I can't believe this. Maybe *she* was the traitor who

informed the Acolytes we'd be at the castle? It's the last person I would have expected!"

"I know," I replied. "I had my misgivings about Ragnhild, but not her."

Ruby's face fell, turning a shade whiter.

"The villagers," she murmured. "When we first saw them in that barn…do you think she was about to do something to them? Before we arrived?"

I hadn't even thought about that. I recalled how the villagers had been so afraid, all huddled in the one barn as if they'd been herded there…and Abelle appearing, as if from nowhere, totally unafraid. What had we stopped? Was it the sacrifice that the human children were now paying for?

"It's entirely possible," I whispered.

"Where is she now?" Ruby asked.

"She's back in the forest—she won't be going anywhere for a while, but we need to get some guards to pick her up and lock her away somewhere safe. I don't want her getting to Queen Trina."

"I'll go and speak to them—and Ash will need to know. Wait here."

Ruby rushed off through the kitchen doors. I heaved a

sigh of relief. I had started to feel the hunger rearing up when faced with Ruby's potent energy, one hundred times more enticing than Abelle's had been. I would need to be careful today, surrounded by Benedict and my friends as we marched to the Seraq kingdom. Very careful.

Tejus

The messenger swooped down, landing on the lawn, and swiftly disembarked. His face looked grave.

"What?" I asked impatiently. I had sent him and a few others off to inform the rest of the kingdoms of our plan, and that we would require their assistance. Most of the messengers had taken too long to return… It didn't bode well.

"I left them deliberating. Corithos has taken over the Hadalix kingdom, unlawfully, but his subjects aren't voicing any objections. I'm afraid I have no firm answer for you."

I nodded, dismissing the messenger. Corithos was Hadalix's son. I had known him as an unruly, spoiled brat who spent most of his time hunting for sport, and had never shown any interest in taking up his father's throne. I could only hope that the boy had come to his senses, and that his father's name wouldn't be shamed in the forthcoming days.

We had only moments before we were due to march on the Seraq kingdom, and I was still waiting to hear whether the Memenion and Thraxus kingdoms would be supporting us. The Demzred kingdom had replied instantly, but the messenger reported that their army was small—they had been hit badly by the earthquake, little of the castle surviving, and King Dellian Demzred, who had failed the first imperial trial by failing to kill his hallucination, was now on his death bed, having fought off an attack by his own mutinous villagers.

"Have you heard from Queen Memenion?" Ash approached, his gaze fixed on the starlit night that would be rapidly approaching dawn.

"Not yet."

Ash nodded bleakly. We both knew that Queen Memenion would be leading the strongest force, made up

of not just her own sentries, but those from the Hellswan kingdom who had needed aid.

"Has Abelle been secured?" I asked.

"In one of the towers. There's little we can do against the Acolytes if they choose to rescue her though. Do you think we should take her with us?"

"I'm not sure. I thought so at first. But I doubt they'll guess we've discovered her, and if this sacrifice is going ahead, then their attention will be diverted elsewhere. I think it's safer to leave her here. Or kill her."

I knew which option I would have preferred.

"We might need her for information," Ash replied quickly—too quickly.

I turned to look at him.

"Ash?" I questioned, my rebuke silent.

"I can't, Tejus," he replied quietly. "Not till I've had an opportunity to question her. I need to know how long it's been going on for—how long she's been betraying us all."

"Betraying *you*, you mean."

I tried to keep my temper in check. I understood what he was going through—I had experienced the same rush of conflicting emotions when Varga had been revealed as one of the Acolytes, but then Varga hadn't directly harmed

anyone I'd loved.

"What if it was reversed?" I asked. "What if it was Ruby who had been taking that potion instead of Hazel?"

Ash was silent.

Grinding my teeth in agitation, I started to walk back to the palace. I needed to do *something*, anything, rather than let my anger at Ash overflow. Combined with my frustration on the lack of support we seemed to be getting from the rest of the kingdoms, my mood was tense and restless. I had already made up my mind as to the consequences Abelle would face if we survived the day—but Ash didn't need to know that. I only hoped he could see the irony of him questioning me on my ability to end the life of Queen Trina when he was unwilling to do the same with Abelle.

Hazel met me at the door. She jumped back a little at my approach, wrapping her arms around herself. She looked pale, and slightly jittery. Her eyes darted too quickly, surveying the landscape behind me, while seeming hyper-alert to my presence.

"How are you feeling?" I asked, wondering if she would tell me the truth.

"Okay," she replied, her voice high-pitched.

"Hungry?"

"No—I'm fine."

"If you can manage to syphon through the door, Abelle is locked in the west tower. You'll need to be quick though, we're leaving shortly."

She nodded her head, then quickly scurried up the main staircase without another word. She must have been starving. I hated seeing her like this—withdrawing from Abelle's potion would have only made it worse. I cursed the vile woman under my breath. I should have trusted my instincts when it came to the apothecary.

Ragnhild and another guard approached me, waiting for their orders. Ragnhild was another one I wasn't sure I could trust…but other than the journey to the temple, where he'd lied to Ruby, I had no cause to doubt him. And time was short.

"Ready the bull-horses and the vultures. All but the badly injured will accompany us—if there aren't enough animals, some will have to walk until we can find more on the journey. Hazel rides alone. Only give the vultures to guards, not ministers—the emperor can have his choice of animal."

I reeled off the instructions, still deliberating whether or

not we should wait for the messenger I sent to the Memenion kingdom to return, but what would be the point? With or without their support, we would be going ahead anyway.

"Anything further, Commander?" Ragnhild asked.

"No—that's all for now. Meet me out front. I will be riding alongside Hazel."

The guards turned away.

* * *

We rode off in the darkness of the night, following the path that would eventually lead us to the main thoroughfare and then all the way to Queen Trina's domain. The moon was high, sickly yellow in the star-studded sky, and seemed to be hovering over the Seraq kingdom—an ominous guide to light our way.

"Did you hear from Queen Memenion?" Hazel asked, her voice barely above a whisper, as if she feared disturbing the dark around us.

"No," I replied. "I have not. I can only hope that the messenger has been detained for some reason, and that the queen has not abandoned us."

As we left the forest that surrounded the path to the

palace, we entered flatter land. Some of the fires started by the earthquake had left parts of the earth still in glowing embers, other landmarks completely eradicated, making the landscape appear alien and strange to even the most seasoned travelers of the land.

"Pick up the pace!" I called back to the rest of the riders, galloping on with urgency as I started to see the faint pinkish hue of the rising sun in the distance. I checked to see if Hazel was able to keep up, reassured when I saw her handling the bull-horse with ease—her eyes focused on the distance, her body moving in smooth motion with the rippling muscles of the beast beneath her.

Her dark hair flew out behind her, her face pale but determined. Her fingers clutched the reins, spurring the bull-horse on. She had forgone wearing a robe, and instead wore her human clothes, though the night air must have been cool against her skin. I wondered if her choice of clothing was a symbolic act; that when she faced Queen Trina, it would be as a human—regardless of the powers she now had, regardless of her transformation.

Watching her now, I could see she was a changed creature from the girl I had taken from Murckbeech Island. The girl who had stood in my living quarters,

demanding that I told her what I was, deriding my actions and hating me with every fiber of her being for kidnapping her and her friends. She had been brave even then, but now her bravery and her courage had been tempered, like steel to flame.

My heart ached with how much I loved her, but at the same time, pumped cold blood through my veins – the fear that she would come to harm haunted me constantly, driving my already inherent need to control everything completely out of perspective. My one comfort was in knowing that wherever our fates led us in the coming hours, my soul would always be entwined with hers. If my body and mind ceased to be, my love for Hazel would continue to be as sure as the setting of the sun and the rising of the dawn. That part of me, at least, would be immortal.

She glanced over at me, her eyes bright and alive. She smiled.

A clattering of hooves could be heard from a distance, fast approaching. As the sound grew louder, I saw a rider holding up a burning torch, its flames lighting up the darkness around him.

"Commander Tejus!" the messenger cried, pulling his

bull-horse to a stop in front of me. The creature reared up, almost knocking the sentry off. He regained his balance, turning to join us as we continued to ride.

"The Memenion kingdom comes not far behind! They're joining us—three hundred in all, guards and ministers mostly."

"Thank you," I breathed, tension easing from my body as I heard the long-awaited news. "Ride ahead, light the way."

The messenger nodded, pride evident on his face as he kicked his bull-horse to the head of the line.

"Did you hear that?" I called back to Ash, riding behind me.

"I did," he replied, and I could hear the grin in his voice. "I'll pass the message on."

Soon I could hear cheers going up from the back of the line. We were no longer alone. I called again for the pace to pick up, and the answering cry and thunder of the herd sounded almost jubilant.

Not long after, we were met by Queen Memenion's army coming from the east. They carried banners high above their heads, the insignias of not only the Memenion kingdom, but Hellswan too. In the hazy light of the dawn,

all were lit by a fiery red, the ground trembling as the bull-horses galloped toward us. Alongside the army, fanged beasts raced toward us, perhaps ten or twenty in total, their howls ripping through the air, their silken coats gleaming. My mouth parted in astonishment—these creatures hadn't left the safety of their forests in years.

"Emperor Ashbik, Commander Tejus!" Queen Memenion called out to us as she approached. "It's a good day!"

Our army came to a halt, and I smiled at the queen. I recognized her dead husband's armor, as well as his weaponry sheathed at her back and waist. The fanged beasts ran amok around us, scaring the bull-horses till they whinnied and reared.

"Are these your pets?" I asked with bemusement – wondering how on earth she managed to domesticate and train such deadly beasts as these.

"They are now." She whistled, calling them back to her. They retreated at her command, coming to stand protectively around her bull-horse. "They left the forests when the earthquakes started – out of fear and hunger they're willing to be loyal. We shall see how long it lasts!"

I recalled Queen Memenion always being a little

eccentric – and her fearlessness had always impressed me.

"Thank you for joining us," I announced sincerely.

"The pleasure is mine. Queen Trina is going to die today, and her blood will be spilled in my husband's name." Her eyes flashed with rage. I nodded, only capable of conceiving a fraction of her loss—not just her husband, but her beloved son, all to the clutches of the Seraq queen.

Their army joined ours, and we rode onward still, fast approaching the palace. Once again, my thoughts drifted to what King Memenion had said to Ash—that I wouldn't be able to kill Queen Trina when the time came. I had briefly considered that he might have been right, but now I knew differently. She would die so that Hazel could live, and she would die so that the sons and daughters of Nevertide who had been slain by her hand would not be lost in vain.

Hazel

The air grew drier as we entered the Seraq kingdom. The morning sun was now blazing down on us, the palace in the distance appearing to ripple slightly in the heat.

"Can you see if anyone's there?" I asked Tejus, pulling out a water flask from my saddle and taking a much-needed gulp.

"It looks abandoned," he replied with a frown. "But it could just be a barrier that I can't see through."

I was starting to feel edgy, like we were missing something. The stillness of the kingdom and the palace up ahead just didn't feel right. Like everything here had been

abandoned days ago.

"We'll ride to the top and disembark," Tejus commented, pointing to the path that led to the exterior grounds of the palace.

"Watch out for nymphs," Ruby muttered.

Tejus rode back down the line, dividing the army into two groups. The first group accompanied us, and the second fanned out to guard the palace while we went to investigate. When we reached the top, I wearily climbed down off the bull-horse. My hunger was starting to rage in the pit of my stomach, and it was taking all my energy to keep it contained. I hoped that Queen Trina and her Acolytes would be here—not just for the sake of the children, but selfishly, so I could have someone to feed off of. My legs felt like they were going to buckle as soon as my feet touched the ground. I'd forgotten what it was like to ride a horse for such a long time, and my thighs ached from the exertion.

We entered the first courtyard on foot. I'd never seen Queen Trina's kingdom up close, and was amazed to find that it was beautiful—extravagantly so. Ruby had mentioned the lavish quarters, but I had only half believed it until now. It was like her kingdom was a world away

from what I'd seen so far in Nevertide, more like an illustration from *Arabian Nights* than a sentry fortress.

Ash, Tejus and Queen Memenion used True Sight to see what lay within the walls. The other guards and ministers spread out around the courtyard, looking for any other soul that might still remain. One by one, they started to shake their heads, looking at one another in frustration and bafflement.

"Nothing?" I asked, walking up to Tejus.

"Nothing," he confirmed. "I'm going to dispatch a group to go inside, but I can't sense any barriers—I think it's truly deserted."

Where the hell is she?

"Help! HELP!" A cry shattered through the air, coming from the side of the courtyard that backed onto the cliff edge. Tejus and I ran forward, peering down through a columned arch to the ocean that lay below.

On narrow steps, carved into the cliff face, Jenus was stumbling about. He did his best to press against the wall, but his feet fumbled, causing rubble to clatter down beneath him, dropping soundlessly into the ocean.

"What's he *doing*?" I asked Tejus. I couldn't see why he was calling for help—there was no immediate danger other

than his own idiocy. “Is he wounded or something?”

“I don’t think so.” Tejus looked disdainfully down at his brother, who had now caught sight of us, waving his arms in the air.

“PLEASE!” he cried. “Tejus, brother, help me!”

“Oh, for God’s sake,” Tejus muttered, sighing in frustration. “What’s wrong?” he called down.

“The wind! It’s fearsome here—I’m afraid I can’t hold on for much longer!”

I looked doubtfully over to Tejus. It didn’t seem windy to me. At the end of the stone steps that Jenus had come from was a small viewpoint, decorated with potted plants and an outdoor bench. It hardly seemed perilous. Maybe Jenus had truly lost his mind.

“Ugh, maybe we should help him.” I sighed. “He might know where Queen Trina is.”

“Or send us on a wild chase when we’re already running out of time.”

Good point.

“Well, we can’t just leave him here, can we?” I asked, hopefully.

“We can.” Tejus shrugged. Then he smirked in my direction. “How hungry are you?”

"Famished." I grinned.

"I'll be back in a moment."

"Be careful," I warned, wondering if this was an elaborate trick of some kind…

Tejus nodded, but he was already starting down the steps. He descended them with ease, and soon reached his brother.

"Thank you! Oh, brother, thank you!" wailed Jenus.

Geez…overkill much?

With a huff of irritation, Tejus grabbed hold of his brother's arm, hauling him up the rest of the way. Rather than help Tejus, Jenus went limp, making the process ten times harder for his rescuer. I rolled my eyes. This farce was the limit—we were wasting time.

I stood back as Tejus appeared in the archway, flinging his brother's body to the floor.

"Where is she?" Tejus demanded, looming over a shaking Jenus.

"Where's who?"

Jenus started to cringe away from his brother, as he noticed Tejus's icy glare.

"You know who! Queen Trina. Where is she? Where are the children?"

"If I tell you, will you take me away from here? Please, Tejus, I implore you. The queen—she is capable of great evil! Don't leave me with her! She has manipulated me—*possessed* me, encouraged me to commit sin upon sin!"

I eyed Jenus with disgust. I was convinced that he was lying, and trying to bargain with us when the kids' lives hung in the balance made me despise him more than I thought possible. I didn't believe Queen Trina would ask him to do anything that he wouldn't happily do with a smile on his face.

"Where ARE they?" Tejus roared.

"A promise that I will be protected, and then I shall tell you!" Jenus beseeched him, spittle forming at the edges of his mouth.

Ash and Queen Memenion came closer. I had hardly been aware of the group that had formed around us, but they all stood watching the wretched creature on the floor as he wriggled like a worm on the edge of a hook.

Tejus looked at Ash, who nodded, looking at Jenus with the same disdain and hate that the rest of us were.

"Fine. You will come with us, and have our word that you can join us at the summer palace." Tejus barked out the promise.

"That you will protect me. Promise that you will protect me!" Jenus cried.

"Fine, you have our protection."

Jenus sighed, closing his eyes briefly. I swore if I saw a hint of a smirk across the sentry's face I would smack it right off him, but he remained earnest, staggering to his feet with a grateful expression.

"The cove—she's at the cove with the rest of the Acolytes. If we hurry, we can still save the children."

Tejus turned to the guard nearest him. "Tie him to one of the horses. Tightly. We need to leave immediately."

Three guards moved toward Jenus. As we walked back to the waiting army, I heard Jenus's wild screams. "I don't want to be tied up! Release me!"

I had no idea if they were genuine or not, but either way, he was getting what he deserved. I would be riding next to him as we made our way back to the cove, finally satisfying my hunger.

"What do we do now?" I asked Tejus. "I'm worried that we're not going to make it in time."

"We just have to hope that we will. We should fly though. It means dividing us, but we'll have to risk it. Hopefully we'll be able to create a diversion at least."

"Agreed," Ash replied from behind me. "We won't make it there on time if we don't hurry."

I ran to keep up with Tejus. His long strides and haste to get to the cove outstrode my much shorter legs…and, increasingly, my complete lack of energy.

"Tejus, I can't fly with anyone. I'm too hungry."

"I know, it's all right," he replied, momentarily slowing down. "You can fly solo—I'll control your bird like last time. Take some of Jenus's energy before we depart. He's not going to be of any further use otherwise."

I nodded, heading back in the direction of the guards.

It was feeding time.

Rose

I paced up and down the chamber, waiting for Mona, Nuriya and my father to return. They had been discussing the stones with some elder jinn in The Dunes whom Nuriya had a decent relationship with—we were hoping they might know what creatures were contained in the stones. Corrine, my mother, Ben and I were due for a meeting with the fae elders once my father returned to join us. We would be asking them the same questions, in the hope that at least one of them had some recollection or knowledge of what creature was considered so deadly that it had to be locked in a stone for all eternity.

All of the delays that had taken place since I'd received the phone call from Caleb to stop opening the portal had made me more and more anxious. If the threat was that bad, then each day that we left the kids alone would put them in more danger. What if we were too late?

Don't think like that! I chided myself. There was no point expecting the worst. I just had to trust that the kids knew how to survive—against the odds.

"Your father's on his way." Caleb entered the chamber, looking stressed.

"And Sherus?"

"He's brought some of the elder members of his council to join us. Apparently, none of the other kings recall the stones—they had completely forgotten that the star existed at all."

"They *forgot* they put fae on a star to wither away to nothing?"

"Tell me about it," Caleb muttered.

As much as I felt for the plight of the Shadowed, I wished we hadn't brought it to Sherus's attention. We'd be in the blocked-off dimension by now, trying to find the kids.

Nuriya entered the room, looking as harassed as Caleb

did. Nuriya's regal stance had dropped slightly—the jinni looked tired and defeated.

"They know nothing." She shook her head in irritation. "Absolutely nothing. At first I thought they were being deliberately obtuse, but we questioned them for hours. Not a soul knows any more than I did—just that the star exists, and the creatures trapped within the stones are dangerous."

"That's more than most of the fae knew," Caleb retorted.

"Where's Mona?" I asked, noticing the absence of the witch.

"She's gone to check on the portal. She will return in a while," Nuriya replied, turning toward the door as my father appeared, his face stern and his blue eyes wary.

"The fae elders will be here shortly. Sherus and Lidera are bringing them here."

I nodded—hopefully we would know something soon.

"I'll take my leave," Nuriya announced. "I'm not overly fond of fae."

I looked at my dad. That wasn't a good idea. I wanted the queen to hear what they had to say—hopefully it might jog some of her memories, maybe she might be able to

recall more of what her grandfather said to her.

"Please, Nuriya, stay. We're still in need of your counsel. You understand the ways of the fae better than we do," my father requested.

"I do not understand the ways of the fae." The jinni sighed, looking at me and then back to my father. "But I see that you probably *do* need me. The fae are tricky creatures."

I smiled with relief.

A moment later, Sherus and his sister entered, followed by four other fae, instantly recognizable as the elders. Their faces looked like bark, cracked, wrinkled and rosy, as if they'd spent ten lifetimes in the wind and sunshine. I wondered how old they actually *were*, but figured it would be impolite to ask. Corrine appeared behind them, keeping her distance from the elders as she came to stand next to me.

"These are the elders," Sherus announced, "the oldest generation of fae."

He bowed low as they came into the room, and we all did the same—it seemed appropriate faced with such ancient men.

"Well met, creatures of The Shade," muttered one of

the elders, his voice raspy and quiet.

"Elders, we have asked you here to discuss the stones—the stones which are guarded by the Shadowed, one of which recently emerged from a portal in the ocean. We wish to understand more about them and what they contain," my dad said respectfully.

The elders nodded, contemplating my father's request. After a long pause, one of them replied.

"We don't know what creatures are held within the stones. It is something that was never shared with us or our forefathers, those who sent the Shadowed to guard them."

Sherus looked as surprised as the rest of us.

"I don't understand," the fae king probed. "Why would they guard something they knew nothing of?"

"It was in exchange for a gift," another elder intoned.

"A gift from the jinn tribe that trapped the creatures in the first place," another elder replied.

"Which jinn tribe?" Nuriya asked.

"One long before your time, daughter of the Nasiris."

"What was the gift?" Sherus asked.

The elders all smiled at their king.

"The waters of immortalitatem," they replied simultaneously.

Sherus nodded, understanding what the elders meant, but none of us did.

"The immortal waters, as they are now known, are a way of preserving life," Sherus explained to us. "Few of the fae wish to use it—we live many years as it is. It is considered sacred...I did not realize it was a gift from the jinn."

The elders nodded. I looked at Nuriya, who glanced back at me in confusion. Clearly she'd never heard of these waters either.

"It is strange that I have not heard of this," the jinni replied slowly, looking at the elders with mistrust.

"It is a magic now lost to your people, I believe. The tribe that bestowed us with the gift died out long ago—they did not use the waters either, having no need to prolong their existence. Only one is reputed to remain alive...but she has not been seen for over a millennium."

It was a lot to take in. Aside from the bizarre revelations that the elders were providing us with, it still didn't seem to be getting us any closer to understanding what was in these stones. The only lead would be the long-lost jinni—but if she hadn't been seen in so long, what would be our chances of finding her in a matter of hours?

My dad was clearly thinking along the same lines as I was,

as in the next moment he changed his line of questioning.

"We were thinking of opening the stones, in a controlled environment," he announced. "Enabling us to understand what they contain, as well as what our chances might be against them if this dimension is revealed to be populated by these mysterious creatures."

"It is sheer madness!" Sherus replied, clearly still convinced that we should leave the portal shut for all time.

"It is risky," one of the elders replied. "I would show more caution than that."

I sighed inwardly. It seemed baffling to me that the fae didn't want to get to the bottom of this mystery. They had been guarding these creatures for all time. Didn't they *want* to know what they were?

My cellphone started buzzing. Making my apologies, I left the room. It was Mona, and I answered it immediately.

"Any news?" I asked.

"The portal's moving…" Her voice came in ragged breaths. "You need to get down here… *All* of you."

With that, Mona hung up.

I ran back into the room, my heart in my mouth as I announced the news to the group.

"We need to go—now," my father said.

"What?" Sherus bellowed.

"It can't open without us there!" my father replied impatiently. "There's more danger that way—we don't know *what's* opening it." My father turned to me, his eyes determined. "We need to gather everyone. You, Rose, fetch Kiev and his siblings, Brock, Vivienne and Xavier, Shayla and Eli—tell them to come at once. Get the rest of the parents together – Claudia, Yuri, Ashley and Landis. I know they'll want to be there for this – but tell Claudia to keep her temper reigned in. Caleb, make sure Ibrahim and Arwen are on their way, I had asked them to meet us here after the meeting. Then speak to the werewolves, let's take three—Micah, Kira, and Bastien. And we might need dragons—talk to Jeriad, Ridan and Azaiah, and whoever else they wish to bring. The more of us the better. I will fetch River, Grace and Lawrence. Corrine, ask the witches for help—there are plenty who will need to be vanished to the island."

We all nodded, moving from the room as swiftly as we could. Before I left I turned to look at my husband in relief. *We're finally doing it.* He returned a small smile, but his eyes were troubled. His look was a reminder that we still had a long way to go till our children were safe—this was just the beginning.

Benedict

The vulture soared across the sky, and I felt sicker and sicker with every passing second as we approached the cove. I had fought with Hazel to be allowed to come, and eventually Tejus had intervened on my behalf, saying that I was safest with them, and not riding with the others. She had eventually relented, letting me fly on the back of Tejus's vulture. I was glad—he rode at the front of the line, faster and more furious than the others. I had to hang on tightly to his robe not to be swept off.

"Are you all right, Benedict?" Tejus turned around, checking I was gripping on.

"I'm fine!" I yelled over the rushing wind.

"She has no power over you—neither does the entity, not anymore. Do you understand?"

He had obviously sensed my fear, but I was grateful for it. I needed to hear those words—I needed to remind myself that I wasn't at their mercy any more, and I was damned if I was going to let Queen Trina and the entity manipulate a bunch of kids the way they'd done to me.

"I understand." I nodded, my heart fluttering with anxiety anyway. I still wasn't looking forward to coming face to face with the queen again, let alone the entity if he managed to rise.

Tejus nodded, turning his attention back to the vulture. I could see the cove appearing in the distance—it was partially blocked by swirls of mist that hung low over the ocean, but I recognized the horseshoe shape of it and the dark forests that surrounded the rocks, leading back all the way to Hellswan castle.

"Don't let anything happen to my sister," I announced suddenly. I needed to say it just in case.

"Never," he replied.

I believed him. As long as Tejus lived, my sister wouldn't come to harm—he would protect her with every

last breath in his body.

“We’re close. I’m going to land behind the cove. We can follow the path up, and that will lead us to the temple.” He pointed at the small one-man track, nothing more than a sand-covered gap in the rocks, that wound its way down to the cove.

“Why are we not landing on the beach?” I asked, confused.

“I want the element of surprise. I suspect Jenus was left at the palace to direct us here, so we need to be cautious.”

That made sense. It also delayed our arrival at the cove, and suddenly I wanted that more than anything—my heart rate was spiking, and I felt like I couldn’t breathe. I desperately wanted to be brave, to be as courageous as Tejus and Ash, but I was terrified.

Tejus swooped down silently, the bird shooting through the air like an arrow.

We landed on a small clearing that led down to the path. The rest of the birds landed, and we all disembarked in total silence. Ruby and Ash had shared a bird, and they walked toward Tejus with questioning eyes. In whispers, he filled them in on the plan—we were to go single file up the path, fanning out when we reached the cove, keeping

them trapped until the rest of the army arrived.

I reached out and squeezed Hazel's hand. She squeezed it back, then released me quickly—I'd forgotten about her hunger.

"I'm sorry," I whispered.

She smiled. "I'll get it under control soon, don't worry."

"I'm not worried."

She was quiet for a few moments, smiling into my eyes. She looked like Mom in that moment, and for the first time I could really see the resemblance between them. I'd never truly noticed it before. Maybe it was because Hazel seemed a bit older to me now. I felt we were much closer than we ever had been. How could it be any different? We'd been through so much.

"I don't want you to be here. I want you to be *miles* from here," she whispered.

"Tough. I'm sticking it out."

"You're stubborn."

"So are you."

My grin faded as Tejus beckoned to us—it was time to get moving.

"I love you," Hazel reminded me.

"I know. I love you too."

I let her lead the way, and we walked swiftly over to the start of the path. Tejus looked at Hazel, his expression unreadable. Then he turned without saying a word, moving silently between the rocks.

The walk down to the cove was a short one. It got wider as we progressed, and soon I could hear noises up ahead. I almost came to a standstill as I recognized the low, melodic chanting. It was the Acolytes. The words, running together as one low drone, were barely distinguishable, but I had heard that sound night after night in my dreams, echoes of it haunting every waking hour. I felt nausea rise up inside me, and the acidic burn of bile at the back of my throat.

The sentry guard in front of me moved out from the pathway to stand along the back of the short cliff face, and I got my first full glimpse of the cove.

The Acolytes, about thirty in all, were kneeling at the shore, all chanting in the low drone I'd heard from the path. Queen Trina stood in front of them, standing at the edge of the shoreline, arms outstretched, facing the ocean with her back to us.

Hanging in the air above her, further out toward the sea, black rags were suspended in the wind. I watched as they fluttered from side to side — tossed about as the

breeze whipped around the walls of the cove and then back again. I squinted, trying to work out what they were. My stomach lurched.

The kids.

The black shapes were children — hanging like rag-dolls in the air, heads bent down to their chests, their arms and legs swaying limply to and fro. They hung in a perfect circle over the water, the formation turning slowly as the ocean roared beneath them.

"They're above the portal—she's trying to open it," Tejus muttered.

No sooner had the words left his mouth than the earth started to tremble. The temple, down in the landslide in front of us, cracked, its stone entrance falling with an almighty crash. I thought the Acolytes might turn around, but they stayed in their trance-like state, droning on. The rocks of the pathway we'd just left started to collapse in on one another, making the gap smaller – if it fell any further we'd be trapped.

Behind the kids, I could see more rips starting to appear in the sky—jagged tears that exposed more of the night's sky, like an endless abyss waited for us on the other side of this dimension.

"We need to stop them. What do you suggest, Tejus?" Ash turned to his commander.

Tejus was silent, looking out to the ocean where the water was being whipped into a frenzy, his face pale. I could see my own fear reflected in his eyes – that we had come too late, that Queen Trina had succeeded in raising the entity.

That we didn't have a hope in Nevertide of getting out of this thing alive.

ROSE

The tar was burping and bubbling, the gap that let in chinks of daylight gradually widening till the tar was drawn back completely, and the bluish, swirling mists of the portal floated upward—the wisps of the portal's tunnel mingling with the choppy waves.

"Do we have any idea who's opening it?" I asked Mona.

She shook her head. "No, which is what I'm worried about."

Maybe it's one of the kids. Maybe they'd managed to find a witch or jinni to help them on the other side.

"We should still take the advantage," my father replied.

"If there is a threat then we need to contain it…and I want to see my grandchildren." My mother nodded, her green eyes anxious but resolute.

"Do we have any idea if the power opening it is a benevolent one? Or is this dark magic?" Sherus asked, still uneasy about GASP's decision to explore the portal.

"I don't know that either," Mona replied. "The only way we'll know is by getting to the other side. The one thing I can tell you is that the magic is powerful…and it feels *old*."

"I don't like this," Sherus muttered.

"You're not the only one," Nuriya muttered. "But what choice do we have? This is family."

Lidera looked sideways at her brother. "Sherus. If whatever is on the other side of this portal is a threat to the fae, then we need to investigate. Our people are relying on us. We can't let them down."

Sherus didn't reply, but with a small nod of his head he acknowledged his sister's words.

"Are we ready?" my father asked, glancing around him one last time at the members of GASP who were assembled. It was a huge operation: Caleb and I, my mom, Ashley and Landis, Claudia and Yuri all standing closest to

the portal, with the witches, jinn, fae, werewolves and other vampires closely behind. The dragons hovered above the portal, waiting for my father to give the signal to go down. We all nodded.

My father went first, followed by my mother, Mona, Kiev and then Caleb and I.

The blue mists spun around us, fast, blocking the light that I had seen emanating from the dimension we were traveling to. The portal started to get darker—the blue mists turned a dark navy, and then a charcoal black…

"What's happening?" I called out, hoping Mona could hear me.

I started to hear the sound of ragged breathing. At first I thought it was coming from *me*, that I was starting to get frightened, but then I realized it seemed to be coming from inside my head, then all around me, till I was hardly aware of anything apart from the deep, laborious sounds of breath.

What is that?

The walls of the portal started to shake. I felt Caleb's hand grab mine. Something was horribly wrong.

In the next moment, I heard a voice. As clear as day, as if, like the breathing, it was coming from inside my own

head.

Welcome, the voice whispered, cloying and soft. *I have waited an eternity for this day to arrive. That you will be here to witness my rise, foolish fae king, means more to me than you could possibly know...*

I tried to spin around in the weightless mist, seeking Sherus out, but he was nowhere to be seen—there were too many of us hurtling down the portal. What I did understand, from the flickers of the shocked faces of GASP, was that the voice had not just been in my own head...everyone else had heard it too.

Fool king, you have brought your own visions to life. Soon my imprisoned children will be released, in this dimension, in your dimension, and on Earth. We will reign with terror you don't yet comprehend, with the ruthlessness of the darkest souls, the glory of what is most corrupt. Prepare for anarchy, for bloodshed, for the tears of your children, your children's children and every generation of the fae until your species is eradicated from the annals of time.

The voice faded away; the portal lightened back to the bluish swirls and stopped shaking. I looked around me wildly, this time searching for my father. His hand was clasped tightly to my mother's, and when our eyes met, his

flashed in a silent warning. He was unnerved—but it wasn't going to stop him reaching the other side of the portal. He wouldn't turn back. Novaks never did.

Hazel

As the earthquake continued to rip and shudder through Nevertide, we stood against the wall of the cliff, all eyes on Tejus as we waited for his command.

"They're opening the portal using the children—we need to break the focus of the Acolytes. Ragnhild, take the guards and attack them from behind. Do whatever you deem necessary to break their trance."

Ragnhild nodded solemnly, removing his broadsword from its sheath. Tejus turned to the ministers, who were staring wide-eyed at the children slowly circling the ocean.

"Catch the children when they fall—they've been

drained completely, if they fall into the water they won't come out alive."

"We risk being seen by Queen Trina," one of them mumbled, and I frowned briefly at the typical lack of ministerial courage, or willingness to take any kind of action that might endanger themselves. Obviously, the queen was dangerous, but the whole of Nevertide was at stake here!

"Leave Queen Trina to me," Tejus replied curtly.

"Shouldn't we wait for the rest of the army?" the minister asked again, then quailed under both Tejus's and Ash's glares.

"We don't have time," Tejus snapped. "The rest of you, guard the periphery of the cove; I don't want any of the Acolytes escaping."

I glanced over at Ruby, taking a deep breath. Her blue eyes calmly met mine, reminding me of the day I had seen her in the trial arena, when I'd thought she was already safe at home. Maybe today we'd get that chance again. We were ready.

She took Benedict's hand, and we fanned out slowly, careful not to make a sound, surrounding the cove. I prepared myself mentally for my own task, one that Tejus

wouldn't be pleased with, but I would do anyway. If any of the Acolytes managed to escape, I wanted to be ready to throw out a protective barrier toward Ruby and Benedict, stopping them from coming to any harm. They were *my* priority. Julian would be arriving with the second wave of the army, and I was grateful—he'd be in less danger that way.

I turned my attention to Tejus. He and Ash stood at the front of an arrow-shaped formation of guards and ministers, ready to attack. Tejus was crouched low, waiting to hurl himself forward when the time was right. He reminded me of a black panther, coiled before leaping to attack its prey. His face was set in a snarl, his gaunt, rugged looks making him appear dark and deadly—once again reminding me of a creature more animal than man.

Ash and Tejus lunged forward, running toward the chanting Acolytes, leading their men. Tejus drew a sword from his back, lifting it up in the air and then bringing it down with a single, elegant swipe. It sliced through the neck of the nearest Acolyte, sending his head flying in an arc through the gray sky.

The fight had begun.

The chanting was replaced by screams. The Acolytes,

with deadly speed, jumped up from their positions and turned to attack the oncoming army. Tejus fought his way past another Acolyte; neither side having much time to syphon, they were relying mostly on the weaponry they had. I'd mistakenly believed that the Acolytes weren't armed—instead, each drew out long daggers from their forearms that had been concealed by the sleeves of their robes. Wielding one in each hand, they launched themselves at the Hellswan guards.

The fight was bloody. The war cries and the high-pitched howls of the injured pierced the air, merging with the ferocious roar of the ocean—and then the throaty laughter of Queen Trina.

Tejus fought off another Acolyte who had attacked him from behind, and ran toward the queen.

She held out her arms to Tejus, almost as if she wanted to embrace him. I watched as he stumbled, almost dropping his sword as the pain of her syphoning tore at him. She continued to laugh, her eyes shining brightly, the dark mane of her hair whipping upward with the wind, making her look more like a vengeful god than a mad queen.

"You're too late, Tejus!" she cried. "It is done! He will

rise—he will rise and end you all!"

Tejus staggered forward, not willing to give in, no matter how excruciating the pain.

"You could have basked in this glory, Tejus – if only you had loved me!" She screeched at him this time, her jubilant mood swiftly being replaced with one of spite and hatred.

Ignoring her cries, he held his sword aloft, determined that it would meet its target. Even from this distance, I could see his face paling and hear his groans of effort as he rose time and time again. Each time she syphoned harder, knocking him back down on his knees.

I can't watch this.

I took one last look at Benedict and Ruby and then crept around the side of the cove, keeping out of Queen Trina's sight. There *must* be something I could do to help weaken her. If she carried on like this, Tejus wasn't going to make it. I could almost feel the power emanating from her as I approached—she must have been taking her energy from the entity, or the children. I'd never been able to sense another sentry's power before. The hunger leapt up inside me. My mouth started to water, my stomach knotting itself. Now I didn't seem to be moving of my own

accord, but instead driven by a much more base, primal need to devour the power and energy contained within Queen Trina. It was a heady sensation, and I could feel my own power raging inside of me, desperate to be set free.

I was behind Queen Trina in a moment, standing between her and the children, the sea lapping up against my feet. In the distance, the rest of the army had arrived, guards and villagers clambering down the cliff edge and the fallen rock to join the battle still raging with the Acolytes.

What now?

I couldn't wait for them. Behind the billowing navy-blue robes of the queen, Tejus staggered to his feet. His teeth were clenched and bared as he fought against her will with everything he had left.

"Today," Tejus panted heavily, "today you will meet the unhallowed creature that made you."

She laughed again, raising her arms higher and sending Tejus crashing back down on his knees.

No!

Instinctively, I took another step forward, willing to do whatever it took to stop her. My fingers rested lightly against the hilt of my dagger, and I prayed for the courage

to do what had to be done.

"Do you think *you* can harm me, vile human?"

She spun around to face me. I could tell by her malevolent, victorious smile that she had known I was approaching. She smiled broadly, as if it was all some great joke to her, as if I was nothing but a small inconvenience that would be easily disposed of.

"You don't have the power," she continued, almost pityingly.

She stepped toward me, closing the gap between us — close enough that I could smell her fragrant breath on my face and the overwhelming frankincense of her perfume.

"But I'm glad that you have come to try, little one." She reached out and ran her thumb down my cheek. I recoiled at her touch. "I would have hated it if someone had ended you, other than—"

She went silent, her expression changing from malice to confusion.

I had let my hunger flow freely, latching on to her dark energy – drinking deeply the bitter, putrid taste of the atoms and molecules that made Queen Trina the twisted being that she was.

"How?" she whispered, feeling me syphon off her.

"You know how," I replied with a smile.

I watched her face twist with hatred as clarity dawned on her; Tejus had given himself to me, had connected us — mind, body and soul. The vehemence of her emotion was instant and brutal.

"He *belonged* to me!" she screeched, the cry tearing from her throat.

"He didn't want you," I replied calmly.

"It doesn't matter," she spat, then tried to regain her dead smile, "you will never get the better of me, Tejus will *never* defeat me!"

She stumbled on the last word, falling toward me – her mouth open in silent horror as she realized what I'd done.

I swallowed, pressing the hilt of the dagger deeper, and then upward to pierce her heart. It had slid in so easily, I almost thought that I'd stabbed thin air.

"You…" she breathed. "How could…"

I released the handle. Taking a step backward, I watched as her hands reached around to cover the hilt, touching it as if she could hardly believe that it was there.

"You underestimated me," I whispered softly in her ear.

I gazed at Queen Trina's impossibly beautiful face. A small trickle of blood appeared at the corner of her mouth

and ran down to her chin. Her eyes, still boring into mine, became glassy. The contorted expressions I had seen her exhibit, from rage to fear, jealousy, lust and vengeance, left her. Her face softened, and I thought perhaps, for just a moment, I was seeing a glimpse of the Queen Trina from long ago—maybe the girl she had been before all of this.

I took a shuddering breath, and my trembling hand reached out again, closing around the hilt as I yanked out the blade. The queen's eyes widened for a second, and then she fell – tumbling to the ground, black tar spilling from the wound where blood should have been.

"Hazel!" Tejus cried, staggering toward me.

Before I had time to react, I was wrapped in his fierce embrace, his mother's dagger falling from my hand. I couldn't continue to touch it in that moment. I closed my eyes against Tejus's chest. My hunger fled, to be replaced with a painful tightening of my chest as I held back sobs of shock and relief.

She was dead. She couldn't harm me or anyone I loved again.

From the comfort of Tejus's arms I heard the ministers dragging the children from the sea, followed by the reassuring sounds of coughing and crying—they were

alive!

I broke away from him, turning toward the ocean.

Presumably, with Queen Trina and the Acolytes stopped, the barrier would now be destroyed…and the portal open.

I looked up at Tejus.

Do we leave?

Ruby

Benedict and I ran toward the ocean. We helped the ministers drag the children out, my heart leaping in my chest as I saw they were all alive. The second wave of the army had just arrived, and I glanced over – back to the passage to see Julian hurrying toward us. He grinned broadly, and I returned the smile. It probably wasn't the time for celebration yet, but this one victory over the Acolytes and Queen Trina made me want to yell and whoop with joy. The children had survived against all odds.

Leaning over one of the young boys, who was moaning

incoherently, I looked up, distracted by a huge burst of light that was coming from the water.

The portal.

It was open.

Julian and Benedict saw it at the same time. They both turned to me, their expressions half-hopeful, half-afraid.

Can we just leave?

I turned back to look at the far end of the cove. Ash was bloodied, with his cloak torn, chaining up a few of the Acolytes that they had kept alive. I wasn't ready to make a choice. I knew that Ash wouldn't come with me—not now, not when he had the entirety of Nevertide to piece back together again.

My gaze shifted to Hazel, staring at the light, standing next to Tejus.

"What do we do?" Benedict called to me over the noise of the waves.

"I don't know!" I replied, my voice sounding desperate.

Suddenly, my body lurched forward. The ground had started to tremble. The Viking remains that littered the cove began to vibrate, cracks appearing in the cliff face and the cries of the army rising up behind me.

"Everybody LEAVE!" Ash bellowed.

I wanted to move, but I felt like my feet had frozen to the shaking ground. The portal was only a yard or two ahead. We could leave Nevertide. Wasn't that what we'd always wanted?

How can I leave Ash?

I couldn't. I wouldn't be able to live with myself. Even if we were to return with GASP, I would have abandoned him when he needed me the most.

"The sea!" Benedict yelled, staggering backward.

I watched, open-mouthed, as a humongous wave built, dragging the water backward from the shore. It grew higher and higher, far over the cliffs of the cove, so high it would have reached the tower peaks of Hellswan castle.

"RUN!" Julian cried.

He picked up the human boy at my feet, flinging him over his shoulder. He grabbed my arm, dragging me backward.

"Wait!" I cried, suddenly aware that the wave had stopped moving. In fact, *everything* had stopped moving. I could no longer hear the sounds of the ocean, or the rumbling of the earth. The sentries behind us were silent too—their run toward the path had stopped as they turned to face the frozen wave.

I looked down at the exposed sea bed. Beyond the cracked shells, tangled seaweed and the spiny bones of dead fish, I saw stones. Millions of them.

"Th-th-the stones," I stuttered at Julian, "look at the stones…"

"Are they—?" he breathed.

"I think so," I replied, mystified.

As we watched, the stones started to glow. They changed from dull grayness to the radiant, multicolored creations that had danced in the locks of the entity. Their colors entwined with the bright blaze of the open portal till the entire ocean seemed lit with a luminous, shining light.

"What does this mean?" Benedict asked quietly.

"I don't—"

I stopped speaking as a sharp crack came from the stones. A second later came another.

"They're opening!"

Something is coming.

"Hazel, what do we do?" I screamed in her direction. Do we try to make it to the portal, for Benedict and Julian's sake? There were thousands upon thousands of stones to cross before we reached it. Could we risk it?

"Get back to the palace, NOW!" Tejus roared. The intervals between the cracking of the stones was starting to decrease—more were opening.

I turned to look in Hazel's direction; I wasn't willing to make a decision that would affect all of us without her. We had to end this together, that had been the plan. She met my gaze. After a split-second pause she nodded, swiftly. We needed to leave. Now.

"Back to the palace," I reiterated to the boys.

"Okay," Julian replied.

"Benedict?" I asked.

"Okay," he replied, glancing at the portal one last time before he turned on his heel, stumbling back toward the departing army.

Ash was waiting for me at the entrance to the path. His hand clasped around my wrist, tightly, without letting me break my stride. Together we ran from the cove.

Derek

Whizzing through the portal's exit, I landed on a hard, stony surface. I leapt to my feet immediately and looked to see if the rest of my family and the GASP team were through all right. Sofia had landed nearby, and my daughter, son and their partners were only a few yards away.

"What *is* this place?" my wife breathed.

I had been momentarily distracted by the sounds of a large group of…humans? Supernaturals? I didn't know, but they were heading off in the distance. I could hear the distinct clatter of horses' hooves, and up ahead in the

distance, huge birds in flight.

Sofia's voice brought me back to our immediate surroundings. I looked down at the ground we had landed on, noticing with unease that we seemed to be standing on millions of stones—the same stone that Rose and her team had seen appear out of the portal, containing the soul of our unknown enemy. Further up the shore line, I could see the remains of shipwrecks, looking vaguely like Viking artifacts…was that a *longboat* I could see?

"Derek, look." Sofia yanked at my sleeve. She was looking in the direction of the portal, her gaze fixed on an absolutely gigantic wave—frozen behind us.

"Everyone, toward the cove!" I yelled out the order, dragging Sofia back with me. I didn't know how long the wave would be suspended like that. If it came crashing down, we'd be dragged out with the tide.

En masse, we hurried to the back of the cove—the only way out was a small pathway between the rocks that looked like it had recently collapsed in on itself. There was still just enough space to get through, but if it sustained more damage we'd be trapped.

"Oh, my God—look up!" River exclaimed, breaking our bewildered silence. Following her awestruck gaze, I

stared once again in baffled disbelief. Across the hazy, nicotine yellow of the afternoon sky, there seemed to be rips and tears running through it, breaking up the very fabric of the dimension's reality. A vast, black night's sky could be seen through the shredding…

What is this place?

"Ibrahim," I said quietly to the witches closest to me, "have you ever seen anything like this?"

"Never," replied Ibrahim. Corrine and Mona also shook their heads, not glancing away from the sight before us.

"Dad?" Rose moved toward me. "Can you hear that?"

I fell silent, waiting to be enlightened. I heard nothing for a while, but just as I was about to turn back to Rose and question her, I heard a sound. It was a resounding crack—like an egg splitting open.

"I think it's coming from the stones," Sofia murmured.

"They're opening," Nuriya asserted, her face paling.

Sherus stepped forward, moving through the group to stand in front of me.

"Derek, we need to depart from this place! If the stones are breaking, then we are all doomed. You heard the voice in the portal—there's no hope for us if we remain here! We need to leave and close it off again before this power

can get out."

I understood the fae's concern, but I would not leave my grandchildren, Ruby or Julian behind. I could not and would not ask that of their parents. Neither was I willing to let the malevolent power remain in this dimension. Evidently it had opened the portal once, and there would be no reason why it wouldn't do so again. No, we couldn't risk it. We would stay here and fight the danger.

"Sherus, I understand if you want to leave. It is probably a good idea to warn the rest of the fae kingdoms of what you have seen here, but I will not be leaving this dimension without our children."

"Derek, this is madness!" Sherus exploded.

"We don't have time to argue," Nuriya snapped at the fae king.

"She's right," I interjected, "we need to get inland as soon as possible. Nuriya, are you able to stop the stones from breaking for a while, delay them somehow?" I asked, willing the jinni to come up with a way to postpone the danger.

Nuriya looked doubtfully at the mass of stones beyond the shore.

"It's such old, ancient magic…I couldn't be sure. I

think it is too great a risk right now—we should leave here, find safety first."

I nodded. It was a good plan in theory, but the chances of us finding a safe haven in this unknown land seemed small at best. The best idea was probably to follow the creatures that I had heard riding off into the distance—from the look of the cove there had been a struggle. Bodies lay strewn about, their appearance human, but strange. Taller and larger than most. They had been killed by swords – that much was obvious. Kiev's team started to check the bodies, while my family inspected the footprints that haphazardly marked the sand. Everywhere we looked, the ground was stained with blood, filling my nostrils with its distinct metallic aroma. If the creatures, whoever they were, were fleeing this place in a hurry, then perhaps they feared the stones as much as we did. At least we would have a common enemy.

"We travel inland," I announced to the group. "We will begin our search for the children as soon as we can—but first we need to find a stronghold where we can protect ourselves from whatever's coming out of these stones."

I led the way through the narrow passage, moving as swiftly as possible, Sofia following behind me.

I didn't know what we would face when we reached the mainland.

I just had to pray that whatever was coming our way, we could deal with it—that GASP would be able to overcome the dangers of this world as it had all the others…

READY FOR THE PENULTIMATE BOOK OF "SEASON 5" OF THE NOVAK CLAN'S STORY?

Dear Shaddict,

The next book, *ASOV 40: A Throne of Fire*, is the **penultimate** book in what has been "Season 5" of the *A Shade of Vampire* series — as we move toward the GRAND FINALE in Book 41!

A Throne of Fire releases February 19th, 2017.

Not long to wait!

Visit www.bellaforrest.net to order your copy.

Thank you for reading.

I will see you again very soon!!

Love,

Bella xxx

P.S. Join my VIP email list and I'll send you a personal reminder as soon as I have a new book out. Visit here to sign up: www.forrestbooks.com
(Your email will be kept 100% private and you can unsubscribe at any time.)

P.P.S. Follow The Shade on Instagram and check out some of the beautiful graphics: @ashadeofvampire

You can also come say hi on Facebook:
www.facebook.com/AShadeOfVampire
And Twitter: @ashadeofvampire